# WAR CRIMES FOR THE
# POLITICAL ELITE

———

# WAR CRIMES FOR THE POLITICAL ELITE

## CHRISTOPHE DOWNES

Matador
9 Priory Business Park,
Wistow Road, Kibworth Beauchamp,
Leicestershire. LE8 0RX
Tel: 0116 279 2299
Email: books@troubador.co.uk
Web: www.troubador.co.uk/matador
Twitter: @matadorbooks

ISBN 978 1800462 274

British Library Cataloguing in Publication Data.
A catalogue record for this book is available from the British Library.

Printed and bound in Great Britain by 4edge Limited
Typeset in 11pt Adobe Garamond Pro by Troubador Publishing Ltd, Leicester, UK

Matador is an imprint of Troubador Publishing Ltd

This is dedicated to Fiona my rock, for wading through the manuscript, Caroline, Clark and Howard. Thank you for your encouragement and support. Also, thanks to all the Puffins for their feedback and constructive criticism and backing.

All the world's a stage,
And all the men and women merely players;
They have their exits and their entrances,
And one man in his time plays many parts,
His acts being seven ages. At first, the infant,
Mewling and puking in the nurse's arms.
Then the whining schoolboy, with his satchel
And shining morning face, creeping like snail
Unwillingly to school. And then the lover,
Sighing like furnace, with a woeful ballad
Made to his mistress' eyebrow. Then a soldier,
Full of strange oaths and bearded like the bard,
Jealous in honour, sudden and quick in quarrel,
Seeking the bubble reputation
Even in the cannon's mouth. And then the justice,
In fair round belly with good capon lined,
With eyes severe and beard of formal cut,
Full of wise saws and modern instances;
And so he plays his part. The sixth age shifts
Into the lean and slippered pantaloon,
With spectacles on nose and pouch on side;
His youthful hose, well saved, a world too wide
For his shrunk shank, and his big manly voice,
Turning again toward childish treble, pipes
And whistles in his sound. Last scene of all,
That ends this strange eventful history,
Is second childishness and mere oblivion,
Sans teeth, sans eyes, sans taste, sans everything.

**William Shakespeare**

# 1977, CYNTHIA'S STORY

---

On a day in April 1977, the same day that German Federal Prosecutor Siegfried Buback and his driver were shot by two Red Army Faction members in Karlsruhe, a young woman left Tottenham Court Road Underground Station and walked down Soho Street to Soho Square. The Curzon Cinema on Shaftsbury Avenue was showing *The Eagle Has Landed*. The private cinema on Romilly Street was showing *Swedish Nympho Slaves*. A cold front had moved south with accompanying winds, but the streets were dry, and her overcoat blew open. She was wearing a short skirt and diaphanous blouse. The cold wind was nipple stiffening.

The woman pulled the coat close round her thin, almost emaciated body and screwed her eyes shut against the dust and papers blowing off the grubby streets. She was cold, tired, and her weary eyes were ringed by dark circles. Her hair was dry from over-dying, and her skin was red and flaky due to a poor diet. She scurried up Waldour Mews to the back door of the club and let herself in with the steel door's turn-key. As she went down the three flights of stairs, she was assailed by that well-known reek of stale beer and pervading cigarette smoke. At the bottom, she entered the back of the club and wondered, as she often did, how they would get out if there was a fire. At that point in her life, she decided that she didn't care. She hung up her coat in the area behind the bar that comprised the cellar and what was laughingly referred to as the 'dressing rooms'.

The *Hoplite Club* was nearly empty, it being a Thursday, and the few punters were more interested in getting pissed than watching the two 'girls' on the stage going through their routine with a bored distraction. They were slouching around on the small stage to Van McCoy's *The Shuffle*. It was still late afternoon so although their ample breasts swung ponderously to the music in a way Mr McCoy had never intended, their sequinned G-strings stayed on. Empty eyes looked at the glitter ball on the ceiling, as though life's meaning lay there.

The woman poked her head round the curtained door off the bar to the back of the club and caught the attention of the West Indian barman. "Is Mick the Greek in, Chalky?" she asked.

The black man looked round and smiled in genuine friendliness, his teeth impossibly white and his gums even more impossibly baby pink.

"Hello, Cyn, love. He popped out, said he had an errand to do. Putting on a bet more like." He loved Cynthia in a way she would find impossible to comprehend. She loved Chalky in a different way, and his affections would forever remain unrequited.

"Quiet now, isn't it?" she observed, watching the distracted punters.

He smiled. "Until you shake your little arse, eh, Cyn?"

She grinned, but knew that she felt as well as looked terrible. She hadn't eaten a proper meal in days. Her nose was running and the backs of her legs and her knees ached as though she was coming down with flu. She badly needed a fix.

"Why don't you have a cuppa before you get ready?" he said in a kindly, concerned way. "Lots of sugar then you can pile on the old slap."

He was discreetly saying that she needed to do something before the night's performance because she looked terrible. Apart from the eyes, hair and skin, the track lines on her thin arms were becoming noticeable, and there was an infected ulcer on her inner left arm. Cynthia made herself a cup of tea with lots of sugar and went into the changing room. The two 'girls' were off the stage and changing into their street clothes to supplement their earnings that night. Cynthia wasn't at that stage yet, but as she looked at herself in the fly-blown mirror, she asked her reflection what had become of the fresh-faced seventeen-year-old who had stepped off the train in Paddington in 1969. The one with a promising modelling and photographic career ahead of her.

Mick the Greek came back about seven that evening and she was desperate to see him. Mick went straight into his office with the huge two-way mirror where he could watch the girls getting changed. When she first started working at the club, Cynthia had thought it strange and rather pervy, but now it was part and parcel of her decadent life. She knocked on the door and went straight into Mick's office. He had his back to the door and the safe opposite was open. Mick was putting wads of fivers into the safe.

"Why don't you just fackin' come in, Cyn?" he snapped at her on turning round.

Mick the Greek was wearing his Savile Row suit that may have been trendy when he was hobnobbing with the Krays, ten years earlier. Now it was faded and stretched across Mick's ample paunch. His bow tie was as greasy as his hair, but he liked to think he still had what it took, and he still made lots of money.

"Mick, I need Horse and I need it badly," she said without preamble, cutting straight to the chase.

"The Apothecary is proving rather difficult to get hold of at the moment. You are running up rather a tab, which is concerning, so I will need you to fack me, Cyn."

"If you want me to perform tonight, Mick, I'll need something to get me through it."

"Your friend may well be popping in later tonight. We have one of Her Majesty's ships docked in the Pool at the moment, and I've been scattering complimentary tickets like confetti. The Apothecary rather fancies getting a lot of new business tonight."

"I need it now, Mick. No Horse, no fucking show! Of any kind."

Mick looked across his desk at her. She had been lovely beyond measure when she first went into the club, but the late nights and heroin had taken their toll. That notwithstanding, she was still eminently fuckable. He opened his top drawer and tossed a small, clear package across to her.

"This Dust should see you through until the Apothecary pitches up."

"I don't like Coke. It really hurts my sinuses and your stage will be covered with snot."

"Rub it on your gums. Just a little at a time. It's what the racing drivers do. Now get your kit off…"

*

The club was heaving by the time Miss Sin was ready to take the stage. Mick the Greek's touts had done a good job and the bar area was packed with the Royal

Navy's finest from the Leander Class frigate docked in the Pool of London. There was a healthy contingent from Heriot-Watt University's rugby club, and already the rugby uni boys were sparking off with the Royal Navy's finest. Chalky and his lovely female assistant with the bathycolpian delights were run off their feet. The punters were paying over a quid a pint, and Mick grinned, tucked away in the darkness. Cyn was so bloody good on so many levels.

Cynthia was euphoric with boundless energy when she hit the lights, wearing a traffic warden's uniform. The opening bass beats of Billy Ocean's *Red Light Spells Danger* boomed out from the PA system as she entered stage left with a notebook, licking the pencil suggestively. Cynthia scrubbed up very nicely with some slap. The boys in the bear pit howled their appreciation. In the next set, she was wearing a hoola skirt and beads, swaying suggestively to Heatwave's *Boogie Nights*. The thong came off and the string of beads was utilised in an entirely inappropriate manner. Mick thought they would blow off the roof.

In the interval between the sets, she rubbed more of Mick's Dust on her gums, but she was still desperate for the heroin. The lights were so bright they hurt her eyes. She saw Chalky look away from her nudity with sad embarrassment but she didn't care. They loved her and the aching legs had gone. The bar was besieged by matelots and rugby aficionados. Invariably, there were tense moments between the two diametrically different groups. At the moment, it was good-natured.

The second set kicked off with Andrew Gold's *Lonely Boy*. She was dressed as a schoolboy, complete with blazer, shorts and a rather fetching cap. Freckles had been heavily applied and a catapult stuck out of the pocket of her shorts. By the time Andrew Gold's *Lonely Boy* had left home on a winter's day in 1969, the first glass had been nudged, the first beer spilled and the first punch thrown. Mick the Greek's bouncers moved in like a prison officer MUFTI team. A prop forward and an operator maintainer were up the stairs and out into the back alley with the bins and extensive bleeding, like corks out of champagne bottles. They pulled themselves to their feet at around the same time and supported each other like lifelong friends, blood and mucus dripping from their mouths and noses. Two men from different classes united in a common British pastime; getting pissed and fighting.

The applause was still deafening when the Apothecary slipped almost unnoticed into the club. Mick shimmied over to him and they exchanged a subtle handshake.

"You got some Horse for my Golden Girl?"

The Apothecary nodded. "But it's potentially hot stuff from a new supplier."

"Put it on my tab this time. Cyn's done me a favour."

The Apothecary looked at Mick with a mixture of doubt and envy. "Then she truly is on the slippery slope."

"Fack you," Mick said, "she can't keep her hands off me."

Cyn's final set was to Glen Campbell's *Southern Nights,* and she was dressed as the sluttiest cowgirl you could ever wish to meet. She treated the frenzied punters to a close up and personal view of her perineum on the edge of the stage at the culmination of her act. As he watched the heaving heads of Her Majesty's Armed Forces and the finest of the British university system, Mick gave silent thanks that he had had the good sense to flee Northern Cyprus before the Turks arrived. He sought out Cynthia after the show and slipped her the package.

"This one's on me, Cyn. You were facking good tonight. The best."

She sniffed. "Never again, Mick."

"We'll see, love. We'll see."

She barely remembered the tube trip back to her grotty flat in Blackwall; just another creature of the night, and what beautiful music she made. Her heart was pounding as she prepared the heroin and tried to find a viable vein. In the end, she gave up and injected between her toes. It took a long time for the intense rush to hit, and she came, as she invariably did. Her heart rate slowed with the intense pleasure that swept over her as she forgot everything. But the cocaine was wearing off, and her heart rate and breathing slowed further. The syringe fell out of her lifeless hand and she looked up at the pool of light above the cheap wardrobe. She was drawn towards it and closed her eyes.

\*

He came out of the light in a confused state. He had been looking down at himself being worked on by the crash team, but now he seemed to be sitting on the top of a cheap wardrobe in an insalubrious bedsit. He was looking at a girl slumped across a bed, naked apart from a pair of tanga pants. She had pissed herself.

*Oh great! Just my luck,* he thought, and came down to step on a hypodermic syringe. *Oh shit.*

For some reason, he knew that this young woman was vitally important to his continued existence. He sat on the bed and shook her.

"Wake up!"

She groaned but made no movement or opened her eyes. He felt for the carotid pulse in her neck. It was very faint and slow. He looked at her body. Very pleasant apart from the mess of her arms. *Oh Christ, a fucking junkie.* He shook her again.

"Leave me alone," she murmured, "I want to die."

"Well, I don't. Wake up, you bitch."

He picked up the phone but the line was dead because she had been disconnected. He reckoned that by the time he went and phoned for an ambulance and got back, she would have gone. He didn't even know where he was. He pulled her up. But she slumped back, floppy, like dead meat. He tried to remember the month's training as a combat medic he had spent in that Birmingham A&E department. Plenty of drugs there, but he had nothing here. What did he need to prevent cardiac and respiratory depression? Stimulus. A shock. He carried her into the shower and toilet cubicle and dumped her in the shower basin. She was so light, nothing of substance. He turned on the cold water, full blast. She opened her eyes and gasped, staring at him with terror. He turned off the shower.

"You have to stay awake. If you fall asleep you will die, and so will I."

"I want to die."

He turned on the shower again and she started sobbing, trying to avoid the water.

"Do I have your attention now?"

He picked her up and carried her back to the bed. He found a towel and dried her vigorously, rubbing hard to get the blood flowing.

"What's your name?"

She closed her eyes, drifting off, so he shook her.

"Your name?"

"Cynthia, Cynthia Penrith."

"Where are we?"

"London."

He looked round the flat, struck by just how unfamiliar everything was. "What year is this?"

She giggled and closed her eyes, so he shook her again.

"1977."

"Christ," he said. "What the hell is going on?"

She had slipped into a dream-like state again and he looked round the bedsit. Coffee, lots of it, strong. The kettle was whistling on the electric hob. He couldn't remember putting it on. He found a tin of coffee; Maxwell House. Yuck. Four tablespoons should do it. He filled the mug with a mixture of boiling water and cold water from the tap, then heaved her upright.

"Wakey-wakey, Cynthia. Time for your medicine."

He pinched her nose and poured a third of the coffee down her throat. She gagged and some came back up, but most went down. She shuddered and then vomited coffee and bile on his lap.

"Thanks. But you're not getting away with it that easily." More coffee went down her neck, and although she shuddered again, this time it stayed down.

She groaned and her head lolled forward onto his shoulder. He knew that it was going to be a long night.

"Right, lady. I've got to keep you alive because if you get the mallet, then so do I. I don't know why that should be the case. It just is. No sleeping until that shit you've injected is out of your system."

He could feel her heart beating slowly and weakly against his chest like a dying bird. "Right, we'll start with what's on the telly every week, the best and worst programmes. Go!"

What seemed like hours later, the little folding travel clock on the bedside table said it was 2:45, and he knew it was the small hours of the morning.

"Right, now listen! The rifle fires one or two more rounds, then stops again. Come on!"

"Cock, hook and look," she slurred without opening her eyes. He shook her.

"No, for fuck's sake, that's the IA drill for the SLR. We're on the L85. The clue is one or two more rounds then stops again. It's a fucking gas stoppage. What are you going to do?"

"Apply safety catch and set the gas plug to emergency," she murmured slowly, and dribbled.

"Good. Now talk me through the stripping and cleaning of the weapon. What size of flannelette should I use with the pull-through?"

By 3.30 am, it was the kings and queens of England. "Right, we've had Henry the Seventh and Henry the Eight. Who came next?"

"Elizabeth the First."

"No you stupid Doris! It was Edward the Sixth followed briefly by Lady Jane Grey…"

At 6.50 am, she opened her eyes and looked at him. "I don't want to do any more capitals of the world. You're driving me mad."

Somehow he knew that the worst was over, and he cuddled her. She nuzzled up to him, the first time for so many years that she had been intimate with another human being without there being a sexual element. She drew back to get a look at him for the first time. He was a middle-aged man with a short beard and long, prematurely grey hair. He had a hard, brutal face with a broken and badly set nose. But it was the harsh, jagged scar on his forehead that was most frightening.

"Are you my guardian angel?" she asked, and then giggled. "It's not very likely, is it?"

He thought about it for quite a while and then everything suddenly fell into place. He could now make sense of the impossible.

"No," he said as the realisation hit him like a sledgehammer, "but I think you could be mine."

She wrinkled her nose. "You're silly. What's your name?"

"Edge."

"That's a silly name. Will you stay with me, Edge?"

He felt an agonising blast go through his brain and knew that his time here was finished. "No. I have to go back."

"Will I ever see you again?"

"Yes. In thirty-three years."

"I'll be dead by then."

"You won't, but you'll have lots of regrets, and so will I."

"Bye, Edge. You're a bloody ugly guardian angel," she said, and fell into a sleep he knew she would wake up from.

"And you'll be a bloody ugly cat minder," he said gently, and returned to his own body, the bright lights of the operating theatre and the pain…

# Chapter 1

# RAGE

———

*Daniel Copeland's Story*

Of course it had been an accident. He hadn't even pushed Glen Collier off the raft. Well, not technically anyway. It wasn't Daz who made him lose his balance on the homemade raft; well, he might have rocked it a bit, but Glen fell in. Glen could easily have climbed back on board; he even held out the plank he had been using as a paddle to help him climb back on. It was an accident he hit Glen over the head with it. Besides, Glen shouldn't have threatened to tell his dad about Daz and Glen's sister, Carly. And nobody was more surprised than Daz when Glen went under and didn't come back up. He spent a long time, minutes or less, calling out for Glen. Of course he hadn't gone in after him; the flooded quarry was supposed to be bottomless. Besides, he didn't want to get tangled with the old crane that reached up to just below the surface. He could have told Glen's parents or another adult, but they would have blamed him and confiscated the raft. He had spent a lot of time making that raft, at least half as much as Glen had, and he had made it work. So it was all Glen's fault really. Anyone could see that…

Daniel 'Daz' Copeland killed his first human being when he was fifteen. He had begun his murderous apprenticeship on vermin, birds, rabbits, then moved on to cats. Even as a child, he took particular pleasure in torturing cats to death. But these were just practice for the cruelty that would become

Daniel Copeland's stock in trade. A dispassionate individual might well have concluded that it would have been better to have drowned the child at birth. It would have at least prevented such misery in the future.

He was born in Andover to a weak, alcoholic and occasionally skunk-addicted girl of sixteen. His father was a soldier from the Tidworth garrison, who really didn't want to get involved with the girl, particularly in view of her drug taking, but she was now pregnant. Her parents kicked her out when they found out, and to be fair to the reluctant father, he agreed to marry her, thus providing her with a home, rather than any hope of a long-term relationship. As a small child, Daniel Copeland could clearly remember his father's absences and his mother's penchant for keeping an open house in the grotty married quarter while he was away.

When the time came for Private Copeland's regiment to move to Germany, his mother point-blank refused to pack up home like, as she put it, a camp follower. She left her husband when Daniel Copeland was nine and moved in with a travelling community. Private Copeland was less than devastated when he heard the news that his wife was gone.

Daniel's mother was drawn to the burling neon and the tacky glamour of the travelling fair, specifically a dark-haired lothario who told everyone he had seafaring roots, but had actually been born in Melton Mowbray, the son of a vicar. They toured with the travelling fairs and Daniel came to love the rough and ready life and the fact he seldom went to school. While they were mainly rough and ready, many were kind-hearted and looked after this stray and her growing son. Daniel could read and write and was taught basic but necessary arithmetic in caravans. He was expected to help with setting up and dismantling the fairgrounds, and he grew up worldly-wise and very strong. He learned how to look after himself and where necessary, he used his fists to establish his place in the travelling hierarchy.

All could have been well but for his amorality and sense of cruelty, none of which was helped by a feeble mother who caved in to his every whim. Unfortunately, Daniel looked to the wrong men as his role models. Puberty also established another of his traits – an insatiable growing sexual appetite, enabled by the lifestyle and the myriads of free and easy girls lured to the fairs in search of a bit of excitement. And at fifteen, and with a tumescent libido, Daniel, or 'Daz' as he now preferred to be known, was only too happy to oblige.

In the long stopover for the Tavistock Goosey Fair, Daz made the acquaintance of local little hard-nut called Glen Collier. Glen had been hanging round, watching them putting up the rides and stalls, and Daz went over to tell him to piss off. But Glen was sixteen, as big although probably not as strong as Daz, and he didn't feel like pissing off. They compromised and started hanging around together, because Daz didn't want to get involved in a fight he might not win. And as a result, Daz met Glen's sister, Carley. An achingly pretty girl with the body of a voluptuous woman, and what Daz wanted, he took. Unfortunately, Carley had just turned fourteen.

On the Monday, the day that the fair folk took off, Glen called on Daz on his bike and asked him if he wanted to help him finish a raft he was building. Intrigued, Daz borrowed (without permission) a bike. They peddled north on the Okehampton road and turned off down a small overgrown lane. After about half a mile, there was a high fence on their left with warning signs: *Danger. Quarry. Keep out.* The fence had gone or had been torn down in one place, which had been extensively used by local builders and traders as a fly tip. The boys pushed their bikes through the gap and stashed them in the new trees that had grown up. Daz followed Glen until they arrived at the disused quarry that was now flooded due to runoff from the moors and the proximity to the River Tavy. It was a beautiful October late-morning, blue sky and a tiny breeze that put cat's paws on the surface of the water.

"This is really cool," Daz said, wide-eyed in almost-forgotten childish wonder. "Where's your raft?"

"Over by that caved-in shed. Come on."

The raft was two pallets lashed together with six empty medium-sized black metal drums with: *Gypsum Products, Dental Plaster*, labelled on them.

"Trouble is, they're too loose," Glen said sadly.

Daz picked one end of a pallet up and lifted. Immediately, it buckled in the middle.

"You haven't tied it diagonally to each corner," he said, knowing a thing or two from constructing rides and stalls. "It needs cross-bracing. Where's some rope?"

They scoured the quarry for suitable ties and strapping. Daz showed him where to tie the ropes. After all, it was Glen's raft. After an hour's endeavours, the raft was relatively sturdy and ready for launching.

"We need to christen it," Daz told him, and proceeded to piss on one of the drums.

"I name this ship—"

"SS Collier," Glen finished for him, giggling.

They carried the raft to the edge of the water and launched it. Without their weight on the pallets, it seemed to float very well and was high up in the water.

"We'll need some paddles," Glen observed, and went rummaging for two planks, of which Daz took the heavier.

They cautiously got on board, and if they kept low by kneeling, the raft was stable. After a few tentative strokes, they got the hang of keeping the raft moving in a straight line. The water had a peculiar greenish-blue shade and was clear down for about ten feet. In the middle of the quarry, they peered down into the depths and saw the derrick of a crane reaching out of the blackness, up to a couple of feet under the surface. Weed festooned the structure, which gently waved in unseen currents. It was a mournful and eerie sight, looking down on the abandoned machinery.

"When they had finished with the quarry, they just left the crane, coz it wouldn't start and was knackered anyway. And then it flooded. There are all sorts of things down there. It's really deep."

It was tiring paddling to keep the raft on an even course, so they had a rest, bobbing near the middle of the quarry. Daz had some cigarettes, which naturally he had pilfered. He gave one to Glen and lit them with a Zippo lighter.

"Where'd you get the lighter from, Daz?"

"Found it on the waltzers, must have fallen out of somebody's pocket. Finders keepers," Daz told him. He had carved DAZ on the body of the Zippo so it was properly his now. He could have given it back to the man, because he saw it come out of his pocket, but the man was with two pretty girls and he hated him for it.

They passed the time in a companionable silence, enjoying the warm sun of an Indian summer. All would have been well had Daz managed to avoid showing off and crowing about his sexual conquests, but because he was a sociopath, he was unbound by normal social contracts.

"Hey, Glen, guess what."

"What?"

"I fucked your sister on Saturday night."

Glen Collier stared at Daz. He dropped the cigarette in the water and it went out with a slight fizz.

"You shouldn't have done that, Daz."

"Why? She loved it, panting like a little dog she was."

"She's only just turned fourteen, you dirty bastard!"

Daz shrugged and stood up. "Well, what are you gonna to do about it?"

"As a starter, I'm going to tell my dad, and he's gonna fucking kill you, Daz."

Glen went to stand up and as he was off-balance, Daz started to rock the raft.

"You bastard, Daz. Stop it!"

The raft was rocking alarmingly now and Glen slipped. As it pitched violently the other way, the boy gave a slight cry and went into the freezing water. He gasped involuntarily as his body reacted and swallowed water. He went under, his parka dragging him down. Glen struggled upwards and broke water.

"Tell your fucking dad now, you prick."

Glen tried to reach for the edge of the raft, but Daz struck him in the face with the makeshift oar. The drowning boy's mouth was an O of surprise, and without a sound, he slipped into the depths, his parka open like a useless parachute. The blackness swallowed him on his journey to the quarry floor.

It took Daz an age to row back to the bank on his own, but it gave him time to get his story straight. He dismantled the raft and scattered the components far and wide, and then Glen's bike joined its owner at the bottom of the quarry. He tried to think who might have seen him leaving the fair with Glen and invented a covering story that he had left Glen because he couldn't cycle up the hills and fell behind, while Glen went on ahead. Not brilliant, but it would do.

The police did call at the fair a couple of days later, with some pictures of the boy. They asked general questions such as if anyone had seen him, but they didn't question Daz. Because of the cold water, it was at least a week before the bacteria and internal gases caused Glen Collier's body to resurface. It was another two weeks before his gruesome remains were found at the edge of the quarry where his body had drifted. The post-mortem found a small contusion on the upper nose and forehead, consistent with a fall into the water. The coroner recorded a verdict of accidental death and sagely warned of the dangers of playing by bodies of water alone.

Daz remained with the fair folk for another season, but his presence, occasional violent outbursts and penchant for underage girls was beginning to try everyone's patience. By the end of the following season, the fair elders made it clear to Daz's mother that while her presence could be tolerated, that of her son could not. People in the community were openly speculating that perhaps he might know more than he let on about the disappearance of the boy in Tavistock. But going to the police with their suspicions was not their way. Daz left with no ceremony and certainly no sorrow. Even his own mother was realising what a foul creature she had spawned.

He headed south-west for what he thought would be rich pickings in the resorts of Cornwall. But winter on the Atlantic coast holds little allure when the holiday bunnies are swaddled up against the cold and the main players are hardcore surfers at places like Newquay. Like everyone and all things Daz envied, he hated and was resentful of these fit youngsters who made riding the waves seem so easy. He spent a miserable winter but survived on part-time jobs. He was also useful with his hands and could pass for someone at least three years older, so he managed to find work and sometimes accommodation on farms.

*

Daniel Copeland was nineteen when he killed again, but that time it really was an accident, honestly. It was midwinter in a dreary, wet and cold Cornwall and he was taking any jobs he could find, supplementing his income with burglary and casual crime. It was the type of crime that came to the police's attention but wasn't worth their expending too much time and effort to catch the perpetrator. Despite the picture-postcard view of the Cornwall of magnificent beaches, cliffs and countryside, the county was and still is one of the most deprived areas in England.

He was staying in a decrepit caravan in a park that was closed for the winter, in exchange for doing odd jobs and maintenance before the season picked up again. The park was on the northern outskirts of Camborne, a town that was in the ten percent most deprived areas of the British Isles, with incredibly high unemployment, particularly in the winter months.

There is a disturbing trend in the British underclass, which is encouraged by the state, and that is to procreate without resources to care for and nurture these unfortunate offspring. There is a reliance on social services to pick up the pieces and expect the taxpayer to reward fecklessness. The two girls were already well known to social services and had been in and out of care homes since they were twelve years old. In many European cultures, the female offspring are regarded as precious and someone to be cherished, the holy cup that will bear and nurture their own offspring to pass on to future generations. In the Camborne underclass, these girls were an inconvenience.

Daz had made their acquaintance well after the pubs' kicking-out time, at a fish and chicken shop on Union Street. He moved in, carefully at first, joking with them and offering to pay for their suppers with his wad of cash. He didn't hurry, just surveying the river before he got out his rod and cast on the waters. He offered to meet them a couple of nights later at a rather grotty nightclub that wasn't too bothered if underage girls frequented it. The girls had a good time, Daz plying them with drink and copping the odd feel in the darkness. He learned that the eldest was called Gabby (or as he called her, Gobby) and the younger was Sam.

He met them again a few days later and asked if they fancied going back to his place; plenty of booze and some pot if they fancied a joint. Gabby had recently returned from a care home in St Austell and her mum didn't much care for her number three offspring being under her feet. Sam's mother was in a fresh relationship and was working part time in a bingo hall. Her mother's new boyfriend unnerved Sam, particularly the way he looked at her. Once he had walked into the bathroom while Sam was in the bath, full of apologies, but she knew it had been no accident. As a result, she would not spend time alone in the house with him, and her mother had been working that night, which was why she had agreed to tag along with Gabby to Daz's 'place'.

It had started well enough because Daz was good company and he had plenty of vodka and cider. Then he had announced, "Okay, girls, let's get this party started. We know why we're all here."

He rolled them a joint for 'relaxation', and in due course he was having sex with Sam, while Gaby watched on, very drunk, stoned and giggling. Sam was no stranger to sex, but the experience with Daz was unpleasant, as he was rough and bit her painfully. She decided that she had had enough, and as her mother would be back from work, Sam decided to walk home to sober up.

"It's late, Gabby. I think we should go."

"You go if you wants, but I'm having a good time."

"Please, Gabby, this isn't right."

"I'm staying. I'll see you tomorrow."

Sam left and walked into the night. She was fourteen and was angry with her friend. She was fortunate to have escaped with her life.

"What a wet blanket," Daz said after she had gone.

"You didn't seem to mind when you was fucking her, Daz."

He laughed and lit another joint. "Now it's your turn."

Presently, he was humping her from behind. Gabby was far more adventurous, not to mention more vocal than her friend, and he knew she was getting near.

"Hey, Gabby, you want to come really hard?"

"Oh, yes. Come on, come on."

He wrapped the belt round her neck from behind and she began to struggle even as the climax built. "Take it, Gabby. Take it!"

She reared up and he pulled the belt tighter as they came. He collapsed on top of her and rolled off panting. "See. I told you it would be good."

He sat up and reached for the partially smoked joint. "We can do it again when I'm ready."

As he blew a contented smoke ring, Daz realised that Gabby hadn't moved and the belt was still wound tightly round her neck.

"Shit!" He rolled her over and her face was contused; her eyes were open and sightless. "Oh fucking shit!"

Panicking, he tore off the belt and shook her. "Gabby. Gabby!"

He knew she was dead by the way she flopped lifelessly, her head lolling back. *This just isn't bloody fair. She said yes, so it was her fault.*

He ran through his options. *Had anybody seen him pick up the girls in his utility truck? No, it had been dark. But what about Sam? Okay, she knew where he lived but didn't know her friend was dead. He had to get rid of the body. Bury it out on the moors? No, someone would find it. Dump it at sea. He would need a boat. This was Cornwall, plenty of boats.*

Daz cleared up inside the caravan, getting rid of the drug paraphernalia. He would put Gabby's clothes with the body, but he needed to wrap everything up and make sure it was weighed down. He headed for the site's storage area and found some old carpet that was to be thrown out. There was also a length of chain, and he dragged the two items back to his pick-up. He was calm now and dispassionately carried Gabby's body outside, where he wrapped it with her clothes inside the carpet. He secured the bundle with the chain and heaved it into the back of the pick-up. It had gone midnight by the time he drove to Hale and headed for the docks. He selected a small boat with an outboard that was moored to a larger fishing boat.

He loaded the body onto the boat and supplemented the bundle with a few breeze blocks, but he needed to wait for the tide. It was nearly 3 am by the time the channel was full enough, and he hotwired the outboard and cast off. Fortunately, the sea was calm as he motored beyond the harbour into St Ives

Bay, the streetlights falling away behind him. Well out from the shore, he put the engine into neutral and very carefully and with some difficulty, he heaved the body and the carpet over the side. It disappeared into the inky blackness of over 200 feet of water with barely a ripple and a few bubbles. A young girl had effectively vanished as though she had never existed.

Daz knew that he needed to vanish as well and reasoned that if Gabby's disappearance caused any issue, it would be assumed that the two of them had run off together. Daz motored back into Hale and re-moored the boat that now had some minor chain striations on the gunwale. He went back to the caravan and re-sanitised it, before packing everything he needed to start a new life somewhere else. He thought about setting fire to the caravan, but that would be suspicious. It was still dark when he headed north-east on the A30. Something else would crop up. It always did.

\*

He gravitated to North Devon, an area that was a holiday hotspot in the summer and had a fishing and shipbuilding industry. He found work in the shipyards during the leaner winter months and with the knowledge he picked up in the yards, he could maintain and repair the fishing boats, operating from Bideford. Because of his psychopathy, he was able to culture a network of acquaintances, and he was not beyond doing a little drug dealing. There was also a plentiful supply of young girls that migrated to the south west in the holiday season, and by the time they'd realised what a violent, degenerate bastard he was, he was long gone. And then he made the acquaintance of a local mover and shaker, a man with his own, rather lucrative business. He had now been given the opportunity to destroy other lives. Unbeknown to him, he was on a collision course with somebody just as violent, but with more control and better training. However, for the time being, Daz Copeland was doing all right, thanks very much.

Chapter 2

# EDGE AND A TEMPLATE FOR A LIFE

———

Billy caught up with Mark in the locker area, opposite the ground floor lavs. Billy was a slightly plump kid, so it was no surprise that he was sweating slightly and a little breathless. But like the trusty dispatch rider that he was for the school's downtrodden, misunderstood or non-conventional, Billy had an important message to deliver. He skittered to a halt as though riding an imaginary horse. All he needed was a cavalry hat and blue trousers with a red stripe. In the Belbin team roles matrix, Billy would have been a resource investigator.

He would have saluted because he liked and respected Mark, as did most of the Non-conventionals. Mark was kind and thoughtful. Mark could help with homework (except maths). Mark knew all about stuff like clouds, where the best hides were in the woods and the difference between the Messerschmitt BF109 E and G variants. (The BF109 G didn't have struts on the empennage and had rounded wing tips.) Mark could easily have slipped in with the Conventionals but chose not to. He was the cat that preferred to walk on his own, and that was dangerous.

"Mark, they told me to tell you. They're gonna get you after school."

"Who is, Billy?" Mark asked, although he didn't really need to.

"Ali Munroe!"

But it wouldn't just be Ali Munroe. It never was. He slammed the locker shut and picked up his PE kitbag, because it was Wednesday afternoon and treble games. The water fountain wasn't working and hadn't been for the last two weeks. Mark was glad he had gulped some water from the taps in the lavs. Belbin would have identified Mark as a Plant with definite Shaper tendencies.

"Why?"

Billy shrugged. "Since when do they need a reason?"

Mark decided to cross the bridge when he came to it, after treble games. With any luck, they would want to go home while he had a shower. Most of the kids in his class didn't bother, preferring to get out of school as quickly as possible. They wouldn't dare start anything in the gym or changing rooms. Mr Jennings took no nonsense.

It was a dry and bright afternoon and Mark fervently hoped that if they were outside, it wouldn't be football. Hockey he didn't mind; even cross-country was okay, but Mark hated football with a vengeance. This was probably another reason why he had drifted into the Non-conventionals' camp. He wished they could do cricket or rugby, but this was a state school in the Midlands, and the boys played football and the girls played netball. Mark hated the team selection and the inevitable: *You can have Edgie, coz he's crap.* There would follow an hour or so of pointless chasing after a soggy ball that bloody hurt when it hit you.

But despite the limitations of the curriculum, Mr Jennings was an exceptionally good PE teacher, one of the few in the school who could control a class of boisterous, hormonal boys. He had served for twelve years as a PTI in the Royal Navy and believed that fitness and training could be achieved in a minimum of space with the imaginative use of equipment. Like Mark, he didn't much care for football, which he regarded as a lazy teacher's cop-out. He had spent his entire lunch hour in the gym, pulling out wall bars, ropes, mats and vaulting horses, which were scattered randomly around the gym. Virtually every piece of equipment had been utilised, and Jennings was bristling with energy.

The boys were lounging in the corridor, changed and ready, when Jennings strode in with his uniform of white singlet and Ron Hills. Some of the younger female teachers rather held a candle for Mr Jennings, which was a pity because it would never be reciprocated.

"Get off the walls and stand up straight, you bunch of reprobates!" he yelled at them, counting heads. "Where are you, Bannister? Got you, stop skulking. All of you in the gym now, two lines facing, six feet apart. Move!"

They moved, and once inside, gazed in muted awe at the myriad of equipment laid out. This was going to be very different.

"Right. We're going to play Pirates. The rules are simple. Anyone I see touching the wooden floor spends ten minutes in the sin bin…"

Some of the lazier boys exchanged smirking glances.

"Doing star jumps!"

"Oh, siiiiirrrr. That's not fair"

"Well don't touch the floor then. It's simple. You can go on the mats, the vaulting horses, bars and ropes. We start with one catcher who will be wearing one of these." He held up a bunch of plastic bands. "Once caught by touching, there will be no rugby tackling or wrestling. The person who has been caught will go to the centre of the gym and put on a band. They then become chasers. Any questions?"

"How do you win, sir?"

"The winner is the last one of you that hasn't been caught. Munroe, you're a fine specimen of a young man. Your mother must be so proud of you. You're the first chaser. Now spread out and start on a piece of equipment. Chaser, you start in the middle and go on the first blast of my whistle. Two blasts, everyone freeze. Ready?"

Jennings blew the whistle and it started. A seething mass of boys diving, ducking, dodging. The chaser easily caught the first of the slower and unfit boys, but they were poor catchers. There were falls, and disputes, which Jennings arbitrated with a double whistle blow. It would never be allowed in today's health and safety-obsessed school environment, but the kids were loving it, shouting and screeching with joy, using sets of muscles they never knew they had.

The PE teacher was a very clever and skilled fitness trainer. The kids were sweating and red-faced with effort, but they didn't notice how hard they were working because they were having fun. It also gave Jennings the opportunity to see which boys needed to be developed and who were the fittest. He became interested in a short, wiry little kid called Mark Edge, who had climbed almost to ceiling height and evaded one of the fitter chasers by swinging from one rope to another. The boy was fast, agile and had surprisingly good upper body strength for one so young. Jennings resolved to find a sport that would suit Master Edge for his fifth year at school. The more he thought about it, Jennings decided that this chap would make an excellent fly-half.

After two hours of this, they were panting and running with sweat, and most of them thought that it had been one of the best afternoons they had ever spent in the school. Billy thought that he was going to die. Jennings blew his whistle for the final time.

"You help me put the equipment away and you can all get off early. After a shower! Got that?"

"Sir, my bus doesn't arrive until half three."

Mr Jennings thought about this. "Do you know what that is, lad?"

"No, sir."

"Unlucky. Now come on, everyone. The quicker you do this, the quicker you can get back to the loving arms of your families."

Mark got back to the changing room and glugged more water from the tap. He saw Munroe and his thick sidekicks saunter out of the changing rooms, shirts untucked in some audacious show of defiance. He dared to hope that they had forgotten about whatever slur he had caused them and took a long shower, without the interruption of having his wretched sister banging on the bathroom door. Mark took solace under the tepid but welcome shower and did what he always did during these moments without the distraction of other people. He wondered what the hell he had been put on the planet to do.

Out of the shower, Billy was waiting for him, sitting red-faced on a bench, and Mark smiled in gratitude.

"Why don't you come home with me? You can cut along the bypass back to get your bus. You don't have to go through the park."

Mark towelled himself vigorously, enjoying the burning itch of the increased blood flow. "Thanks for offering, but I have to get home. They will have gone by the time I leave."

Billy wasn't so sure. He was a faithful dispatch rider but totally unsuited to standing in the corner of the infantry square next to Mark.

"See you tomorrow, Mark?"

"Sure you will, Billy. Keep the faith."

The final bell hadn't yet gone when Mark left the school. He thought about waiting and slipping away with the throng, but that seemed wrong for some reason. The park and playing fields were quiet this time of the afternoon. The earlier brightness had given way to a dull, late spring afternoon and the trees along the Wem Brook were getting their full livery of early bright green leaves. The only other person in sight was an elderly dog walker, some 300 yards away. He could see the traffic moving on the A4254, where his bus stop was.

A later version of Mark Edge would have admired the simple efficiency of the ambush, and that later version of Mark Edge would have known how to deal with it. Ali Munroe appeared out of a clump of dogwood shrubs, about 50 yards ahead of him. Belbin would have categorised Ali Munroe as a sociopath. Mark weighed up the options of a right-flanking move, but one of Munroe's henchmen appeared out of the Wem Brook woods on his three o'clock. The third one had been waiting near the school and was tracking down the path on Mark's six o' clock. The park's tall wire fence blocked his left flank.

He knew what would follow and knew that he was outgunned and would be outfought. So he went on the attack and sprinted towards Munroe while the others were still too far away. Munroe was much taller and stockier, but Mark caught him on the right shoulder with his forearm. It hurt his elbow, so it must have hurt the soft, fleshy area around Munroe's subscapularis muscle. He turned and received a fist to the side of the head. Mark reeled but managed to get a fist into Munroe's gut and another to his nose before the other two were on him. Inevitably, he went down and had to protect himself from a fusillade of kicks.

He was saved by the dog walker, who ran towards them and slipped his dog, a very lively boxer. The man yelled and the gang looked up and saw him running towards them. It was the large dog that decided the day and saved Mark from what would have been a severe beating. The few punches he had managed to get in had been telling, and if it hadn't been for the bounding boxer, they would have finished the job. Munroe and his gang headed for Wem Brook and the woods, hotly pursued by an exuberant dog barking in joy at this new game.

"Are you all right?" the man asked, helping Mark to his feet. He looked at his face, grazed by the sole of a shoe, and a nostril that was trickling blood. The boy was grateful to this courageous elderly man who hadn't looked the other way.

"I'm all right, thanks, mister. Thanks for saving me."

He handed Mark some tissues from his pocket. "Do you know those kids?"

He nodded.

"Then you should tell one of your teachers."

The boy mentally shrugged. If it didn't happen on the school grounds, they didn't give a toss. Instead, he said, "I will, mister."

"Where are you going?"

"To my bus stop on the road over there."

"I'll come with you 'till it arrives."

He had some trouble retrieving his dog that like Royalist Cavalry preferred hot pursuit to going back on the lead. Eventually, it came to heel, and the man was as good as his word, waiting with Mark until his bus came. That elderly man had performed a kindness that had restored a youngster's faith in humanity. A corner of the blanket of his depression had been lifted. As Mark stared gloomily at the unlovely sprawl of the town, he decided that he fucking hated Nuneaton and would leave it the first opportunity he had.

*

He was lying on his bed, drawing. It was Saturday, so his dad was playing golf with his cronies from the Jaguar works. His sister was out shopping with her gang of plastics, as he called her friends, due to the amount of makeup they wore. As they were sixteen, they had little time for a runty, insular younger brother. Mark was drawing a Junkers 88 night fighter stalking a Halifax bomber from below. He was having a few problems getting the Junker's tail right, not helped by the fact he was using a plan and elevation plate in a book to render a three-dimensional drawing. But the Halifax was just right and the night sky competently finished with his drawing pencils of varying hardness.

There was a gentle knock on his bedroom door and Mark's mother came in. He was really worried about his mum, because lately she seemed to have sadness about her. It didn't help that she was overshadowed by an overbearing husband and a daughter who on occasions showed an astonishing level of disrespect. She was the constant in Mark's life and he loved her. Both his father and sister called him a mummy's boy.

"I managed to get the mud out of your blazer and I've stitched the seam at the shoulder." She sat on his bed and gave him a wan smile. "Is there something you want to tell me, Mark?"

He rolled over, deciding to give the tail fin a rest. "Don't think so, Mum."

"Are you being bullied? It's just that's the third time you've come home with damage to your school clothes."

Mark felt his face begin to burn with shame and embarrassment. One of the most pernicious effects of bullying was it turned the victims into apologists for their own misery. His mother ruffled his hair because she didn't need to ask any more questions.

"Keep Tuesday and Thursday nights free."

"Why, Mum?"

"Because we're going to put a stop to this."

\*

He had expected to hate the evenings in the Karate *dojo*, and the first few times he felt terribly self-conscious, in his school sports kit, while the other kids were a maelstrom of kinetic energy in their *dōgi*. He had been frightened of having to chop planks and screeching like Bruce Lee, but the experienced *sensei* took the newcomers through the basics, concentrating on the *kihon*, the fundamentals of self-discipline and the endless training of his runty little body. After his first week, he ached in parts he never knew he had. Much to his surprise, this was the part that appealed to Mark's inner self, and he felt like bursting with pride when the *sensei* presented him with his *dōgi* after the first few weeks.

The karate he practised at the *dojo* placed emphasis on fitness and self-development for the younger members, rather than fighting in its purest form. They practised with punch bags and mannequins before being allowed to fight each other, and by the late summer, Mark had attended his first grading and reached the grade of yellow belt. By the autumn, he was an orange belt and would attain a green belt, or 6th kyu, in the following February. The *kata* he had to master were becoming increasingly more difficult and he barely noticed how fit he was becoming. By now, he didn't need his mother to drive him into town and happily got the bus, looking forward to Tuesday and Thursday evenings.

His father was dismissive. "Why can't you do a proper sport like boxing or football instead of all of this stupid Chinese wrestling?"

His sister would take the piss by imitating a very bad Bruce Lee routine with all the screeches, or she would call him the 'Karate Kid'. As far as school went, he and his fellow Non-conventionals endured a low level of insurgency bullying, but one evening, after practising for the school play, Billy was ambushed by the Munroe Gang as he left the school. Billy was subjected to a violent assault where he was kicked in the head and lost an upper left lateral incisor. Martin Bleeston (another Non-conventional) caught up with Mark at lunchtime.

"Edgie, have you heard about Billy Walsh? He got beaten up by Munroe last night after the play."

"So that's why he wasn't at school this morning. Bastards."

"His mum came to the school this morning and complained to the headmaster."

"They won't do anything. They never shitting well do!" Mark said with feeling. Fuck was still very much in the fuel-air explosive grade of swearwords. The C-word was of course the nuclear option that would result in probable excommunication.

Mark pondered the fate of Billy Walsh all afternoon. Affable Billy, who wouldn't hurt a fly, and whose crime was to be fat, or 'big-boned' as Billy's mother said. The Non-conventionals' convoy system could never work all the time. Billy returned to school the next day and scurried around, taking cover with other available Non-conventionals, like a wounded zebra on the periphery of the herd. He had the beginnings of a black eye, a grazed cheek that bore the imprint of a training shoe and a hunted, frightened look.

Mark felt the familiar stirrings of his deep, seething bouts of anger that always seemed to be dormant within him, like geothermal activity under Yellowstone National Park. His anger was a symptom of anxiety, overcompensated for by violence. Mark associated anxiety with cowardice, and his anger was a coping mechanism for deep-seated anxiety. Yes, sure he was angry with Munroe and his gang, who were swaggering around the school environs like petty gangsters, but he was angrier with the teachers in his school who were in loco parentis and were supposed to have a duty of care over their charges. They seemed indifferent or wilfully blind to someone who had obviously suffered a serious assault. Only Mr Jennings seemed to notice Billy Walsh's contused face and stopped him in the corridor.

"William Walsh. You appear to have been in the wars. Is there anything you want to tell me? I might be able to help, you know." It was like he knew, because he did.

And Billy so wanted to tell Mr Jennings, and Mark who was with him so wanted Billy to tell him as well. But that would break the code. That would be a long social suicide. Jennings knew it. Billy certainly knew it, and Mark knew it, because he went through school life like a middle-rank Bomber Command crew, halfway through their first tour. While the German night fighters were attacking a lone Sterling, coned in the searchlights, the Mark Edges and Martin Bleestons could slip unnoticed into the clouds. Billy shook his head and Jennings smiled sadly.

"You know where I am, lad."

That afternoon, lost in the boredom of Alpine transhumance in double geography, Mark Edge decided that he was fed up of being a middle-rank Lancaster crew and decided to become a Serrate Mosquito night fighter.

The following week, Mark had a dental appointment at 14:30 (tooth hurtee as his fellow losers giggled). It was only for a check-up, but his mother's note didn't specify that, and Mark had no intentions of returning to school. He headed for the Horeston Grange area of Nuneaton and waited patiently around the Wadebridge Wood. He had already conducted two surveillance operations on Ali Munroe's trip home from school, a walk of about a mile and a half. He noticed one of Munroe's wingmen peel off for the bus station, while the second headed for Hill Top. Mark guessed Munroe would take the short cut through the Maltings and across the disused railway to Etone College Sports Fields. It was quiet this time of the afternoon, the period between the primary school runs and the returns from work. Mark spotted him heading towards Wadebridge Wood, and his anger was dark and seething in his soul. Munroe passed his ambush position and Mark moved swiftly, approaching from Munroe's five o' clock.

The first inclination Munroe had that anything was amiss was when the flat palm of an open hand smashed into his right ear. It was a massive blow that sent a shockwave of air into his middle ear that dizzied him, and in agony, Ali Munroe staggered and fell over. Mark was on top of him, straddling him and keeping his arms pinned down with his knees. He pressed his index and middle fingers down behind Munroe's collarbones and pushed his fingers in hard, behind the clavicles. Mark's fingers were bony and rock hard after continually pounding a basin full of building sand. Ali Munroe started to wail then scream with pain.

When he was satisfied that Munroe was incapacitated, Mark clenched his fist and started to batter his face, not with the knuckles, but hammering down with the padded bottom of his fist. Munroe's nasal cartilage went, but he kept going. Mark Edge subscribed to the IDF version of deterrence. You can't argue with violent entities who want your destruction. The anger had taken over; the red mist. It had taken less than thirty seconds and Munroe was barely conscious, leaking watery blood and mucus.

The red mist dissipated and Mark felt fear. He stood up and ran to where he had left his coat and school bag in the trees. He risked a final look at Munroe, who had pulled himself up on one elbow and was trying to stand up. Munroe was snivelling and wailing like the child he still was. Heart thumping with dread, Mark disappeared through the trees, sobbing with guilt and fear. Unknowingly, he had laid out the template for the rest of his life.

Mark spent an agony of three days before Ali Munroe returned to school. Every day and night, he expected the police to come to his school, or knock on his parents' door, and spent sleepless nights tossing and turning, racked with guilt. When he returned, Munroe wore his facial scars and broken nose as a badge of triumph. He was a celebrity because he had been beaten up by a gang of big, very big kids. He told how he had tried to fight them off, but they had knives and he was lucky they hadn't killed him. But the bottom line was, even kids like Munroe have a code, and he would have been destroyed if anybody found out he had been beaten up by Mark Edge, the school's loser-in-chief. But he was also afraid, because he had met a far more violent person than he could ever be. Munroe hunted with a gang, but Mark Edge was the solitary tiger burning brightly in the night. Ali Munroe was afraid, because he had seen the deadlights in Edge's empty eyes.

Mark also noticed a remarkable and distasteful phenomena; the fact that certain females seemed naturally drawn to violent, sociopathic bullies. Irony passed his fifteen-year-old self with barely a whisper, but again this would come to haunt him in later life. There was name-calling, random unpleasantness, but not one of the Non-conventionals was ever singled out for violent attention ever again. In truth, as they grew older, other distractions got in the way...

Mark's year was one of the last in English schools to sit GCEs and he had done well. Bs in English, history, woodwork and technical drawing, Cs in geography and Spanish, a disappointing D in mathematics and an F in religious studies, in an era when other faiths were identified but still not studied with fawning slavishness. England was still a country in contact with its core beliefs and values.

There remained the problem of what he was to do when he left school. Mark had always had an interest in all things military as a child, from making rather a good job of Airfix kits, to drawing aircraft. He had watched, in stunned fascination, the Armed Forces of the United Kingdom and Northern Ireland fighting a war over and in a small group of islands at the bottom of the world. He had lived with Irish Republican terrorism as a fact of life and knew a significant number of people and their families in the West Midlands that supported the IRA. Collection jars were often found in pubs frequented by the Irish Republican community, not the first destructive parasites the English were forced to tolerate. He despised them.

Mark had an uncle whom he really liked, and he often wished that he had been his father. He would have been astonished to find out that his Uncle Jack was indeed his father, at a time when his mother was a vivacious and attractive woman, before being browbeaten by an overbearing husband and an over-indulged, obnoxious daughter. His father never talked much about his brother, but his mother did, always with a little faraway glimmer in her eye. Jack Edge had been a corporal in the Support Company of the 1st Battalion of the Royal Leicestershire Regiment from 1951 to 1952, during the Korean War. Uncle Jack had been in the sniper platoon. On the rare occasions he visited, Uncle Jack had shown a keen interest in young Mark. Uncle Jack was the hero Mark so badly needed, and at seven years of age, Mark decided he wanted to join the Army.

One evening, his 'father' brought up the subject of Mark's future and employment prospects. "I've managed to enrol you in an apprenticeship at the Jaguar works, in the body and design shop. Your exam grades aren't too bad, but I had to pull a few strings to get you in. They'll even grant you release to college to get the maths you ballsed up."

Mark knew a storm was brewing. "That's very kind of you, Dad, but as I've told you, I want to join the Army."

His father was contemptuous. "What? A bloody mummy's boy like you. The first time the IRA shoots at you, you'll shit yourself."

"Possibly, but I have no intention of working for the rest of my life in a car factory."

"Why? Not good enough for precious little Mark? Well, working in a bloody car factory has put a roof over your head."

"I thought that was the Council."

"Which regiment? The Queen's Own Airfix Kit Makers?" Edge Senior chortled at his own joke.

The sniping continued for over a year because Mark's father refused to sign any paperwork that would have allowed him to join the Army, prior to his eighteenth birthday. Mark got a part-time job in a garden centre off the A5, lost his virginity and learned to drive. He honed his fitness levels and achieved *Nidan* level black belt. His mother remained supportive despite her misgivings, and wore down his father who agreed to sign any paperwork the Army required. Frankly, he would be glad to see the back of his disappointment of a son.

At seventeen and seven months, Mark Edge was attested into the Worcestershire and Sherwood Foresters Regiment (29th/45th Foot), issued with a travel warrant to the Army Training Regiment at Pirbright and two days' pay. The day he left home, his father was at work and his sister told him he wouldn't last the week. His mother drove him to Nuneaton railway station.

"You will write."

"Yes, Mum."

"And make sure you have breakfast every day."

"Yes, Mum."

"And for God's sake, take care of yourself."

There seemed little to say as the two of them waited for the London train. As it came into view, his mother hugged him tightly. She felt as frail as a bird.

"Goodbye, Mark."

"Bye, Mum. Don't worry."

She didn't wait for the train to pull out, giving Mark a last wave and a sad little smile. The tears were streaming down her face by the time she got back to the car. She was crying over the loss of a son, and the years she had wasted living with an empty, overbearing bully. How she wished she had followed her heart and the only man she had ever truly loved. It started to rain.

## Chapter 3

# EDGE – FIRST CONTACT

———

Lisanelly Barracks in Omagh, County Tyrone was a scattering of old War Department buildings and more modern, but just as dilapidated, buildings from the 1960s and '70s. Surrounded by a double security fence and guard towers, the barracks were close enough to the meandering Irish border to warrant a strategic importance in support of Operation Banner. It offered a certain degree of comfort and relative luxury compared to the operating bases nearer to the border; small, uncomfortable and isolated, like Foreign Legion outposts in Vietnam. Both sets of troops were fighting a similar war, separated by forty years.

A Wessex helicopter taking off from the parade square rattled the windows of the medical centre. The platoon sergeant was chatting with the Royal Army Medical Corps ward manager of the Role 2 bedding-down facility.

"So what's wrong with him and why can't he go out with the team tonight?"

"Chickenpox."

"Chickenpox? I thought that was supposed to be something kids get, and isn't everyone supposed to be vaccinated against it?"

The RAMC medic was preparing the notes for the next morning's ward round. He looked at the sergeant and shook his head. "Chickenpox is a relatively harmless virus in kids, but it can knock an adult for six. There can be complications such as pneumonia or meningitis. That's why we've admitted him so he can be kept under observation."

"So how long is he likely to be off for?"

"At least a week, and then he'll be waving a light duties chit for a month."

Sergeant Wood swore and went in search of his platoon officer, Lieutenant Attwater, who was skulking in the company office, pretending to be writing annual reports, instead of drinking tea and reading the *Sun*, which was hidden under the report folders. Wood went through the military niceties on entering an office where an officer was present.

"Sir, I've got a problem."

"Well, the orderly sergeant did say you had gone to the medical centre."

"Very droll, sir. It's about tonight's OP operation. Private Abdi has gone sick, bloody chickenpox."

The lieutenant looked alarmed. "I hope it's not catching. I remember one winter when norovirus swept through the camp. There wasn't a man left standing who wasn't shitting through the eye of a needle."

Wood sighed mentally. "No, sir. Most people have had it as kids. It would appear that Private Abdi didn't."

"And you're going out for forty-eight hours?"

"Yes, sir. A covert OP near the border overlooking Dunshaggin Farm. The Brigade tasking, you remember?"

"Of course I do," Attwater said with a slightly hurt tone. But he had forgotten under the deluge of a thousand and one tasks that junior officers had to cope with. "What about taking Private Edge? He's a steady sort of chap and a bloody good fly-half. He'll be in the Brigade team, you mark my words."

This time, Sergeant Wood sighed out loud. "With all due respect, sir, Private Edge's prowess on a rugby field is not a totally accurate gauge of how he will perform on a forty-eight-hour covert OP operation. Besides, he's a rook."

"He was bloody good during that riot in Strabane last week. And don't forget, Sergeant Wood, you were a rook yourself once. Let's give the lad a chance, eh?"

The platoon sergeant realised that further argument was pointless. He saluted as he left and went to find Private Edge to give him the good news.

*

It was dark outside when the four of them assembled in the drill shed, waiting for the helicopter. Sergeant Wood checked their equipment meticulously, making sure that both of their water bottles were full, their two twenty-four-hour ration packs were stowed in their respirator haversacks and that all loose equipment that could have made a noise was taped with the pervasive green bodge tape. He paid particular attention to Edge, making sure he had camouflaged his forearms and neck as well as his face and hands. They wore woollen headovers rather than Kevlar helmets, and most wore the much lamented, black, leather Northern Ireland gloves with the padding, rather than the new Gore-Tex gloves that always seemed too tight. They each carried the SA 80 rifle with 120 rounds of 5.56mm ammunition. Sergeant Wood sadly missed the 7.62mm SLR with its awesome stopping power.

A Puma swept in over the security fence, showing no lights, and flared onto the parade square. They all knew that the base was being well and truly dicked, and that the surrounding telephone kiosks were full of bottom feeders, waiting to phone the players to tell them a covert op was underway. They clambered on board and the RAF loadmaster checked they were strapped in with a right-angle torch with a red filter. The helicopter lifted off and headed north towards Londonderry for a few miles, before making a sweeping turn well east of Omagh, then heading for the salient of land that jutted into the Republic.

The crew flew with night vision goggles (NVGs), the streetlights a hazy bright green blur in the artificial light. The Puma headed west into the salient and the lights on the ground became few and far between. This was bandit country, and Edge felt his stomach muscles tighten and his testicles draw up inside his body. He knew that the tendrils of fear were brushing him, and unobserved in the darkness, he concentrated on breathing from below his solar plexus.

The loadmaster warned them they would be landing in two minutes; the slipstream blasting in through the open door was joltingly cold. They felt the helicopter descend and gently touch the Tyrone turf. As they went out, the loadmaster wished them good luck. The four-man patrol went out about 50 yards and the Puma lifted off. Covered by the noise of the engines, Sergeant Wood gave the order to load. Edge reached into his left-hand ammunition pouch and pulled out a magazine. He felt the rounds on the top to make sure they were properly seated and gently but firmly pressed the magazine into the housing under the weapon.

The helicopter was by now a low hum in the distance, but they waited to orientate themselves with the night. Finally, Wood gave the order to move out, him leading, Edge next and close enough for Wood to keep an eye on him, then Private Henderson with Lance-Corporal Odling bringing up the rear. They moved at a fast pace that covered the uneven ground, well spaced and irregular, just like the infantry training manual. Their boots were hissing through the long, wet grass and soon, rivers of sweat were running down their bodies, inside their clothes. Edge was glad he hadn't worn his Buffalo jacket; it was tied round his waist, tucked into the trousers underneath his smock. They had all studied their maps carefully, so they all knew roughly where they were. The border was less than two miles away when they crossed a narrow road, pushed through a hedge and started to move steeply up a hill.

By now, the arable countryside had given way to moorland and large plantations of coniferous trees. They skirted a wood to their right and crossed another road into rough ground. Wood slowed the pace right down and they went into covert patrolling mode. Moving slowly, carefully, and making the minimum amount of noise. Ahead was open land, scattered with small, deciduous copses, and Wood led the way towards one of them. It was late winter, but the new growth was coming and there was still plenty of cover within the environs of the copse. The sergeant halted them on the far edge of the copse and they moved into cover. Wood murmured to them in a low voice, setting out landmarks in the darkness by pointing with his hand.

"Five-two mils, at two hundred metres, farm. Our target. Cavan road to our right, five-eight to one-six mils. Wood beyond the road. Five-eight mils to three-four mils Cam Road to our left. Second farm beyond Cam Road on four-eight mils at four hundred metres. Our secondary target."

At midnight, Wood put them into their watches, four on, four off, making sure either he or the lance-jack was always on with Edge. Quietly in the darkness, they

camouflaged themselves and their hides, setting up a central bivvy area for the off watch. They were under hard routine; no noise, no lights and no hexamine stoves for a brew, and no fags. It would be cold rations out of the bag, and they would bag and take everything with them on exfiltration, including turds if they were unable to cork it.

Edge was on from 02:00 to 06:00, overlapping Wood first and then Odling. He was warm and comfortable because like most British infantrymen, he had spent over £500 on supplementing his personal equipment with superior kit from the commercial market. His boots were Gore-Tex Danner from the US. The Buffalo wicking jacket was now next to his skin, under the smock, and he wore Carhartt wicking long underwear. Under the smock was a German Gore-

Tex lightweight jacket, because the British Army hadn't got round to issuing troops in Northern Ireland with fit-for-purpose waterproof clothing yet. (Please note that other proprietary brands of outdoor clothing are available.)

After his first stag, Edge crawled into the bivvy. He tried to sleep but the excitement made it impossible, so he lay calmly and meditated, lowering his conscious state. He was back on at 10:00, and by now, low cloud and a miserable drizzle obscured the tops of the hills. He could barely see the farm and had to peer through his rifle's Sight Unit Small Arms Trilux (SUSAT) with its x4 magnification. The second farm that he was observing was a miserable collection of single-storey buildings, constructed mainly of corrugated iron. It was absolutely deserted, and a bare handful of vehicles passed on the Cam Road, despite this being a rat run to the border.

Soon he was soaked to the skin, despite the Gore-Tex second layer. A hardy field mouse, probably driven out of hibernation by hunger, jumped up on his arm and then up onto the rifle. It paused and stared at the immobile soldier, probably suddenly realising that this was a human being. It groomed its whiskers, jumped down and disappeared into the long grass. Edge smiled. The little cameo had lifted his soul.

At the end of Sergeant Wood's stag, he visited Edge before getting his head down. Edge barely heard him as the sergeant very carefully wriggled up next to him.

"How's it going, Edge?"

"Okay, Sarge."

"Right, what have we got?"

Edge briefed the NCO on his arc from left to right, what he had seen, numbers of vehicles that had passed on the road and their types.

"I've seen no people on foot or in or around the farm, but I did see a number of fallow deer, including calves, near the farm outbuildings."

"What's the significance of that, Edge?"

"Fallow deer are very shy and skittish, which probably means that the farm is unoccupied. And there's been no smoke."

The sergeant clapped him on the back. "Good lad, Edge. Keep it sharp."

And that was why Edge had joined the Army, for the comradeship and similar values, forged in adversity, a common sharing of beliefs. A sense of belonging. The real kind, not the ersatz kind portrayed in the Army's current ridiculous and offensive recruitment campaign. It was a sense of belonging that spanned time. From the men-at-arms and archers sheltering from the rain on the eve of Agincourt. To the men on the gun deck of the *Temeraire* closing on the French and Spanish fleet off Trafalgar. To the crew of a Lancaster, jossing and bantering as they put on their kit and waited for the WAAF-driven truck to take them out into the night, to their dispersal where 55,000 lbs of fuel, duralumin, steel and high explosives waited for them to clamber inside. It was a sense of belonging and loss that could make the eyes of frail, old men, weighed down with medals, well up on certain Sundays in November.

But the truth of the matter, despite sounding so glamorous with a frisson of danger, manning a covert observation post in Ireland's border country was crushingly and mind-numbingly boring. There was a distraction on the second day when a van approached from the border along the Cavan Road. It seemed to swerve and ended up partially against the fence nearest to their position, level with the corner of the woods. Two men got out and one started shouting at the driver. Sergeant Wood whispered to Henderson to wake the other two up to stand-to. Carefully, they wriggled out of bivvy bags and into stand-to positions.

By now, the fracas on the road had developed into the beginnings of a fight, with pushing and shoving. The soldiers who could see watched the incident with amusement. It was a pity they couldn't see the three men slip out of the other side of the van and disappear into the woods. Eventually, the situation calmed down and the two men seemed to be surveying damage to the front offside of the van. They bent down and started working on the front, but they were out of view behind a hedge. The troops assumed they were pulling the front wing off the tyre after the collision with a fence post. It was all over in about fifteen minutes, and the van disappeared down the road in the direction of Castlederg.

It was the only noticeable incident during their forty-eight hour stint. Whatever intelligence had been received concerning the two farms, they seemed unoccupied and nobody went anywhere near them. At 23:00 on the second day, they covertly packed up and sanitised the site of all traces that they had ever been there. Dead on midnight, Sergeant Wood led them out of the copse towards the road and the corner of the wood. They were using a different exfiltration route, but the first 100 yards were the same as the route in. By the gap in the hedge, they paused, adjusting to the night. The moon was behind the clouds, which was a pity, because Wood may have spotted the gossamer-thin tripwire in the moonlight. He stood up and went to move through the hedge.

Wood bore the brunt of the blast and fragments of the exploding pipe bomb. Edge, who was about 10 feet behind the sergeant, bore the brunt of the heat from the weed killer, sugar and fertiliser-improvised explosive device. His trousers were scorched off below the knees, and the right side of the Buffalo jacket melted and stuck to his skin. Partially blinded, burned and agonised, Edge dashed towards the gap in the fence, reasoning there would be no secondary devices in the same place as the first. He went down and crawled into a new position, realising with guilty revulsion that he had just put his hand in Sergeant Wood's entrails.

A few seconds after the explosion, the ambush came down on top of them, from two positions in the wood on the other side of the road. Closest to his position was the fast, occasionally faltering and intermittent rattle of an M60 machine gun. Fifty metres to his left, what sounded like an M16 rifle being fired in short bursts at the hedge line.

*A bloody mummy's boy like you. The first time the IRA shoots at you, you'll shit yourself.*

Edge felt real and tangible fear, but he also felt his overwhelming anger erupting like boiling magma. The fear never had a chance. At least Odling and Henderson were still in the game and were firing into the woods from the other side of the hedge. But they were separated from Edge by 70 or so metres, and their options of manoeuvre were limited by the hedge and fence line. Additionally, Odling was encumbered by the heavy Clansman radio. Soldiers, sailors and airmen are drilled constantly to react to effective fire in a manner that flies in the face of common sense. No amount of drilling and training can prepare a man or woman for the reality of coming under effective fire for the first time. It's a tribute to the selection, training and conditioning that most will continue to function. But until it happens, an individual has no way of knowing how they will react.

Edge's anger had trumped his fear. He went forward, dashing across the road to the flank of the woods and then pushed into the trees. It was heavy going in the densely packed, evergreen plantation. Ahead of him, the machine gin was firing the odd burst before stopping, but beyond that, the M16 kept up a steady rate of fire. As he moved closer, he could hear two men cursing and swearing in broad Irish accents. They were trying to operate the M60, a new toy gifted from Irish Americans, thanks to NORAID, but seemed to be having problems with the weapon's belt feed.

*PPPPPP*, Edge thought grimly to himself and closed in on them from the flank. They were less than 4 metres from him, bent over the top of the weapon, trying to fit the top slide down over the belt of ammunition.

"I told you we should have left this fucking thing behind and brought the AKs," one of them complained bitterly.

"It worked perfectly well yesterday. You don't have a clue what you're fucking doing!"

Edge raised his rifle and sighted with the iron sights on top of the SUSAT, knowing the optical sight was useless in the dark. He pumped fifteen bullets into the two men, who never knew what had hit them, making the last two head shots. He pushed through the wood to where the M16 was firing. Now it was risky because rounds being fired by Odling and Henderson were cracking over his head and around him. Edge bent double, moved forward and saw the man at the same time as he saw Edge. He was wearing a combat jacket and ski mask and he swung the M16 round to face this new threat. He fired one round before Edge, which ripped through his collar. Edge fired two rounds in quick succession. The first hit the man in his upper arm and he spun round with the force of the impact, the M16 thrown from his hands. The second round missed.

"ODLING, HENDERSON, STOP!" Edge yelled, but another round cracked past.

"CHECK FIRE. THIS IS EDGE."

The fire from beyond the road finally stopped, and Edge looked down at the man, who was in obvious pain.

"Okay you, Brit bastard, you got me. Now get the po-lice and a fucking ambulance."

Edge smiled unseen in the darkness, more of a grimace, and put a 5.56mm round through the terrorist's head.

"ODLING, HENDERSON. I'M COMING OUT ONTO THE ROAD. DON'T FIRE."

Edge emerged from the trees, bent double, and threw up. The other two emerged cautiously from cover.

"Where've they gone?" Odling asked when they joined Edge on the road.

"They're dead. Three of them."

"You sure?"

Edge vomited again. "Two over there, one just behind me."

The lance-jack was aghast. "I'll need to check the bodies. See what you can do for the Sarge."

Sergeant Wood was beyond any help they could give him, and while Henderson prepared a bivvy bag to carry the remains of the platoon sergeant, Edge knelt down on the road next to the body.

"Eternal rest grant unto him, O Lord, and let perpetual light shine upon him. May the souls of all the faithful departed, through the mercy of God, rest in peace."

As they slid Wood's body into the bivvy bag, Henderson said gently to Edge, "I didn't know you were a God-botherer, Edgie."

"I'm not. It just seemed the right thing to do rather than just pouring him into a bag. When you were in the firefight, did you ask for help?"

"I might have done," Henderson said guiltily.

"It's nothing to be ashamed of. No atheists in a firefight, or so they say."

When Odling returned, he took Edge to one side. "Yeah, they're all dead and they've all been shot through the head."

Edge shrugged. "Lucky shots."

"We need to get out of here. It'll be crawling with players soon and the radio isn't working, so I haven't been able to send out a contact report."

By now, Edge was in considerable pain due to his burns, and between them, they carried the body over a mile back to the helicopter RV. At two in the morning, they heard the helicopter, and Odling flashed the signal using a pre-arranged blue filter. A Wessex landed in the darkness and they clambered on board after unloading their weapons. It flew directly to the Tyrone County Hospital, where Wood's body was placed in the morgue and Edge had the burns on his legs and side treated. He had lost his eyebrows and eyelashes, but fortunately only in one area of his leg was the burn to full thickness.

As he mooched around the hospital, bored and aimless, he started to dwell upon why their operation had been compromised. He had no way of knowing that they had been caught up in a turf war between MI5 and Army Intelligence, specifically the protection of a tout being run by MI5. It wasn't the last time Edge would be involved with the dirty dealings of the intelligence services.

But the hardest part was when he lay alone on the guarded military ward, during the small hours. He had killed three men in the space of minutes, one of whom he had slaughtered in cold blood. He could pass off the two on the machine gun as making sure, but the third could not be so conveniently filed. In the years that would follow, Edge would kill many men and probably women, but it was the man in the Tyrone wood, with the M16, that would haunt him for the rest of his life.

# Chapter 4

# EDGE, THIS
# SPORTING LIFE

———

The regiment moved from Northern Ireland to Cyprus in 1991 and in the September, an extremely promising fly-half, Lance-Corporal Edge was selected to play for the 3rd Infantry Brigades rugby tour of Germany. The team, reserves and assorted skivers and camp followers were bussed to RAF Akrotiri, where a C130 was waiting for them, its two inner engines running on the hot pan. Like expectant and excited children boarding the bus on a school trip, the Army rugby tour walked towards the rear ramp and were swallowed up in the aircraft's cavernous interior. Edge was assailed by the heady aroma of Cyprus trees and AVTUR, with the heat shimmering off the concrete. He marvelled at the accomplished scruffiness of the RAF ground crews, in their clumpy desert boots, impossibly short khaki shorts and long socks. He was pretty sure they should have been pulled up to the knees, not rolled over the top of the grimy, scuffed desert boots.

Although Edge had flown in helicopters during training and in Northern Ireland, he had never flown in an RAF transport aircraft. The four rows of canvas seats and the red netting were a novelty, so he followed the lead of the more experienced and picked a seat on the starboard side, facing inwards. While they strapped in, the movers loaded pallets and lacon boxes and nets of baggage into the fuselage, and the loadmaster strapped them down to hard points on the aircraft's deck. The rear ramp went up with a whine of hydraulics and the outer engines were started. The loadmaster came round with a box full of cardboard packets, containing yellow cylinders (Plug Ear NATO Serial Number 6515-01-603-3450).

Edge felt a surge of excitement as the aircraft taxied and turned onto the runway. The engines were run up to full power and they got close up and personal with the person next to them as the Hercules accelerated down the runway. Edge craned his head round to look out of the small window level with the propellers. The saltwater lake and the telecommunications base slid past below as the aircraft climbed out. It turned gently to starboard and he was looking down at Paphos and the azure sea. The roar inside the cavernous fuselage was deafening. It was the first time Edge had flown in a C130, but it sure as hell wouldn't be his last.

They all watched with interest as the loadmaster climbed up on their shoulders and the stretcher stanchions, pulled the insulation away to reveal a myriad of pipework and started to inspect the wires and pipes with a right-angled torch. He pushed his gloved hand into the spaces and inspected the fingers.

"What you looking for?" someone yelled in question.

"Stuff that shouldn't be there," the loadmaster replied, moving with the agility of a monkey onto the next area.

"What, like holes?"

He gave the Army bod a pitying look. "No, like oil and hydraulic leaks."

Some exchanged worried glances. The aircraft was over twenty years old and had had a busy life.

"But don't worry. I'll give you a shout when we fall out of the sky."

At 12:30 Akrotiri time, the loadmaster started to distribute the white butty boxes, their packed lunches. Then followed the inevitable bartering and swapping of items so that all tastes were catered for. Edge opened the box with expectation: a cheese and ham pasty, tuna sandwiches, a packet of beef crisps, an apple, two custard cream biscuits in a wrapper and a small bag of compo boiled sweets.

"Edgie, I'll swap you my cheese and pickle sandwiches for your tuna."

"Done."

After lunch, the pilot cranked up the internal temperature and most of them slept as the C130 tracked up the west coast of Italy. There was some clear air turbulence with associated air sickness skirting the Alps, and then they were over Germany and beginning the final approach into RAF Wildenrath. The restricted view out of the window showed green fields, clumps of houses with numerous tree plantations. As the aircraft came in on finals, Edge spotted Phantoms and their hardened aircraft shelters (HASs) tucked into the trees. The Phantoms would soon be gone, victims of the so-called 'Peace Dividend'. The base would close the following year.

The troops cheered like kids as the Hercules kissed the runway and rumbled to a running pace, turning off onto the taxiway and heading for a hangar that served as the terminal building. The rear ramp whined down and they poured off the aircraft, some making improper comments to the WRAF mover in her florescent tabard who was marshalling them towards the terminal building. A whiteboard in the building informed all members of 3rd Inf Bde Rugby Tour that their transport had been delayed for two hours. Some moaned, some cursed, and some tried to find a bar that was open this time of day. Edge decided to take some surreptitious photographs of the Phantoms, despite the *No photography* warning signs in the terminal.

*

Mr Jennings had done a good job in introducing Mark Edge to rugby union. He soon realised that Mark was not only extremely fit, but he had a quick mind, very fast and sound reasoning and good communication skills. It seemed obvious that the youngster was destined to be a fly-half, as his spatial awareness was first-rate. Although rugby wasn't taught or played at Mark's school, Jennings, a former RN player, coached the local grammar school team on Wednesday evenings and Saturday mornings. He invited Mark to join them, and he became an outstanding junior fly-half. He even, quite inappropriately, played in a couple of games for the grammar school, but he was good and the boys didn't care. Mark Edge was a force multiplier who could win a game when he spotted the opportunity.

But Lance-Corporal Edge was just that, a lance-corporal, and an effective fly-half has to efficiently direct the flow of the game and provide a crucial link between the forwards and the backs. In a hierarchical organisation like the Army, more senior team members took a pretty dim view of being directed by a lance-jack. And there was a WO2 established fly-half who had played for years. Unfortunately, he was approaching forty, was slow, as thick as a whale omelette and had the spatial awareness of a deaf bat in a bell foundry. So for most of the tour, Edge was on the bench, waiting for the established fly-half to get knackered, which he usually did, halfway through the second half, and feign injury for a substitution.

Edge played in a couple of the warm-up games against RAF Germany teams from the Clutch Airfields, games that the 3rd Infantry Brigade easily won. But the Army team was roundly thrashed in a Rugby 7s game with the RAF Hospital, Rugby 7s being a very different game. Like all military rugby tours, the boys from the Brigade played hard on the field and hard off it. The night life of Germany and its beer was a strong pull, and they headed east like a marauding cohort. On the pitch, some they won; off the pitch, nobody cared. They lost some due to injury, others due to overenthusiasm in embracing the night life, followed by incarceration by the military police. They swung back west for the final games against the tankies in Bielfeld, which was won easily, and the RAF at Gütersloh, which was a different story.

There was a lot of history at RAF Gütersloh, which Edge was keen to find out about. The day before the game he would be playing in, he went to the station education centre and started reading up about the base. Construction of the base began in 1935 and from 1943-44 it operated JU88 night fighters of Nachtjagdgeschwader 2 in the defence of Germany. The base now operated Harrier GR5s of Nos 3 and 4 Squadrons and Chinooks of No 18 Squadron. The buildings on the base had an old-world feel to them, like Bavarian hunting lodges, tucked away in the pine trees. There was also a lot of the RAF personnel wearing field kit rather than their normal blues. He read the station arrival magazine and found that RAF Gütersloh was the home of the Harrier Force, where aircraft and their ground crews deployed into the woods and hides around Germany and continued to conduct armed air operations in support of the BAOR, including operations with the WE 177. He wondered if the German people would be happy to know thermo-nuclear weapons were deployed to woodland hides, but decided he couldn't give a toss, given their previous track record.

It seemed as though a good contingent of RAF personnel had been given the afternoon off, to watch 3rd Infantry Brigade give the Crabs a good pasting. As it was an easy game, the Army fielded their standby fifteen and Edge played fly-half from first kick-off. It was a carnival atmosphere at the station's playing fields that afternoon. Hundreds of the RAF contingent had turned out to watch; there was even a beer tent. Just before the kick-off, a Harrier screamed in from the airfield, came to a halt in mid-air above the pitch, pirouetted and bowed to the crowd. Then the aircraft stood on its arse and roared upwards at an impossibly steep angle. The noise was visceral and was a harbinger of the game to come.

From the first three minutes of the match, it became obvious that this RAF side was not going to be a walkover. The back row of the home pack was not only powerful, but very fast. The RAF inside centre was over 6 foot, but powerful with it, and he seemed determined to stamp his authority over the Army team's backs. Within the first ten minutes, the RAF's inside centre had sacked Edge in the lineouts, moving as fast as the Army's scrum half could move the ball out to the backs. It was like being hit by a windmill, and Edge got a good view of the turf on Gütersloh's playing field. By half-time, 3rd Inf Bde was trailing 6 points to the RAF's 10 and were a try down. Edge had been outclassed in the scrum, failing to get the ball out to the backs before the opposition inside centre hit him time after time with monotonous regularity.

At the half-time break, it was obvious that the touring had taken its toll on the fitness of the Army team. At the team talk, Edge made his views known to the captain.

"You've got to get the balls out of the scrum and lineouts more quickly. Their back row is shit hot and all over us like a rash. We've got a stronger pack. Try hanging on to the ball and drawing them in while we get organised at the back. And backs need to come in tighter. They're fit and fast and able to intercept the longer passes."

"Yeah, thanks for that, Edgie."

"You want to beat the bloody Crabs, don't you?" There were no dissenting voices. "So let's tighten things up."

The second half was a turgid affair, with both teams slugging it out in the metaphorical trenches. The RAF scored a second try and converted it, but thanks to some sterling work by the Army inside and outside centres following a good feed from Edge from a lineout, the Army responded with an unconverted try in the extreme right of the try line. The Army forwards must have listened to Edge and doggedly kept possession, forcing the RAF to concede two stupid penalties in their own half. With less than two minutes left to play with the score tied at 16-all, the ball was fed back from a ruck by the Army's scrum half. Edge had space on the right and prepared to launch a shit-or-bust drop goal.

He had enough time and time itself seemed to slow. He looked at the opposition inside centre bearing down on him. He still had space, but there was an angle and Edge was left-footed. The uprights beckoned. To his left and slightly behind, his full back was in a perfect position, but his kicking had proved unreliable throughout the tour. Lieutenant Carter was a decent enough bloke. Edge ran through the options as he heard the opposition inside centre's boots pounding on the turf. He presented the ball for the drop kick. The opposition was committed…

Edge flipped the ball one-handed high to his left. It was a perfectly judged pass, straight to the full back. Lieutenant Carter took it like he had been presented with the crown jewels. Edge never saw the kick, as he was being buried by the RAF's inside centre. Late tackle? Possibly, and the knee on the side of his head stunned him, but Edge saw the ball's parabolic curve between the uprights and heard the referee's whistle, followed by the double whistle for the end of the game.

Edge sat up and spat mud and gum shield out of his mouth as his team eulogised Lieutenant Carter like he was the new messiah. The RAF inside centre pulled Edge, who had been forgotten by his teammates, to his feet, in their celebration of a damned close thing well run.

"You could have kicked it. You had plenty of time. Why?"

Edge shrugged. "Wrong foot. He was in a better position."

"Quite the hero now, isn't he. I bet he's a Rupert."

Edge smiled ruefully but said nothing. He didn't need the opposition to tell him he'd just won the game for the 3rd Infantry Brigade.

The RAF had laid on an all-ranks function in the NAAFI club and it was exceptionally well attended. The home team was gracious in their narrow defeat and they proved to be good hosts. The beer was flowing and the distinctions between the ranks were being eroded, at which point the Army officers and SNCOs perhaps wisely decamped to their own messes. The Hercules flight back to Cyprus wasn't until the following afternoon, so Edge was quite happy to soak up the more relaxed atmosphere of the RAF and get slowly, but steadily, pissed. In the early evening, his opponent from the match weaved his way across to where Edge was chatting with a corporal from the touring side. He had three girls in tow and another male, a gawky individual with heavy glasses and an air of terminal virginity swirling around him.

"Brought you a beer, for being such a shit rugby player," he said with a good-natured grin. "This is Alicia, Becky and Sharon. I'm Orinoco. This sad twat is Scooby."

"Rut row," said Scooby.

"I'm Mark Edge. This is Danny."

"Hello, Edge," said Orinoco.

"Hello, Mark," said Alicia, and promptly sat down next to him.

"Hello, Danny," said Becky, and sat down next to him. So Danny was sorted. Orinoco and Sharon were obviously an item.

"Why Orinoco?" Edge asked reasonably.

"All us squadron engineers are named after Wombles. Stupid, I know."

"What about Scooby?"

"He's a scribbly. He wouldn't know a pitot from a jet pipe. He comes out into the field with us to write chits and make the tea."

"Ass Hright," Scooby confirmed.

Edge smiled at the girl. "Alicia, what a frightfully posh name. You must be in the RAF."

1991 was a strange time for those serving in British Army of the Rhine and RAF Germany. The First Gulf War was still fresh in military minds, and the more astute military planners and watchers realised that things would never be the same again. Of course, the politicians saw the new world order as an ideal opportunity to cut defence spending to the bone. German reunification was well in progress and the tens of thousands of NATO troops on German soil had outlived their purpose and welcome. But the drumbeat of the Cold War still held sway for those who were serving on the former Cold War front line, and the *live for today, for tomorrow you could be gasping and drowning in chemical blood agents* attitude still prevailed. Alicia was the epitome of this philosophy. She had watched Edge play rugby, had admired the cut of his jib even if he was in the Army, and decided he would do very nicely for one night only, but who knew what else the fates had planned? A pretty shitty hand as it transpired.

As the evening wore on into the night, Orinoco suggested that they should hit the bright lights of Gütersloh and then perhaps round the evening off at a *schnellimbis* for some *pommes frites mit ketchup*. Danny declined politely. He had decided to sample Becky instead. Once outside, the air sobered Edge up as they waited for a taxi. He had come to the conclusion that the RAF were completely mental, that Orinoco was a very pleasant and naturally charismatic young man. The insular part of Edge envied him. He couldn't make out their Klingon friend, Scooby, who was obviously intelligent and could hold a conversation. He was like an insecure child, who had gone through school making people laugh rather than getting beaten up. He would have made an ideal Non-conventional, except this wasn't school and he didn't know when to stop. Alicia was uncomplicatedly lovely and he knew he was going to have uncomplicated sex with her, in her room that night. Poor Edge. It was never to be.

Once they arrived at the centre of the city where the nightlife was concentrated, it became apparent that other members of the military community had decided to sample the local attractions. Groups of at the moment good-natured but noisy Brits toured the narrow precincts looking for entertainment, singing and chanting. Orinoco led the way to a boisterous bar overlooking a park, and drinks were ordered. The two men had a slightly drunken *résumé* of the rugby match they had played that afternoon.

"Your pack was better than ours, but our backs were better. We scored more tries."

"But we won, my Womble friend."

Scooby, who had been regarding Alicia's cleavage, suddenly seemed to become more animated. He grabbed Edge's arm. "No, no. You won with that pass. Even Orinoco couldn't stop you."

"Stopped him making the kick though, didn't I? Anyway, let's get some schnapps chasers," Orinoco said, and caught the attention of a German girl who was collecting glasses.

"*Fünf Bier, fünf Pfirsichschnaps bitte, mein Teutonic lieblich,*" Orinoco said in apallingly accented German. She raised her eyes, collected the empties and headed for the bar.

Alicia put her hand on Edge's, raised her finger in warning and gently shook her head. She nuzzled against the side of his head and murmered: "Orinoco is a pisshead. I don't want you falling asleep on top of me later."

Edge turned to her. "I've had a hard match this afternoon. You'll be doing all the work."

Her eyes narrowed but he smiled. There was something about the quiet, serious Mark Edge when he smiled. Alicia playfully dug him in the ribs. But she was right. Orinoco was a pisshead and fairly soon, he, Sharon and Scooby were well drunk. Edge managed to dump his schnapps in a nearly empty beer glass when nobody was looking. By 22:00, the bar was heaving with Brits, including Army supporters from the Bielefeld garrison.

"Come on, Mark. Time we were heading back," Alicia told him. Sharon and Orinoco were eating each other's faces, but there was no sign of Scooby.

"Where is he?"

"Probably gone to the toilet," Edge suggested.

Orinoco came up for air. "Said he was going out for fresh air and to howl at the moon."

"Oh shit!"

"Alicia?"

"Look, I know he's a liability, but he's our bloody liability. We need to look for him."

Edge reluctantly followed her outside. By now, there were clearly more police on the streets, who were keeping a close eye on the thickets of drunken Brits as they made their unsteady way from bar to bar. But there was no sign of the unconventional Scooby.

"Let's try the park."

Edge was becoming frustrated. This missing clown was preventing him and Alicia from making the beast with two backs. Reluctantly, he followed her into the park. It was cool in the moonlight and the trees were dappled with silver. Edge wondered if Alicia was up for some *al fresco* action, but they soon saw some action of a far more ferocious nature.

A member of the German Landespolizei in his distinctive pea green peaked hat, pea jacket and khaki trousers, was bent over a huddled body on the floor. The German copper was laying into the prone figure with what looked like an iron bar, and the victim of this beating was crying out and wailing with pain, trying to shield his head from the blows. It would appear that Scooby may have gobbed off to the wrong person at the wrong time. In a way, Alicia was right; Scooby had suddenly become his liability as well.

"What the hell are you doing?" Edge yelled and sprinted towards the policeman. "He's on the ground, helpless for fuck's sake!"

He had intended to grab the bar off the policeman, but as he closed in, the Landespolizei, who was using the weapon left-handed, whipped it round and smashed Edge across the face. Edge felt his nasal septum and left cheekbone break and reeled back, stunned. He tasted the blood that was running down his face and the back of his throat. Edge went into a half-crouch, his left hand up in defence. The policeman faced him side-on, the bar, which Edge now knew was an ASP extendable baton, drawn back behind his head ready to strike again.

Edge felt visceral fear, but again the boiling magma of his anger drowned it out. The policeman was watching Edge's face.

"*Fick dich, verdammter englischer!*" the German policeman snarled.

He should have been watching Edge's feet. The sole of Edge's left foot hit the side of the German's left knee. The kick had the force of over 3,000 newtons behind it. A human femur can withstand a force of over 25,000 newtons, but the knee is a modified hinge joint, the largest joint in the human body. No matter how remarkable it is, the human knee is not designed to pivot sideways. The policeman's lateral condyle broke away; the lateral meniscus was crushed between splintered bone and the tibial lateral ligament was torn apart. He went down screaming and the ASP clattered onto the footpath. Now Scooby wasn't the only person screaming.

Edge checked he wasn't going to get up again, then went to help Scooby, who had at least stopped screaming in preference for wailing. He was joined moments later by Alicia, who looked at the German policeman on the floor who was groaning in pain. On a whim she didn't understand, Alicia picked up the ASP and tucked it inside her coat.

"Herro Ejjie," Scooby slurred through broken teeth.

"Please just fucking button it, Scooby. Give us a hand to get him back to the bar, Alicia. We can call an ambulance from there."

Edge was sorely tempted to lay into the prostrated policeman, but settled for stamping on his hand as he tried to grab at them. Out of the park, there were more police about, and a small group spotted the two of them emerge supporting Scooby. There were four more Landespolizei, but one of them was female.

"Just go, Alicia."

"What are you going to do?" she asked, in tears by now.

"Turn myself in."

She looked at the approaching police. "Oh, Mark, I'm so sorry."

"Story of my life. It's all right, I don't think they'll give me a kicking, with one of them being a woman."

She sobbed and he looked at her sadly.

"Wasn't to be, was it?"

Edge watched her half-carry Scooby into the bar where there was safety in numbers. He stood in the harsh streetlights, waited for the police to approach and held his hands away from his side. He would see Alicia once more, but never get to speak to her, hold or touch her again.

## Chapter 5

# THE BARRISTER'S STORY

———

Horace Cutler stared out of his office window at the imposing walls of Lincoln Castle and stirred his coffee thoughtfully. On the front page of the *Daily Telegraph*, the Prime Minister John Major was outlining his vision for a 'classless' British society at the Conservative party conference, and Vauxhall had just launched the new Astra model. Cutler looked at the front page photograph of an extremely unprepossessing John Major and said "Bloody idiot."

Mr Cutler was a notable barrister who specialised in court martials, specifically in getting military personnel off through the incompetence of the prosecuting authorities and utilising every loophole in the book and many that hadn't even been written. He was waiting for his 10:00 appointment with the mother of yet another squaddie who had fallen foul of military law. Horace Cutler mentally groaned, being in no doubt that this young soldier would be a paragon of virtue who loved his dear old mum. While not being totally cynical, Cutler had heard it all before, and he wanted to make sure that there was a genuine case to be made against the charges. He had built his reputation on representing those genuinely wronged and had no truck with liars and time-wasters.

At 09:50, Cutler moved to the window and looked down onto St Paul's Lane where he saw a woman approaching from the direction of the Cathedral, looking at the plaques on the business properties. She was trim and well dressed and stopped in front of the brass plaque on the wall of his business.

"Mrs Edge, I presume," he said quietly, and went to his desk to tidy away the newspaper and take a good swig of coffee.

Today, Cutler was wearing his best shirt, multicoloured waistcoat and gold-rimmed spectacles, rather than the *pince-nez* he sometimes wore in court as an affectation to wind up his legal opponents. A few minutes later, the intercom went off and his PA/general Girl Friday came on.

"Your ten o' clock appointment has arrived, Mr Cutler."

"Thank you, Sharon. I'll be out shortly."

He made sure the Dictaphone was working, that the two chairs were set corner-on to the coffee table and that he had the ability to take notes. He took a last look at himself in the mirror, adjusted his cravat and opened the office door to the reception area.

"Good morning, Mrs Edge. Do come in."

Cutler showed her to one of the chairs by the coffee table and he sat on the second. He didn't speak for some time as he prepared himself, scrutinising his client. Mrs Edge was a small, slight woman in her forties. She seemed to have a slightly melancholic air about her, but she maintained eye contact as she shook his hand.

"Mr Cutler, thank you for seeing me at such short notice."

He bowed his head politely and because he had an eye for such things, he concluded that Mrs Edge was a dammed fine-looking woman. "Mrs Edge, I believe your son Mark, who is a lance-corporal in the Worcestershire and Sherwood Foresters Regiment, is in a spot of bother."

"No, Mr Cutler, my son Mark is in a great deal of bother. He is accused of assaulting a German police officer, occasioning him grievous bodily harm. The incident occurred during a rugby tour in Germany, while he was defending a military comrade from a violent and unprovoked assault by the policeman. The incident happened very quickly, during the course of which my son's face was smashed with an iron bar wielded by the policeman and he was subsequently beaten after his arrest by several of the policeman's colleagues, during his detention."

As soon as he heard the term 'rugby tour', Cutler felt his heart sink. Sports tours inevitably involved copious amounts of alcohol, and he had the dreadful feeling that his defending this woman's son at a court martial was going to be a non-starter. The fact that an injury to a foreign policeman had occurred made this case almost undefendable. Perry Mason couldn't get Mrs Edge's son off this one.

"Do you know the nature of the policeman's injuries, Mrs Edge?"

"He is unable to walk without crutches and he may never walk again unaided. His injuries were so severe that he is being invalided out of the state police."

Cutler was amazed at her candour. He unnecessarily took off his glasses and polished them with a silk handkerchief, desperately wondering how to let her down gently. However, she wasn't prepared to be let down gently.

"Mr Cutler, I know exactly what you're thinking. You think that my son is a violent thug who deserves everything that he gets. You believe that he was in a drunken frenzy, that he was incapable of rational thought and picked a fight with an officer of the law, carrying out his rightful duty."

"Mrs Edge. Have you ever thought of taking up law yourself?" He smiled in what he hoped was a disarming manner. The woman regarded him with a flinty stare, and Horace Cutler, scourge of the court martial system and the squaddie's friend, was unnerved.

"Mr Cutler. My son Mark is five foot seven inches tall and weighs under twelve stone, and on that night he was unarmed. The policeman who assaulted him with an iron bar is over six foot five inches. The policeman was beating a semi-conscious and unarmed man who was cowering on the ground, again with the iron bar. My son went to stop the assault and was hit across the face with the weapon and required surgery in the maxilla-facial department of an RAF hospital in Germany." She went into her handbag and pulled out two photographs, handing the first one to Cutler. "This is what my son looked like before he was violently assaulted."

The barrister took the photograph. It had been taken at Mark Edge's passing out parade, probably in his room the night before. He was looking at the youthful and pleasant face of a teenager, staring proudly into the camera in his No 5s. Cutler had seen scores of such pictures, but there was something about the handsome, unsmiling face looking at him. Mark Edge had inherited his mother's striking but melancholy features.

"This is what he looks like now."

The youth had gone and a dour and battered face stared up at him. The nose was twisted and badly set and the right cheekbone was slightly displaced. There was still something about the young man, but under the vulnerability was a frisson of contained violence. Some women would be attracted to that face; the ones who never listened to their meow or their friends and ended up in refuges.

"Although I don't blame the RAF surgeon who did his utmost almost a week after the assault, that was the best he could come up with after operating on Mark for over five hours. That's how severe his injuries were, so you see, Mr Cutler, I don't feel a single iota of sympathy for that German policeman."

Cutler removed his glasses again and massaged the bridge of his nose. "Would you like a cup of tea, Mrs Edge?"

"Could I have a cup of strong coffee please, Mr Cutler? I had to leave the house at four o'clock to make the first train from Nuneaton. Changes at Leicester, Newark. I didn't think there were any hills in Lincolnshire."

"You came by train and walked from the station?"

"My husband needs the car for work, you see."

That single sentence told Cutler a great deal about the dynamics within the Edge household. He stood up and opened the door through to reception. "Sharon, could you please make a pot of strong coffee for us."

Once the coffee had arrived, Cutler started to question Mrs Edge. "Where is your son now?"

"He's in Cyprus at RAF Akrotiri, under open arrest."

"And he is being represented by the Army's legal department?"

"Yes, and I've read that they're pretty useless," she said pointedly.

"And the court martial is being held in Cyprus?"

"No, Germany. The German authorities insisted."

"Mrs Edge, you've been very honest with me up to now. Do you believe beyond reasonable doubt that your son is telling you the truth and the whole truth, without omission or elaboration?"

"Mr Cutler, my son is no angel. He did all the normal stupid things that children and adolescents do. He has a rather cavalier attitude to sexual relations, which I have found distasteful because I am a religious person, but fundamentally, I have brought him up to demonstrate the values of loyalty, empathy, kindness and humanity. I know he has killed people in Northern Ireland during a terrorist ambush, an action for which he was commended by his commanding officer. He is brave, sometimes foolhardy, which is why he was involved in a violent altercation with a German policeman. He has never lied to me and he loves the Army. Please save his career, Mr Cutler."

He sipped his coffee thoughtfully, his mind racing. *This is a bloody no-hoper, Horace. But do you believe him through her? Probably. Does this young man deserve a chance? Yes, they all do. Can she afford it? Who cares?*

"Mrs Edge, if I take on the defence of your son, there will be a cost."

"I have savings."

"I may not be successful."

"That's a chance I'm willing to take."

"Very well, I will visit your son in Cyprus and start to prepare a defence. The caveat being that if I don't find your son's version of events compelling, I will not proceed with his defence. Do you agree with my terms?"

She nodded, looking down.

"I will contact the Army's legal department and tell them that I will take the brief, subject to the conditions I have mentioned."

When she looked up again, her eyes were glistening and Cutler felt the power of a mother's love for her son. He went out into the reception while Mrs Edge composed herself.

"What appointments do I have this afternoon, Sharon?"

"Three. Prentice verses Prentice at two. Manning verses Anglian Water at three thirty and your friend, the amorous policeman, at five."

"Cancel the Prentices and rearrange a time and date with my apologies. It will give them some extra time to sort out their differences. I will run Mrs Edge home because she's had rather a gruelling morning. I should be back by three."

"Mr Cutler?" Sharon said warningly.

"I need to find out some more about my client. I have a feeling that defending this lady's son will be rather like the RAF Brewster Buffalos going into action against the Japanese Zeros over Malaya."

"I often wonder what you think about, Mr Cutler."

"History, Sharon. Just History."

\*

Flying from RAF Brize Norton by VC10 was always a novel experience for Cutler, especially before take-off, when he watched four ground crew jumping up and down on the wing in order to get the side cargo door closed. The rear-facing seats were also a novel experience, and he wondered how these clapped-out relics could still be the second fastest passenger aircraft flying. He was processed through the small terminal fairly quickly and noticed a very young-looking female flying officer scanning the passengers as they came through the control. She clocked Cutler and looked down at a piece of paper then walked towards him.

"Good morning, my dear. Are you waiting for me?"

"Mr Cutler? I'm the station adjutant. There's a room booked for you in the officers' mess where you can drop your kit off. I believe that Lance-Corporal Edge will be waiting for you in the Station Education Centre, and we've called for the accused's friend."

"Hmm," said Cutler doubtfully.

She drove away from the airfield towards the main drag, fighting with second gear on a couple of occasions. Cutler decided to give her the benefit of the doubt; it was an extremely old Land Rover. He booked into the officers' mess and she promised to wait for him in the anteroom. While he freshened up, the adjutant sat down with a cup of coffee and read the papers that had been unloaded off the VC10 and delivered to the messes. Cutler returned about ten minutes later and joined her.

"Very kind of you to look after me, my dear."

"That's okay, sir. I'll give the Education Centre a ring to see if he's there yet."

When she returned, Cutler was reading a copy of *Air Clues*. "Whatever happened to Wing Commander Spry?"

She smiled uncertainly and the barrister wondered why the RAF gave such junior officers so much responsibility as the role of an adjutant. It was one of those things the RAF just did, probably to wind up the Army.

"He's there, sir, but his friend hasn't turned up yet, but he's on his way."

"Huh, some friend," Cutler observed. "We'll wait. Have you attended a court martial, dear?"

"Err, no. It's one of the things I need to do as part of my development programme. Like a promotion board and doing the OC admin job on a small detachment. Then I've got Junior Officers' Command and Staff Course."

Cutler nodded thoughtfully. "I would be delighted to explain the workings of a court martial, and of course the role of defence barrister, over dinner this evening. What is your name?"

"It's Ona. Gosh, would you? That would be really helpful. The station commander will be so pleased. Is he in a lot of trouble, Lance Edge?"

"I'm afraid that he is. He's drowning in it."

She put her cup on the table and a hovering steward took it away. "That's a pity. We've been looking after him and giving him stuff to do. OC Admin says it's so he doesn't brood. I like him, for what it's worth, and hope you can get him off. He doesn't seem capable of doing what he did. I'll drive you to the Education Centre."

"Thank you, my dear," he said imperiously to the RAF education officer and scrutinised the two soldiers in the room. "Lance-Corporal Edge, I presume?"

He looked at the officer. "And who are you?"

"I'm Lieutenant Gardner. I'm the accused's friend."

"How nice. Now in the nicest possible way, bugger off."

Gardner bristled angrily. "I'm here to advise and look after Edge in a pastoral rather than a legal sense. And just who the hell do you think you are?"

Cutler gave a start as though the question was the most grievous impertinence. "Why, I'm Horace Cutler QC. I have been commissioned to represent Mr Edge during his upcoming court martial. Now, Lieutenant Gardner, I'm glad that you have Mr Edge's best interests at heart, however, whatever you call yourself, you are part of the system. You are therefore the enemy. What I have to say to Mr Edge is privileged information that is only to be shared by a legal representative and his client. Be so good as to leave, would you?"

It was clear the lieutenant was fizzing as he left the room. "I'll be outside when you've finished, Lance-Corporal Edge."

Mr Horace Cutler looked at a bemused Edge and smiled. "Sit down, laddie."

He took the chair opposite on the other side of the table. "Now, your mother, who is a charming and remarkable woman by the way, has commissioned me to represent you at your court martial. And take your bloody hat off. You're indoors now."

"But what about the Army's legal defence that was taking my case?"

"About as much use as Doctor Crippen's defence team. I, on the other hand, could get you off. But only if that's what you want. I don't believe in wasting your mother's money."

"Of course I want to get off. What sort of question is that? And where did Mum get the money from?"

Cutler opened his briefcase and removed a Dictaphone, lay it on the table between them and started to record the conversation. "Edge, I want you to tell me everything that happened that night, including the assault of the German policeman and what happened after it until you were released back into British custody."

Edge did his best, but it wasn't enough. He shrugged and stared miserably at Cutler's watch chain. Cutler suspected that his client had buried the visceral and what must have been terrifying violence and the events of that evening in his subconscious. It was a military coping mechanism, but it wasn't helping him, or indeed Edge in the longer term. He knew that what he would do next was not strictly scrupulous.

"Look carefully at the back of the watch," Cutler said, holding it up by the chain in front of Edge's face. "You can see the inner workings. Aren't they beautiful?"

Edge looked more closely at the tiny cogs with their jewelled movement, and he began to tell Cutler every little detail of what had happened. He spared nothing. He told him about his final game winning pass. His desperation to stay sober so he could make love to an RAF girl called Alicia. The moon on the trees in the park. The jolting violence perpetrated by the German policeman on the helpless Scooby. The pain as the ASP smashed into his face and the sound of a knee joint being destroyed by a karate kick. The beating in the cells. The reconstructive surgery on his face at the RAF hospital and his aching longing for Alicia, who had picked up the policeman's ASP, and her friend called Orinoco, who had tried to get him drunk to make recompense for a late tackle.

Edge looked away from the watch and blinked. "It's no good. I'm sorry, Mr Cutler. I just can't remember."

"Your mother was right. There is something about you. Yes, I know all mothers say that about their little soldiers, but in your case it's true. Although she may be rather shocked to have known about her son's intentions with Alicia."

"Are you going to represent me?" Edge asked, wondering how the QC knew about Alicia.

"I'll see you in Germany. Keep calm, try not to worry and don't do anything silly."

Cutler thanked the education officer and phoned the extension he had been given for the station adjutant. While he waited for her to pick him up, the barrister formulated his plan. He wasn't going to defend Edge. He was going to destroy the prosecution's case and, if necessary, the German policeman. After what he had heard, he would enjoy that.

*

The senior engineering officer (SENGO) had been working late on a Tornado GR1 that had gone unserviceable on the route from the UK to Ali Al Salem in Kuwait. It was late and he was tired, but at least they had found out what was wrong with the damned thing and he was confident they could fix it. He was too late for the bar, let alone a meal, and decided to turn in. As he walked past the wing of the officers' mess that contained the guest suits, he saw Ona, the station adjutant, coming out of a room and then the fire door. She froze when she saw him.

"Hello, Ona."

"Hello, sir." She scurried off in the other direction.

The SENGO was too tired to wonder why the adj had looked so guilty…

\*

Back in Lincoln, Cutler gathered his three associates, or as he called them, his elves. "Whatever you're working on will need to go on the back burner for a few weeks. Monica, I want you to go to Germany, specifically RAF Gütersloh, and track down three people, all of them in the RAF. Firstly, SAC Alicia Meredith, who should be able to help you find a gentleman known as 'Scooby' and another chap, an engineer who is known as 'Orinoco'. I want to find out everything that happened that day and night. Meredith and Scooby are the ones to concentrate on. Get Sharon to help you all she can, booking flights and suchlike.

"Stephen and George, I want you to concentrate on the policeman, Polizeiobermeister Brauer. I suspect that someone who is as violent as Mr Edge says he is would have a string of complaints levelled against him. Start with some of the law firms in the Bielefeld area and see what you can throw up. Oh, and press the Landespolizei. I want them to know that we're after them because Edge was assaulted while in their custody. I want the Boche bastards to be sweating, all right? I also want a progress report every day while I go into action with the Judge Advocate General's department."

"Mr Cutler, why are we expending so much time and effort on what is effectively an open and shut case against this squaddie?"

Cutler took off his glasses and stared at Stephen. "Because he is innocent of a heinous assault on a policeman. In fact, he is the victim of an assault. Once by the policeman and then a cowardly beating while in German police custody, and I want to nail the bastards."

"Can we be sure?"

"I can. I've met him."

\*

A week later, Cutler called for a progress meeting. If George had a tail, he would be wagging it. Monica was hiding her light under a bushel and Stephen had some news regarding the Bielefeld Landespolizei. Sharon was taking notes.

"Right, Elves, what have you got for me? You first, George. It looks like you can't contain yourself."

"Mr Cutler, there have been several complaints against Herr Brauer for heavy-handedness from both British civilians and Service personnel."

Cutler shrugged. "So what? There are tens of thousands of British Service personnel in that area, and they ain't no plaster saints, as Kipling so perfectly put it. They drink a lot and get lairy. I'm afraid we'll need a lot more, George."

The associate smiled. "Is beating someone to death enough for you?"

Cutler took off his glasses. "Spit it out, George."

"A couple of years back, Polizeiobermeister Brauer was accused by a German woman of beating her fiancé to death, outside a football ground in Bielefeld. The lady's name is Edda Schuster and her fiancé was a Timothy Nowell, English, working for the Stadtsparkasse bank. The attack was unprovoked and she alleges that Brauer used an iron bar to beat Mr Nowell while he was on the ground. He died in the hospital when they switched off his life support apparatus. He never regained consciousness.

"Ms Schuster tried to bring a private prosecution against Brauer with the help of a civil rights lawyer, who specialised in cases of police brutality, but there were no witnesses, and other police said that Brauer had been with them outside another part of the stadium. The case was dismissed by the federal prosecutor."

"Will she appear as a hostile witness against the prosecuting advocate's case?" Cutler asked.

"She will be glad to, Mr Cutler."

Cutler grinned. "Well done, George, and you too, Stephen. I'm sure you did a lot of the digging as well. What can I say? Over to you, Monica."

Cutler thought he detected Stephen giving Monica a slight smirk, as if to say: follow that.

"I managed to track down Senior Aircraftswoman Alicia Meredith who agreed with Mr Edge's version of events. She witnessed both the policeman assaulting the chap called Scooby and the single blow to Mr Edge's face. Scooby is in fact a Senior Aircraftsman Scotton, and he has been severely physically and mentally traumatised by the beating he received from Polizeiobermeister Brauer, in the park that night. I'm afraid Orinoco, or rather Corporal Rigley, is no help. He remained in the bar with his girlfriend when the assaults took place. He did ask me to say to you, Mr Cutler, that 'Edgie is a bloody good bloke for a pongo' and he hopes you get him off, and he's sorry about the late tackle."

"Will Meredith and Scotton appear as witnesses?"

"Yes, Mr Cutler."

"Good girl and well done! Right, we have our lines of attack. I will need to fly out to Germany and school our two witnesses, and I would also like to meet Ms Schuster if that is possible."

"Mr Cutler, there is something else. Alicia Meredith has in her possession the weapon used to assault SAC Scotton and Lance-Corporal Edge. The policeman dropped it when our client 'took him out' and Alicia picked it up. It is an ASP, one of those telescopic steel batons. They are strictly illegal in Germany."

Horace Cutler rocked back in his chair. "Oh, Monica. That's absolutely outstanding. You have done splendidly, Elves, and that includes you, Sharon. Dinner will be on me this evening, *The Bowl Full* at nineteen hundred hours. No excuses, as this is a three-line whip."

The day after Cutler got back from Germany, just before lunchtime, Sharon came on the intercom. "Mr Cutler, I have a call from a Mr Finegold from America on line one. He wants to speak with you as a matter of urgency, regarding your court martial case. He says he's from the Simon Wiesenthal Centre."

Cutler was both surprised and intrigued. "Then you had better put him through."

He heard the click and the slight hollowness from the satellite. "Good morning, Mr Finegold. Horace Cutler speaking. This is an early call for you."

There was a slight delay. "Good afternoon, Mr Cutler. My name is Hiram Finegold, and I am phoning from the Simon Wiesenthal Centre in Los Angeles."

"Well, this is a surprise, Mr Finegold. What could I possibly do for you?"

"It is I who can do something for you, Mr Cutler. Let me explain. I believe you are investigating a member of the German Landespolizei, a Polizeiobermeister Brauer. I am not interested in the details of the case, although I believe you are defending a young British soldier. You see, we also have an interest in Herr Brauer, or rather his family, specifically his father, who is deceased but unlamented."

"Riiiight," said Cutler, slightly confused now.

"Mr Cutler, we have tracers on every person of interest that the Centre is concerned with. This triggers a notification if these individuals are being investigated. When your associates made enquiries into Polizeiobermeister Brauer, a member of the German law firm notified us that a person of interest to us was being investigated. Hence my call to you today."

Cutler remained slightly bemused, but now this was tinged with a feeling of unease at just how far the tentacles of the Jews, which meant in all probability MOSSAD, stretched. It was as though Finegold had read his mind.

"Don't waste any time worrying about Herr Brauer, which is not his real name, by the way. He is a thoroughly unpleasant individual who was fed with his mother's milk hatred for my people. But he hates the British, especially members of your armed forces much more. A visceral hatred because his father was killed by a British soldier in 1945. Let me tell you about his father, Mr Cutler, and you will understand."

And he did, and Horace Cutler knew that he could save Lance-Corporal Edge, but in the process comprehensively destroy the German policeman, his reputation and his family. Cutler thought it a price well worth paying.


## Sennelager Court Martial Centre, Germany, April 1992

Cutler's first German witness, Edda Schuster, had certainly been impressive and had heavily dented the credibility of the prosecuting advocate's case, but she had not landed the killer blow. Cutler was trapped by the horns of a moral dilemma: whether he should use Finegold's information or not. However, Polizeiobermeister Brauer's demeanour when giving evidence convinced Cutler to use the nuclear option. He would, he decided, rather enjoy it.

"Judge, I am concerned that this case might be fatiguing for the witness. I was hoping to resume after the lunchtime recess."

The judge advocate sighed. "Will this take long, Mr Cutler, and if not, ask Herr Brauer if he minds continuing."

Cutler duly did.

"No, not at all. I'm rather enjoying this."

Cutler peered at him. "In which case, Herr Brauer, you'd better fasten your seatbelt because this is going to be a bumpy ride." He didn't translate this for the benefit of the court.

Cutler opened his briefcase and handed out four folders, one to the judge advocate, one to Ms Campbell, one to the German and one to the board.

"Polizeiobermeister Brauer, I'm not going to ask you why you hate English people so much, particularly those in Her Majesty's Armed Forces, because I already know why.

"You are rather proud of your family history, are you not? Your father who died heroically at Seelow in 1945, defending the Reich. It must have been so cruel for you as a child of five, to have your father snatched away in the last weeks of the Second World War. At least you have the knowledge that your father died nobly defending the Reich. What was his regiment, Polizeiobermeister Brauer?"

"303rd Infantry Division," Brauer said, but he looked uncomfortable.

"And his body was never found among the tens of thousands who died on the Heights. Judge, Gentlemen of the Board and Herr Brauer, kindly open your folders and have a look at the top photograph."

The photograph showed seven German SS Officers standing for a posed photograph, in front of a series of wooden single-storey huts. "Herr Brauer, which one of these fine upstanding specimens of the Master Race is your father?"

"None of them."

Cutler took off his glasses for dramatic effect. "Really? Are you sure? Let me help you. That officer standing second from the left in the greatcoat is your father, isn't he?"

"No!"

"He is in fact Untersturmführer Adalhard Günther. Your father and mother registered your birth in 1940 and you were baptised as Clemens Günther. If I can draw the court's attention to the next document, which is the register of births for March 1940 from Buchholz in der Nordheide. And there you are, Herr Brauer, or should I say Günther, fifth name from the top. Thank heavens for German efficiency at record keeping. If your birth had been registered in Hamburg, the records would almost certainly have been destroyed in the bombing, and no one would have been any the wiser.

"You see, your dear old dad managed to raise quite a bit of interest due to his military service, if I could dare to call it that. In fact, the Simon Wiesenthal Center in Los Angeles has quite a file on your father and indeed you and your mother by association. I must thank the Centre for their kind cooperation in this case.

"Your father did not die a heroic death at the Seelow Heights, and the furthest east he served was in Belzec Extermination Camp. In fact, that photograph with his chums was taken in 1943 at Chlemno Death Camp."

Cutler paused and looked at Brauer, who now had a noticeable shake. "So why do you hate the English military so much, Herr Günther? Is it because when the British Army liberated Nauengamer Concentration Camp in 1945, a dispatch rider from the Royal Corps of Transport, a Corporal Alfie Mullins, was so incensed with what he saw that he didn't take kindly to your father trying to pass himself off as one of the inmates? Do you hate them so much because your father tried to remonstrate with a lowly corporal, when he knew the game was up? And that corporal drew his pistol and shot your father through the head, twice for good measure. You hate the British military, particularly the English, because your father was a gutless swine. A mass murderer of women and children. A lowlife Nazi who got his comeuppance from a bloody lowly corporal."

"No!"

"Your mother took you north and across the border into Denmark, and a few months after the final surrender of Nazi forces, the pair of you recrossed the border back into Germany, where you posed as displaced persons with no ID documents. And you became Clemens Brauer. And all would have been well, apart from your father's disgusting war record and the long memory and reach of the Simon Wiesenthal Center.

"Timothy Nowell just happened to be in the wrong place at the wrong time. You thought he was in the military, so you beat him to death. Your life and police career is built on a lie and the bodies of emaciated concentration camp victims. You are a vile piece of ordure and you are not fit to clean the boots of my client, Lance-Corporal Edge."

Cutler almost hurled his *pince-nez* on the table and without bothering to look at her, snapped at Ms Campbell, "Your witness!"

To her credit, she did try to extricate the faeces from out of the fan, but Cutler had eviscerated the main prosecution witness. The mangled phrases from the translator didn't help, and by the end of it, former Polizeiobermeister Brauer was on the verge of a breakdown and the German police observers had left the court. Edge looked as stunned as Brauer.

The court took a late lunch and reassembled at 14:30 for Edge's sentencing. Cutler had wisely taken himself off on his own, where he pondered who he was most angry with. The German policeman for his lies and violence, or Ms Campbell prosecuting, for making him destroy the man in court.

Lance-Corporal Edge had by his own omission assaulted a German policeman occasioning grievous bodily harm, but the presiding judge and board of officers were in no doubt that Edge had acted in justifiable self-defence. He could not be admonished, so he was sentenced to the minimum of twenty-eight days of military correction and reduced to the ranks. This would have no adverse effect on his future army career and was a calculated insult to the German police.

Cutler asked to see Edge alone before he was taken to the cells for the onward journey to Colchester. They stared awkwardly at each other and Edge smiled.

"Thanks, Mr Cutler. I don't know how you managed to find out that stuff about Brauer, but I'm grateful. I'll pay the fees once I leave the glasshouse, but it'll have to be a bit each month, if that's okay with you."

"I'll phone your mother and let her know what's happening later today. Edge, I would like you to do me a favour once you get out and rejoin your unit."

"Sure, Mr Cutler, anything you want."

The barrister handed Edge his card. "I would like to hear from you regularly, about how your life is progressing. You can either phone or write, but I want to hear from you."

"I will, but why?"

"Because I think you're a remarkable young man, Mark Edge, and I think your future will be most interesting. Promise?"

"Yes, I promise, Mr Cutler. And thanks again."

"Contact your mother as well. Soon as possible. Until we meet again, Mr Edge."

They shook hands and Edge began his twenty-eight days of incarceration at the Military Correction Facility.

## Chapter 6

# EDGE, EMBROILED IN THE BALKANS

---

Edge hated Banja Luka Metal Factory. He hated the cold, draughty accommodation tents that had been erected inside the factory's precincts, he hated the boredom, and he hated the dull and monotonous food. But above all other things, he hated having to go out patrolling in the light blue helmet covers. As one of his section had succinctly put it as they loaded up in the loading bay by the camp's main entrance, "Tell you what, Corporal, why don't we paint a fucking target on our backs? Then all sides will know exactly where to shoot us."

Corporal Edge was sitting at a trestle table under the leaking roof and was writing a bluey letter home to his mother. He knew that she worried when he was on operations and loved to hear from him. Unfortunately, he found it difficult to know what to say. Edge had repaid his debt to a corrupt German police department and served his period of Purgatory, while the regiment grew to trust him again. He now had his two stripes and they were stitched on. He had actually enjoyed his brief stint in the glasshouse, even the repetitive drill and PT, where he didn't have to think very hard. He left Colchester as fit as a butcher's dog and had studied back with the regiment where he finally passed his maths GCE as well as O-levels in economics and English literature. It's a pity he hadn't studied European history, which might have been useful for his current tour.

Another of his pet hates was being cooped up in the back of a Warrior APC, stalled at many of the illegal checkpoints the Serbs threw up to hassle and hamper the British IFOR patrols, while the grown-up in the lead command vehicle negotiated with the gangsters. The chief gripe of all the Toms, apart from the lousy food and accommodation, was their pathetic rules of engagement on their Card Alpha, which seemed to have been produced by a *Guardian* columnist and was an incitement to get abused by the locals. To their east, the Americans in their zone could hose down the local warlords' private armies for looking at them in a funny way. Some wag from the paras had produced their own version of the Card Alpha, which seemed to be pinned to every noticeboard on the base.

Edge looked up from his bluey at the runner from the ops room who had blundered into the table. He was a big Fijian lad whose grasp of English was at times colourful and other times hilarious. Out beyond the wire he was a dynamo of a soldier, never tired, never complaining and always grinning.

"Corpse Hedge, major ops man wants to see you. Right now, he says, PDQ."

"What's it about, Rishi?"

The Fijian private rolled his eyes. "You think he'd tell me, Hedgie?"

"No, I suppose not," Edge said, agreeing at the implausibility of it. He folded the bluey and put it into his smock pocket to finish later.

The Operations Section in Banja Luka Metal Factory (BLMF) was a number of Portakabins joined together and divided off into offices for the various headquarters' disciplines: G1 Personnel and Admin, G2 Intelligence and Security, G3 Operations, G4 Logistics, G5 Plans, G6 Communications and IT and G9 Civil Affairs and Cooperation. G8 Finance and Contracts was co-located with the G9 cell. The G7 training cell didn't usually deploy on non-established operations.

"Which one, Rishi?"

"G9, at the back."

Edge went round and found the door marked: *Civil Secretariat. No Unauthorised Entry*, and knocked on the door. It opened and he was hit by a blast of hot air as he went into the office. Inside, there were four civilians, including a man wearing blue UN body armour, a major from G3, a female lieutenant from G1, Captain Gardner, his 'friend' from the pre-court martial and newly promoted. There was also a sergeant and corporal from the Royal Military Police (RMP), who looked at Edge suspiciously as he went in. His reputation had obviously preceded him.

Captain Gardner looked at Edge as he came in and grinned. "Ah, Corporal Edge, we have all, especially you, been selected for a special mission that, the Major tells us, requires a great deal of tact and diplomacy. As we will be dealing with the locals. I especially asked for you, because of your proven track record regarding the host nation, especially their police forces."

Edge's face was deadpan, but the RMP sergeant looked at the captain as though this was no place for levity. Edge often wondered about Captain Gardner. He could be and often was kind to the soldiers, but seemed to view them with laconic contempt. Perhaps Edge might have been surprised to find out that Gardner came from far humbler roots than he did, and the lackadaisical veneer was a way to hide the officer's own anxieties and lack of confidence. They were incredibly alike.

The ops major outlined the task they had been given. To the south-west of Banja Luka, near a town called Ključ, the locals had told the UN IFOR forces that there was a mass grave in the woods. IFOR had requested a small British military presence, as the area lay within the British zone of control, to liaise with the UN team that was investigating the site. Their presence was to be low-key, to provide a police presence, hence the RMP involvement, and be small enough not to disturb sensibilities in the area. Ključ lay on the fault lines between the Serb, Bosniac and Croat communities, and a delicate touch would be required. They would have more robust rules of engagement, and Edge was heartily gratified to hear that they would not be wearing the hated blue helmet covers. There would be the four of them in two vehicles: a Land Rover (camouflaged, not white) for the RMPs and a Land Rover FFR for Gardner and Edge. Edge was surprised to hear he would be drawing an LSW as well as a Browning pistol.

The Major outlined the mission: "You'll set off at zero eight thirty hours tomorrow and rendezvous with a member of the UN team in the Risović Comerce in Ključ. We'll send a Warrior patrol ahead of you so you don't have any problems with illegal road blocks. You'll be accommodated in local housing that's now empty and you'll be given an allowance for food. And gentlemen, a mild warning to you. This isn't a bloody holiday, so stay on your toes. I'd like an evening sitrep from you, Captain Gardner, at twenty hundred hours every evening and any time you run into any problems.

"Any questions?"

"What's the duration of the mission, sir?" asked the RMP sergeant.

"Until the UN team have furnished enough initial evidence. Less than a week or it could be up to a month. Right, if you could stay behind, please,

Captain Gardner, I'll give you your full orders and you can brief the others later this evening. And don't forget to pack some civvies just in case."

\*

The two Land Rovers left Banja Luka and headed approximately due south on the R411. The RMPs were in the lead vehicle, the FFR following 200 metres behind with Edge driving. His LSW was clipped between the two seats next to Gardner's L85. The LSW was similar to the L85 rifle but had a longer barrel with a bipod for sustained fire. Edge would have preferred to have been issued with the FN Minimi. Gardner was rolling a cigarette and when finished, inspected it. Not too bad. He handed it to Edge.

"Cheers, sir." He lit it deftly, one-handed with a Zippo, and slid the side window open. "Question for you, sir. Despite the endless amusement I obviously provide you with, why me for this job?"

Gardner didn't answer until he had rolled his own cigarette and clicked his fingers for Edge's Zippo. "Because you're bored, aren't you? Patrolling for the sake of it and not being able to do anything kills a soldier. It's killing me. There's only so many times you can read *The Green Mile* and *Bridget* fucking *Jones's Diary*. Even the porn is shit. Bored soldiers worry me. Especially bored soldiers like you, Corporal Edge. Just getting away from that dreadful place, can't you feel your soul lift?"

He had to agree that he could.

"And you never know what's round the corner."

And that was true, and probably for the better.

\*

The UN teams were digging several sites in the open and sloping forest. In a clearing, they had erected some large tents where the first rudimentary post-mortems could be performed. The rains had gone and there was something of an Indian summer. Out of the breeze and in the sun it was pleasantly warm. Apart from the sickly, cloying stench of death.

Gardner was talking to one of the heads of the UN team. The two RMP were helping to record some of the forensics as they had been trained to do. Edge was supposed to be looking after them, so he prowled unobtrusively through the trees, just acting like their eyes. He was briefed that the dig was being conducted over a number of sites, including one isolated site north of the road. Occasionally, he stopped and noted some of the wildlife. Biting insects that were so big they seemed to disturb the air as they went in search of his blood. Thank the Lord for Avon's *Skin So Soft*, as recommended by his uncle, the Scottish Gillie. As he prowled through the forest, Edge was struck by just how happy he felt. He was alone, trusted to do something in a regime that was extremely relaxed, compared to the miserable existence of BLMF.

North of the road, Edge came across the smaller dig. A little tent had been erected and three people were excavating the site; two women and a man. The man looked up at Edge and nodded, before going back to photographing the trench. The elder woman was hefty, difficult to tell her age because of the scarf wrapped round her face because of the smell. The second woman was dark-haired, tied back, some of which fell into her face. She was wearing a t-shirt and dirty shorts and seemed to be concentrating on something in the earth. She looked up at Edge, who smiled. She scowled and went back to her work in the trench.

*Charming*, thought Edge, and went back to his slow, random and thoroughly enjoyable patrol of the site. An hour or so later, he was back at the same spot again. The man had gone. The older woman was sitting against a tree, smoking a cigar Edge was amused to see. The other woman ignored him.

"Afternoon, ladies," he said pleasantly.

The younger woman turned to the other one smoking under the tree and said something in a language he couldn't understand. They both cackled with laughter. If Edge could have given a shit, he would have been embarrassed. Instead, he meandered off to enjoy the afternoon, the smell of the forest away from the graves and the dappled sunlight coming through the trees.

*

Captain Gardner had insisted on an established routine. They would all meet at 18:30 for a report on the day, any update on their orders and then have a communal meal. From then on, when Captain Gardner went to do his daily sitrep on the radio to BLMF, the time was their own. The house they were staying in was large, although partially damaged in the fighting of three years before. Gardner had his own quarters. The RMP sergeant should have had his own, while the two corporals shared the largest bedroom. But the scuffers had elected to stay in the same room, so Edge had his own room with a proper bed.

The local café kindly provided coffee, tea for their flasks, rolls, meats, cheeses and pastries in the morning, before they drove out in the two vehicles to the dig sites. To Edge, this life was heaven on earth.

Even the return of the rain the next day couldn't dampen his spirits. He prowled the forests with a new resolve, his LSW front slung so he could spot the wildlife with the weapon's SUSAT. Inevitably, he was drawn once again to the small site north of the road. The old Babushka was carrying items from a UN pick-up on the road into the small tent. The man of the previous day was not there, and the other woman was in the trench, oblivious to the rain and the mud that had plastered her hair to her face. Edge went closer and smelled and seemed to taste the stench at the back of his throat. He looked down into a jumble of twisted limbs, tangled and matted clothing, bones, skulls partially covered with flesh, with the rictus grin into eternity. This was no heaven; this was the inner reaches of hell in a Balkans forest.

"Jesus!" said Edge.

She rocked back against the slimy side of the trench and looked up at him, a trowel in her hand. "Are you glad you've satisfied your curiosity? Happy now?"

Her English was good, clear but heavily accented. He looked at her properly for the first time. The wet t-shirt clung to her thin, oh so bloody thin body. It was obvious just how cold she was. Her pinched face looked at him like she felt hatred for him and his kind. Her eyes seemed to bore into his soul.

"Now you've had a look, why don't you fuck off."

Edge stepped back, unslung the LSW and his daysack. He crouched down, opened it and pulled out a Gore-Tex jacket, putting it on the parapet of the trench.

"Okay, I'll fuck off. But this is for you to wear. You're bloody freezing, and if you want to join them," he indicated to the corpses, "then crack right fucking on. Don't bother thanking me, because me and my kind have done shit jobs like this for hundreds of years, so I don't, I really don't, need your fucking thanks."

Edge moved away, feeling a strange emotion, like anger but more of a kind of disappointment. He remembered his words to her and began to feel a little bit precious. She watched him move away into the trees until he was lost in the rain. She picked up the Gore-Tex jacket and pulled it on. Predictably, it was too big for her.

*

The next day, Edge avoided the site north of the road, skirting it but keeping it within his patrol area. Captain Gardner noticed that Edge seemed rather quiet and over a tea asked him what was wrong.

"Nothing really, just that bloody woman digging in the site on the other side of the road. What an unfriendly bitch."

Gardner pinched one of Edge's cigarettes. "Oh that's the lovely Ms Jozica Marić. She doesn't really get on very well with the rest of the UN people here."

"Really, sir? You do surprise me. Now why ever would that be?"

"Well, it's all these people in the mass graves. The UN desperately want it to have been the Serbs who slotted them, but Ms Marić has a different take on it, and what's worse is that she's a local. It's all politics, Mr Edge."

"So she's a Serb."

"No, she's a Croat from the University of Sarajevo, some sort of forensic anthropologist. She was involved in the war between the Croats and Serbs back in the early nineties. Complicated, isn't it?"

A few days later, Edge swung in past the site north of the road again. The woman was supervising the moving of the bodies from the trench, into cardboard coffins then onto a truck. When it was full the truck drove off, and she sat against a tree alone.

"Is that all the bodies?" Edge asked. She looked up at him, not exactly brimming with friendliness, but at least she didn't scowl at him.

"No. There's another grave over there we're just starting to excavate."

"Who were they, Ms Marić?"

"So, English soldier, you've found out who I am. Did they tell you all about me?"

"Only the nice bits."

She frowned then looked away. Edge could tell she had the beginnings of a smile. "Are you really interested?"

"I could always fuck off if you want."

"They were Bosnian Croats. My people."

"Were they killed by the Serbs?"

"Is that what they told you?" she asked, suddenly animated.

"No. I made an assumption."

She looked at his asymmetric nose and cheekbones that gave him a brutal look, but there was something else behind those eyes that weren't cold anymore. "Okay, English soldier. You know my name, what is yours?"

"Edge."

"Hedge," she repeated, having a problem with pronouncing the vowel at the beginning of his name.

"No, huh, just Edge." He grinned.

"So you think it so funny how I speak?"

"Oh, please wind your neck in. I'm not at war with you."

"I'll tell you what, Meester Hedge, assumptions are dangerous round here. You all come here with your preconceived notions, poking your noses into something, hoping it will fit your agendas. You don't know the first thing about our countries, our people and our history!"

"I'll *tell you* what, lady. I really can't be arsed listening to your pathetic whinging. We all have our jobs to do. I think your problem is you've spent too much time with dead bodies and can't relate to real people anymore." He stalked off in a state of high dudgeon.

"Hey, Hedge, do you want your jacket back?"

"Keep it! Stick it up your scrawny arse, and the same goes for the record collection!"

That afternoon, Edge was lying on a hillock from where he could observe the main dig site, their vehicles and the road. His LSW was resting on its bipod and he was eating a cheese and sausage bread roll he had pilfered from the café that morning for his lunch. He was upwind from the smell of death. There seemed very little birdsong, and even the wildlife gave this place a wide berth. He was enjoying looking at the dappled sunlight dancing through the trees, and then stiffened. A familiar figure stalked into the site from the other side of the road. Edge watched her seek out Captain Gardner and engage him in an animated conversation.

After a few minutes, the woman strode off and Gardner yelled: "Corporal Edge, on me!"

"Fuck!" said Edge, and lugged up the LSW, doubling down the hill towards the Captain.

"Sir. What did Dracula's daughter want?"

"For some bizarre reason, she wants you, Corporal Edge."

"Me?"

"Apparently she was trying to explain something to you, when you took the hump and disappeared. Ms Marić would very much like to speak with you, to further your education, as she put it."

"Captain Gardner, she's completely mental."

"Better not keep her waiting then."

Edge reluctantly trudged away and sought out the dig site north of the road. Jozica Marić was sitting on the tailgate of a UN Toyota, legs swinging, and she was smoking a small cigarillo.

"What do you want?"

"Corporal Hedge, you flounced, is that the right word? Flounced off while I was trying to explain something to you. I want you to understand something about this country and us. I want to explain to you why everything isn't black and white."

"Why the cigars?"

She looked irritated because he had put her off her flow. "They stop the smell, so you stink of cigars instead of… Well, you know what."

"Am I really thick and in need of education?" Edge asked, not ready to declare a ceasefire just yet.

She sighed, flicked the butt of the cigarillo away. "Why not sit next to me and put that gun down? You make me nervous."

Edge reluctantly complied, but he leaned the LSW next to him within easy reach.

"Did they tell you anything about Bosnia and Herzegovina before you came out here to save us from ourselves?"

"Not really very much," Edge admitted. "Just that it was an ethnic mix and that Tito had kept the lid on you lot, until he died."

"Croatia and Serbia?"

"Some things about Greater Serbia and Serbian ethnic cleansing."

"And the Ottoman Empire?"

"Nope, nothing. Oh, I remember from school that Archduke Franz Ferdinand got slotted in Sarajevo and that started the First World War."

Jozica Marić sighed again. "So basically, we all lived in peace and harmony for hundreds of years, until a tired old communist dictator died and like naughty children, we were at each other's throats."

Edge looked away, slightly embarrassed. "Pretty much, Ms Marić. So who killed all the people in this forest and who are they?"

"They are mainly Croats, a very few Serbian women and children. As to who killed them, it's obvious that some were killed by Serbian militias, but just as many were likely to have been killed by Bosniaks, or Mujahideen who have infiltrated in through Kosovo and Macedonia from Turkey. There are some Bosniaks buried over there where we're just starting to excavate. They were probably killed by Croats. Not so easy to pick sides now, is it, Hedge?"

He looked away, knowing that it was a rhetorical question. He was interested, but annoyed that this woman was lecturing him like a student.

"And of course these mass murders have to have been committed by the Serbs, because the Serbs are the current bad people. Be in no doubt, Hedge, some of the Serbs are evil, just as evil as the mujahedeen or the Croats who shot those people at the edge of the graves they made them dig. But only the Serbs are allowed to be evil in this new world order. President Clinton and your Prime Minister Blair have decreed it."

As she brushed the hair out of her eyes with annoyance, Edge regarded her profile. She could have been attractive, but never beautiful, if only she didn't have an air of perpetual annoyance and impatience. How old was she? Older than him, that was for sure, but not by that much. He looked at her body in shorts and t-shirt, but by God she did look undernourished, seeming to exist on cigars and nervous energy. He looked down at her legs, the scrawny side of muscular, and caked with dirt. She turned to look at him and saw he was gazing at her legs.

"Like my legs, Hedge? Just as well you're not a tit man, you would be disappointed."

"You've picked up a tick on the back of your left calf, just above the sock."

She lifted her leg to have a look at it. "Little bastards. I'll burn it off with my lighter."

"No," Edge said urgently, pulling off his daysack. "As it dies in agony, all the shit and diseases in its body will be regurgitated into you. That's Lyme disease and encephalitis, and you could end up with an infected sore."

He pulled a tobacco tin out of his daysack, opened it and found a pair of surgical tweezers. "Hold this tin and put your leg on my thighs. You'll have to turn away so I can get to it."

She complied, and while he had a good look at the tick, she went through his survival kit in the tin. There were fish hooks and line, a wire saw, flint and striker, four-by-two weapon cleaning flannelette, puritabs, modelling knife blades, para cord, tripwire from a claymore for snares, suppositories, antiseptic wipes and a couple of condoms. She waved one in front of his face.

"Ohh, Hedge. You are well prepared, like a good scout."

"Shut up. This might pinch your skin a bit." He pressed down on either side of the tick and grasped its head, then rotated it as he pulled it out. He held it up for her to see, its tiny legs wriggling under its growing body.

"Eagh," she exclaimed with disgust. He threw it down and stamped on it. Edge wiped away the small bead of her blood with an antiseptic wipe.

"Thank you, Doctor Hedge," she said, but at least she was smiling. He smiled back awkwardly, suddenly feeling shy.

"I must get on," he said.

Chapter 7

# LOVE AND DEATH
# IN THE BALKANS

———

Life could have been idyllic except for Jozica Marić and her irritating ability to get under Edge's skin. Whenever she was around, cropping up at the other dig sites or talking to Captain Gardner, he felt awkward. He hated the way that Captain Gardner and she would be talking, then suddenly look at him and smile at one another. If he passed her dig site, she would look at him and then say something in Croat to whoever she was with, and they would share a joke. It was as though he provided her with permanent amusement and he was getting sick of it. She would sometimes say: *Good morning, Hedge,* and then chortle, *look, no nasty ticks.*

Bored one evening, lying on his bed and listening to the BBC World Service, Edge tried to work out why she seemed to treat him with such contempt. Okay, so admittedly he knew absolutely nothing about Bosnia and Herzegovina, apart from what he had been told during the pre-deployment training at Tidworth. It had always been Yugoslavia as far as he was concerned. Edge was willing to bet she knew fuck all about Warwickshire, Bosworth Field (was that in Warwickshire? Edge wasn't sure) and the county coat of arms of a bear shagging a tree.

He had tried to be nice to her. He had given her his best Gore-Tex jacket. Well, actually not his best one. That was an American jacket he'd swapped for six twenty-four-hour ration packs. For some reason, the Yanks went mad for them. He'd given her his issue Soldier 95 jacket. And he had spotted that tick and stopped her from burning it off. He suddenly remembered the feel of her legs on his thigh and buried the thought.

And she was an ugly, titless, scrawny bitch. Lank hair, bony cheeks. And she smoked bloody cigars. She had dirty nails. She was patronising, lecturing him like a particular dullard of a student. She was rude, her English was crap and she couldn't even say his name properly.

*And I so badly want to fuck her.*

*Pull yourself together!* Edge went and had another shower, got changed into his civvies and went looking for a bar. He found the Caffe Bar Ključ and ordered a beer. He knew he shouldn't have gone out alone, but he didn't feel like socialising with RMPs, and Captain Gardner was, well, an officer. He sat in a corner and watched a Bosnian quiz show that seemed to involve lovely, underdressed women answering questions to win a holiday with some Balkan studmuffins.

A group of men in a mixture of combat trousers and mufti regarded him with interest, and one of them waved the proprietor over. It was obvious that they were asking him who Edge was. He hoped that nothing was going to kick off, but had taken the precaution of bringing his Browning, which against regulations and all disciplined weapon handling best practice, was tucked into the rear waistband of his jeans, the barrel pointing down towards the crack of his arse. He reasoned that wearing the holster in plain view would have been asking for trouble. Edge finished his beer unhurriedly, left some money on the table and went out into the night. He waited up a darkened alley to see if anyone had followed him, but nobody did.

Back at the patrol house, Edge grabbed some brown biscuits and tinned meat paste from one of the ration packs in the kitchen. He tossed them on his bed and unloaded the Browning, putting it back in the padlocked ammo box that was D-locked to the bed frame, along with the LSW. He lay on the bed and slowly ate the biscuits and paste, wondering how the hell he was going to pluck up enough courage to make a complete fool of himself.

The following morning, Captain Gardner told them he had to go back to Banja Luka for a mail run and to pick up supplies, returning the following morning. He would take the RMP Land Rover along with the RMP corporal. He gave the RMP sergeant and Edge their daily orders, told them not to have any wild parties and reiterated that the sergeant was to radio in a sitrep to BLMF at 19:00.

At the dig site, Edge spent more time than usual skirting the encampment north of the road. On his fifth unobtrusive pass, he finally saw that Jozica Marić was on her own and that the UN pick-up had gone. In agonies of self doubt, Edge made a final shit or bust pass, but she wasn't there.

"Fuck!" said Edge. *Where the hell has she gone?* He almost physically recoiled as she stepped out from behind the trees.

"Fuck? Fuck, Mister Hedge?"

"Where the hell have you been?" he blurted out.

She regarded him with puzzled amusement. "Hedge, this is a forest and it's a long walk to the Portaloos. What do you do when you need to go?"

"Err, sorry. My mistake. I'll be off. Just worried that you weren't around."

He turned away, his face burning, cursing under his breath. *Fucking blown it, haven't I?*

"Hey, Hedge. Have you got any of that tea in your flask that melts dental fillings?"

"Err, yes. You want some?"

"Sure."

He slung off his daysack and they hunkered down under the trees as a light drizzle fell, pooling as huge droplets that ran down the fir branches and dripped onto the needles. They sat against the bole of a tree and she sipped the tea. The steam fogged the air in the suddenly chill morning.

"It is so sweet. Lovely. Reminds me of being a child again." She pulled out a tin of cigarillos and offered one to Edge. He felt too self-conscious to refuse and he lit them both with a Zippo. They passed the time in companionable silence, but he was writhing inside. *What do I do now? What do I say? She's older and cleverer than me.*

"Now, Hedge. Why the hurry? You seem to have something on your mind."

"Nothing really. I was just wondering where you sleep. *Damn, that sounded so fucking stupid.* I mean, where do you stay when you're not...?"

"In a hotel. The Hotel Ključ, which is about six kilometres up the road from here. It's a nice hotel, good UN rates, and they love having us, because we pay five times more than everyone else. But how I hate the UN," she said with passion.

"Oh, so where do you eat?"

"It depends. Sometimes the Ključ kod Ramadana or the Kula, depending what the others are doing, so I can avoid them."

Edge felt his heart sink. *I'm trying to chat up a bloody misanthrope,* he thought bitterly. He felt his resolve leave him, but remembered Horace Cutler's words to him at the court martial... *but you have gone face to face with IRA bastards and prevailed.*

"Why are you so concerned about my sleeping and eating arrangements, Hedge?"

"Because I want to ask you if you would like to have a meal with me," he blurted out again.

Jozica Marić stared at him in surprise, smiled, and then began to laugh. Edge stood up quickly and grabbed the cup of the flask off her, emptied it out and stowed the flask in his daysack.

"Okay, okay, I know the fucking drill. And I am fucking off right now." He grabbed the LSW and stalked away.

"Hey, Hedge," she called after him.

"What!" he yelled, turning round.

"I thought you were never going to ask."

\*

They had shared a bottle of red wine, which was nearly finished, so Edge ordered another one. The meal had been simple, consisting of *ćevapi*, a form of kebabs served on a flatbread, and meat and rice served in grape leaves. Edge felt the alcohol and her company lift his soul. The Kula restaurant wasn't busy and they were tucked away in an alcove, which had amused them. They were waiting for the cheeses, and Jozica was continuing Edge's education in European history.

"You English don't understand how lucky you are. While you were fighting two civil wars, interfering in European affairs and building your navy, the Bosnians were either fighting Islam or ruled by the Ottoman Empire. The Muslims enslaved our people for four centuries while you were carving out an empire in India and the Americas. We were a frontier province between Islam and the Christian West and we have known nothing but war for over five hundred years. And eventually the Austro-Hungarians pushed back the Ottomans and once again we were enslaved, but with new masters. But the Muslims never really went away. They stayed and 'integrated', but they have never truly integrated.

"And during the Second World War, you English bastards played one off against the other. You armed the Chetniks, Serbs, who killed Jews, Croats and anyone including the Muslim Bosniaks. The Chetniks wanted a Greater Serbia, but the Bosniaks were no better, killing 340,000 Bosnian Serbs with German weapons, forming the first non-German SS Division in 1941. Tito at least tried to form the Partisans along multi-ethnic lines, and the Bosnian War of 1992 to 1995 was just a continuation of the wars that have been fought since the fifteenth century. And your fucking Tony Blair sends poor, clueless boys like you, to a place you do not understand the first thing about!"

Edge put his hand on hers. "I'm not your enemy. I've already told you, I'm not at war with you. I'm just here and you lot don't need any help from me to pick enemies."

Over the cheese and more wine, Jozica asked Edge about England, where he came from and why he had wanted to join the Army, when the English weren't at war with anyone.

"Not strictly true," he told her. "We are at war with Irish republican terrorism."

"Ireland is not England. Just let the Irish have it."

So Edge proceeded to give her a lesson on the bitterly intertwined histories of Ireland, Scotland and England, and it was her turn to be educated, albeit from the perspective of a humble British soldier. It was nearly 22:00 by the time the wine and cheese had gone. He tried to pay for the meal, but she wasn't having any of it, explaining that her allowance for one meal was over three times what they had both been charged for it.

"I'll walk you back to your hotel. The patrol house is over the other side of town."

She looked at him evenly, a serious and soulful expression in her eyes. "Hedge, there is a certain inevitability for moments such as these. They are brief, like a shooting star in a dark morning sky. If you miss it, you won't even know that it was ever there."

*

She was lying with her head on his shoulder, her thin body curled into his for warmth. Edge lay on his back, looking at the pre-dawn light above the curtains and decided that he needed a pee. He gently moved away so as not to wake her.

"Where are you going, Hedge?"

"To syphon the python."

71

"Huh, some python. Don't be too long and wash your hands," she said sleepily.

"Yes, miss."

When he slid in next to her again he regarded her body, so thin but she had a hunger that had astonished him, a very noisy hunger. She went up on one elbow.

"Hedge, what happened to your face? You could be such a pretty boy apart from that nose. It makes you look like a killer, and those eyes of yours. When I first saw them I thought you wanted to kill me. You seem angry sometimes, like a volcano waiting to erupt."

"Some German policeman didn't like the look of me and decided to rearrange my face."

"Germans," she scoffed, "biggest bunch of bastards in Europe. They should have been kept partitioned. They will try to take over Europe once again if you Brits and the French let them."

"Do you know why the French roads are lined with trees?" Edge asked her. She shook her head.

"So the German army can march in the shade."

She giggled and lay back on the bed, totally unashamed, and he traced his finger down over her flat stomach.

"While we're on the subject of personal questions, Jozica, what do those strange tattoos just here signify?" he asked, indicating with the finger just above her mons veneris. To his surprise, she turned away angrily.

"Don't ever ask me that again, Hedge! I don't want to talk about it. Never again, you understand?"

"Okay, calm down. Just asking. Jeeez." He looked at his watch and it was half five. "I'd better be heading back before I'm missed."

"Please don't go just yet," she demanded, wrapping her arms round him. "I can make sure you want to stay."

And she did.

\*

They were insatiable, the original Martini couple. Edge would try and stay away from her dig site, but she sought him out at lunchtime and they would disappear into the forest. He knew he was being unprofessional, but he couldn't help himself. As well as the obvious lust, they both had other feelings and tender moments together. He hadn't slept at the patrol house for nights and Captain Gardner was no fool. One morning as they drove from Ključ, Gardner gently warned Edge.

"I know you can't keep your hands off each other, but for God's sake be careful."

Edge stared at him in astonishment.

"It's bloody obvious how you feel about one another, but it's doomed, Edge lad. Enjoy it while you can, but there will be no happily ever after."

Edge scowled. "You don't approve, sir."

"No, Mr Edge, I bloody well don't. I'm the officer. I should get the totty," they both smiled, "but I mean what I say. Don't disturb the delicate balance of this place, because we're just passing through while you're ploughing your furrow."

And within a few days, everything had changed. Edge was watching the main dig when he heard a vehicle on the road come to a halt and the sound of doors slamming. Cautiously, he advanced through the trees, the LSW side slung to look unthreatening, but from where he could quickly bring it up into a firing position. The vehicle was a UAZ light utility vehicle, formerly of the Yugoslavian army. About six men were around the UAZ, wearing dark combat clothing, black head caps and armed with LAWs and the ubiquitous AK range of assault rifles. One of the men, the leader, was talking to Jozica Marić. The situation didn't feel right.

Edge moved cautiously into view and he could see the badges of the Serb militia with the two-headed eagle. Some of the men he recognised from his evening in the Caffe Bar Ključ. The man talking to Jozica also had a nasty-looking dog on a leash, some kind of Doberman Pinscher hybrid. It was straining on the leash and constantly growling. As Edge moved down towards the road, the Serbian militia unslung their weapons. Edge moved the LSW to high port.

"Good morning, gentlemen. Can I be of assistance?"

The Serb leader looked at Edge and grinned. "Hey, Englishman. I am talking to my lovely friend here, making sure she does not say any bad things about my brothers, regarding these poor unfortunate people."

"Nevertheless, this site is under our protection. I think you should go."

"Englishman. This is my country. It is you who should go." The dog was growling and slavering, straining to get at Edge. "And even Radić agrees with me, don't you, boy?"

"This site is under our protection and I will take all necessary measures to protect these people."

The Serb laughed and bent down to slip the dog's leash. In the time it took to let slip the dog and for it to bound forward, Edge had cocked the LSW and brought it into the aim, not easy given his left hand had to reach across the weapon for the cocking handle. The dog was airborne, jaws open to rip out his throat, when Edge fired a three-round burst. The 5.56mm rounds were small but travelling at supersonic speed. They began to break apart and tumble as they destroyed the dog's head, causing massive cavitation with the shockwaves. The dog's entrails and spinal column were blown out of its anus. As the dead animal thudded onto the ground, Edge advanced until his weapon was pointing directly at the Serb leader's head.

"Tell your pals to point their weapons away from me. Otherwise, your fucking head goes the same way as your fucking dog's. And I will slot you the instant I hear a safety catch going off."

He accepted that it wasn't a strictly legal warning, given the wording on his Card Alpha. But now Edge was in a Mexican stand-off where neither side could back down. Jozica shouted something in Serbo-Croat, but the militia leader merely snarled, his eyes never leaving Edge's. From behind him, he heard the sound of SA80s being cocked and Captain Gardner's voice booming out.

"Stand down, gentlemen. You as well, Edge."

He lowered the LSW. The Serbs looked uneasily at their leader and lowered their weapons.

"Be so good as to get back in your vehicle and fuck off. There's good gentlemen."

The Serb militia leader indicated that they should comply, but spoke a final few words to Edge in a low voice: "You killed my dog and you will pay for it! I will remember your name, Edge."

As the vehicle backed up the road, Jozica asked him what he had said.

"Just that he didn't like me very much." As she turned away, there were tears in her eyes.

"God's sake, Edge," Gardner said to him once she was out of earshot, "if you're not fucking the locals, you're shooting their dogs."

But Gardner was worried by this development, very worried, and reported it on that night's radio sitrep to BLMF, asking if they would consider sending some extra men.

That night, Edge and Jozica spent a long, tender night together, once the imperative of their lust had been satisfied.

"Who was that Serb bastard this morning and what did he want with you?" he asked, and she sighed.

"His name is Jakovljević Milorad, and he is a prominent leader of the Army of the Republika Srpska. He and his men were very active during the first of the new wars. He is evil. They have come back and have set up in an old hostel in Velagići."

"He seems to know you." Jozica sat on the edge of the bed and lit a cigarillo.

"I wish you wouldn't smoke those bloody things. It's like kissing Winston Churchill."

"Those little marks on my body are Cyrillic numbers. He put them there. I was his Croatian whore."

"My God!"

"No secrets, Edge. I was used as his whore until I escaped, but you never really can properly escape. He wants me to say that those people in the graves were killed by Croats and Bosniaks."

"But I thought you said that they were, well, some of them."

"He is paranoid, and you, today, killed the most important thing in his life."

"This country is fucked up. Why don't you leave?"

"And go where, Hedge?"

Come back to England with me. I'll come and get you when I go on post-operational leave. We'll meet in Dubrovnik and you can lecture me all about its history."

"You won't."

"I will, I swear it. I love you!" he exclaimed, and then felt foolish. She was too intelligent for the likes of him.

"Perhaps I do as well. You never know. It might work…"

The following morning, she still hadn't appeared by 10:00 and Edge was worried. He asked the Babushka in the trench and the old lady shrugged. She still hadn't appeared by the evening and Edge ignored Gardner's instructions and went to the hotel, where eventually he tracked down someone who could speak passable English.

"She left this morning and hasn't returned, mister. Sorry, I don't know where she is."

The next day, Edge was frantic, pacing anxiously round the site. He couldn't eat and he was operating on nervous energy. Gardner tried to placate him to no avail, and even the RMP were considerate towards him, telling him not to worry.

At 11:00 that morning, a UAZ swept past on the road, slowed down, and a bundle was dumped out of the back, before the vehicle sped off. Gardner yelled at the RMPs: "Sergeant Clements, Corporal Waring, find Corporal Edge and make sure he doesn't come anywhere near this. Arrest him if you have to!"

Gardner went down onto the road and stared in horror at the naked corpse of Jozica Marić. There wasn't an inch of her frail body that hadn't been burned, cut or bruised. A piece of paper had been rammed into her mouth and he pulled it out and unfolded it. It said:

*EDGE*

*YOU KILLED MY DOG. I KILLED YOUR BITCH. WE MADE SURE IT TOOK A LONG TIME FOR HER TO DIE. REMEMBER THAT.*

Her dead eyes stared at him from eternity and he gently closed them, pulled a poncho out of his daysack and covered her remains.

\*

Edge picked up the keys of the FFR from the kitchen and lugged the LSW out to the Land Rover. He placed the LSW in the passenger's seat and as he climbed into the driver's seat, the spare magazines in his smock pocket clunked on the metalwork. He was going to die that night, but Jakovljević Milorad and as many of his henchmen as possible were going to go with him. He put the vehicle keys in the ignition.

"Don't do this, Edge," said a voice from the rear of the vehicle.

"With all due respect, sir. Fuck off and let me get on with it."

"Sorry, Edge. I can't let you do this." Captain Gardner placed the muzzle of his Browning in the nape of Edge's neck. "I will use it if I have to."

"Why?" Edge demanded, hammering the dashboard with his fists.

"Because I'm not letting you off the hook with suicide by Serb. You have to live with the consequences of your actions. You killed that woman as surely as if you had put a gun to her head."

"But what else could I have done?" Edge almost howled in anguish.

"Probably nothing, but every decision you take in life has a consequence. You should know that as a soldier. That's why it's such a shit job. It's called the butterfly effect, chaos theory, and this place is a perfect example of chaos theory in action. Except you didn't step on a butterfly, oh no, you blew a warlord's dog's brain out through its arse."

"I loved her," he said miserably, too ashamed to weep.

"I know you did, lad. And she loved you. She told me that almost from the start. She so wanted you to speak to her, but she was shy as well, probably why she gave you such a hard time. That's why we used to laugh, every time you haughtily stalked past, looking like the universal soldier. I really am so very sorry, Mark Edge."

"What happens now? How can I live with this?"

"You unload your weapon, give me the Browning and we'll discuss your options. I have a bottle of good quality malt in my room. You can help me finish it."

# Chapter 8

# EDGE, FIGURES
# ON A LANDSCAPE

---

Much meaningful business within the Armed Forces is conducted at the senior NCO or warrant officer level, sometimes circumventing slower, official channels that take a great deal of time to catch up. The telephone rang in the RSM's office at Tidworth and the RSM answered it. He exchanged formalities with the person on the phone.

"Good morning, Frank. I'm Sergeant-Major Steve Brayford, Selections Cell at Stirling Lines. Are you well?"

"Morning, Steve." They had never met but both knew of each other and what this was about. "I suppose this is about the pair of our lads going up for selection?"

"Yes, tell me about them. Warts and all."

The RSM wouldn't have had it any other way. "They have both completed the Special Forces Briefing Course, passed the CFT, navigation and first aid with flying colours. Sergeant Paul Cavendish is a good soldier, steady career, but he's getting on. He's thirty-two and reckons this will be his last chance at making the selection. He's been working hard on his fitness and aptitude, but honestly, I think he may struggle on the hills. I'd be grateful if you didn't break him. He has years of good service left and should make Warrant Officer One easily in our pond."

"Okay, what about the corporal?"

"Ahh yes, Mr Mark Edge. Again, an outstanding soldier, very intelligent, kept his head on Banner and Op Grappel, although something seemed to have happened to him in Bosnia. He's come back a different person. More focussed, colder, but he's put in a lot of work and is incredibly fit. I think it'll be down to whether you want him, and you must know about his court martial."

"Yes, we've heard about that, and our legal team have looked into it. We don't think it should ever have gone for court martial and it shouldn't disbar him from being eligible for selection. Frank, I suspect a 'but' here."

The RSM sighed. "Let's put it this way, you either like Corporal Edge or you don't."

"He's got a good write-up from this Captain Gardner, he ticks all the right boxes, yet I suspect you don't rate him."

"Oh, I rate him. I just don't like him."

The SAS sergeant major was doodling on a pad on his desk. "Thank you, Frank. I appreciate your honesty. We look forward to seeing both of them next week. And thanks for your time."

The sergeant major hung up and watched some troopers abseiling from a Lynx onto the flat roof of the old RAF station headquarters.

"Arsehole," he said quietly.

*

Edge had trained hard for two weeks on Dartmoor, as all candidates had been warned to within an inch of their lives to avoid the Brecon Beacons. Edge had leave owing and he took it in Devon and spent his days and a few nights on the moor. It was potentially easier to navigate the more recognisable features on Dartmoor, but the weather was as unpredictable as the Beacons, and the valley terrains with their mires as much of a challenge. He averaged 25 kilometres a day, the same as he would have to complete on the first part of the hill phase at Sennybridge. In the second week, he completed a march of 65 kilometres, carrying a bergen of 30 kilograms and a piece of scaffolding tubing to simulate carrying a rifle. The march was completed in nineteen hours, twenty-one minutes and his navigation had been spot-on. Edge knew that barring accidents or sheer bad luck, he could complete the four-weeks hill phase.

But he was under no illusions. Edge knew that the directing staff (DS) would be watching the candidates' every moves, both on and the few hours off duty. Edge remembered how to smile and be cheerful again, an act he found more difficult than the hills. He spent the long hours brooding darkly about a love he had lost as he pounded the Brecon Beacons, and the pain he felt in his joints and back was nothing to the pain he felt in his soul.

He completed the Long Drag well within time but struggled slightly on the SF Swimming Test where he had to enter the water from height in full battle order, swim 25 metres, tread water for five minutes, hand out his kit and then swim 200 metres with the final 10 underwater. The DS passed him, but warned he would have to work on his swimming.

The pace was unrelenting and the candidates were flown out to Belize for the nine-week jungle warfare and SF Standard Operating Procedures phase of the selection process. They had lost over half on the hills of the Beacons and a further 30% in the jungles and bush of Belize. The remaining candidates were put under extreme pressure, including sleep deprivation, to test their soldiering skills. Edge found this more difficult than the hill phase, and he was shocked at how much he had forgotten and the standard of soldiering skills required.

One morning in the final week of the jungle phase, an RAF Puma helicopter circled the clearing in the jungle and flared into land. Edge, who was trying to tie a bivouac into the tree canopy, saw the Puma pass above and thought: *There goes another one, probably a casevac.* On the landing point, the loadmaster jumped out and went to find the detachment commander, carrying a priority signal. Ten minutes later, a member of the DS sought out Corporal Edge and stared up into the tree.

"Edge, come down, the Boss wants to see you."

He felt his heart sink. *So bloody close. Shit!*

He abseiled down from the tree. "Collect your kit but not your weapon. Things are going to be moving fast for you."

"What's going on?"

The DS smiled sadly. "The Boss will explain."

The detachment headquarters was an eighteen by twenty-four foot tent. Edge pushed through the flap and was surprised to find the ops room was empty apart from the major. He waved him in and gave him a mug of very sweet tea.

"Sit down, Edge," the major said gently.

*Shit, this is very bad. I must have fucked up royally.*

"Mark, I am so very sorry I have to tell you this. I'm afraid that your mother has died. She passed away last week after a short illness, in the George

Eliot hospital. For whatever reason, your family failed to notify your parent unit until yesterday morning. We have to get you home as quickly as possible. The Puma is going to fly you to Belize City Airport, where you have been booked on a flight to Gatwick. An RAF flight will pick you up there and take you to Coventry Airport.

"I understand that this must be a profound shock to you and there is little I can say to minimise the shock and sadness you must be feeling. We are all truly sorry and wish you the best in the days ahead."

"Thanks, sir. I don't know what to say."

The major shook his hand. "Good luck, Corporal Edge."

After the helicopter had left, the major called in the chief instructor. "You heard about Edge?"

"Yes, Boss. A really tough break. Poor lad."

"Does this mean we'll have to scrub him?"

The senior NCO thought about it. "No. He's doing okay and will just miss one anti-ambush exercise. Most of the next few days will be wash-ups and Character Assassination Groups. I don't think he would have gained much from that, given his personal circumstances. He's put in a lot of effort, but he's quite insular and difficult to read, but I like him. No bullshit or deflection from Edge. If he fucks up, he holds up his hand and is always willing to help the strugglers."

"Thanks, Geordie. So once he's got this bereavement out of the way, we'll put him through to Employment Training and SERE. That's if he makes the window."

*

Edge felt like a package being swept along by events totally out of his control. The Puma landed close to a Cessna Caravan at Belize City Airport. The flight had been held back specifically for him to get on it, and the impatient passengers looked with a mixture of annoyance and curiosity at this soldier still wearing his jungle camouflage kit and webbing. The flight to Cancún on the Yucatan Peninsula took just under three hours. Edge was waved through the controls straight into the VIP lounge, where the rich and famous looked incredulously at this grimy apparition who had been in the jungle a few hours previously.

He was escorted onto the Thomas Cook flight to Gatwick and made comfortable in the first-class cabin. The more-camp-than-a-scout-jamboree, extremely kind and attentive senior steward made sure he was comfortable and provided him with a meal. Edge sat in bemused confusion, wondering what the hell was wrong with him. He felt an emptiness, but he hadn't shed a single tear for his mother or for a Croatian woman he believed he had truly loved. He was angry and disgusted with himself for being unable to show emotion. *Fuck, I'm just a robot.*

At 20:00 local, the Airbus rumbled onto Gatwick's runway, and at the terminal, Edge was first off the aircraft. He was directed to a van by a ground handler wearing a fluorescent tabard and driven a short distance, to where an HS125 of the Royal Flight was waiting for him, its engines running. The RAF loadmaster patted him on the shoulder in a kindly manner and brought him a cup of tea in a paper mug. *Not finest china for the likes of me.*

The 125 took off and turned north, heading for the Midlands. Edge stared distractedly out of the window at the brightly lit motorways and road network below. He tried to think about his mother, but it was just too painful. Then he wondered how his father would cope. *I hope the old bastard appreciates her now she's gone. Too fucking late.* And then he analysed whether he had been such a dutiful son. He could have visited more often. But he escaped to join the Army. He drained the tea that tasted as bitter as his thoughts.

The 125 landed at an almost deserted Coventry Airport, taxied to the terminal, and the front door and steps went down. The cool evening air cut through his jungle fatigues.

"Good luck, son. So sorry for your loss," said the loadmaster.

A buxom lady in another tabard was waiting for him on the pan. As they walked towards the darkened, glass-fronted building, she put her arm around Edge's shoulders, and it was such a gesture of kindness and common humanity that he did almost feel tears prickling in his eyes.

"There's a taxi waiting outside for you." She gave Edge a faxed piece of paper. "Give this to the driver and it's got a telephone number and website he can claim the fare from. I don't suppose you have any money, do you, dear?"

Once outside, the smooth mechanics of the military repatriation process seemed to come off the rails. Outside in the harsh glare of the neon lights, a taxi was waiting, its driver smoking and pacing. He was a Pakistani with a beard, probably in his twenties, and he looked aghast at Edge, looking him up and down.

"Man, you're filthy. You're not coming in my cab like that."

"It's dry. The loose stuff has gone. If it's good enough for first class and the Queen's Flight, it's good enough for your fucking taxi. Note that it's a taxi, not a fucking cab. Stop making a fuss and drive me to Nuneaton, like you have been contracted to do."

Edge got in the back and dumped his webbing and daysack on the seat next to him. He realised with shock and amusement that his fighting knife was still taped to the webbing riser. The taxi left the airport and the driver turned up the radio, listening to Radio Panj, a cacophony of wailing Asian crap, and very rude to his passenger. Edge looked at the rear side of the driver's head and thought about calming his rising annoyance. On the outskirts of Nuneaton, the driver said without looking at his fare:

"What address?"

Edge told him an address five streets away from his old house. The taxi stopped and Edge grabbed his kit. He passed the faxed sheet to the driver. "This is the phone number or website where you can claim the money for this fare. I've got no money on me, I'm afraid."

"You shitting me, man?"

"I presume you were told why you were picking me up?"

"Some bollocks is what they said."

"There you go then. Thanks for the lift."

"No, no, no fukin' way, man. You fukin' pay me now. No money, I'll drive you to a cashpoint and get out fifty quid for double fare and pissing me about. Makin' a mess of my cab, you kufar soldier bastard. You're gonna fuckin' pay me for—"

Edge grabbed the driver's beard and hauled his head through the gap between the front seats. Their faces were inches apart and Edge's twisted face was visible in the interior light. Edge's eyes were dead.

"I think you are mistaken," Edge said very quietly, "because I think you're going to phone the number on that sheet tomorrow morning. Meanwhile, I am going to get out of this taxi. Then you are going to drive away and we will never see each other again. If you think that's not the case, then I have no alternative other than to rip your fucking face off. Do we understand each other?"

The driver saw the camouflaged handle of the knife on the webbing and realised that this man was very dangerous. This was no drunk punter he could overcharge, or drop off somewhere in the town to get beaten up by his 'brothers'. This was Iblis personified.

"All right, but I'll fuckin' remember you."

"You had better," said Edge, and got out. The taxi sped off before he had closed the door.

He was so tired. He hadn't slept properly for weeks and the lights of exhaustion were dancing on his peripheral vision. All he had to his name was his wallet, ID card, passport and the mud of Belize on his boots. His car, keys and civvies were back at Stirling Lines. Edge walked for ten minutes through the estate, meeting not another soul. A cat jumped down from a wall and approached him, tail in the air, and he avoided it. He wasn't fond of cats because they reminded him too much of himself.

He stood for several minutes outside his old house, which had always felt like a prison. The only reason he had ever had to visit it had gone forever from his life and was lying in the Co-op funeral parlour's chapel of rest. The front garden was getting overgrown and his mum would have hated that. There was a single light on upstairs, probably the landing light. Edge sighed. There was no point in putting off the inevitable. He opened the gate and went and knocked loudly at the front door. It needed repainting. He waited a long time and knocked again, louder and heavier this time. Another, brighter, light went on upstairs and he saw movement on the stairs.

"Who is it? What do you want?"

"Dad it's me, Mark."

The door opened and Edge looked at his father. He seemed much older than when he had last visited, and in a way, diminished. He hadn't shaved for several days and he looked unkempt. Edge suspected he had been drinking heavily.

"Mark, you'd better come in."

The sitting room was untidy, a half-finished whisky bottle and official documents on the coffee table. His father slumped in a chair, and Edge moved some papers to sit on the sofa.

"So you finally bothered to come."

"Dad, less than twenty-four hours ago, I was in the Central American jungle. I only heard about Mum dying this morning. When did she die?"

"Anne said she tried to get hold of you last week. Last Wednesday she went. She'd only been in hospital a week, some cancer that women get down…"

Edge felt a bubbling anger. "Did you try to notify me when she was seriously ill? I could have got back."

"Anne's been dealing with everything." Edge's father poured another whisky into a tumbler that was grimy and heavily fingerprinted. "Well, she's had to, seeing as how you weren't here."

Edge looked around the room and into the kitchen, with a sink piled high with dishes. "It's a pity she hasn't been dealing with the housework."

"She does have her own life, now that she's married."

"When's the funeral?" asked Edge. "And can I have a whisky, please, Dad?"

"Day after tomorrow, and help yourself."

He went into the kitchen and eventually found a clean glass. When he got back, to his horror, he saw his father was crying. "Dad, I'm so sorry I wasn't here, but I think Anne could have tried harder to find me. Mum had all my addresses in her book. What about the death certificates, her savings accounts, stuff like that?"

"Anne and Ronnie have taken care of that. Ronnie has really been a tower of strength. I don't know what I would have done without the pair of them."

Ronnie was his sister's husband. Edge thought he was a camp, mincing prick, whom he had disliked instantly the first and only time he had met him, at his sister's wedding. He poured himself a whisky and drained it quickly. At least his father seemed to have pulled himself together and was staring vacantly at a dead bunch of flowers on the sideboard. Edge felt like a bastard, suddenly realising that his father had lost everything. *You don't know what you've got till it's gone.*

"Why don't you go to bed, Dad? We'll get this place sorted tomorrow."

"I'm sorry but your old room's not been made up. I couldn't find the bedding and we didn't know if you were coming."

*I suspect my fucking sister did everything she could to make sure I didn't.* "Don't worry. I'll sleep on the sofa for tonight. You get to bed."

Edge watched his father shuffle away with an empty sadness. He seemed diminished; the big, bluff, hearty, hail-fellow-well-met stalwart from the Masonic lodge had gone. The shop steward from the Jaguar works who had held court in the local pub, now just a shadow. Edge did feel a degree of pity for him, but it had been hard. In truth, he felt more pity for himself.

The next morning, Edge woke early and gutted the downstairs, cleaning and dusting, putting on the washing. He suspected his father didn't know how to operate the washing machine. He would hoover once his father was out of bed, then do the same for the bathroom and spare bedrooms. His was pretty much how it had been the last time he had visited, although the bed hadn't been made. That afternoon, he borrowed one of his father's golfing jackets and went into town to buy shirts, jeans, black shoes and a dark suit with a black tie.

That evening, he cooked a meal for the pair of them, having had to borrow his father's car and get in some essential shopping. They ate it in a companionable quiet, skirting round the subject they didn't want to discuss.

His dad steadily sank four cans of bitter, and Edge polished off a bottle of red wine.

"I'm glad you made it home, Mark. Your mother thought the world of you."

"I know she did, Dad. And she thought the world of you." His father looked at him doubtfully. "Just think of the little things she used to do for all of us. Even Anne, although she treated her like shit."

"She didn't even tell me she was sick. Why didn't she tell me, Mark?"

"Don't know, Dad. She never told me, either."

"But you were never here!"

"I wrote every week, wherever I was."

"I bet she told that bloody priest every time she went in the TARDIS for the absolution of her sins," his father said bitterly.

"She had her beliefs and her faith, Dad. She never insisted that we were brought up Catholic. Confession is a sacrament to reconcile mankind with God. It's one of the tenets of the Catholic faith, not a quick wash-spin cycle to rinse away naughtiness."

"Do you believe that crap, Mark?"

"It doesn't matter what you or I believe. Mum never lost her faith and she believed it."

"Where was her God when she was dying in hospital, grey and gasping for breath?"

"We've all got to die sometime, Dad," said a young soldier who had been prepared to commit suicide by Serb in Bosnia the previous year.

*

After the requiem mass in the Catholic church and the cremation, the wake was held in the lounge bar of a local pub, which Anne had booked at short notice. It was a ghastly and inappropriate venue to celebrate a person's life; a grim, sprawling drinking factory on the edge of a housing estate. The priest showed his face, self-consciously sipped an orange juice and left. His mother's female friends and acquaintances made similar apologies and left shortly afterwards. His father's cronies stayed longer, and the only relatives were Edge, his sister and her husband and his Uncle Jack who had travelled down from Perth. Edge was struck at just how few words his uncle and father had exchanged during the day and how upset he seemed to be over his mother's death. Edge chatted with his uncle.

"Did you know she was ill, Uncle Jack?"

He looked at Edge's father at the other end of the bar and said quietly: "Yes, she told me as soon as she was diagnosed."

"Why didn't you tell Dad or me?"

"Because she didn't want me to. Your father couldn't have coped, and she told me you were going through selection."

"This doesn't make any sense, Uncle Jack."

"It makes perfect sense, Mark. She had terminal cancer and knew when she was going to die, almost to the week."

"I wish I had known. To have the chance to say all the things I should have said to her over the years."

His uncle put his hand on his shoulder. "Life is seldom convenient like that, Mark. She was so proud of you. Are you still in the running?"

Edge shrugged. "Depends. I had almost finished the jungle phase. Who knows?"

Later, his sister and her husband sidled over to speak to him. It was obvious that Anne had drunk quite a lot. Her husband, Ronnie, minced behind her, looking like he wished he could be somewhere else. He was wearing a dinner jacket with a normal tie, because it was the only dark suit he possessed.

"So you finally made it," Anne said nastily. "Good of you to make the effort."

"You didn't let the Army know about Mum until the day before yesterday, did you? You bitch."

"Now wait a bloody minute," Ronnie said in righteous indignation. "You can't speak to my wife like that!"

"Fuck off, Ronnie, you mincing, gay-bar loiterer." Edge turned on his sister. "And you've done nothing in the house, you lazy trollop. Dad was living in squalor till I got home."

"Oh, precious little Mark. Mummy's boy who made Mum squander her savings, hiring an expensive lawyer to get you out of trouble. That cost her entire savings, because you're just a violent thug."

That wasn't strictly true. Mark had paid Horace Cutler back in £200 instalments every month since the court martial, and Cutler had shredded his mother's cheque.

"She doted on you and you pissed off as soon as you could. She died of a broken heart, because of you."

"Anne, you are a rancid bitch and you are incapable of having children, thank God. Which one's the Jaffa, you or Larry Grayson here?"

"Right, that's it. You, outside now!" said Ronnie.

Edge's Uncle Jack was between them in an instant. "Ronald, stand down. He'd do you serious harm. Mark, outside with me. Now!"

Outside, Edge was pacing with nervous energy. His uncle pulled him round the corner, out of sight.

"Mark. Get a grip! It's not Anne's fault your mother died. It was no one's fault. It was her time."

"The bitch should have told me!"

"She did you a favour. You will look back and understand that. There's nothing more you can do here. Go back and finish your selection and training. And I want a letter from you every month, telling me how you're getting on. Make peace with your sister at a later date. Things are too raw now."

Edge made himself absent from the rest of the wake, which had effectively run its course. Before he left, he asked the publican if the room had been paid for. Unsurprisingly, it hadn't, so Edge paid by debit card. In the past three months, he hadn't had a great deal to spend his pay on anyway.

The following morning, he said goodbye to his father and took a taxi to Nuneaton railway station. He was back at Stirling Lines in Hereford by 16:00. He had been on authorised absence for just over seventy-two hours. He was glad to be home.


This is dedicated to the outstanding Service personnel and civilians of the Joint Casualty and Compassionate Centre (JCCC). They are responsible for the management of British armed forces casualties and compassionate cases 24 hours a day, 7 days a week, and 365 days a year. The work they do on behalf of British Service personnel deserves far more recognition than it gets. The JCCC provide support to Service personnel and their families during what is for many a distressing and difficult time. I thank and admire all of you.

Chapter 9

# ON THE EDGE, STEPPING OUT INTO THE COLD

On an evening in October 1998, a C130 Hercules of RAF No 47 Squadron, Special Forces Flight, took off from RAF Leuchars, north of St Andrews in Fife. To the residents on Meteor Avenue, behind their triple glazing, the passing Hercules was a drone, barely heard above *BBC Scotland News*. Their homes would be shaken much later, when a Composite Air Operation (COMAO) of four Tornado GR4s and four Tornado F3s would blast off and track through the valleys of Scotland, in an attempt to attack the naval task force located off the Mull of Kintyre. The Falcons of Cobham Aviation Services were already airborne, weaving their deceptive electronic webs, confusing and trying to blind the radars of the task force's ships.

In the noisy and cavernous rear of the C130 was an air dispatcher from the Joint Air Transport Establishment, an RAF loadmaster, two RAF parachute jump instructors (PJIs) and sixteen members of Nos 22 and 23 SAS. As soon as the Hercules turned south after the climb-out, the sixteen SAS and two PJIs went on to oxygen from the black cylinders strapped to the seating stanchions between them. They were breathing pure oxygen to purge their body systems of nitrogen to prevent decompression sickness. Tonight, they would be jumping from over 28,000 feet and would have to change over to their integral oxygen supply prior to the jump.

This was the final operational jump for the men, all men, no women, male privilege, of the High Altitude Exit, Low Opening (HALO) and freefall, covert insertion parachute course. Although they were part of a NATO exercise, for the parachutists, this was the culmination of a long and vigorous course. They were still under evaluation, which was why the RAF PJIs were jumping with them. The lighting in the rear of the Hercules was dimmed. Some tried to sleep; some stared vacantly at some meaningless inanimate object and tried to concentrate on breathing slowly to avoid hyperventilation.

Edge was reading with a small torch: *We Wish to Inform You That Tomorrow We Will Be Killed with Our Families*, not exactly a rip-roaring, light-hearted romp or cosy travelogue of Rwanda, but a sobering insight into the barbarism of mankind. It had been on the suggested reading list for his intake and Edge was catching up with it. It was very hard going, because it reminded him too much of Bosnia. He felt the aircraft bank gently to starboard as it tracked south of the Yorkshire Moors.

He felt hot, even though the air dispatcher's and loadmaster's breath was misting in front of their faces. The cabin temperature had been deliberately kept low to avoid thermal shock as they left the aircraft. He was wearing long silk underwear tops and bottoms next to his skin, an expensive purchase from a skiing equipment shop. Silk inner socks and Marino wool outers. The thick-soled boots were Haix's finest (Edge's personal favourites). Silk inner flying gloves and outer Arc'teryx Sabre skiing gloves. He had three layers under the radar-absorbent smock, including Gore-Tex, and two under his trousers. The bergen was between his knees with a radar-absorbent cover; an M16 was strapped to his left-hand side, attached to the parachute harness, muzzle pointing down. The rear sling swivel was tied with paracord to the left riser of his chest rig with a carabiner. The reserve chute, oxygen bottle, altimeter and rate of fall gauges were attached to the main harness on his chest. He had a GPS indicator on his left wrist. Edge was wearing a Kevlar ballistic helmet and goggles, with oxygen mask connected to the small oxygen bottle under the reserve chute. He was dreading the ecstasy of fumbling, as they donned and checked their kit prior to the jump.

The Hercules banked again about twenty-five minutes later and headed north towards the Isle of Man. Edge watched the loadie go up to the flight deck and knew that soon it would be ShowTime. He stowed the book and torch in a sealable polythene bag in one of his bergen's side pockets. What seemed like an eternity later, the loadie came back down from the flight deck and he and the air dispatcher went onto their own portable oxygen supply. The

PJIs started to get them ready, although unlike their SAS trainees, they were unencumbered by bergens and weapons.

Edge stood up and turned his bergen upside down, stepped in front of it and put his legs through the shoulder straps. His buddy-buddy helped him haul it up and attach the heavy rucksack behind his knees to his parachute harness, with two quick-release carabiners and a length of webbing strapping. Once his parachute had opened (God willing), Edge would release the bergen to drop 10 feet below on its webbing strap. It would hit the ground first and slow his descent. He had taped the cleats of his boots with green bodge tape to prevent them tangling with the straps as it dropped away. The process was repeated with his buddy and now none of them could sit back down. The mutual check of equipment lasted a long time. Their lives depended on getting it right. Edge's final essential piece of life support equipment was tucked in his smock's inner pocket. A small, well-loved and rather grubby koala bear, called Skippy, that his mother had given him when he was five. The PJIs went round and double-checked the thoroughness of the buddy-buddy system. If anything was found, the buddy got a cuff on his helmet for missing it.

The loadmaster told the PJIs that the aircraft was getting ready to depressurise and the eighteen jumpers went onto their integral oxygen supply. This was the difficult time. Any faults with the oxygen and the parachutists would not be allowed to jump. By the time faults were sorted, the parachutist would have breathed in normal air. Even a brief few breaths would in theory be enough to induce decompression sickness. Edge held his breath and felt the puffs of oxygen from the mask against his eyes. He clipped the mask on and pulled down his goggles, giving one last wink to his buddy.

Up on the flight deck, the crew were on their oxygen supplies and the Hercules depressurised. The loadie came round and showed all the parachutists a whiteboard. On it was written the wind speed and direction at their current altitude, at 10,000 feet and ground level. The cloud base and height was annotated along with the zero degree isotherm, which was 8,000 feet. Edge groaned inwardly; they would be freefalling through freezing cloud.

The red lights went on above the two para doors, although they would be exiting from the rear ramp. Edge was in the first stick of eight and they waddled towards the rear of the aircraft, laden with over 100lbs of kit. One of the PJIs was with them, to assess them for the final jump. All had luminous numbers on their helmets for identification. The two going out first lugged the 'bundle', a padded container carrying their specialist equipment. The bundle was fitted with a drogue chute to give it a degree of stability and allow it to drop at the same rate as the rest of the stick. These two would accompany it, keeping it stable and away from the other parachutists. Looking after the bundle was a shit job.

The rear ramps went down and up with a whine of hydraulics and nine stepped onto it. Edge could see the lights of Ramsey far below through the clouds. The sun was still setting and the tops of the clouds were dusted with orange and pink. The horizon was a deep purple. The second stick formed up just off the ramp. They had a different landing zone and a different target and mission. The air dispatcher was right on the edge of the ramp, next to the bundle, his trousers and smock flapping in the slipstream. He was tethered to the aircraft with a long strop, facing in. The loadie gave the thumbs-up.

"Stand by!"

Edge was watching the lights above the para doors as they went green.

"Go!"

The bundle and its handmaidens were out first. Edge counted one thousand and one, and he leaped off the ramp, pitching top downwards, his legs coming up. He was inundated by the screaming of four turbo-jet engines and the gut-wrenching sensation of falling felt in his shoulders and abdomen. As he spun, he saw the Hercules disappearing above away from him and got into the freefall starfish position. The freezing coldness was like lying naked on a fishmonger's slab, and his testicles disappeared to what felt like his throat. A boot swept past his face as another freefaller swung in too close. There were others above, one within touching distance, and the bundle with its snaking drogue chute some way below. They seemed to stand out against the clouds like flies on a tablecloth.

The much more manoeuvrable PJI formatted facing him and raised his thumbs in question. Edge gave a thumbs-up in reply, but became conscious his breathing was too rapid and shallow. He slowed it down, concentrating on breathing from below his diaphragm. As his anxiety subsided, Edge became aware of just how beautiful the setting sun and the clouds were, still thousands of feet below him, and he forgot how cold he was. He subconsciously recollected a poem, *High Flight,* which was composed by Pilot Officer John Gillespie Magee Jr, particularly the line *I've chased the shouting wind along.*

He lurched into the slipstream of the 'bundle', which jolted him out of his spiritual reverie, and Edge closed his legs slightly to reduce drag and back away from the disturbed air. *Concentrate, you arsehole!* His altimeter registered 12,000 feet and the clouds seemed to be racing up to them. A long way to their north,

Edge fancied that he could see the tiny dots and vertical slipstreams of the second stick above them. He glanced at his GPS indicator on his wrist, which showed he was still over the sea, although the coastline was close, unseen below the clouds. Their forward momentum would take the stick to the coast around 5 kilometres south-east of Portpatrick. Then with the ram parachutes open, they could make the 3 or 4 kilometres to their designated drop zone. As the top of the clouds approached, the stick moved apart to avoid collisions in the reduced visibility.

Edge's altimeter indicated 9,450 feet as he went into the cloying wetness of the stratus clouds. It felt colder and the lack of visibility was disconcerting. He prayed that his instruments wouldn't ice up, as the first of the ice crystals formed on the material of his smock. At 4,500 feet, he put his left hand on top of his helmet and the right hand grasped the D-ring of the parachute ripcord. At 4,000 feet, he said a silent prayer and pulled firmly. There was a flapping from behind and something clouted the back of his helmet. There was a violent jerk, his legs swung forward and Edge stared up. The square canopy looked good; thank you, God. No riser lines over the top to blow the periphery. They had popped the chutes at 4,000 feet because at that height, the sound of the canopy opening was inaudible on the ground.

Next he pulled the paracord attached to the pins to release his bergen. One of the straps caught on his foot, so Edge wriggled his boot and the heavy rucksack dropped away. He felt the jolt as it came to the end of the strop and it was now dangling 10 feet below him. His GPS indicated he was tracking north, and he pulled on the handle controlling the right risers of the chute, to make a turn to starboard. He came out of the clouds at 1,500 feet and it was nearly dark over the Scottish countryside. Edge went silently over what looked like a farm below and seemed to be coming down in a shallow valley, with woods following a burn to his north.

The ground was coming up fast and Edge chose his landing site. The bergen hit the ground, instantly slowing his descent. He flared the chute and hit the ground gently, immediately twisting under the shrouds to kill the canopy. Edge struggled out of the parachute harness and bundled everything together as neatly as possible. He hid the folded canopy, reserve and his helmet and oxygen kit deep in a hedge, marking the position according to GPS. At a later date, it would be retrieved by support staff to save the long-suffering British taxpayers some money.

Edge worked out his position and reckoned he was some 750 metres away from the rendezvous point, a copse just west of Stoneykirk. He shouldered his bergen, picked up the M16 rifle and set off at a gentle jog, being careful of the uneven ground. Some ten minutes later, he was with the rest of his stick, holed up in the copse, under a gentle but annoying drizzle. Everyone was accounted for and there were no injuries.

"We'll need some help to bring in the bundle. It's about a click and a half away, but we hid it first."

The PJI gathered them together. "Right, any problems?"

Heads were shaken in the darkness.

"Number four, you looked like Korky the Cat. Arms out to the side, please, and don't be afraid to spread those legs. Nothing's going to fall out. Well done, you chaps on the bundle. All in all, an excellent jump, good exit and obviously good landings because you're all here in one piece. Good all the way. Right, if you'll excuse me, it's back to Leuchars for tea and medals for me. You lot can crack on with being hooligans."

"How will they know where to find you?"

"By the miracle of modern technology, also known as a mobile phone. Don't do anything I wouldn't do," he said, and left them.

*

They were holed up in a wood known as Grenoch Square, about 2 kilometres from RAF West Freugh, their target and primary objective. The Blue forces had set up two forward operating bases for their helicopters and fixed wing air assets, one at RAF West Freugh, the other at Castle Kennedy. The Blue fixed wing aircraft were still on *HMS Illustrious*, but West Freugh was home to eight CH 53 Sea Stallion helicopters, and Castle Kennedy, the objective of the other team, was operating RAF Puma and Chinook helicopters. Edge's team were Orange Special Forces, tasked with destroying the CH 53s on the ground. Lieutenant Colquhoun tried not to feel despondent, but the news from his recon team wasn't good.

"It's almost as though someone has tipped the bastards off. The airfield is crawling with patrols. If anything, there's more of them at night."

"What about coming in from the seaward side?" asked Colquhoun.

"No chance, they've strung out motion sensors and they do investigate every contact. Some deer set them off last night and a patrol was out in a few minutes. They are bloody good."

"Okay, it looks like it's Operation Certain Death, then."

"Not necessarily," Edge observed, looking closely at the lieutenant. "Boss, you're a Jock, aren't you?"

Hamish Gideon Colquhoun, Ninth Earl of Kilochewe, stared at Edge as though he had just made an inappropriate comment about his mother.

"Say something in Jockanese."

Reluctantly, Colquhoun complied.

"Hmm," Edge observed. "What do you think, chaps?"

A trooper called Mickie Keeble, who was dangerously ginger even with his camouflage, gave his verdict in a Devonian drawl: "Not too bad, Boss. But do you think you can do it a little less Doctor Finlay and a bit more Rab C Nesbitt?"

Colquhoun tried for another five or so minutes until:

"I think he's got it! By George, he's got it!"

*

That lunchtime, a farmer near Lochans had his meal interrupted by a knock on the kitchen door. He opened it to two strange apparitions who were dressed in camouflage clothing, with blackened faces, heavily armed and festooned with camouflage hessian strips. The nearest one dragged off his woollen hat politely.

"Good afternoon, sir. This may seem like a strange request, but please may we borrow a tractor and a trailer for a period not exceeding four hours."

"And some sheep, probably six will do, and some straw. Dirty ones, the dirtier the better," said the second stranger, "but not in that sense, if you see what I mean. We may have to borrow them for a bit longer, but none will come to any harm. Emotional or otherwise."

"Och aye?" replied the farmer, as if this were an everyday occurrence around these parts. "And may I be so bold as to ask you why you wish me to provide you with a tractor, a trailer and some sheep, the dirtier the better?"

"And straw, sir."

"And a Barbour jacket or coat if you have one. We're a bit 'obvious' dressed like this."

"Well, why?"

"Sir, I regret that if we told you, we'd have to kill you." He smiled to show he was joking.

"I'd like to see you try, laddie, with those blank firing attachments on your fancy American rifles."

*

That afternoon, a tractor pulling a trailer of bad-tempered ewes chugged up to the security checkpoint of RAF West Freugh and was waved to a halt by two American combat security policemen. The gate was also covered by a machine gun in a concrete sangar.

"Sir, this is a restricted area and I'm afraid you'll have to turn round and go back."

"Get lost, sonny. This is where I graze my sheep and this is where these girls will graze."

"You can't graze sheep on here. This is a goddamned major military exercise."

The man driving the tractor looked pointedly across the security fencing to where sheep were contentedly grazing. "And how do you think those sheep got in? By teleporting?"

"Shit!" exclaimed the security policeman, "get that Limey liaison officer here. Let him sort it out."

The man on the tractor contentedly sucked on a pipe and waited until an MoD police van turned up at the main gate. The MoD Plod got out and officiously pulled on his cap.

"What seems to be the problem?"

"This farmer gentleman says he has the right to graze his sheep on the airfield."

The MoD policeman looked at the trailer that was covered with trampled sheep shit.

"Baaaaa," said an irritable-looking ewe.

"Technically, the local farmers do graze their sheep on the airfield. It keeps the grass short and saves the cost of mowing."

"Jeeez," said the American military policeman.

"If we stop him, there will be ructions in the local community. They moan enough about the noise of the aircraft. I'll escort him on and off and we'll keep well clear of your helicopters."

The tractor followed the MoD police van, and the two American policemen looked at each other. "The last century? It's more like going back to the Dark Ages."

The tractor pulled off the perry track and the driver started to unload the trailer. The ewes scampered off happily enough while the driver unloaded some of the straw. He paused as though tired and went to chat to the MoD policeman, pointing at the helicopters in the distance. While the MoD Plod was distracted, four straw men lugging bergens slipped off the trailer and lay in the long grass, indistinguishable from the dry grass around them. The 'farmer' finished unloading the straw and followed the MoD van off the base, waving cheerfully at the Americans as he chugged past the security checkpoint.

\*

Edge followed Sergeant Pedlow, flanked by Mickie and another trooper towards the flight line. They went down and crawled the last few yards towards where a sentry and a dog patrolled around the first four CH 53s. Mickie raised the air rifle and aimed at the dog. Normally, they would have used the silenced .22 'Hush Puppy' pistol to dispatch both the dog and the sentry, but this was an exercise. The tranquiliser dart hit the dog on its rump. The German Shepherd yelped and staggered. As the sentry bent down to see what was wrong with the dog, Edge and the other trooper bundled him onto the ground, jammed a rag in his mouth and cable tied his arms, knees and feet. They bundled the sentry into the grass and waited until the yelping dog fell over, before carrying it to join its handler.

Edge bent down next to the sentry, who was mumbling indignantly behind his gag. "Right, if you promise to play the game and stay nice and quiet, I'll get rid of the gag and untie your hands. Your pooch is fine. He'll wake up in an hour. Do we have a deal?"

The American sentry nodded and spat out the rag while Edge cut the cable tie on his hands. He gave him a bar of chocolate. "Now be good while we do our naughty stuff."

Each one of them took a helicopter, moving quickly in the darkness. They all placed a simulated explosive on each aircraft in exactly the same place, then ran thunder flashes with tripwires from helicopter to helicopter. Before they moved off, Edge jogged back to where the sentry was lying.

"Everything all right?"

"Guess so, you Limey bastard."

"Good man," said Edge, patting him on the shoulder. "Nice and quiet, remember."

The four of them cautiously moved around the back of the buildings to get to the second package of four aircraft, some 400 metres away. Every few yards, they paused and set up thunder flashes with tripwires on every doorway they thought would be appropriate. They almost ran into the second sentry, who was having a surreptitious cigarette at the side of a hangar. He dropped his rifle and opened his mouth to shout when Edge and the sergeant hit him. This one fought and tried to shout, while his dog took chunks out of Mickie's legs as he fumbled for the air rifle. The dart hit the dog between the shoulder blades and it eventually keeled over, its jaws still locked around Mickie's calf.

"Do these fuckers have rabies?" he asked in a low voice as he prised the dog's jaws open.

"No, just Ebola."

There were no niceties with this sentry. He was gagged and trussed with bodge tape and dragged into the shadows with the snoring dog.

They went to work with the dummy explosives and thunder flashes on the second batch of helicopters, same routine as the first. Once finished, they doubled back towards the control tower, their secondary objective, and waited in the shadow of a fire and rescue truck for the fun to start.

There was a flash and loud explosion from the direction of the main gate, followed by the rattle of automatic gunfire. Simultaneously, gunfire came from the other end of the runway and a Schermuly flare spiralled into the night sky. Edge was first through the main door of the control tower and fired a short burst at someone running down the stairs, staring at them in shock.

"You're toast," Edge told him.

Sergeant Pedlow and Mickie cleared the ground floor with gunfire and thunder flashes. Up on the next floor, Edge tossed a thunder flash into a room and watched people scatter. The trooper cleared it with short bursts, then they were up to the top floor and the control gantry itself. Two thunder flashes went in, followed by Edge and the trooper, their guns chattering. It was bedlam and the duty crew were on the floor, cowering in terror.

"Thank you for your cooperation, gentlemen, oh, and lady as well. Evening, Ma'am. My apologies if you were startled."

As they withdrew north towards the perimeter wire and their escape route, the thunder flashes started to go off round the helicopters as the tripwires were triggered. They could hear random and uncoordinated return fire, then they hit the fence and turned right, tracking along it until they found the non-notional hole that had been cut in the fence. As they ran towards their rendezvous, Mickie started to drop behind. Edge and the other trooper helped to keep him going.

"Fucking dog," Mickie gasped, and then in the distance they heard the helicopter.

The other four were waiting for them on the landing point, and the Sea King from 771 Naval Air Squadron flared and landed just north of the B7077.

"Well done, chaps," said an extremely chuffed Lieutenant Colquhoun. "Probably the most fun you can have with your clothes still on. I trust that none of that fine gentleman farmer's sheep were harmed by your display of thuggery."

"They were all well when we left them, Boss. Almost wistful."

"Mine made me promise to write."

The Sea King headed north to HMS Gannet at Prestwick Airport and the bar was open. They poured in to get a drink and wait for the Hercules back to Leuchars, while Mickie had his legs cleaned and dressed and a tetanus booster. They were feeling full of themselves, pumped up with adrenaline and testosterone, and Lieutenant Colquhoun threw open an invitation that he would later regret. He tapped on a glass to gain everyone's attention and stood up solemnly.

"Now as you are all aware, next week I am getting married, and I would like to invite all of you to my evening reception."

"Are you sure that's wise, sir?" said Pedlow with his best Sergeant Wilson impression.

"Of course it is. We can even invite the Crabs, whom I noticed pissed off when it got a bit wet and uncomfortable."

Later, Sergeant Pedlow asked Edge if he was going to Colquhoun's wedding.

"I'm not sure. What do you think?"

"His future missus will kill him. I wouldn't miss it for the world."

"Then count me in," said Edge with a grin.

\*

Whoever had been left of the bride's family had made themselves scarce, tut-tutting as they left, wondering what the hell she had let herself in for. He had always felt like an outsider looking in and had grown bored with the military rutting rituals. He spotted a girl who had been talking to Mickie and was unattached, judging by his surveillance. She was dark, looked slightly vulnerable, and she was fucking gorgeous. Edge moved in on the beautiful young woman who would become his wife and saviour. But first he said a sad little prayer: *Please forgive me, Jozica, but I have to move on. May God keep you, and you know that I'll always love you.*

# Chapter 10

# ANGELA'S STORY

———

Angela Keeble knew that she had made a mistake as soon as she said yes, but like most things in her life, she reasoned that she could manage the situation. At twenty-one, she was an independent woman with her own place, a reasonable job, and had no need to rely on anybody but herself. And what harm could it do? she asked herself. He was good-looking, had a roguish charm and plenty of money to splash around, and he did manage to get his hands on a regular supply of Puff the Magic Dragon's finest. Angela was quite partial to the odd tonk, as were quite a lot of youngsters in North Devon. Let's face it, there was sod all else to do. She told her friend Moira at the glass factory where they both worked the next day.

"And you said yes?" Moira asked incredulously.

"Yes, why not?"

"Somebody said he takes drugs."

"So what? Most of us do round here. We can't all live with our rich mummies and daddies in a very big house in the country. It deadens the monotony."

Moira frowned but knew that what Angela said was true. She wished she lived closer to where she worked so she could socialise more, but it was an excuse. She had her own car and had been driving since she was seventeen, and Angela had offered her the sofa in her flat on several occasions. Her dad got her the job in the glass factory, straight into the sales department, because of his contacts. Angela had come from the estate near Torrington's secondary school and had started work in the packing department.

Angela was not only very sharp; she wanted to get on after the complete cake and arse party she had made of her years at school. She soon moved up into the administration department and she had no doubt that she would be office manager, once the lazy, useless and incompetent old bag that ran the admin team could no longer drag her fat arse up the stairs. She was three years older than Moira, pretty without being beautiful, but she was vivacious and well liked. She dyed her hair blonde, because she had the ginger gene, and there was no way she wanted to look like her brother, who couldn't have given a toss.

"I can't help but think, Moira, that you're somewhat underwhelmed by my news."

Moira was simply jealous. Daz Copeland worked in her father's business and he was very popular. He was a risk-taker, a rough and robust man with a shock of dark curly hair, very tall and strong and very popular among her father's workforce. But her father was especially fond of him and had tried to engineer his going out with his daughter on at least a couple of firm functions. Moira was a coward, but more importantly she felt a danger when she was around Daz, and bizarrely, she found that most appealing. If the truth were known, she would have liked to rake her nails down her friend's face.

"There's just something about him. Something a bit…"

"A bit daring," Angela scoffed. "A bit different to the boring farts and inbreeds round here."

"I like some of the glassblowers," Moira protested.

"Have you ever been out with any of them?"

Moira shook her head.

"Most of them come from Scandinavia. Most of them are married, even the ones who say they aren't, and they like shacking up with us, because they're just so lonely. My brother Mickie calls us 'bergen brides', like the second wives that Marines have in Norway. They drink like there's no tomorrow. They are morose, and when you finally get round to some horizontal gymnastics with them, they fall asleep on you mid-hump."

Moira's eyes were round saucers of shock and the desperation to find out more, from her worldly-wise friend. Moira was still a virgin.

"Has that ever happened to you?"

"Never you mind. But I'll take my chances with Daz Copeland, coz he has shitloads of money and I can deal with his cock-like tendencies."

She was very much mistaken and soon came to realise that she had chosen to ride the tiger. Or let him ride her.

*

It was all fine to begin with. Daz was attentive, generous and willing to share his skunk stash in return for some uncomplicated sex, to which Angela was rather partial. But she soon found out that Daz Copeland had extremely tumultuous moods and he could change in the blink of an eye. If Angela couldn't make a liaison, he wanted to know why, who she was with and why she wasn't with him. On one occasion when she told him she was going shopping in Plymouth, she was convinced that she saw his black pick-up following her car south, trailing her Astra some vehicles behind.

But it was the sexual side of their relationship that concerned Angela the most. She was no prude, but began to realise that there was no shared tenderness, respect or love from Daniel Copeland. Sex was merely a means of satisfying himself and exercising coercion and control over Angela. She concluded that sex was merely an extension of his violence, and the time had come for her to bang out of this toxic relationship. But Daniel had other ideas about relationships, which were more about possession than synergy and mutual respect.

She would later admit that she hadn't picked her moment very well. Daz was in a particularly foul mood because he had travelled down to Plymouth to watch Plymouth Argyle lose 0-3 to Derby. They hadn't agreed to meet that evening, but Angela heard a hammering on the door of her flat above the pub at around 7 pm, and her heart sank. *Bastard told me he was going to Plymouth*, she said to herself. She reluctantly went down the stairs and opened the door and Daz barged in.

"Useless, they're all fucking useless," he raged.

"I take it Argyle lost," she said unhelpfully.

"Three-nil. Three fucking nil to Derby!"

He stomped up the stairs and shoved himself into the flat. "Daz, I thought we were having the weekend off. I thought that's what you said. It was your idea."

It was obvious he had been drinking heavily. He scowled at the television, sneered at Noel Edmonds, and switched it off.

"I was watching that! Have you been drinking, Daz?"

He slumped on the sofa. "So what if I have?"

"Where's your pick-up?"

"Outside."

"And you've driven from Plymouth in that state? Are you mad?"

"Yeah, and? Filth daren't touch me. Got too many things on them."

"You could have killed someone!" she said incredulously.

"Stop having a nag at me. You'd better be nice to me, coz I'm really pissed off, and I mean really, really nice."

Angela sat down on a chair and folded her arms. "We agreed no sex this weekend, and you know very well why. And why is it we have to have sex all the time anyway? There's more to a relationship than constantly rutting."

"Coz you like it."

"I can't this weekend."

Daz sighed and looked up at the ceiling. "In which case you can fix me a drink. You'd better have one as well to get that mouth of yours nicely limbered up."

"You can piss right off, Daz. Get out and don't bother coming back until you're sober!"

Something dark and dangerous came across his face; his eyes were glazed and empty. Daz stood up and walked over to the chair, then suddenly grabbed her hair and stood in front of her, pinning Angela in the chair with his strong legs. He pulled her head towards him.

"Don't you fucking defy me, you bitch! Now you're going to be nice to me."

He had unhitched his belt from his jeans and wrapped it round her neck in a quick move. The belt was two inches wide of hard leather and it dug into her neck. Angela screamed.

"Stop your fucking noise! Now, get ready and be nice. If you bite me, I'll choke the sluttish life out of you." Daz Copeland yanked her towards him with the belt and unzipped the fly of his jeans. "And you had better be fucking good!"

*

When she heard the street-level front door slam, she stood up unsteadily and pulled up her pyjama bottoms. She limped into the bathroom and stared at her face in the mirror. The bruise on her cheek could be covered with makeup on Monday, but she would have to wear a scarf to cover the wheals and bruises on her neck. Her voice was hoarse anyway, so she could say she had a sore throat.

Angela scrubbed her teeth and finished the best part of half a bottle of Listerine to get rid of his foul taste. She hobbled back into the sitting room and poured half a glass of neat gin with trembling hands. The drawing pain in her back passage made sitting difficult.

She wondered what the hell she was going to do. Daz had made it clear the police were his 'friends' and wouldn't believe some little slapper from the council estate. She thought about telling her mum and dad, but her dad was bloody useless in a crisis and her mum would probably say she had egged him on. Angela's track record wasn't exactly as clean as the driven snow. She thought about telling Moira, her friend, and almost laughed out loud. Moira was still a child in her head and wouldn't have a clue.

"I bet she still thinks babies come from storks," Angela whispered croakily, and then felt a guilty sadness. It wasn't Moira's fault she had got tangled with a psychotic bastard.

Then she thought of Mickie. Golden boy Mickie, Mum and Dad's favourite, her elder brother. Mum had been distraught when he left, and so had Angela. Mickie was everything she wasn't. He was fit, handsome – apart from that bloody hair of his – and clever, so very bloody clever. He was driven, kind and never had a bad word to say about anyone, even Angela when she pranged his car. Three A-levels, two at A and one at B, but no university for Mickie.

She had been about five and Mickie was ten on Saturday, the 1st of May 1980. Mickie was lying on the floor, reading one of his books while she was playing with her Barbie and his old Action Man. Their dad was watching the snooker, when the programme went off for a live broadcast from London, reported by Kate Adie. Mickie sat up and watched the television, knowing the report was coming from outside the Iranian Embassy.

"What's this bollocks? his dad asked. "What's happened to the bloody snooker?"

Mickie had stared with fascination at the black-clad figures, scaling the balconies, the blasts from the windows, the rattle and flashes of gunfire and the smoke beginning to billow out of the second-floor windows as the curtains burned. In those few moments, Mickie had realised that he didn't want to be a Fleet Air Arm pilot after all.

Angela smiled at the memory of seventeen years ago and went to the phone. She dialled a Hereford number and a switchboard operator asked her what extension she required. The phone rang a long time before a man answered it.

"Can I speak to Corporal Keeble, please?"

She heard the man shout out: "Has anybody seen Mick Hucknell, that flame-haired minstrel of soul?"

"He went downtown an hour a couple of hours ago."

The man came back on the phone. "Sorry, love, he's out."

"This is really important. I'm his sister and could you tell him something terrible's happened," she sobbed, because she couldn't help herself.

"Okay, love. I'll make sure he gets the message. Are you all right?"

"Yes, thanks. Just please ask him to phone me. I'll give you my number just in case…"

Her brother phoned back at just after midnight and it all poured out, between the sobs and the weeping. He asked and re-asked several questions, but his voice didn't betray any anger or emotion.

"Ange, I've been drinking so I won't be able to come until tomorrow morning. I'll put in for some compassionate leave with the duty clerk tonight. I'll borrow someone's bike, it'll be quicker. Lock yourself in and I'll see you at around one tomorrow. We'll sort it."

*

He made his preparations on Sunday after making sure his sister was all right and then began the first of a number of surveillance operations. He asked Angela for Daz's usual haunts and routine and would take him when the best opportunity arose. On the Monday morning, he asked Angela to follow him in her car while he stashed and camouflaged the borrowed motorbike deep in some woods. On the Monday evening, the King's Arms public house overlooking Bideford Quay was very quiet. Quiet, that is, apart from the three men at the bar, engaged in a noisy conversation. One of them was holding court, telling the other two a story, and they were guffawing along with the unfolding tale.

The bar door opened and a man walked into the pub. He was carrying a newspaper, and at first, nobody paid him the slightest attention. The big man at the bar paused in his tale and looked round at the stranger's shock of ginger hair. He sniggered and the other two grinned. The man ordered a half of lager, which caused more mirth, and then went and sat down. He could have sworn he heard "Ginger tosser." He opened the newspaper and pretended to read while he overheard how the big man at the bar had orally raped and sodomised his sister that Saturday. He didn't finish his lager and went out into the night, followed by a guffaw of laughter.

An hour or so later, Daz Copeland climbed behind the steering wheel of his pick-up, started the engine and leaned back with a satisfied sigh. He felt an imperceptive movement from behind and the point of a knife drew blood as the point jabbed into his neck. The voice from the back seat was calm and low. There was a trace of a West Country accent, but the voice was dangerously pleasant.

"In case you're wondering, Mr Copeland, the knife at your neck is an Applegate-Fairbairn combat knife. I spent most of the afternoon sharpening it. Just for you. Now, you're going to take me for a nice evening drive. I've noted that you have a rather cavalier attitude to drinking and driving, so no sudden braking. It'll go right through your neck and you'll be wearing your tongue like a Bolivian necklace. Drive south, keep quiet, and think about dying. Slowly."

The man gave Daz instructions and they headed south towards Torrington, turning right towards Putford, where it became heavily wooded.

"Slow down and turn right up the forest track. The gate's open."

"You're gonna fuc—"

"Shut up!" and Daz felt pain and blood trickling down his neck, into his shirt. "Stop here and turn off the engine and the lights. Don't try and turn round."

The silence in the dark wood was suddenly terrifying. Daz started to plead for his life.

"Shut it, you filthy bastard! In the few moments you've got left, I want you to reflect on what you've done and why you're here."

"Look, she said it was all right. She likes it a bit rough..."

The man hit him twice on the back of the head with a Maglite torch he had found in Daz's tool box. Daz slumped onto the passenger's seat. He was fit and strong, but Daz was a big man and it took him a while to drag the body out of the pick-up and lay it across the bonnet. Daz showed signs of coming to, so he was hit on the head again. The man got busy with Daz's clothes, cutting them off, then he produced some ropes he had purchased at a chandler's that afternoon. When he had finished, he looked at the Maglite and smiled horribly. Daz grunted in pain but didn't regain consciousness. There were a number of flashes as the man took photographs. Daz never heard the motorbike starting up and heading back to the road.

The Forestry Commission Land Rover pulled onto the track and followed the tracks the anonymous caller had said would be there. Sure enough, he could see the back of a black pick-up pulled off the track. He stopped, got out of the vehicle and approached it cautiously. He nearly choked with laughter at the sight of the man, slumped over the pick-up's bonnet, whose arms were tied to the wing mirrors and his spread legs tied to the pick-up's bull bars. But it was the torch that was the most incredulous sight he had ever seen.

"Now then. What sort of hanky-panky has been going on here?"

Daz opened his eyes. He had almost been driven insane by the cold, his head was throbbing, but it was nothing compared to the agonising pain in his anus. He looked at the Forestry Commission worker with fury.

"Fucking cut me free, you bastard. Otherwise, I'll kill you!"

The worker folded his arms and grinned at Daz. "I'd be a little more polite if I were you, mate. You're in no condition to threaten anybody, and I'm not the one with a torch sticking out of his arsehole. I'll get a knife."

Daz groaned in pain and stared at the windscreen of the pick-up. Sprayed in white paint was:

*IF YOU CAN'T POT THE PINK, GO FOR THE BROWN. TOUCH HER AGAIN AND I'LL KILL YOU.*

"Bastard!" said Daz. "I'll fucking kill you."

# Chapter 11

# FURY, DANIEL COPELAND'S STORY

———

Like all sociopaths, after a few years Daz Copeland had built up a network of contacts and acquaintances due to his superficial charisma and undoubted skills of a handyman. By now, he had gravitated to North Devon, where the winter work was better and more varied. Holiday lets needed constant maintenance and there were the fishing boats as well. Working on the fairground rides and machinery had provided him with a profitable skill set, and Daz found he had rather a knack with marine engines.

But Daz well and truly fell on his feet when he was recommended to do some work for a local businessman called Frank Tremain. He was a real mover and shaker in those parts, as well as a major employer in his agricultural supplies business. Daz Copeland was a master at charm, knowing when to butter someone up and all the while exaggerating his credentials, but still making them seem plausible. There was something of the sociopath in Frank Tremain as well, which is probably why he was drawn to this rough-diamond chancer. By the time Daz had finished the work at the large, sprawling house outside Barnstaple, Frank Tremain had offered him permanent employment in his business.

It was an offer Daz couldn't refuse. Frank Tremain's daughter was a beautiful and slightly vulnerable young woman. He knew she worked in the glass factory at Torrington where one of his exes, Angela, also worked. But Angela was a worldly-wise girl who had swiftly seen through Daz's superficial charm and had a brush with his more unsavoury tastes. Moira was in a different league. She was the daughter of his future boss, and Daz decided that what he wanted he would take. The offer of employment was a ticket to future wealth. Daz was almost licking his lips with anticipation. He was going to enjoy the debauchment of Moira Tremain.

And inevitably because of her naivety and the cosseted upbringing she had received, Moira fell for this charming sociopath; hook, line and sinker. He introduced her to a world of danger, a life that was slightly edgier than living with her staid parents. Daz got her drunk, got her high and got her to do things she never knew existed. It seemed so exciting at first. Angela her friend remonstrated with her, knowing how this would end, but Moira was besotted and was drawn into the life like a moth to a flame. But the flame became a blowtorch.

She was staying with Daz for the weekend in his ramshackle house out in the wilds off the A3124. It had been almost derelict when Daz moved in, but at least half of it was inhabitable now and he was slowly doing it up, and it had Calor gas and a generator. It was set back off the road, in trees up a narrow track. Secluded and perfect for what he wanted.

Moira was more than a little drunk and stoned. Daz had been drinking and had taken some weed as well, but he was more used to it. He only wanted to do one thing now, and sat next to Moira.

"Let's fuck, Mo."

"Is that your idea of foreplay, Daz?" she asked, and giggled.

He pulled up her t-shirt to feel her breasts and she pushed away. He grabbed her hair and tried to kiss her, but she turned away.

"Daz I'm too pissed and stoned, not tonight."

He tried to grab her again but she pushed him away again, harder this time. Daz felt the stirrings of anger because he needed to dominate, to win. He hit her backhanded across the face, but Moira retaliated and caught him across the nose with her nails; the graze started to bleed.

"You fucking bitch!" he yelled, and pulled back his fist.

Then she realised and saw in his eyes the danger she was in. She ducked away and ran for the door, then went out running into the darkness and the trees. He followed her to the door and laughed. "Where do you think you're going, you stupid bitch? I've got your coat and handbag."

Daz thought about getting his powerful spotlight and going out into the night after her. But he ran through the options in his mind. At the moment, he could pass any 'awkwardness' off as a lovers' tiff. But he knew that if he found her, he would beat her into a coma or perhaps kill her, because nobody should ever dare to defy him. That would be harder to explain. There were lots of lonely woods in this part of the world, and the idea of torturing and killing her was becoming more attractive. But there was Frank Tremain and the financial mother lode to consider. Daz could milk that for years to come, so he settled for rifling through her handbag, taking the cash out of her purse, throwing her coat and bag out into the yard and trampling them into the mud. He went back inside and tried to extinguish his seething anger with three-quarters of a bottle of Jim Beam.

Moira fell over several times but made it to the main road. He didn't follow her but she could hear him continuing to rage. Eventually, she flagged down a passing car, heading for Torrington. The elderly female driver was concerned.

"Is everything all right, dear?"

"Could you please take me to Torrington?"

The lady driver could smell the drink and another, cloying odour. "Well…"

Moira looked frantically over her shoulder. "Please, I'm in trouble."

"All right, but the police station is closed."

"It's okay, I can go somewhere."

The worried lady dropped her off in the town but seemed reluctant to leave her. "Are you sure you're all right?"

"Positive and thank you."

Moira walked to the glass factory where the night shift were working, freezing in just jeans and a t-shirt. It wasn't cost effective to shut down the kilns and furnaces overnight, and there was a skeleton shift that tended the furnaces and prepared the materials for the following day. She splashed water on her face and drank what seemed like gallons, then put her head down to sober up. She woke at five with a monstrous headache and fortunately had her car keys in her jeans pocket. Her car was in the car park where Daz had picked her up last night. Moira didn't want to, but she had to go back to get her handbag and coat. She would risk it because she guessed that Daz would be sufficiently out of it to allow her to creep into his house. She left the car halfway up the track and sneaked towards the house. In the pre-dawn light, she saw her belongings lying trampled in the mud.

"You bastard," she murmured to herself, picked them up and crept back to her car.

When she went through her purse, she saw that about thirty pounds was missing. Moira called him a bastard again and drove home, still well over the drink-drive limit. She reckoned that thirty pounds was a small price to pay for the narrow escape she had had. She wouldn't tell anybody what had happened, because she couldn't bear to hear 'told you so'. Moira would say that Daz had been seeing someone else, which wasn't so far from a lie, because she was pretty sure he had been. As she drove, Moira cried bitter tears, but by the time she had got home and crept into her parents' house, she was grateful that Daz Copeland had been exorcised from her life. She and her future family would find out just how wrong she was.

*

Daniel Copeland dismissed Moira Tremain from his life. She had been given a chance and had blown it, which was rather a pity for her. She was frigid anyway and frankly not worth bothering about. There were plenty more fish in North Devon's pool, and Daz Copeland moved through the ecosystem like a pike. And it was true; there was no shortage of girls drawn to this big, curly-haired charmer with an easy wit, and who always seemed to have plenty of money to throw around. He certainly knew how to show a girl a good time, if you could put up with his violent sexual urges. Many could, but a few would not.

Nobody should ever defy Daz Copeland. Glen Collier had been stupid enough to threaten him and he ended up at the bottom of the quarry with his bike. Which was a pity, because Glen's bike was a good one. A couple of punters at the fairs had tried it on with Daz a couple of times, but a tyre brace in the shadows soon sorted them out. It was all a question of respect. Daz had built up a following of a few good men and true, who shared his partiality for living life to the full and taking what they wanted, as long as it was all right with Daz. True, they weren't the brightest bulbs on the tree, but they were useful, and Daz called them his posse.

After Moira, there had been Tina. A fair handsome mare she was too, and she had her own flat above a surf shop in Westward Ho! She had a liking for the odd joint or three, which suited Daz down to the ground, plus she could be incredibly dirty when the mood took her, which was often. She could have been almost perfect if it wasn't for her cat, Tilly. *Tina and Tilly, bloody ridiculous,*

Daz thought. Dirty thing jumping up on the kitchen surfaces and hissing at Daz, but Tilly was Tina's baby and it made him fair sick to the stomach to watch her and how she spoke to it. But the damned cat was a small price to pay for Tina's dirtiness, her remarkable ability to get her hand on quality weed and her own place. *Who needs Moira fucking Tremain?* he asked himself.

But Tina made a mistake. She defied him. It was in the spring before the hordes of Grockles descended on the beaches, still too cold and windy, except for the hardcore surfers and kite surfers. *Stupid twats* was Daz's opinion of kite surfers. Tina had a cold, which had gone on for a few days. She was complaining that her joints ached, stupid fuss about nothing was Daz's considered opinion and he knew just the thing to perk her up, his new interest in all matters carnal, a spot of autoerotic asphyxiation.

"Come on, Tina, it'll put the colour back in your cheeks… Or perhaps not," he chuckled.

"There's no way, Daz. I feel like shit. No sex and certainly not that bloody strangling bollocks."

But Daz had been walking round with a semi all day and he was in need of relief. He wheedled, coaxed and eventually threatened, getting angrier all the time. But what amazed and infuriated Daz was that her angry defiance was growing. This wasn't supposed to happen, so he overpowered and took what was his as a right. She fought him despite her weakened state and started to scream and he was just forced to cram her pants into her mouth to shut her up. It didn't last long and thank God he hadn't tied the bathrobe cord around her neck. While she was in the bathroom being sick, he made inroads into his post-coital Jim Beam.

Tina had shut the cat in the spare room out of the way as soon as Daz had barged his way into the flat earlier that evening. She remained in the bathroom, sobbing, until she heard him snoring from her bedroom due to the effects of bourbon. She pulled her aching and bruised body to its feet and headed for the kitchen where she opened a utensils drawer.

Daz was lying on the bed on his side, snoring slightly and reeking of bourbon. The meat tenderiser hit him on the side of his head. It was just as well Tina was in an exhausted and weakened state, because it was a metal tenderiser with a nasty serrated surface. Daz opened his eyes, his temple throbbing.

"Whatderfuck?"

She hit him again before Daz could raise himself out of the alcoholic stupor, and then a third time.

"You fucking piece of shit!" she screamed at him, raining blows on his head.

Daz raised his arms in protection, so she landed a good one in his groin. The semi had long gone. He fell off the bed and vomited bile and foul-smelling bourbon on her carpet.

"You filthy, stinking bastard!"

A blow to the back of his head made him see stars and he fell face down in the puke. Daz was mortally afraid and he knew he had to get the hell out of there before she killed him. He pulled himself up, the quilt slipping off the bed and into the puke. Tina caught him again between the shoulder blades and on his right kidney. Panicking now, Daz headed for the door to the stairs. He was half running, half falling down them, and she caught him a couple more times before he was able to wrench the door open and fall out into the street in the early hours, wearing just his boxer shorts. Tina slammed the door behind him and double bolted it. Shaking with anger and fever, she went upstairs to wreak havoc on his clothes and boots with a carving knife. Daz had been extremely lucky she hadn't decided to use it on him. When they looked like they had been put through an industrial shredder, Tina threw them out of the window onto the street below. That night, she slept on the spare bed, cuddling Tilly, who had been as frightened by the commotion as Tina.

"What the hell happened to you, Daz?" one of his posse asked him the next Tuesday in the pub.

"I got into a bit of bother outside a nightclub in Exeter," Daz told him. "Fucking marines from Lympstone."

"You got done in by baby marines?"

"There were three of the bastards, and two of them won't be doing the assault course this week."

"You never told us you were heading to Exeter for the nightlife this weekend. I thought you were seeing Tasty Tina?"

"Miserable bitch had a cold, and Christ, did she go on about it. Got fucked off with it, so I've blown her out. Listen, Paulie, can I borrow your car for a couple of nights? My Ute's playing up."

"Err, okay, Daz, so long as you don't use all the petrol."

There was nothing wrong with his 4x4 utility vehicle. He wanted a car that Tina wouldn't recognise.

*

She could sense there was something wrong the moment she opened the door to the flat upstairs. Tina delved in her bag for the pepper spray and made a cautious ascent up the stairs. She listened for a long time outside the inner door, then cautiously opened it. Her flat had been trashed, cushions and pillows slashed, but what made her wail and sob in desperation was the sight of her cat, Tilly, who had been nailed to her bedroom door. Next to the clearly dead cat was a crude handwritten note:

> *YOU DIFIED ME YOU STUPID BITCH AND NOBODY DIFIES*
> *ME.*
> *YOU TELL THE FUCKIN POLICE IF YOU DARES*
> *BUT PEOPLE WILL SWEAR I WAS WITH THEM*
> *POLICE WONT BELIEVE A JUNKIE LIKE YOU.*
> *IF I DO GO AWAY IT WONT BE FOR LONG*
> *WHEN I GETS OUT ILL BE LOOKING FOR YOU*
> *AND YOULL END UP LIKE YOUR FUCKIN CAT.*
> *NOBODY DIFIES ME YOU BITCH.*

Tina began howling in impotent grief.

# Chapter 12

# MOIRA'S AND EDGE'S STORY

---

When Angela found Moira it was obvious that Moira had been crying. Her dark mascara had run from her eyes in blue streaks, and those eyes were puffy and reddened. Even her hair looked slightly dull and listless, as though the spark had gone to be replaced with self-indulgent misery. She was sitting on the loading bay, pretending to smoke a cigarette. Moira was drawing in with a huge suck, the cigarette end glowing like the tip of an inquisitor's poker, then she let out the smoke in gentle puffs, because it was obviously too hot for her oral membranes. Inhaling was out of the question.

"For Christ's sake, Moi. What the hell are you doing?"

"Leave me alone," Moira sobbed, and then hiccupped. It was the cigarette smoke.

Angela gathered her work dress, voluminous with nice white buttons, and sat down on the loading platform next to her.

"Moi, why are you sitting out here? It's bloody freezing and you don't even smoke."

She hiccupped again and threw the cigarette away.

"Who gave you that?"

"Charlie."

"Oh," Angela observed dryly. "So that's why he was laughing."

"So you're all just laughing at me."

Angela sighed. Sometimes her friend could be very high maintenance and she blamed Moira's cloying and overbearing mother and father. "What is it this time, Moi?"

Cue another round of sobbing. "It's Daz, I've dumped him."

Angela's mouth was set in a thin line. "Good, because he's a cock!"

"But I love him."

Angela knew very well what a bastard Daniel Copeland AKA Daz could be, because she had spent a long, exciting but ultimately frustrating six months with him, intimately. It was Daz's wandering eye and controlling demeanour that did it for Angela. He was like all men of his ilk: dangerous, exciting, but not somebody you'd spend the rest of your life with. A big, violent and aggressive fish in Great Torrington's little gene pool.

"Whose idea, your mum's or dad's?"

Moira dabbed her eyes. "Mine. Dad thinks he's wonderful. He works in Dad's company."

"What did he do this time?"

Moira's tears flew freely now. "He's been seeing someone else."

"By seeing, do you mean shagging?"

She nodded.

"If it wasn't now, it would have been next week, next month, or next year for the rest of your time with him. You've had a lucky escape, love. Come on, let's go in."

They went back to the offices through the glassblowing area, bathing in the heat from the furnaces. The two young women stopped to admire the easy skills of the glassblowers.

"I wish I could do that," Moira said as she watched one of the makers blowing through the hollow steel tube, an amorphous mass of molten glass on the other end. He made it look so easy, but she knew it wasn't.

"I thought Daz would have made sure you'd have plenty of practice by now."

Moira laughed reluctantly, but she knew Angela was only half joking.

That lunchtime, Angela put a suggestion to Moira. "Listen, I've got an invite to a wedding up near Bristol, this weekend. Do you fancy coming with me? My car's just failed its MOT and I know it's cheeky, but you could take us in your car. I've got a hotel booked and we could share the room, unless one of us cops off with someone, then we'll arm-wrestle for it."

"Who's getting married?"

"A friend of my brother's. You know, Mickie, my elder bro, who's in the Army. Well, he's Mickie's company commander, an officer."

"Do officers normally invite their soldiers to their wedding?" Moira said doubtfully.

"They do in my brother's regiment. They're a bit 'special'."

"Like slow-witted?"

Angela giggled. "Bloody hell, Moi. I think the special one is you sometimes. No, not that kind of special."

"I don't know. I'll have to ask Mum and Dad."

"For God's sake! You're nineteen, nearly twenty. Grab life by the balls! What do you have to lose?"

"I'm not sure what to wear."

Angela put her head down and pretended to beat her head on the desk.

*

The reception was full of young people, a large number of which were in uniform. It was around 75/25 Army to RAF. This clearly wasn't a family wedding. Moira was enjoying herself chatting to Angela's brother, who had the greenest eyes she had ever seen and a shock of ginger hair. She had drunk rather more than she was used to and Daz was a distant memory, like the unfortunate repercussions of a bad meal. Mickie was charming company, but it was obvious he had come with someone else who was in the mood for dancing. He wasn't and was happy to chat to his sister's friend.

"Who are those boys over there in the grey-blue uniforms?"

They're RAF PJIs."

"PJIs?"

"Parachute jump instructors."

"I wouldn't have thought you'd need much instruction to jump out of a plane."

Mickie smiled at her naivety. "You'd be surprised. We have to give back the parachutes that don't work to someone."

She sussed he was pulling her leg. "Oh, you."

As the evening wore on and the slower dance tracks started, Moira was un-partnered, but she wasn't too bothered as she had had enough of men and relationships. She decided to get what would be her last drink at the bar and was resolved to spending the night alone in the shared hotel room. Angela had copped off with one of the PJIs for a night of uncomplicated sex in his hotel, so she had the room to herself.

He had been watching the girl from the scrum of unattached males, whose wedding reception was one of boozing rather than dancing and courtship displays. They were getting into their stride with the unofficial regimental song, Chumbawamba's *Tubthumping*, complete with actions and a signaller singing the chorus in a *sotto voce*. Whoever had been left of the bride's family had made themselves scarce, tut-tutting as they left, wondering what the hell she had let herself in for. He had always felt like an outsider looking in and had grown bored with the military rutting rituals. He was unattached and so was she, judging by his surveillance. She was dark, looked slightly vulnerable, and she was fucking gorgeous. He moved in to the fight-through.

Moira became aware of someone reaching the bar just before she did.

"Could I have…" then he noticed her. "Oh, I'm sorry, I've pushed in."

Moira smiled shyly. "It's okay."

"Let me get you a drink. It's the least I can do."

The barman, who had seen it all before, raised his eyes. "Bacardi and Coke for madam?"

Moira nodded.

"Sir?"

"Red wine, Merlot or Shiraz, it doesn't matter."

She looked at him surreptitiously. Smaller than she would have preferred, compared to… Fuck him. Very fit-looking and smart in his Number 2 dress uniform. Hard face with grey eyes. A nose slightly displaced to the side. Two stripes, a corporal? He looked unsafe and appealing for it. His voice was quiet and temperate compared to some of the ruck who were getting more boisterous. She reckoned this was a man who was comfortable in his skin.

His hair was quite long for a soldier and a bit tousled, like a naughty little boy, she thought to herself. Although he was smiling, he seemed to have a slight air of sadness, as though life had dealt him a pretty poor hand. And looking at his face, it had. There was a frisson of danger about him that attracted Moira, much like that bastard Daz, but in his case, the danger seemed controlled.

He gave her the Bacardi and smiled, raising his glass. "Your good health."

They toasted each other. "It looks like we're a couple of spare wheels. Do you mind if I join you?"

She hesitated so he started to back away. "Sorry if I'm being a bit forward. I'll leave you—"

"No, it's okay. We can be spare wheels together. Can we sit down, only my feet are killing me in these shoes."

They found a quiet table and the chat came easily. He was genuinely interested in her and asked lots of questions about where she came from and what she did.

"You work in a glass factory? Stupid question, but do you make stuff?"

She giggled. "No, silly. I work in the sales office. I'm Moira Tremain, so hello."

"Moira Tremain," he said, mulling the name over. "That's very *Lorna Doone*. Lorna Tremain from the glass factory."

We export stuff all over the world. I've told you my name, now what's yours?"

"Edge."

"Like the guitarist in U2."

There was a brief, fleeting trace of anger in his eyes, but she knew it wasn't directed at her. "No, not like the guitarist from U2. He's The Edge. I'm just plain old Edge."

"Your Christian name, please."

"Mark."

"Right, Mark, now I want to know something."

*Here we go*, he thought. The inevitable *have you ever killed anyone?* question.

She touched the bright blue parachute wings on the top of his right sleeve. "How come your badge is much prettier than those RAF boys' badges?"

He laughed. "Because they're not allowed to wear them, unless they are in the Regiment."

"So you're better at parachuting than they are?"

He smiled and then chuckled into his Merlot. "No, they actually teach us on the HALO course. We've just finished it. That's why my badge looks so bright and new."

"HALO?"

"High Altitude exit, Low Opening."

"What height do you jump from?"

"That's classified."

She pouted and Edge guessed that despite her obvious beauty and sexual attraction, Moira was a spoiled little girl.

"But you can see the curvature of the earth."

They drank more and now as they talked of cabbages and kings, their heads were close together, hands touching occasionally. There was nobody else in the big room as far as they were concerned. Eventually, she dragged him up to dance to *Kiss From a Rose*.

"C'mon, Mark, I like this one."

"No, I've got two left feet."

She pulled him to the dance floor and they melted together. She smelled as good as she looked, and a song popped unbidden into Edge's mind, wiping out Seal: *Year of the Cat – Al Stewart*.

*

Moira wrapped the sheet round her tender body as the sweat cooled, and she went up on one elbow to study the man who was lying next to her. Edge lay with his eyes closed, breathing gently. His body was covered with old and some newer scars. There were scabs on his knees and elbows, like a little boy. It was the hardest body she had ever felt, a by-product of a hard and violent occupation, rather than a narcissistic obsession in a gym.

"What time is it?" he asked without opening his eyes.

"Just after six in the morning."

"I suppose that I really should have a shower and get ready."

"Have you anything to get ready for?"

"Not until Monday," he admitted. Edge went up on his opposite elbow and they stared at each other. "What about you?"

She decided that his rather hard face with the slightly twisted nose was the most handsome she had ever seen. "Work on Monday."

"Glass factory?"

"Are you mocking me, Mark Edge?"

"No. I'm here looking at you and I can think of no better reason not to go to work. Ever."

"I never managed to blow a vase or glass, but it was valuable practice," she said, and tracked down his stomach with her mouth.

By Sunday evening, Moira's friend Angela was feeling disgruntled because she had to go home by bus and train. Moira had met the man she wanted to marry and was suffering from a mild case of honeymoon cystitis. Edge decided that Moira was a good catch and he would be a fool to let her go. He also had a torn frenulum.

"What happens now?" she asked as they packed that evening.

"I go to France to do some parachuting with the French Army. You give me your address and telephone number and when I can, I'll be hotfooting it to North Devon for some more glassblowing instruction. I haven't quite got the hang of it."

\*

The course of true love never runs smoothly, and Edge and Moira's relationship was no exception. His visits were infrequent due to the tumultuous situation in the Balkan States of the Former Republic of Yugoslavia. There were the logistical difficulties of travelling down to the West Country and limited periods of leave, but Edge came to love the area and Moira. Moira became more worldly-wise and mature. She was infatuated with her little soldier, as she called him, much to Edge's disgust.

For his part, Edge learned to share his life with someone else, well, most of it. Like all ordinary people who do extraordinary work in the service of their country, Edge had compartmentalised his mind. It was like a library he could delve into. Romance; non-fiction. Travel; non-fiction. War and conflict; non-fiction. Happily ever after; fiction. But Edge truly loved Moira and he was absolutely happy and contented in her company. He just wasn't very good at showing it.

Moira had a lot of preconceived notions about the Army, a view shared by her parents with an absolute certainty. But Mark Edge refused to fit stereotypes and he constantly surprised her. He was vigorous and harsh, but on occasions tender and artistically very talented. He would sit opposite her, doodling on a pad, and after five minutes produce a beautifully executed portrait in biro. His watercolours of birds and landscapes were exquisite, but photography was his real talent. He took endless pictures of the Taw and Torridge whenever he visited her. Edge had a passion for books and was well read.

She learned more about the countryside she had lived in all her life from Edge, in the days and weeks they spent together. They would go for walks and disappear into the undergrowth. Edge always knew where to find dry and secluded hides where they would make love like forest animals and return to Moira's parents' house, looking flushed and dishevelled.

Moira's parents, particularly her father, disliked Edge with a vengeance, and it was a source of endless conflict between them.

"Mark, why won't you even try to meet them halfway?" Moira asked him in his hotel room in Bideford. The situation regarding Edge and her parents had become so toxic that he felt obliged to stay in a hotel when he visited Moira rather than stay under their roof.

"Because I have a delicate and sensitive nature and I don't like it when people don't like me and go out of their way to make me feel unwelcome."

They were lying in a four-poster bed in a hotel that overlooked the medieval bridge over the Torridge. Her head was tucked on his shoulder and Edge was paying gentle attention to her right nipple. She brushed his hand away irritably.

"You won't even make the effort!"

"All right then, let's look at the evidence. Your dad is a big noise round these parts. He runs a large business which employs a lot of people. All credit to him. And you, you lucky girl, live in a six-bedroom house. You're an only child, and to put it bluntly, Moira, you're a spoiled little bitch.

"And then along comes Edge, a violent killing machine who likes nothing better than despoiling Daddy's little girl. I bet they've gone out of their way to dissuade you from having anything to do with me. I bet you haven't even told them I'm here. How am I doing?"

She said nothing, but he could tell by her breathing and heart rate he had hit the nail on the head.

"Okay then, let's think about Daddy's lovely six-bedroom house. Along comes Edge, Percy Pongo. Is there any room at the inn? No, Percy Pongo gets to sleep in the annex above your daddy's nice double garage and workshop. 'We thought it best for you,' says Mrs Tremain. 'You can come and go as you please.' As long as it's nowhere near our darling daughter's bedroom. Much more fitting for the lower orders, don't you think? Far enough away to stop him giving his little girl a good seeing-to."

She sat up and slapped him, not hard and rather half-heartedly because she knew he was right. Edge started to laugh and her face changed and she punched him, harder this time. She found herself on her back with her arms pinned over her head. By God, he was fast and strong. His face wasn't angry, just set and determined.

"We have to sort a couple of things out, Moira Tremain. Do you want to marry me?"

"You must be joking. No, I do not!"

Keeping her arms pinned, he moved down and blew on her right nipple. He knew that was the more sensitive.

"You bastard, Edge! I suppose so."

"A proper marriage, just you and me living together. Not with Mummy and Daddy."

"I've told you. I'm not following you around in damp, shitty married quarters like some chattel. I've got a job and family here. I could make a home for both of us here. You won't be in the Army forever."

"But not with Mummy and Daddy. Those are my conditions. Tell me, Moira, did Daddy buy you a pony when you were little?"

She pouted like the spoiled girl she was.

"He did, didn't he?" Edge said with a laugh.

"Fuck off, Mark."

"I disapprove of such unladylike language," he told her, and nibbled at her nipple.

"You are such a bastard!"

He stopped and studied the tactile reaction. "What if I tell you that I've seen a cottage on the river, well, obviously up a bit from the river? What if I tell you I've got enough money for a deposit and what if I tell you we could both live in it? Not me all the time, of course."

"I don't believe you. Where?"

"Weare Giffard. Less than three miles from here, but just conveniently far away from your mummy and daddy. And closer to your work."

"I don't believe you."

"I've got a viewing tomorrow. You can come if you want."

"I might not want to."

"Okay," he said. "I may have to persuade you a bit more…"

\*

A few hours later, someone was hammering on the wall and yelling for them to: *Keep the fucking noise down. Some of us have to get up tomorrow!* They collapsed in each other's arms, laughing. And Edge necked half of the bottle of champagne that had been cooling in a chiller.

"Did you know that the original champagne glass, called the 'coupe', is reputed to have been modelled on two of King Louis the Fifteenth's mistresses, Madame de Pompadour and Madame du Barry? They are said to have created glasses from their breasts for the king's lips only. Napoleon's wife, the Empress Josephine, is rumoured to have created breast glassware for her own personal use, while Helen of Troy allowed Paris to make wax moulds of her breasts to turn into *coupes* for his own pleasure."

"They couldn't have had that much in the booby department back then," Moira observed pointedly.

Edge scrutinised her breasts and picked up the chilled champagne, then poured some on them and proceeded to lick it off. It was a decadent action but the coldness followed by the warmth was exquisite. She couldn't believe that she was doing this, with a person who had just proposed to her in such an odd way. But as he grinned at her, she knew that for better or worse, they would be together. She was getting on a rollercoaster.

## Chapter 13

# EDGE, BACK IN THE BALKANS (SAME SHIT, DIFFERENT DAY)

---

They were lying in a hide under the trees, about halfway up the steeply sloping valley. From this vantage point, they could see the Pristina road and the River Iber winding through the valley below. The two of them had prepared the hide two days previously by making a shallow scrape and draping over the top a well-camouflaged tarpaulin. Their hide was indistinguishable from 2 metres away. Aircraft were rumbling overhead, but otherwise the valley was peaceful, almost idyllic, with very little traffic on the road below.

Minty was on stag, but Edge was awake and gently ruminating on a piece of chorizo sausage and hard cheese, his favourite munchies during the interminably boring OP watches. He cut a piece off the top of the chorizo and offered it to Minty on the end of his Fairbairn Sykes knife. Minty put down the field glasses and shook his head with a grimace. He went into the pocket of his smock and pulled out a slack handful of Haribo Starmix, blowing off dust and debris.

Edge murmured in a low voice: "I'll kill myself with salt and fat. Your choice is sugar and gelatine."

Minty looked at him, munching on the sweets. "What's wrong with gelatine?"

Murmuring was better than whispering, because a low murmur didn't carry as far as a higher-pitched whisper.

"It's made from the boiled-up bones, tendons and spinal columns of pigs and mad cow-ridden cattle. You'll go raving mad, Minty, but worse, you'll be mooing by the end. You'll wake up at five every morning, demanding to be milked."

Minty grinned. When they told him he was going out with Edge, all his mates had commiserated, saying that Edge was a nasty, miserable bastard. In their forty-eight hours of close confinement, Minty had got to know the seething, angry myth that was Sergeant Edge quite well. Minty may have been a signaller and forward air controller, but he was good at reading and understanding people. In a previous life, he had been a registered mental nurse with a degree in psychiatry, but became disillusioned with 'issues' and the victim culture. He had joined the Army late and qualified for Special Forces even later, against all the odds.

Edge wasn't angry, at least not all of the time. The Edge he was sharing this hide with was considerate, thoughtful and reflective. There wasn't anger within Edge; there was a profound sadness. But unfortunately, a Kosovo forest hide wasn't the place to set out his couch and ink blots.

Edge cradled a .338 L115 A3 sniper rifle, well wrapped with hessian, and a LAW anti-tank rocket launcher was lying next to him. Minty had his L119A1/A2 individual weapon, but between them on its tripod was a SOFLAM (Special Operational Forces Laser Air Marker) laser designator and a radio set. They were waiting for Serbian tanks that had been expected to move up from the south and deploy to cover the river crossing. The Serbs had become masters of evading NATO airpower by using the terrain and woods to hide, where airborne laser designators couldn't lock-on.

A laser designator is used to project an intensely focussed beam of light on a target. This is known as 'painting the target'. A sensor on an attacking aircraft's bomb or missile detects the laser beam as it bounces off the painted target. Upon release, the laser-guided munitions follow this aim point, effectively homing in on the beam's reflection. The laser beam is 'coded' which means it shines in specific patterns of pulses. This coding enables the air assets to ensure they are being guided by the correct designator. Laser designators can effectively be used to paint targets for aircraft operating at medium- to low-level altitudes.

Minty was the forward air controller and he would be directing precision-guided munitions onto the tanks hiding under the trees. The only problem was that the Serbian tanks hadn't pitched up, because they seemed not to have received the memo. He had never directed an air strike in anger before, so Minty was champing at the bit. Edge was far more sanguine. He cut off a chunk off the salty, hard cheese, closed his eyes and remembered being lectured by an undernourished but infinitely lovely and bitterly missed Croatian forensic anthropologist, about goodies and baddies in unnecessary wars of choice. Kosovo was the prime minister's second major war of choice, and when clueless politicians get a messianic complex, people like Edge had to go out and kill or be killed. He knew the score and would never ask for pity or even sympathy. It was an outdoor life and the cheese was particularly good, while the chorizo was disappointing.

They spent a totally uneventful night and Edge decided to give it twenty-four more hours and then they would bug out. They would be running short of water and Edge's old kidney and bladder problem, courtesy of a couple of Anglophobic German policemen, would flare up.

The following morning, Edge was asleep, having been on stag for most of the night. He enjoyed the feel of the darkness and listening to the wildlife, while Minty snored gently. Now Minty was watching the mist gently roll through the valley, following the course of the river. It was beautiful and almost impossible to identify the wooded valley as a war zone. It was too early for the NATO pilots to get out of bed and Minty lay and watched the view, accompanied by the backdrop of birdsong. He remembered his previous life and the frustration of dealing with people with 'mental health issues', but really they just had unrealistic expectations of life. The really mentally ill patients were zombified with pharmaceuticals and should have been in secure units that didn't exist. Minty's family and even Minty himself were at a loss as to to why he had ever elected to go into the caring profession, particularly as a registered mental health nurse.

He liked nothing better than the smell of the earth and forest, sharing a covert hide with such a complex kindred spirit as Sergeant Mark Edge. It was the nature of their job that they might never operate together on a solo mission such as this again, but everyone knew everyone in the Special Forces, except that is for the boys and girls of the 'Det', who kept themselves very much to themselves. It the truth were known, some of the people in the 'Det' frightened the hell out of the blades.

At 07:30, Minty heard vehicle engines from the valley below. He estimated there were three vehicles but no sounds of tracks. He tried to peer down into the mist, then used the IR on the SOFLAM, which confirmed an eight-wheeled armoured personnel carrier and two technicals. The imaging was poor through the moisture of the mist but sufficient to count vehicles. The vehicles' engines were still running, but they had pulled off the road, under the trees by the bridge. He gently nudged Edge's boot with his own.

"What is it, Minty?"

"We've got company down by the bridge. The wrong kind. Two pick-ups, technicals and an APC."

"How many bodies?"

"Can't tell. The IR isn't powerful enough to pick out body heat through the mist."

Edge started to pummel his legs to get the circulation going, then peered through the SOFLAM, down into the valley.

"Okay, well, this definitely wasn't in the script," Edge said, picking up his rifle. "I'll go down and have a shufti. The mist should give me enough cover, but if I'm not back in twenty, get the hell out."

"That wasn't in the script, either, Edge."

He grinned at him and wriggled out from under the tarpaulin. "Whatever you do, Minty, don't talk to any strange men."

Minty sighed and looked at his watch, then tracked Edge's progress down through the trees through the SOFLAM, until his thermal image was lost in the mist. By the time he had made it back some eighteen minutes later, the higher sun was beginning to burn off the haze. Edge wriggled in and pulled off his headover. He was sweating with the exertion of clambering back up the slope.

"I think either them or us are in the wrong production. They're bloody mujahedeen. There must be around fifteen to twenty of them."

There were around 1.6 million Muslims, 150,000 Serb Orthodox and 60,000 Roman Catholics in Kosovo at the time of the Kosovo war of 1998-99. Once again, it had been spun by the US president, Britain's prime minister and a supine and compliant media as a war of Serbian aggression against ethic Kosovars, i.e. Albanian Muslims. As in the Bosnian War, this was at best an over-simplification, a snapshot in time of over 500 years, or a deliberate attempt to weaken Serb and therefore Russian influence in the Balkans. The Kosovars attacked Serb military positions and undertook ethnic cleansing to remove Orthodox Serbs and Catholics from the state. The Serbs retaliated, and it was to this retaliation that politicians arm-twisted an effectively useless NATO that had lost the *raison d'être* for its existence, into retaliating. The Serbs were the baddies in the Camp David world of high-fiving and towel flicking. The Kosovans were the poor, oppressed Muslims (except the M word was never mentioned in news reports) that NATO had a duty to protect. The more astute cynics noted that the war in Kosovo was more of a tactic to divert attention away from the US president's penchant for using the vagina of a young intern as a cigar humidifier. And we all fell for it, hook, line and sinker. Well, not all of us. People like Edge and Minty, the people on the ground, understood the grim realities of ethnic and religious civil wars.

"What do you reckon, Minty? Bug out or stay?"

"Jeez, Edge. Why do you ask me? I'm the magic fairy who talks to the pilots. You're the steely-eyed killer."

"Because we're a team."

"Let's see how it pans out then."

It was to pan out very badly as it turned out.

By mid-morning, the sun had burned away the mist and the two of them could just about see the technicals drawn up under the trees. An attempt had been made to camouflage the APC which was recognisable as a BTR 60, and they could watch the mujahedeen make a meal and dig in.

"We could call in an air strike to whack 'em," Edge suggested belligerently.

"The trouble is, they're not the bad guys. It's Serbian tanks we're after. We can't break radio silence until the approved bad guys turn up."

By 10:30, the situation was further complicated when a decrepit Kosovar bus, that looked more like a 1970s British coach, trundled down the valley from the north. The armed mujahedeen stopped the vehicle at gunpoint and ordered everyone off.

"Minty, this is going to get interesting in a bad way," Edge said grimly, watching the tableau unfolding through field glasses.

It was mujahedeen SOPs the world over, whether a bus on the Somali/Kenyan border or a convoy in the Lebanon, the armed men separated the passengers into two groups. It wasn't hard to guess which religious factions the two groups were comprised of. Edge grabbed Minty's sleeve and talked to him forcibly face to face.

"The killing will soon start. They will slaughter all the non-Muslims. Our mission is compromised and we must extract. You will have to lug the designator and the radio and head for the primary pick-up point. If you are in trouble, destroy the Krypto, but you must make the primary pick-up. I'll distract them and head for the secondary pick-up within twelve hours. But you must go now!"

"Bollocks, Edge. We'll both do this."

"I'm the steely-eyed killer. Remember, you told me that. You're the important person now. I'll wait until you're clear before I ruin their day."

"Edge?"

"Just fucking go, Minty. And you had better tell them to come and get me. Can you manage the radio and designator?"

Minty, who was built like a brick shithouse, glowered at him.

"Good luck, Minty."

"Fuck you, Edge."

Edge shook his hand and slithered out of the hide, lugging his sniper rifle and the LAW rocket launcher. He made it down about 50 metres before the first shots came from the road below. He went down behind a tree, half sitting, supporting the rifle on his knee. He looked down at the vehicles through the Schmidt and Bender telescopic sight and evaluated the main threats. The men from the bus and some of the women were kneeling by the ditch at the side of the road, while a mujahedeen in a headscarf was shooting them in the back of the head. What he assumed were the Muslim passengers were filing back on the bus. A second group of younger women were partially in the woods and were being forced to strip by two armed men.

Edge took aim, steadied his breathing, and the head of the man who was shooting the kneeling passengers exploded. Less than two seconds later, one of the men who was forcing the passengers to undress went face down as the .338 Lupa Magnum round hit him between the shoulder blades. Amid the confusion down on the road, Edge changed position, tracking down left, crossed the river and then sprinted across the road. He was desperately and silently willing the non-Muslims to make a run for it, but they seemed stupefied by events.

He moved stealthily through the trees, pretty sure that Minty should have been well clear by now. He unslung the LAW and knelt behind a tree, extended it, raised the sight and switched off the weapon's safety. Edged aimed at the APC; the BTR's commander was in the top hatch of the hull, swinging the heavy machine gun towards the slope on the other side of the road. At around 200 metres, the APC was at the limit of the LAW's effective range. Edge aimed just above the middle of the wheels and pulled the trigger. The percussion cap ignited the LAW's rocket motor and the projectile left the tube, its fins unfolding. The missile hit the APC just in front and below the turret at 145 metres/second. At first, he thought he had missed, but the BTR 60 lurched and Edge was gratified to see the vehicle commander shoot upwards at the tip of a column of flame from the turret hatch. He threw away the now useless LAW tube, grabbed the rifle and ran north along the side of the road. At last, some of the passengers were running for their lives into the woods.

From behind, he could hear the sound of the technicals' engines starting up. It seemed as though the mujahedeen attention was now focussed on whoever had destroyed the APC. Edge went to ground in a ditch overhung with trees. He couldn't see anything down the road from where he had come, and sidled forward to peer out just as a technical fired down the road towards his position. The fire was inaccurate, but it was a heavy machine gun and proved that they had a pretty good idea where he had gone. This was bad. He was stuck on the wrong side of the river and road, with an enemy that seemed pretty good at their craft, rape and murder aside. He aimed prone at the gunner on the nearest technical and fired. What seemed like a puff of dust erupted from the man's shoulder and he folded behind the pick-up's cab. Then he was on his feet and tearing across the road, through the vegetation and down into the river. It was deeper and faster-moving here, and as Edge held the rifle out of the water and half kicked and swam across to the other side, heavy calibre rounds and tracers streaked and cracked overhead.

He would be vulnerable as he clambered up the riverbank and into the trees. Edge looked to his left and saw several mujahedeen fording the river to cut him off. He fired leaning on the riverbank and dropped one and fired again at the windscreen of a technical moving up the road towards him. The vehicle slewed to a halt and Edge was up the bank and zigzagging into the trees. Heavy machine gun rounds and tracers reached for him, and a round hit the trunk of a tree next to his head, partially blinding him with wood and bark fragments. *This was bloody bad*, Edge concluded as he wiped blood out of his eye and ran up the steep slope into the trees.

*Who are these bastards?* Edge asked himself as he raced up the slope, ducking and diving around trees. Part of him knew. These were no Saudis or Syrians looking for a bit of fun-filled Jihad. These had to be Chechens, fighters who loved nothing more than mixing it with the Russians, and Edge concluded that he was in serious shit. He had lost the advantage of range that the sniper rifle had afforded him. He was in the forest where the fighting would be close in and he had the wrong kind of weapon, which had five rounds left in the box magazine and a further ten rounds in a magazine in his chest rig. Once again, Edge's noble (or stupid) intentions had dropped him in the shit, and he was convinced, as he was on many occasions, that God was having a laugh with him. In reality, Edge was having a laugh with himself.

He stopped to listen, his pulse throbbing in his temples, chest heaving. Little black dots were dancing in front of his eyes, like thunder flies on a hot summer's afternoon. He could hear the movement of several bodies in the undergrowth down below. No voices or shouting, they were too good for that, and then there was silence. Edge felt a cold chill in his guts. They had stopped to listen for him, or at least some of them had, while the others pressed on silently. He did the same, moving as swiftly and as silently as he could, half running and half climbing up the steep slope.

Higher up the forest slope, the trees thinned and he crossed a firebreak or track that showed signs of logging activity, judging by the heavy tyre tracks in the mud. In the trees the other side, Edge went to ground, selecting a depression that gave him a degree of cover and from where he could cover the track. He could hear them coming up the slope and thought he saw a figure pause in the undergrowth about 100 metres away, before crossing the track. Edge peered through the sight and saw grass and fern fronds move. He aimed low and sent down two rounds. Two mujahedeen burst from cover to dash across the track. The first made it; the second didn't, going down with a puff of bloody dust from his chest. Edge fired his remaining two rounds into the vegetation to keep the others pinned on the other side of the track, then changed magazine. Apart from his Sig pistol, tucked inside his chest rig, he was down to ten rounds for the rifle.

The mujahedeen bracketed his position with suppressing fire, short bursts to keep him pinned while their brothers worked through the trees towards him. Edge realised that his position had outlived its usefulness, and trying to ignore the rounds cracking over and past him, he pressed on up the slope. By now, he was becoming exhausted and debated doubling back, but that would lead him back into danger and away from his pick-up point. While he was fitter than they probably were, there were at least fifteen of them in pursuit. Edge had woefully underestimated the numbers of mujahedeen during his first recce in the mist. He decided to find another position, perhaps on the crest of the hills, make a determined stand, then leg it down the other side, hoping to outdistance them. The only problem was, there were more of them than he had rounds.

By now, Edge's left eye was throbbing with pain and he had lost some central vision. A pine marten jumped between two trees as he laboured up the slope, but he knew he was getting near the crest of the hills because the trees were thinning. Before he broke cover, he saw the ground clear and gently slope away to a cluster of buildings about 400 metres away, which he guessed was a meteorological station. There was absolutely no cover between the treeline, the buildings and 500 metres beyond the buildings, the forest starting again to slope down into the next valley. A verse from a poem slipped into his desperate thoughts, unbidden, but a strangely comforting poem by Thomas Babington Macaulay about *How Horatio held the bridge*.

*But it doesn't work, does it?* Edge thought grimly. *I need two more to hold the bridge.* He went into a comfortable firing position and prepared to sell his life dearly. He loosened the Velcro on the inner pocket of the chest rig, pulled out the Sig, cocked it and slipped it back in. *That one's for the end and may God forgive me.*

He spotted the first one, just paused by the edge of the forest, about 150 metres away. *They are bloody consistent, I'll give them that.* They moved towards him in a skirmish line, staying on the verge of the forest, but spreading out and moving towards the area where they were pretty sure he was. The instant he fired, Edge's position would be compromised, and although he could get two, perhaps three, there were still at least ten, and unlike him, they weren't afraid of death.

One of them leaned just the wrong side of the tree he had been using as cover, and Edge blew off his shoulder and left arm. He killed a second just as he raised his AK-47, but then the rounds were coming down. Despite the flash eliminator, they had pinged him, probably by the dust kicked up by the rounds exiting the muzzle. Edge aimed for a muzzle flash whenever he could see one, but figures moved out of the trees on each flank, crawling and using the minimum natural cover most effectively. They had already guessed the limitations of his weapon.

"And now I really am fucked," he mumbled to himself. One of the mujahedeen forgot to keep his arse down while he was crawling, so Edge obligingly shot him through the buttocks.

*Can I make four hundred metres to the buildings?*

*Doubtful, but let's just suppose that you make it. What then?*

*Fucked if I know.*

Edge fired off the last three rounds at the crawling fighters, or at least where he thought they were. He dropped the rifle and leaped to his feet, sprinting in a zigzag towards the buildings. The Gillie suit was slowing him down. It was like sprinting in soft sand wearing a wet clown's suit.

*But I can make this, I can fucking do this!* He couldn't.

The 7.62 round passed through his left side at around 700 metres per second. Fortunately, it missed his kidney and descending colon, but the round nicked the top of his hipbone's iliac crest. The sonic wave and cavitation ripped his side open like he had been hit double-handed with the blade of a claymore, and that is exactly what it felt like. Edge was bowled round and dumped in the dust.

Unconsciously, he grabbed the Sig, held himself up on one elbow, knowing that the round's damage made further running impossible, and made ready to die. He didn't bother with any *why me?* or bemoan the damned unfairness of it all. There was a mujahedeen within 15 metres approaching him cautiously with one holding back, covering with his AK. They obviously wanted him alive, which boded badly for his future health and would probably mean a special appearance on Al Jazeera, wearing an orange boiler suit.

Edge dropped the nearest with two shots and fired at the second, who went to ground. He closed his eyes and stuck the muzzle of the Sig in his mouth.

*Sorry, Moira, my love. It wasn't to be and you had a lucky escape.*

*Be with you shortly, Jozica. Get ready to have your bones rattled.*

*Receive, Lord, your servant into the place of salvation, which he hopes to obtain through your mercy.*

"Edge!"

The bursts of fire were closer now. Fast but very controlled, too fast for an AK-47. Edge opened his eyes and stared into the dead eyes of a mujahedeen who was glaring into perpetuity. A man approached, a bloody big man. Every so often, he would pause and fire at something on the ground, constantly going down and sweeping the treeline. As he got closer, he looked at Edge.

"I'd put that down if I were you. You might hurt yourself."

"Minty? I thought I'd told you to fuck off."

"Oh, don't bother thanking me, Edge."

Edge slumped down, shaking with fear and sudden exhaustion. The Sig fell from his hand. "My rifle, it's over by the trees. Could you get it for me, please?"

Minty cut away the Gillie suit around the spreading and impressive patch of blood and applied Edge's first field dressing. "That might not be such a good idea, Edge. There may be one or two still knocking around and I doubt they'll bill you for it."

"CSAR?"

"It's on its way. I'm the magic fairy who talks to pilots, remember?"

Within minutes, they could hear helicopters, and Minty activated a smoke flare to mark the landing site and wind direction. A CH-53 Sea Stallion swept along the treeline, hosing it down with its miniguns before flaring into land. The SEAL team went into all-round defence while the medical team of four approached with a stretcher. They continued to work on Edge in the back of the cab back to the deck of the *USS Theodore Roosevelt,* and he was operated on in the ship's Role 2 enhanced medical facility, to debride the wound and stitch it back up with a drain. He was also given an injection of broad spectrum antibiotics. Edge had been extremely lucky; apart from a bone chip that was removed and some muscular damage, his vital organs were untouched. He had fragments of wood removed from his eye and wore a patch while it healed. Minty visited him that night in the sickbay's ward.

"Ahahahahaaarg. How are you feeling?"

"Okay and thanks, Minty. I owe you big time."

Minty pulled up a chair and sat next to the ward bed. "I can't stay long. A chopper's going to fly me to Gioia del Colle and then home with any luck."

Edge looked at Minty out of his good eye and smiled. Once again, it was a different Edge, the kind and sad version.

"Sorry you didn't get to do your job and talk to the winged master race. I know you were looking forward to it. But you more than did mine."

"Edge?"

"What?"

Minty had wanted to ask him why there was such melancholy in Edge's life, and why it seemed as though he had wanted to kill himself. But he lost his nerve.

"Err, it doesn't matter."

*

After their reports, specifically Minty's, Edge was recommended for the Military Cross. This was blocked at prime ministerial level, because Edge and Minty had been fighting and prolifically killing the 'wrong' baddies. Edge, for his part, insisted that if there were to be any awards, they should go to Minty. The political spin machine had reckoned without the very forcible intervention of the regiment's colonel-in-chief, who threatened to raise the spectre of the whole flawed reasoning behind the Kosovo War and British involvement. Edge and Minty were gazetted in September of that year. Edge was awarded the Military Cross and Minty was mentioned in dispatches. Edge always maintained that, if anything, it should have been the other way round.

He was admitted for a short rehabilitation at Headley Court and went to Devon on sick leave. Moira spoiled him and called him (when he showed her the medal with its purple and white ribbon) her 'brave little soldier'. Edge would grimace at her and try not to think about just how terrified he had been. He married Moira in the October of that year.

# Chapter 14

# MOIRA AND EDGE'S STORY, HOLY MATRIMONY

———

Like most of the important milestones in Edge's life, his marriage was in the autumn, October the 14th of 2000 at St John the Baptist Church, Instow. It was and is a beautiful church, nestled into the gentle folds of the hills above the estuary of the Rivers Taw and Torridge. Moira Tremain and Mark Edge were married at 13:00 under a glowering sky and predictably it rained all afternoon. He was smart in his No. 2s, a sergeant now with a Military Cross adding to his impressive tally of medals. Nobody asked him and he felt no need to publicise it. Moira knew and she also knew the toll on his mental health being awarded that medal had cost him.

His best man was a handsome man of average height and build. He was a staff sergeant, also dressed in No. 2s. His name was Henry Morrison and like Edge, they had both reverted to the headwear of their donor regiments for security reasons. Edge's was the Worcestershire and Sherwood Foresters Regiment. Morrison wore that of 2 Para. Their reception was in a hotel on the outskirts of Barnstaple. Moira's friend Angela seemed destined to be the perpetual bridesmaid, but never the bride. She had conducted her own close reconnaissance on the best man and was executing her own plan of manoeuvre on him.

The wedding meal was a rather stilted affair on the top table, and a lot of Morrison's jokey anecdotes fell rather flat with the audience. At one point, Edge caught Moira's father looking up at the ceiling. He got busy with a biro and a paper napkin, not on the nice linen ones, and drew a quick picture. When Moira's father was distracted, he slipped it under his plate. When the waitress came to clear the plates, the napkin fluttered down and landed in front of Moira's father right way up and around. He stared down at an uncannily accurate drawing of him wearing a smug expression, an Elizabethan ruff and two horns growing out of his head. What made it worse was that the waitress giggled. He angrily ripped it up and threw it on the floor while Edge turned away, sharing a joke with Morrison.

This was very much a family wedding, or to be precise it was a wedding for Moira's family. Edge's mother had died in late 1998 but his father was there in the church, remained for the wedding meal and then disappeared around 16:00. Edge hadn't even noticed. They would have been lucky if they exchanged more than fifty words.

"Where's your dad?" Moira asked.

Edge shrugged.

"Mark, it's a bit rude."

"Did he speak to you?"

"Only to say, good luck, you'll need it."

"So there you go. Missing but not missed."

"Sometimes, Mark, I just don't understand you. He's the only family you've got."

"I have a sister as well, but she couldn't make it. Probably washing her hair. Oh, and I've got an uncle, but he's too frail to travel from Scotland. The Edge family have never been what you would call close, unlike your mum and dad."

Before the evening function, Edge and Morrison made use of the hotel's pool and chatted before going up to their rooms to get changed into Mufti. In the warm water, they watched other guests splashing about while the rain lashed down on the roof.

"Where you going on honeymoon, Edgie?"

"I hear Dubrovnik is nice this time of year."

Morrison stared at him. "You are bloody joking."

"Of course I am. I've bought a three-bedroom cottage on the River Torridge, about ten miles south of here. So money's a bit tight. I'm going to introduce Moira to the delights of the Scottish Monroes."

Morrison stared at him with a strange half-smile playing at the corners of his mouth. "I would never have thought it of you, Edgie. You are so lucky. Moira is gorgeous. Please tell me you won't fuck it up with that temper of yours."

Later, they would both have cause to reflect on Morrison's plea from the heart with a certain amount of irony. No wedding is complete without a family row or a good fight. That evening, Moira was doing the good hostess bit and chatting with the guests. She was sitting next to Angela, and Morrison had his back to the room, listening politely, hoping in the nicest possible way that Moira would piss off so that he could continue schmoozing. Suddenly Moira looked over her shoulder and she froze.

"Who the bloody hell invited him?" she demanded.

Angela turned round, following her icy stare. "Oh Christ, it's Daz! Torchy the Battery Boy," she added, and giggled.

Morrison turned round and looked at the man who seemed to have a couple of friends in tow. He was tall and well-built with dark, curly hair. Almost like a traveller who had settled down somewhere where the pickings were easy. He didn't know just how accurate his appreciation was. The man looked round the room and caught Morrison's eye. He winked and nodded sarcastically.

"My bastard father," Moira said, and scurried off to find him, incandescent with rage.

"Who's that?" Morrison asked Angela.

"His name's Daniel Copeland and he is a complete cock. I prefer to call him Torchy the Battery Boy. You should ask Mickie why. I'm afraid that both Moira and me have gone out with him in the past."

Meanwhile, Moira was venting her anger on her doting daddy. "Why the bloody hell did you say he could come?"

"Because he's a good man to have in the business and I count him as a personal friend. He's loyal, hard-working, and you could do a lot worse than settle down with a man like Daz Copeland, oh hang on, you already have."

"If there is any trouble, it will be your responsibility!" she hissed at her father and stormed off to warn Edge. She could envisage a disaster looming over the evening.

Edge tolerated the reception but really wanted to whisk Moira away to a hotel they had booked further up the coast for a bit of wedding night passion. He kept a wary eye on Mr Copeland, who seemed rather well known to Moira's family and associates. He was being really good and even bought Moira's father a drink. Predictably, he went for an expensive single malt.

"Edge raised his glass. "Your very good health. Mr Tremain."

"Frank, please."

"Just think, Frank. Next time I take Moira to heaven and back, it'll be legal."

Mr Tremain's eyes darkened. It wasn't a long conversation.

Later, a tall, thick-set man grinned at Edge. "So you're the lucky groom. eh?"

"You are?"

"Daz." He didn't offer his hand to shake. Neither did Edge. "Lucky, lucky you. Me and Moi used to be a bit of an item."

"So I believe," Edge said evenly, although he wanted to smash his glass in this leering prick's face.

"I hear that you and Moi are staying at some place in Weare Gifford." Edge said nothing. "And that your new wife is staying in it all alone when you go back to the Army. Puts a lot of strain on a marriage, does that."

"Are you Marjorie fucking Proops?"

"Just saying, that's all. Keep your hair on. I'm sure she'll be well looked after."

"I tell you what, Daz. It'll be me giving Moira a good old looking-after tonight and for long, long nights to come. You must excuse me while I mingle."

An hour or so later, Morrison was at the bar getting some drinks. "We'll be off soon, Henry. Thanks for coming and doing your stuff."

"Good luck, Edgie. Remember what I said and treat her nice. I'll see you in a couple of weeks."

When Morrison went back to the table with the drinks, Daz was sitting next to Angela, who was looking uncomfortable. Daz put his hand on her forearm and she dragged it away sharply.

"I really don't think the lady is appreciating your attention, Mr Copeland."

"Piss off, Pongo. You don't come from here," Daz said, and tried to kiss Angela, who slapped him across the face.

"Bitch!"

Morrison grabbed a fistful of Daz's curly hair and bent down close to his face. He said quietly so the girl couldn't hear, "You and me outside now, you bastard!"

He walked out of the room, past the toilets and conference rooms, down the long corridor to the reception and the car park. He scanned the walls and ceiling for security cameras. Meanwhile, Daz had gathered his posse. At intervals along the corridor the fire doors were open on magnetic locks, but the end ones were shut. He pushed through them and when he heard the fire doors opening behind him, Morrison turned and ran at them, hitting them with all his weight and momentum. He was moving very fast.

The heavy door with its fire glass hit Daz in the face, ramming him backwards. Daz became entangled with one of his wingmen and went down. Morrison went down on top of him like a cat and smashed the heel of his right hand into Daz's face, three times in quick succession, aiming for the sensitive area under his nose, the philtrum. He wasn't going to risk breaking knuckles on this piece of shit. He was on his feet and going for the second most obvious threat, Daz's wingman, who had composed himself and looked as though he wanted to be tasty. As he advanced on him, Morrison pointed upwards. He couldn't help himself and looked up and Morrison's knee smashed upwards into his groin. He went down with an ooohff and puked beer onto the carpet. Morrison looked at the third man and smiled grimly. The man decided that Daz wasn't that good a friend and ran back towards the back door to the pool.

Morrison didn't have long. He went back to Daz, who was bleeding profusely from both nostrils.

"Listen to me, you piece of Pikey shit. If Moira Edge or Angela are touched, hurt or looked at in the wrong way, I'm coming back here and I'm going to kill you very slowly. Do you understand, Daz?"

Daniel Copeland was past understanding for now. Morrison went back to the reception room and smiled at Angela, sliding in next to her. He had been gone for less than three minutes.

"Are you all right? Where's Daz?"

"He and his mates have gone. Where's Edgy?"

"He and Moira have gone too."

"Didn't see them come past my way, which is probably just as well because Daz was feeling a bit under the weather."

She gave him an old-fashioned look. "They sneaked away about half an hour ago. Moira's mum isn't very happy about it."

"In which case, let's finish these drinks and make use of the sauna and pool. They should be quiet now."

*

Edge, despite his absences, was a constant in Moira's life, as she was in his. She made a home for them and decorated the tired décor of the cottage with the help of Angela's friends. She also had two wood burners installed, one to heat the water, and during the fitting she found that the roof by the chimney needed some attention. Moira's father suggested Daz do the work at first, but his daughter's violent reaction stunned him. In many ways, Frank Tremain was a thick, insensitive bastard. She weaned herself off her mother to a degree, but still visited for Sunday dinners.

Unfortunately, Daz was also one of the constants in Moira's life. He would unexpectedly just happen to 'bump' into her in the town, in the supermarket; he would find an excuse to pop round to see her father on a Sunday. If he was hoping to wear her down, he was having the opposite effect. Angela told her that he had picked a fight with Morrison at her wedding, and when she heard what had happened, she laughed. What neither of them realised was the depths and intensity of Daz's hatred towards the British Army, Moira's husband and their best man, who had shattered the roots of his two incisal front teeth. The cost of bridgework was beyond Daz's means, so he wore a cobalt-chrome framework denture to fill the gap. He fantasised about raping Moira and strangling her with bailing twine as he came. The toxicity of his thoughts frightened even him sometimes.

"Serves him right!" Moira said with feeling. "He came in spoiling for a fight, so he got what he deserved. I hate him! Anyway, what about you and your beau?"

Angela looked at her sadly. "I really like him. Really, really like him. But I'm afraid that he's just not the marrying kind. Ever the bridesmaid, that's me."

The other constant in Moira's life was Edge, who came home whenever he could. When he was away on operations, she knew but never asked where he was. Sometimes he would phone her on a satellite phone from God knows where. She would hear helicopters or vehicles in the background.

In 2002, Moira realised she was pregnant, and in early 2003, Edge went incommunicado on Ops. She didn't even have to try to guess where in the world he was this time. He made it home for the birth of his daughter Sarah in the late summer and was outwardly delighted. But for all of his delight and cuddling of his daughter, Moira detected a subtle change in Edge that became more noticeable over the next few years. Whatever had happened during his tour in Iraq in 2003, he wouldn't discuss it. Edge had always liked a drink or three, but now he was medicating with it to sleep.

But they were still very much in love, passionate, and his son was born in 2006 after his second tour in Iraq. Edge had got his way with naming Sarah, but Moira insisted on calling the boy Francis. They skirmished over the issue rather than declaring open warfare and she got her way.

While having a spot of leave in 2008, Edge was gathering wood for the winter and became slightly alarmed at the amount of vermin occupying the cottage's outhouses. They hadn't made inroads into their home yet, but it was only a matter of time. He discussed it with Moira.

"Why don't we get a cat?" she suggested.

"I don't like cats."

"It can be like a farm cat, which lives outside. We probably won't even see it, except to feed it once a day. I've heard you have to give them some food to stimulate hunting."

Edge reluctantly agreed and Moira came home with a tabby kitten in a shoe box. Sarah and Francis were delighted and wanted to call him Willum after Pusscat Willum. Again, Edge put his foot down and Monty, Ratter Class One joined the family. Predictably, he became a pet with part-time rodent prevention duties, but he was spoiled. He showed his gratitude as a kitten by pissing on Edge's Buffalo jacket.

As the end of Edge's Army career approached, he elected to return to his donor regiment for resettlement, as he wanted to avoid security jobs. Or rather the Mercian Regiment, as the Worcestershire and Sherwood Foresters Regiment no longer existed. He was a stranger in their midst and widely distrusted because of his background.

As his terminal leave approached, Edge became despondent, as he had promised Moira that they would settle in Devon, and being effectively rootless, it was his home as well. But jobs were of a seasonal nature in that part of the country and permanent jobs were few and far between for a man of Edge's 'talents'. Like very many ex-Service men and women, he was poor at selling himself and found it difficult to transfer his experiences and training into key outputs and core skills required on the job application forms.

Moira's father had made a very successful business supplying agricultural machinery and products to the smaller farms with smaller, enclosed fields in that part of the world. His daughter moved into action, hinting, badgering and in the end, begging her father to give Edge a job. Her father relented as much for his daughter's sake as the desire to see Edge dependent on him. He offered him the job of delivery driver; take it or leave it. Edge took it and hated himself for it. Part of him resented Moira as well.

He was sitting in front of the wood burner, cradling a large glass of red wine, staring morosely into the flames. He was due to start work the following Monday. Moira sat next to him and stroked his cheek affectionately.

"Don't worry, Mark. It's a new chapter of your life opening, a safer one." She nuzzled in close to his neck.

Edge played with her ear and smiled at her, but she noticed that lately, the warmth never seemed to reach his eyes.

One hot August day, Edge was sent on a longer delivery run to Cornwall that would take a couple of days. Moira was off work because the glass factory was temporally closed, as the furnaces and kilns were being reconditioned. She had been tidying the children's bedrooms while they were at school. She didn't hear the pick-up drive into the yard, but became aware of someone hammering on the cottage door. She went down to open it. It was Daniel Copeland.

"Oh, it's you. What do you want, Daz, and what are you doing here?"

"Your old dad asked me to keep an eye on you, seeing as how Mark's away for a couple of days."

"As you can see, I'm fine. How did you know I wasn't at work?"

"Like I said, your dad asked me to make sure you're okay, and here I am, making sure."

"I'm truly grateful to both of you, now if you'll excuse me."

"I've driven all the way from Tiverton and I could murder a drink, Moira." She hesitated and he could hear the doubt in her voice.

"Well…"

"Just a quick cuppa," he wheedled.

"You'll have to make it quick coz I'm very busy, Daz."

"Thanks, it's hot out there and I'm parched."

She made him a tea that he would never drink. In the end, she ejected him from the house at knifepoint, him with a bleeding neck and torn shirt, her with a bruised and aching breast. She decided never to tell Edge what had happened, because she feared the repercussions. It was the worst mistake she ever made.

Chapter 15

# THE LITTLE GIRL
# FROM DERBY

———

Afarin Khan had never been blessed with the type of cleverness required to ingest, sift, collate and then regurgitate information onto an examination paper. If anything, as far as the British state education system was concerned, she was cursed with a questioning and interrogative mind. She took nothing at face value and questioned established wisdom at every cut and turn.

"Why are we concentrating on the Native Americans and black people in the 1930s, miss? Surely the depression affected all poor and working-class people? What about the Chinese immigrants to America?"

"Why do we call the Nazis 'right wing' when they were called the National Socialist Workers' Party?"

"Why is it when we've been sending millions of pounds to Africa over the past sixty years, do they still send their kids loads of miles with a manky plastic jerry can to gather water from a polluted river and then complain because they can't go to school? Why don't they boil the water or move the village a bit closer to where the water is and dig a few new, clean wells?"

Afarin Khan was blessed as well as cursed. She certainly ticked the right diversity boxes; she was Asian, she was a 'she', she was a Muslim and therefore came from a very special and protected niche of liberal society. Her teachers expected very little of her because of her 'disadvantaged' background, but in their heart of hearts, her kindly liberal teachers with a social justice agenda hated her guts. She was roundly and secretly detested, and had she been a white working-class boy, she would have been excluded at the drop of a Pussyhat. Unfortunately, they had been hoisted by their own politically correct petard.

It was late spring in the secondary school in south Derby and the GCSEs were coming up. A clump of the more right-on teachers were in the common room, drinking fair-trade decaffeinated green tea and discussing Afarin Khan's prospects of achieving a reasonable set of examination grades.

"I don't suppose we should expect too much. It's quite surprising that she's still in school to be honest."

"I find her quite disruptive in the class," the religious studies and citizenship teacher observed with a trace of rancour. "She constantly interrupts me when I try to explain the six articles of faith in Sunni Islam and five roots of Usul ad-Din in Shi'a Islam."

They were joined by the physical education teacher, a rather strapping young woman with close-cropped hair, interesting tattoos and numerous piercings, both visible and hidden. Because she was a lesbian, she also fell into a 'special' and therefore protected category.

"Are you lot talking about Ms Khan?"

They nodded with pained expressions.

"Ah, she does present somewhat of a challenge, doesn't she? But I quite like her. At least she isn't constantly menstruating like the other girls in her year. She will expend some effort and will at least take a shower after PE, unlike the other skanks."

There were pained expressions around the group and the terribly camp arts and drama teacher looked like he was having a touch of the vapours.

"She just lacks application."

The PE teacher drained her coffee. "No, she doesn't. Her problem is that she has a questioning and independent mind. The kiss of death for kids in state education. Now if you'll excuse me, I have some year eights to brutalise in the gym. Circuit training for the little bastards."

Afarin always wore a hijab to school, not because she wanted to, but because it was expected of her by her community, her female relatives and the oh-so-liberal teachers. She hated it and pulled it off whenever she was at home. One afternoon on leaving the school, she saw a group of girls hanging round a pimped-up Mercedes parked outside the school gates. The girls were mainly year eights and nines and came from what their teachers and social workers called rather euphemistically, 'troubled or challenging' backgrounds. Their white male classmates called them 'skanks'. The men in the Mercedes, who would have been called by a reluctant media 'Asian men of Pakistani heritage', called them 'fresh meat'.

Afarin Khan walked up to the car and sneered at the young men inside. Her father and her family originated from the Hindu Kush area of Afghanistan, so her first language was Pashtu. Afarin was also fluent in Arabic, Urdu and Bangla. Although she considered them to be of a lower social caste, she addressed them in Bangla.

"Looking for some little white girls for a spot of fun, are you?"

"Fuck off, you Afghan whore," the driver said to her in English.

"Yeah, piss off, you Taliban bitch," one of the white girls said to her.

Afarin shook her head with incredulity. "You do know what this is about, don't you? What's it been up to now? CDs? PlayStation games? Some fags? Soon it'll be booze, then drugs, and then you'll end up staring at the ceiling in some grotty hotel, while their uncles, fathers and grandfathers queue up to fuck you. They don't care."

She looked at the young men in the car and her face screwed up with disgust. "مشيمة الخنزير." She spat at them.

Afarin crossed the road as a police car drove slowly past. Despite looking into the parked Mercedes and at the underage girls outside a school, the coppers did nothing, and the police car disappeared around the corner.

*

Her grades were predictably disappointing and she went home in tears. Her mother and sister were quite sanguine about it, because academic results meant little in their world. It was the reaction of her father that she was terrified of. Eventually, she caught him alone and told him, fearing the worst. They spoke in English as he insisted, even in the home.

"Father, I messed my GCSEs up. I only managed a B in Science, a B in Art and Design, a C in Geography, a C in Computer Science, a C in History, a C in literature but two Es in English Language and Maths. I am so sorry."

Her father smiled sadly at her. He and his wife and elder daughter had fled Afghanistan when the Russians invaded. He had been a high-ranking member of the Civil Service but had carved a new life for himself in England. He deliberately avoided the Pakistani ghetto towns in the West Midlands and the

North, and settled in Derby. He ran his own carpet business and he loved his middle daughter with all of his heart. There was something about Afarin that stirred his soul. She was just so unique and he wanted the best for her.

He had argued with his only wife when the child was small.

"No, she will not be cut. It is a barbaric superstition from the Swat valleys. Afarin will leave this world in exactly the same way as God brought her into it. I will not allow her to be mutilated. If you go against my wish, you will go back to the home country without me."

He knew the problems his daughter faced, being torn between two different cultures. And he knew he didn't want her to be in an arranged marriage with what he considered some inbred wide boy from Pakistan.

"Come on, Afarin, let's look at this dispassionately. You have two subjects with good passes, one of which is science. You have three other good passes. Unfortunately, you have not done well in the two most important subjects, the ones potential employers care the most about. What shall we do about it?"

"I could go to college and get a part-time job."

"You could, and so you shall."

She hugged her father, still crying, tears of gratitude now. "I thought you would be so cross, Daddy."

"What's the point? But I do worry about you. I won't always be here and I want you to make a good life for yourself. One that will provide you with the opportunities this country offers, but nevertheless, a life that pays homage to your background, religion and culture. As a girl, Afarin, it will not be easy. Do you have any idea what you want to do?"

She shook her head. "I literally have no idea."

"Then think. The choices you make now will be the most important for your future life."

Afarin Khan went to college and struggled once again with English and mathematics, but the difference was that now she was in a class of men and women who actually wanted to be there. The disruptive morons had gone and at last she was able to concentrate, instead of waiting twenty to thirty minutes for an ineffectual but oh-so-liberal teacher to gain a modicum of control over the class.

A few days before she took the examinations again, there was a display in the entrance hall of the college by a group from the Armed Forces Careers Office (AFCO). The Army display was quite impressive with lots of radios and technical stuff; no guns allowed but lots of boys' toys. The two men and the woman from the Royal Navy looked really good in their best uniforms, and the looped video showed ships and helicopters and was slick and professional. The Royal Air Force display had two females; one was a medic with an impressive tally of medals on her No.1's breast pocket. The other was a pretty woman with long auburn hair, tied in a high ponytail. She was wearing a green flying suit, with wings and two tiny, thin, light blue stripes on her epaulettes. She was sipping coffee from a black metal insulated mug. She exuded confidence and easily batted aside the boys' attempts to make a pass at her. Afarin looked shyly at her and the RAF lady caught her gaze.

"Hello."

"Hello," Afarin said shyly. "What do you do?"

The woman put down her coffee and smiled. "Well…"

"Afarin. Afarin Khan."

"Well, Afarin, my name's Louise and I fly one of these," she said, pointing to a picture of a helicopter on the display board.

"Cool. I bet you've got a degree or something."

The RAF pilot nodded. "Yes, but if you join up, you just need GCSEs and then apply for aircrew duties. If you pass the aptitude tests."

She handed her a leaflet. "This tells you what you need to have for exams and how to do your homework before you apply to join."

Afarin could have got lost in those hazel eyes and she felt hot with embarrassment. Louise had that effect on both sexes. She took a long time to read the paperwork on the bus and by the time she got home, Afarin Khan knew what she wanted to do. Unfortunately, her father was not happy about her decision when she told him.

"Have you taken leave of your senses? You are placing yourself at odds to two communities, neither of which will ever accept you. The kufar will always distrust you and your own fellow believers will ostracise you. To our community you will be dead!"

She was shocked by his negativity, as he had always seemed such a beacon of tolerance, but it would appear that if the veneer was scratched off, the lie of multiculturalism was revealed. In truth, she was deeply disappointed with her father and her stubbornness kicked in. Now would not be a good time to tell him that she found the entire premise of a supreme being to be nothing more than a ridiculous throwback to the Dark Ages.

Afarin passed GCSE English with a B and Mathematics with a C, and the previous week she had celebrated her eighteenth birthday. That afternoon, she put on her best job interview clothes, collected her educational certificates, birth certificate and passport, and walked into the Armed Forces Careers office on Sitwell Road in Derby and made an appointment. She sat the first of a raft of aptitude tests, interviews and initial medical PULHEEMS. Seven weeks later, she was attested into Her Majesty's Armed Forces as an intelligence analyst (subject to successfully completing Recruit Training and the sixteen-week course, in the fundamentals of intelligence with the Joint Intelligence Training Group, Chicksands in Bedfordshire). She was initially paid over £13,000 pounds a year, a figure that was beyond her wildest dreams. Once her training was finished, she would learn to drive and buy a little car.

*

She could have written the script herself. Her transit through Recruit Training at RAF Halton was laughably easy because the race, religion and 'special category' card was played at every opportunity. Not by her, but by the directing staff who were terrified of failing to show 'cultural awareness'. In the end, she became so pissed off with it, she asked for an appointment with her flight commander. Of course it was immediately granted.

"What is the problem, AC Khan?"

"I want to be treated like everyone else in my flight and not picked out for special attention, sir."

The instant worry in his eyes was almost comical. "Has anyone—"

"Sir, you don't understand. I want the instructors to stop tiptoeing round me like I was a delicate little flower. I want to be shouted at and sworn at like everyone else. In the past week during kit inspections and my weapon-handling drills, I have made mistakes that anyone else on my flight would have got restrictions for. I want to make it by my own merits, not because I tick a diversity box."

He looked at her with a slight smile and thought: *Right, you bitch. Be careful what you wish for.*

Another major irritant for Afarin were the recruiters who wanted to photograph her at every cut and turn so she could be a pin-up for diversity at the AFCOs.

Relaxing on her bed, "Can you wear one of those headscarf thingies for the photos?"

"Do you mean a hijab?"

"Yes, one of those."

"No!"

"What about a picture of you sitting at the table, reading the Koran?"

"Get stuffed!"

She was the only person on her squadron who had no friends or family attending the ceremony. The problem was what to do during the two weeks' leave before she started her Phase 2 training. It had been made clear to her that she was not welcome at home, mainly due to the attitude of her mother and sisters. But the craven weakness of her father left an emptiness in her soul. She approached the *padre,* who managed to persuade SSAFA to let her use the emergency married quarter, put aside for families who were *in extremis* due to family break-up or major problems in a married quarter, such as flooding. It was a lonely existence, but Afarin had found that all of her life. Some people make very great sacrifices in order to serve their country.

Afarin struggled with the more academic elements of the Intelligence Analysis course, but she was good at analysis and with the help of her instructors, she graduated, and her first posting was to RAF Marham, a huge main operating base in the wilds of Norfolk, close to Swaffham, much beloved by Harry Hill. Afarin learned to drive in eight months and explored the area in her little Corsa, a part of the country she had never been to. King's Lynn was interesting historically but had seen better days. Norwich was a fine city that she enjoyed visiting, but the less said about Swaffham the better.

She made friends on the station and socialised with them, but the boys were reluctant to get too close. Afarin was a strikingly beautiful young woman but the barriers were there, and she hadn't erected them. So, surrounded by thousands of people, she remained lonely and unfulfilled.

She also found out that the route to aircrew through the ranks was much more difficult than direct entry from civilian life. Serving RAF personnel had far more hoops to jump through than keen youngsters coming in from university and sixth form college. There were always excuses when she tried to apply. *We've had our quota from the ranks this year. You really need a degree or your work can't spare you.* It all led to an increased level of frustration and dissatisfaction, but she had made her bed and would have to lie in it.

On September 11th 2001, Islamic terrorists from Saudi Arabia decided to fly passenger jets into the Twin Towers in New York, and the Pentagon. President George W Bush decided to bomb a country stuck in the Dark Ages back to the Stone Age. The special forces of all English-speaking countries piled into

Afghanistan to hunt another Saudi called Osama bin Laden. These units required a massive amount of logistics support, and the airfields that had been bombed to destruction suddenly needed to be reactivated to support counter-terrorist operations. Which was why in February 2002, Senior Aircraftwoman Afarin Khan stepped off the rear ramp of a C130 at a provincial airport a few kilometres south of Jalalabad, east of Torkham on the Afghan/Pakistan border. She was part of an enabling force of force protection, engineers, EOD technicians, flight operations, medics and chefs who were going to reactivate the airfield. It had been built by the Russians, bombed by the Americans and repaired by the Brits.

They set up an operating base of tents on the edge of the airfield. The bitter rains turned the talcum powder sand to a muddy mush, and temperatures would regularly fall to the minus twenties at night. The heavy equipment arrived a few days later by Antonov 225 and the hard work started, but nor for Afarin, whose real work wouldn't start until the Tornados and their RAPTOR (Reconnaissance Air Pod Tornado) arrived in theatre. She joined the RAF regiment patrols that pushed into the local area and did a bit of hearts-and-minds stuff with the women and children. The men obviously shunned her.

A few Groundhog Days after she started patrolling with the gunners, a Land Rover that was bristling with heavy machine guns, anti-tank missiles and crewed by pirates trundled onto the airport and headed for the operations tent. There followed a one-way discussion with the senior RAF officer and a runner was sent to the mess tent to find SAC Khan.

"Station master wants to see you, Affi."

"Oh no, why?"

The runner shrugged.

The wing commander was waiting for her along with four men who were dressed in a mixture of British, American and Afghan clothing. They scrutinised her like she was a particularly unusual specimen. The man who seemed to be in charge of the pirates smiled at her.

"You speak Pashto fluently?"

Yes, and Arabic, Urdu and Bangla."

The man in charge of these strange visitors looked at her. He regarded her with a critical eye, a sardonic half-smile playing around his mouth. But despite the headscarf and the mean-arsed demeanour, by God he was handsome and he knew it. He had taken the time to shave, unlike his companions, and his eyes never left Afarin's. She stared back at him defiantly. It was as though he expected something of her.

"SAC Khan, these gentlemen have requested that you be seconded to them for a few weeks, and they have paperwork that is signed off by the Directorate of Special Forces, which rather trumps the Air Component Commander."

"I see," although she didn't. "When?"

"Now, treacle," the chief pirate said. "Get your kit, luv, but don't bother with your personal weapon. You won't be needing it."

*

Afarin Khan was used as an interpreter by the patrol teams that operated from a tiny forward operating base (FOB) in the mountains that spanned the border. The base was a small cluster of tents, a prisoner holding cage, satellite dishes, guard towers and Hesco bastions. It had an airstrip just long enough to operate C130s, and a Chinook, two Black Hawks and an Apache were based there. The accommodation was luxurious compared with where she had come from. She had her own tent and ablutions. A proper bed with a mattress. The mess tent had armchairs and sofas and a TV showing the American Forces Network; God knows where they had come from. She had everything apart from their trust and companionship.

One morning, Afarin was sitting alone with her knees drawn up, leaning against a Hesco bastion blast wall. She felt miserable and the cramps in her stomach were drawing and painful. One of the blades saw her sitting and sauntered up.

"Hello. You look deep in thought. Everything okay?"

She looked up. It was Jarvis. She liked Jarvis because he was kind and never said anything unpleasant to anybody. She had never seen him lose his temper or even swear. He was wearing a black woollen hat that partially hid his long, wavy and luxuriant hair, and he smelled particularly good. Jarvis was very nice to look at, and unlike Henry Morrison, he didn't know it. She could have liked Jarvis a lot and perhaps under different circumstances, she might have. But he was a Blade. Unreachable. Too good for the likes of an ugly little Afghan bint like her.

She shook her head and he sat down next to her, his carbine clouting her shin. "Sorry. What's up? Tell Uncle Guy."

Afarin looked at him and decided to be awkward. "Well, Mr Jarvis. I have something of a 'condition'. As Mr Morrison would delicately put it, I have the painters in. It's been a few months and this time it's heavy and painful."

"Oh," he said and stood up. "Wait there."

She watched him stalk off and felt a degree of disappointment and contempt. These roughty-toughty men, running at the first hint of a woman's monthly cycle. He returned about fifteen minutes later and gave her a bag. "A strip of Co-codamol, which should last you about four days, and four chemical adhesive heat pads. Don't put them on your bare skin, because they'll burn you."

"Where did you get these, Mr Jarvis?"

"The medical tent."

"You didn't tell them… Did you?"

"No, I said I'd pulled a muscle in my back."

Afarin could have cried at this unexpected kindness. "Thank you. Mr Jarvis, why does everyone hate me?"

He sat down next to her. "Afarin, nobody hates you. It's just that we're a pretty insular bunch and you're an unknown quantity. I realise that we're not making the best use of your language skills and you didn't ask to be here. But here you are and you should make the best of it. Stand up for yourself. You're as good as everyone else, just a little bit different."

"What you mean is I'm not trusted because I'm like them out there, a Raghead."

He patted her knee in a friendly platonic manner. "No. It's worse than that. You're a Crab. What you need to do is push back. Get noticed and have a go at any numpty that treats you with contempt. The only way is to make them respect you. Stop being a grey woman."

She laughed and smiled at him. "You're like a big brother, Jarvis. Thank you again."

He smiled back and looked away shyly. If only she knew what he really felt about her, and what his advice would unleash.

Afarin would go out with them on the WMIK as part of the support troop on patrols. She was always unarmed, always accompanied, and she was only allowed to question women and not suspects who had been captured. The questions they told her to ask were clumsily framed and showed a hopeless understanding of the people and culture of the area. She bore it for weeks and finally erupted with frustration during a morning's O-group meeting.

Because of the small number at the base and the nature of their operations, everyone except those on essential duties attended the weekly main O-group meeting in the Ops tent, round the 'Bird Table'. Not everyone, however, was

154

expected to have a speaking part. The command group would run through commander's intent, scheme of manoeuvre, the latest Int briefing, weather for the aircrews, a logistics briefing and command and signal codes. The colonel would finish with a pep talk and then any questions from the main players. Just before the colonel turned to leave, Afarin stuck up her hand.

"I've got a question, sir."

The battle captain moved to behind the colonel and made a chopping motion at his throat to signal to her to shut up. She ignored him and ploughed on.

"Why am I regarded as somebody who is here on sufferance? Why have I not been issued with a personal weapon of any kind? Are you worried I'll shoot myself, or some of you lot? Why do you only allow me to speak with local women with questions that have the most dumb-arsed framing so they can only be answered yes or no? Why am I referred to as 'Genghis Khant', the 'PONTI Paki' and my personal favourites, the 'Tinge with the Minge' and the 'Gash with the 'Tache'? Why am I wasting my time and your time here, when I could be gainfully employed analysing data from RAPTOR Pods? You lot treat me with contempt and frankly, sir, I'm sick of it."

The colonel's face was white and pinched. The grown-ups looked shocked and embarrassed, while some people were smirking. She thought the battle captain was going to spontaneously combust.

"Don't worry. This Paki's going to pack."

She went outside and entered the MT compound, sat on the ground leaning against the wheel of a Land Rover and lit a cigarette. She was watching the Ops tent, waiting for the hammer to fall. One of the RAF Chinook pilots walked purposefully towards her after he came out of the Ops tent. His face was grim and as he reached her, he dragged her roughly to her feet and gave her a tight, warm hug.

"Very big balls, SAC Khan, and an attitude the size of a planet. Good luck and I'll help you if they get arsey. I don't think they will."

Nobody spoke to her until the next day and she had packed her kit and lay moodily on her bed, which she would miss. She heard someone moving outside her tent followed by:

"Knock, knock."

"Come in. I've packed."

Morrison, the man who had been in charge of the party who collected her, came into her tent. He was holding a Colt L119AW short rifle and a pistol in a holster.

"Are you going to shoot me?" she asked, only half joking.

"No, I'm going to teach you how to fire these. We've got all day and every time you get it wrong, I'll kick your magnificent arse."

They went to the makeshift firing range on the other side of the airstrip, which consisted of sand-filled oil drums in front of a bund.

"We'll be firing at two hundred metres. Any further and you'll be wasting your time. This is our weapon of choice," he said, holding up the short rifle. "The Colt Special Forces Infantry Weapon. 5.56mm calibre, same as the L85 that you're used to. Single shot or fully automatic. Forget the single-aimed shot bollocks. You're not gate guard at RAF Little Snoring now. You fire short bursts, three rounds max. Got that?"

She nodded with beautiful wide eyes.

"And stop looking at me like that. Otherwise, I won't be responsible for my actions. Now. Loading your magazine. When you're on the range, do you count your shots?"

"No, I always lose count."

"Me too. So this is how we know when to change magazines." He held up a round with a red tip to the bullet. "This is a tracer round and it goes into the magazine first. Then three normal rounds. Then a second tracer round and then all the rest. Only put twenty-eight rounds in each magazine so you don't knacker the spring. So you're firing away in short controlled bursts and you see a tracer round go down. What does that tell you?"

"I've got four more rounds left."

"You've got it. So when you see that first tracer round go down, you yell MAGAZINE and get ready to change. You make sure you can reach the pouch, make sure you can open it, but you don't look down and take your eyes off the action. Got it?"

"Yes."

"Why do you yell MAGAZINE?"

"So everyone knows I won't be able to fire for a bit."

He smiled. Underneath the stubble, he was a very handsome man.

They spent all day on the range. First, Afarin learned the weapon-handling drills and how to strip them down for daily cleaning. Then she zeroed the rifle with single aimed shots at a Figure 11 target at 50 metres, before moving back to 200 metres. He ran her through short bursts, fire with movement and firing while moving position. By the end of the first session, she was sweating like an adulteress in Kabul and was covered with ingrained grime and dust.

"I'm hungry."

He opened his daysack and produced a halal ration pack. Afarin scowled at him. "So you bastards had these while I've been eating rancid, processed fucking cheese sandwiches."

"We found them in stores." At least he had the good grace to look embarrassed.

In the afternoon, they moved on to the pistol, which was a Sig. He thought it would suit her because it was so small and easily concealed, but she was having a great deal of trouble cocking it with sweaty, slippery hands.

"Okay, you weak and feeble Crabette. Let's try the Glock." He produced a chunky, plastic block of Lego that looked like it should have been attached to the bottom of a Johnny Seven toy gun. She loved its non-slippery tactile grip and was a natural with the chunky but very light automatic pistol. Each magazine held seventeen rounds and she fired twenty of them, from cover and on the move.

"Bloody hell, Ms Khan, you're a better shot than me," he said as they sat sharing a coffee and watching the sun pour itself into the Kandahar Plains.

"What's your name?" she asked, enjoying his company.

He turned his head to meet her inquisitorial gaze. She had the most beautiful eyes he had ever seen, almost violet and flecked with hazel dots. She was small, lithe, and he had to admit, she was in possession of the finest arse it had ever been his pleasure to view from behind. Her hair was black, cropped short out of necessity. A dusky Joan of Arc. He wanted to pull her towards him, but she was to him still a kid, an innocent abroad. He would learn just how wrong he was. He was captivated.

"Henry, as you well know," he said reluctantly.

"But I wanted to hear it from you. Well, Henry, you bunch of bastards could have been a bit kinder to me when I first got here. I never asked to come."

"Yeah, you're right. Sorry, for what it's worth, Treacle."

"So what happens now?" she asked, lighting a cigarette.

"Those things will kill you. You come out with us, still in the support WMIK, but we might have to ask you to speak with the bad guys. Do you mind doing that?"

"No."

"You'll still have someone keeping an eye on you and you may have to hide your ample charms a bit, but a chest rig over the Osprey should help to conceal your lady-bumps. I realise that it will be impossible to stop you walking and running like a girl. You need to cover your hair as well. I know it's short but very nicely styled. I presume you don't want to look like Medusa. Do you have a shemagh?"

"Yes, I wear it round by neck to stop the Osprey chafing my neck."

"Of course you do. Well, wear it round your head. I'll show you how to wrap and tie it tomorrow."

It was almost dark by the time they walked back across the airstrip to the camp in companionable silence. The sky was purple and the stars looked like a van Gogh painting of Arles.

"Do I put these guns in the armoury?"

"No, you keep those weapons with you at all times from now on. They are your responsibility now, so don't leave them in one of the traps when you do numbers one or two. They should be made safe while in the camp and in vehicles. I will be doing random checks, and if I've found that you've made ready, I will do unspeakable things to you."

"What about when I have a shower?"

"Put a poly bag over the working parts and hang them on the hooks above the shower head."

"So that's what they're for. I thought it was a bloody silly place to hang a towel."

As they came to part company, she sensed a sudden awkwardness come over him.

"Err, me and the boys are having a few beers and watching baseball on the American Forces Network. I know you probably don't drink, but you're welcome to join us for a Coke or something. It's our way of saying sorry."

"I don't drink," she agreed, "but it's nothing to do with any religious sensitivities. You see, when I was fifteen, I got blind drunk on cider to piss my mum off. I thought I was going to die. I don't ever want to feel like that again. Thanks, I'll be glad to join you." She reached out and briefly squeezed his hand. "And thank you for teaching me how to fire these gu... weapons."

There were a few, a very few, other women on the base; a chef, a crypto analyst, two signallers and an RAF battlespace manager. Their company was much in demand in the mess tent. There was a proper bar but no spirits, it had cans and bottles. They did have wine in a carton. Henry made room for her when he spotted Afarin push open the door flap tentatively. He beckoned her over and made a few proper introductions. The driver was a Brummie called

Wayne. He nodded shyly and apologetically. She learned that Wayne was a stand-in for their usual two IC, a sergeant called Mark Edge, who was currently recuperating after a severe wound received in Kosovo and he had also recently got married. Afarin got the distinct impression that Jarvis didn't like this Edge very much. The WMIK gunner was a corporal called Cooper. His number two was Guy Jarvis, whom she already knew. He was the only one who had shown any time for her, and Afarin knew she could trust this soldier, explicitly. He was a gently-spoken man from somewhere in the Midlands, Lichfield, as she recalled. He seemed particularly smitten with Afarin's performance at the O-group yesterday.

"Loved it. 'The Gash with the 'Tache'. I thought the Colonel was waiting for the ground to swallow him," he chuckled. "I told you that you needed to stand up for yourself. I'm glad you did, but was the neutron bomb really necessary?"

"Well, I'm still here and not buried out in the cuds," she told him, and Jarvis gave a slight shudder.

"I'll tell you what wouldn't be a bad idea," Henry muttered in her ear, looking at the bar, "going over and apologising to the Colonel. Clear the air. And don't call him sir, address him as Colonel."

"But he's only a lieutenant-colonel, same as a wing commander."

Henry chortled. "Err, not quite. Go on, big balls."

Reluctantly, she went over and stood next to the most senior officer on the FOB, "Excuse me, Colonel."

He looked round and scowled at her.

"I apologise for speaking out in a manner that you would class as inappropriate in an O-group."

He chose to ignore the semantics, realising this was half an apology. He smiled ruefully. "Well, Ms Khan, I realise that the Royal Air Force may do things slightly differently, but I wouldn't do it again at a bird table, if I were you."

"Oh, I wouldn't, Colonel. Unless it were an operational imperative."

He huffed in amusement. "Well, having delighted me with your presence, I think your friends who put you up to this are waiting to hang on your every word."

When Afarin got back, Henry was taking ten dollars off the RSM.

"You put a bloody bet on me not apologising to him?"

"No, on you not getting thrown off the base."

"You lot really are bastards," she said, trying not to sweep drinks off the table with her slung SFIW (Special Forces Individual Weapon). She had only just realised she was the only woman carrying a weapon.

"Why am I the only girlie lugging bloody gu… weapons around with me?"

"Because you're the only girlie who's going off base with the blades and we want carrying and being confident with a weapon to be second nature to you."

Suddenly Afarin felt humbled. They actually trusted her.

"I bet your mum and dad would be shocked if they could see you now."

"To be honest, Henry, they wouldn't give a toss. I'm dead as far as they're concerned."

He felt a lump in his throat. "Why? Because you're here?"

"No. They haven't known where I am for over a year. They didn't want me to take the Queen's shilling. It's not the done thing in my community, apparently."

He felt a desperate sense of sorrow for the young woman and gave her a manly, non-sexual hug. Her rifle clouted his shin.

"Well, fuck 'em!" was the only constructive thing he could think of to say.

Chapter 16

# THE GIRL
# FROM THE RAF

———

Afarin became another cog in the machine and made a conscious effort to fit in and not piss them off. Her real skills came to the fore while they were interrogating Afghans; both villagers and suspected Taliban. While the blades sometimes went in in their size ten boots, she would hang back slightly and observe, listening quietly. Sometimes with a suspected Taliban fighter she would take over the interrogation, talking softly and gently with the often frightened and disorientated men, some who were much younger than her. The blades were struck by just how angrily she would verbally attack village elders or Taliban who treated her with contempt because she was a woman. The troopers were astonished at the rage this diminutive woman could conjure up when she was riled.

On the long patrols under hard routine, the five of them would sleep under ponchos slung from the WMIK, Afarin in the middle because she wasn't expected to go on stag. They would huddle together for warmth in the bitterly cold Afghanistan nights and sometimes it would snow. When they met up with other units, they would share the ground with the war dogs; incredibly brave animals that would go down into the Taliban cave and tunnel systems to root them out. The Taliban hated these dogs in their Kevlar armour, but they seemed drawn to Afarin and would curl up at her feet. Despite the danger from the Taliban, she would never feel as safe as she did sharing hardships with these four men. One night, she woke up and realised that she was nestled in close to Jarvis. She opened her eyes in the bleak pre-dawn light and realised he was awake, looking at her with an odd expression on his face.

"Sorry, Mr Jarvis," she murmured, and rolled over with her back to him.

"Now you've left a cold bit," he whispered, and spooned up against her back, wondering whether he dared put his arm around her.

\*

She was lying in a small depression behind the cover of a bush and clump of rocks. About 50 metres behind her, the four Land Rover WMIKs were drawn up nose to tail in a battle line, well spaced, half the crews operating the vehicles' support weapons, the other half providing a protective skirmishing screen ahead and behind the vehicles. They were occupying a frontage of about 500 metres; Wayne, their driver, occupied a position about 50 metres to her right. She could only see him when he moved, but she suspected that he was keeping an eye on her.

In the clear, blue sky, the circular vapour trails of the B52s wound like the Olympic symbols as the bombers circled, waiting to be called in to drop their JDAMs. She could feel the visceral thuds of the 8,000lb munitions as they pulverised the cave complexes of Tora Bora in the Spin Ghar mountain range. She also felt the heavy, slow thuds through her torso of the WMIKs' .50 Cals firing over her head, and watched with awed fascination the bobbing, jinking fiery trail of the TOW missiles, heading towards the Taliban trench and sangar system.

They were providing fire support to a unit of US Navy SEALs who were clearing the outer trenches before moving into the main cave complex. Afarin shook her head with bemused wonder. *This little girl from Derby is in the middle of a battle in her ancestral homeland. Bloody hell!* She turned round and looked at her Land Rover. Henry and Jarvis were stripped to the waist, operating the support weapons.

Henry was singing tunelessly as he sent the rounds down from the 50 cal singing, *that's the way, I like it,* by KC and the Sunshine Band.

Henry saw her looking at him.

"Face your bloody front and scan your arc!" he yelled at her. Afarin turned back and smiled to herself. She had decided that she liked Henry very much.

From about 300 metres ahead of them, she heard the fast rattle of automatic rifle fire and the thuds of grenades as the SEALs started to roll up the trench system, clearing it metre by metre. Their weapons of choice seemed to be war dogs, grenades and fighting through with automatic fire. The WMIKs ceased fire and the remaining crew members dismounted to provide all-round cover. The JDAMS continued to pound the caves, 2 kilometres away. It took about two hoursThe skirmishes in the trenches until billows of purple smoke denoted that the first line of enemy defence had been cleared.

A group of figures appeared out of the smoke, moving steadily towards the WMIKs. As they came closer, they were revealed as multiple SEALs leading a hooded prisoner, who had his hands tie-wrapped behind his back. The British officer went out to meet them.

"Can you guys process this joker for onward move to Bagram? He decided he didn't want to go to paradise and meet his seventy-two virgins today." The SEAL swung round and punched the prisoner in the side of the head. He fell over in the dirt. "We think this piece of shit is a Saudi mercenary."

Watching from a few metres away, Afarin was shocked at the way the American Special Forces treated the prisoner. In her headscarf and dark goggles, she was indistinguishable and looked like the others. She turned away in disgust and found Henry standing just behind her. He had put on his smock and Osprey.

"You have to remember, these guys have just gone eyeball to eyeball with some of the fiercest fighters the world has produced," he said to her in a low voice. "This fighter is lucky that he's still alive, particularly if he isn't an Afghan. Walk a mile in their boots."

The British agreed to take the prisoner back to the FOB and decided to use Afarin's WMIK. She was grateful because it meant she would be sleeping in her comfy bed tonight, rather than in a depression in a sleeping bag. She was briefed to make note of anything the prisoner said on the way back, but he just lay on the floor, hooded and tied, and never made a sound. Back at the FOB, the intelligence officer was waiting in the tent inside the POW holding pen. The British weren't exactly gentle with him, either. They sat on the vehicle, listening to the intelligence officer (colloquially known as green slime) yelling at the prisoner in appalling Arabic.

"He sounds like the Arabic version of Officer Crabtree from 'Allo 'Allo!" Afarin remarked to the captain who had been leading her patrol. "Why don't you let me have a go?"

The Captain looked at her doubtfully.

"Go on, Boss. Just yelling at him won't cut it," Henry said in support.

"Okay, I'll ask."

"But it's just me alone with him in there. I understand how their minds works, so we'll do it my way. It's my way or nothing. That's the deal."

"So what's the plan, Stan?" asked the Captain.

They walked away from the POW holding pen and she explained to him.

"If this guy is a Saudi, he will almost certainly be a Wahhabist. They are so ultra-conservative that women disgust them and are regarded as unclean. If a fighter is killed by a woman, they believe that he will be disbarred from paradise. The seventy-two virgins thing is a load of crap and is a mistranslation. But he has to believe that I will kill him. That's why I need to fire one round."

He waited until the intelligence officer came out of the tent, seething with frustration, and had a word with him. They both looked at Afarin doubtfully, but he reluctantly agreed.

"All right, but the guard stays in there."

"No." She was adamant. "Just him and me."

"Why?"

"Because I don't want to be involved in his long and drawn-out torture, which is what will happen to him once he leaves our protection."

In the end, they reluctantly agreed. She gave her rifle to Jarvis and took off everything apart from her boots, trousers and t-shirt. She wasn't wearing underwear because it was pointless in the field. The scarf had gone, so had the dark glasses. She unholstered her Glock.

"Bloody hell, where did they come from?" Jarvis said, unable to take his eyes off her breasts.

"Let's go, sir," she said to the intelligence officer. Her heart was pounding.

Inside the tent there was a table and two chairs. The prisoner was sitting on one chair, still hooded, head bowed. The guard stood behind him, rifle at the ready.

"Will you please take off his hood and then both of you leave. Do not come back in until I have done what you requested."

They did and she sat down at the opposite side of the table. She was holding the Glock. The prisoner refused to look at her while she scrutinised him. He was definitely a member of the Saud; she could tell by his ratty features.

"They have told me to kill you," she said to him in Arabic.

He sneered without even looking at her. She cocked the pistol.

"They know what is written in the Holy Koran, that if a man is slain by a woman, he shall never enter the gardens and vineyards and meet his young, full-breasted maidens of equal age, with a cup of wine."

She leaned forward to accentuate the fact she was a woman.

"So I want you to look at me before I kill you."

"You are nothing but a vassal of the Kufar, whore!"

She pointed the Glock at his head and pulled the trigger. The round ruffled his long hair and deafened his left ear. The 9mm bullet went out of the tent and harmlessly across the airfield. The guard came back in with a tearing hurry.

"Get out!" she screamed at him, "until I have killed him." She was guessing the prisoner could speak English. She was right.

The prisoner wailed and fell on the floor, moaning and shaking. Afarin stood up and pressed the pistol hard into his head.

"No. I want to talk to the man, not you, not you…"

She left the tent and looked at the intelligence officer. "I think our Saudi Arabian friend wants a chat now, sir."

Henry was looking at her with a strange expression. "Jesus, Treacle. You forgot to tell us you're a fucking psychopath."

She was shaking with emotion and Henry took the Glock out of her trembling hand and unloaded it, fired off the action, put the ejected round back in the magazine and then back in the weapon. He tucked it into the holster on her thigh, then put his arm round her shoulders.

"You will never cease to amaze me, Ms Khan."

"Do you know what the worst thing is? I could so very easily have killed him."

*

Four months after she arrived at the FOB, the blades were rotated with a fresh mobility troop unit. By now, she was part of the fixtures and fittings and nobody questioned her right to be there, but she badly missed Henry, Jarvis and Wayne, her oppos. Before he left, Henry gave her a couple of phone numbers.

"When you get back to Blighty, give me a call. We can catch up."

Despite not really having anything to go home for, Afarin wondered when her tour would be up, but if anything she was getting busier and was loaned on several occasions to American and Australian SF units. The Americans were very polite but reticent towards her. The Australians were outrageously friendly and desperate to 'initiate' her into their unit. She had a pretty good idea what form the 'initiation' would take. As well as starting to miss the cool, wet UK, Afarin noticed that the Taliban were getting better as their tactics evolved. They were using more IEDs and instead of shooting and scooting, they were setting up sophisticated ambushes.

She was in the back of a Land Rover FFR with two diggers and a couple of war dogs that were as friendly but only just slightly more slobbery than their handlers. They were on the main Jalalabad to Kabul road, designated as Route VIOLET but known as 'Route Violent' because of the numbers of burned-out military vehicles and oil tankers that littered the side of the road. Two Land Rover FFRs and two versions of the Australian WMIKs were well spaced, the gunners on top cover with the .50 Cals. She couldn't see much out of the back of the FFR, but she certainly heard and felt the deep boom of the IED that rocked the vehicle. She followed the digger who was tumbling out of the back of the FFR while the top cover waited for the inevitable ambush. She went prone on the road and cocked her Colt SFIW, waiting to follow the lead of the rest. She made a very fast tactical appraisal of the situation. She had been in the third vehicle. The second Land Rover WMIK, or at least half of it, was burning in a crater in the road. The first vehicle, an FFR, was 300 metres away. The radioman of the command FFR was sending a contact and METHANE report.

"Afi, mate, check the casualties. Come on, luv, move your arse!"

It seemed futile to point out that she wasn't a medic, so she got up and dashed, zigzagging towards the wrecked WMIK. The rounds started spattering off the road and cracking overhead. Nothing, absolutely nothing in the world could have prepared her for the scene of carnage that was waiting for the little girl from Derby. The front axle and engine block were 10 metres from the crater. There were two men near the back of the wreck. One was unconscious, the other *compos mentis* and returning fire. The driver had taken the brunt of the explosion from the conduit under the road. There was nothing describable left of him, and she blanked the image from her subconscious. The vehicle commander had lost his right arm and leg and was staring up at the sky, muttering, "Fuck, fuck, fuck."

Afarin tried to remember her Common Core Skills Aid Memoire and the casualty triage algorithm. She shook the man who was returning fire.

"Okay?" she yelled,

"Deaf," he shouted, sending the rounds down.

She moved to the unconscious man. HRABC. Hazard – pretty bloody obvious as a round clanged off the roll bar next to her head. Response – no to shouting. She pinched his earlobe and heard a low moan. Airway – she checked for at least ten seconds. Breathing – she felt a gentle breath on her cheek so he was breathing. Circulation – fast but regular but he was bleeding from his ears. No point in checking pupils because she couldn't have done anything anyway, so she rolled him into the recovery position.

The driver's remains made her retch, so she dragged the commander by his webbing slowly into cover. *Now what the fuck do I do?* She found his morphine autojet round his neck and jammed it into his good thigh. His leg stump was spurting and she tried to tie her *shemagh* around his thigh. So Afarin did the only thing she could do, while the gun battle raged around her. She cuddled the digger and talked to him softly. He stared up into her eyes, shivering with the pain and morphine. They were the most beautiful eyes he had ever seen. Like his wife's, only darker and flecked with violet. He smiled at her and died four minutes later. They were the longest four minutes of Afarin Khan's life.

Time telescoped until a Pedro Black Hawk with two Apaches riding shotgun blasted the Taliban back under their stones. The Pedro retrieved the casualties along with Afarin. She was checked over in the US MTF in Kabul and was ascertained as suffering from mild combat stress. The Americans flew her back to the British FOB that night. She was tortured with the thought that had she gone to assist the vehicle commander first, he might have survived.

The following day, she begged to borrow the ops officer's sat phone and called one of the numbers Henry had given her. She told him everything that had happened and couldn't stop herself from sobbing.

"Henry, I've had enough. I can't take it anymore. I go out on nearly every patrol and I'm terrified that I'll fuck something up and get someone killed. Everyone says I'm indispensable, but surely someone else must be able to speak Pashto?"

"Leave it with me."

Twenty-four hours later, she was on a USAF C17 out of Kandahar to Ramstein. She was met at the US air base by a charming lady USAF Captain and an MT vehicle to take her to Frankfurt Airport. Her flight had been booked to Heathrow, where a Q-car from Hereford was waiting for her. She was back at RAF Marham less than forty-eight hours after she had made the phone call. The British Special Forces do tend to look after their own when there is no

Civil Service involvement. Afarin had been in almost constant frontline action for seven and a half months.

*

Two days after Afarin had returned to RAF Marham, an Army staff sergeant pitched up at the main gate and booked himself on to the camp.

"Purpose for visit, Staff, or do you have a sponsor?"

"I've come to collect SAC Afarin Khan, who's won a two-week holiday. Do you happen to know where she's accommodated?"

"Sorry, no, but the two female accommodation blocks are located behind the Med Centre. I can't give you the combination, but ring the door and someone will answer and get her for you."

He didn't need to ring the doorbell of any block. As he drove down the main drag, he saw a young woman jogging on the grass at the side of the road. The arse was instantly recognisable. He followed her, parked up and chased after her.

"Hello, Treacle. Going my way?"

She turned round in shock. "Oh, Henry," she cried, ran up and hugged him.

"You are on post-operational tour leave, correct?"

"Yes."

"Can you do brickwork pointing or plastering?"

"Err, I dunno."

"Do you want to find out?"

She smiled shyly. "Oh yes."

"Ten minutes. Pack light."

That night, they had dinner in the Lions of Bledlow pub on the Oxfordshire/Buckinghamshire border. Henry explained his project to her.

"It's an old barn that I managed get for just over eighty grand. The hardest bit was getting the plans through the planning department, but they gave the go-ahead after I made a few changes to the design. I've got a mate who's a builder and the roof has just gone on, so it's weathertight. The external brickwork needs pointing and there's a dry stone wall that needs rebuilding. That's where you come in.

"I've got a good-sized caravan in the grounds where I'm living, with hot and cold water and power, so you won't have to crap in a bucket."

She drove his car back from the pub because he had a few drinks with his dinner. In the fading light, he showed her round the barn. Immediately, she could see its potential.

"It will be lovely when it's finished, Henry, and the view is beautiful." He was like a dog with two tails as he showed her into the caravan.

"Here we go. All mod cons."

"Henry, where do I sleep?"

"Well, this sofa can double as a bed. Or you can sleep with me."

She looked at him and felt her cheeks burning.

"Henry, I'm not very good at this because… well, I'm just not."

He cuddled her as they sipped coffee. "No worries, Treacle. We've got two weeks."

Later, the owls screeching and hooting frightened her, so she padded to the other end of the caravan and slipped in next to him. He was still awake and hugged her close.

"Ah, listen to them, the children of the night. What music they make!"

And they did.

She slipped out of the bed at dawn and looked through the window at the rising sun on the Chiltern Hills. The beech trees were beginning to turn and the slopes were dusted with yellow and orange. She was crying with happiness…

Chapter 17

# THE LONG SHOT

---

Just before midnight on a late October evening in 2005, a Puma helicopter took off from Basra Air Station and headed north. The aircraft showed no lights, a contrast to the city passing on its starboard side and the gas and oil separation plants in the desert that were lit up like Christmas trees. Once clear of the city, the helicopter swung right and picked up the River Tigris that wound its convoluted path through the desert, south-east towards the Persian Gulf. The Puma was heading in the opposite direction, north-northwest towards Maysan Province.

In the rear of the helicopter, the loadmaster sat behind the right-hand door's 7.62mm GPMG, his lower legs dangling in the warm slipstream. Four other men were sitting in the dull-red canvass seats. They were all armed and wearing clothing that was festooned with strips of hessian and dirty rags. They only had fighting order webbing with extra water bottles. None carried bergens, but all had personal role radios and three were armed with L119A1/A2 individual weapons. The fourth man had a long rifle across his knees and cradled in his arms to protect it from the vibration of the aircraft. Parts of the rifle and its telescopic sights were also draped with strips of hessian.

This four-man team had spent the last few days in the relative luxury of Basra Air Station, studying their mission notes and poring over hundreds of photographs that included aerial shots of the outskirts of a city and its buildings, in high definition, taken from a Tornado GR4's RAPTOR pod. There were also about thirty photographs of a man wearing a variety of clothing, both Western and Arabic, with him in various situations: talking with other men, leaving buildings and getting out of various vehicles. Those photos hadn't been taken by a RAPTOR pod, but incredibly brave undercover men and women of the 'Det'. The man was in his forties, dark hair with a luxuriant moustache very much of the Saddam Hussein fan club variety. He was handsome with a hooked, aquiline nose. A proud father with two sons, three daughters, two wives. Prosperous and successful. He was also a high-ranking official in the Jaish al-Mahdi. The four passengers in the back of the helicopter were going to kill him, but only one was going to pull the trigger.

From the photographs, the team had identified their drop-off point, the route in, the secondary rendezvous point, the observation and firing position and most importantly, the safe route out. The helicopter aircrew also studied the photographs and agreed that the approach and way out of the drop-off point was clear of obstructions. The rules of engagement were agreed, rations and ammunition issued and the team had relaxed in an air-conditioned Corimec and waited for nightfall.

The RAF loadmaster didn't know the names of his passengers. He didn't know their cap badges and he wouldn't dream of asking. They were just pax, cargo. Cooper and Jarvis were the back-stop. The force protection. A jovial tag team, a double act that would be expected to die if necessary to protect the shooter. Morrison was the spotter. He would help the shooter set up the shot, call windage and do everything except pull the trigger. He didn't much care for the shooter, but few did. Edge was the trigger man. A glacial, introverted, swept-up killer with a lot of pent-up aggression. Sometimes they could see it in his eyes. Cooper had once remarked to Jarvis that if ever a mission went totally tits-up, he would take great pleasure in slotting Edge before going down. He was only half joking.

The city of Amarah was ahead of the helicopter, its lights sparkling off the muddy River Tigris. The river was more of a dribble this time of year at the end of the dry season. The rains of March were months away. The Puma's cockpit was backlit by the eerie glow of the pilots' night vision goggles (NVGs) and they avoided looking at the most brightly lit parts of the approaching city. The British base at the old airfield of Al Amarah was south-west of the city. The helicopter headed for a southern suburb with low-quality housing and ruined blocks of what would have been flats for the oil workers. Its grid pattern showed up harshly in the NVGs and there were few lights in this district.

The RAF loadmaster turned round and tapped one of the passengers on the leg, extending two digits from his fist. Two minutes. The team became alert and started to check their equipment. They didn't have NVGs, just their night vision. While essential for pilots, NVGs tend to give the wearer a sense of tunnel vision that overrides all the other, equally vital, senses. They would need all of them once they were on the ground. The pilot headed for a pool of darkness on the outskirts of the district and flared to lose speed. By now, the loadmaster was flat on his belly, hanging out of the door and calling out the height.

"Twenty metres, fifteen, ten…"

The four men were crouched behind him in the door.

"Five, four, three, two, one…" He thrust his arm out, pointing.

The four-man team disappeared into the dust thrown up by the rotor blades. The loadmaster broke a cyalume stick and shook it, sweeping the floor of the helicopter to make sure no kit had been left behind.

"They're clear."

The Puma's pilot applied collective and cyclic control and the helicopter pitched forward, accelerated and gained height, before turning left and heading towards the base at Al Amarah. The wheels hadn't even touched the ground. The team waited immobile for the noise to disappear and the dust to settle, their senses stretched taut. A dog barked in the distance and a child wailed. It was cool out in their element and they waited until they were sure. Then slowly they stood up and made their unhurried, cautious way north towards the distant buildings. Well spaced and moving in total silence, they were like creatures of the night.

\*

It was their second day in that dangerous, decaying block of flats. The oil workers had left in 1990 and the local inhabitants had at first looted the building, partially burned it down then used it as an open sewer. The building was now in fact such a disgusting mess, that nobody in their right mind would go anywhere near it, even the local kids on their motor scooters.

Edge stared over the top of the rifle's telescopic sites at the road that ran left to right, left of arc to right. Three-quarter left was a petrol station and small market, range 650 metres. Half-right was another, smaller, petrol station, range 950 metres. Traffic on the road was light; the odd lorry, motorbikes and a few ubiquitous Toyota pick-ups. Edge massaged his tired eyes, his face invisible under the netting headscarf draped over his head. He was partially lying on an old kitchen unit they had dragged into the main sitting room with its large glassless window and balcony. The table was as far into the room as they could get it, while maintaining sight of the two fuel stations. Morrison sat behind and to the left of Edge, his telescope close to the rifle, but he used a pair of binoculars to scan their arc of fire on the fifth floor. The telescope was to help Edge set up and take the shot, when the time came.

On the floor below, Jarvis and Cooper kept watch on the back and flanks of the flats, making sure that their escape route was un-interdicted. They were both tired and thoroughly bored. The highlight of their previous day had been watching a bunch of little savages drag a dog behind a motorbike and then stone the exhausted animal to death.

"Practising for when they're married," Cooper had observed to Jarvis, wishing that he had the rifle.

Edge was feeling uncomfortable and knew that he had to take a piss, even though he had been trying to remain hydrated. He was concerned as he was down to his last water bottle.

"Sorry, mate, need a piss." Edge slid off the table with glacial slowness and once out of sight of the window, crawled on his hands and knees to what had been the bathroom. The lavatory had gone and there was just a rank hole in the floor. This room had no windows, so Edge stood up and fumbled with the front of his ghillie suit. He pissed in the sink and was horrified at how brown his urine was, how much it stank, and how much it burned coming out.

"Bollocks," he exclaimed quietly. A urinary tract infection was the last thing he needed. Anxiously, he went back to his post with a stinging bladder.

Back at the table, Morrison was gently chewing a few nuts and some dried fruit he had packed into one of his smock pockets. Chocolate bars would have been a useless mess in this heat. Trouble was, nuts made him feel thirsty.

"Better?"

"No, I'm in fucking agony."

"You should drink more, keep hydrated."

"Prick!"

They had a false alarm at 14:00 when a couple of pick-ups approached the garage left-of-arc and stopped in the parking area away from the pumps. Morrison stirred and nudged Edge, who had been catnapping. Two men got out of the first pick-up and one man from the second. They came together and seemed to be chatting and sharing cigarettes. Edge looked through his telescopic sight and Morrison was peering through the telescope.

"I don't recognise him."

"What about Mr Headdress?" Morrison asked. "Guy on the right. He has a Saddam moustache."

"His nose is wrong. Not our man."

They watched the three Iraqis finish their cigarettes, then one of them wandered into the petrol station and came out with three cans of Coke.

"It's the real thing," Edge observed, "but unfortunately, they aren't."

\*

The light was going and the air was cooling when Edge spotted a Toyota Land Cruiser pull into the further petrol station. It stopped short of the pumps but no one got out. A minute or so later, a second pick-up drew level with the first. One man got out and appeared to be talking with someone inside the first. Two more men got out of the first vehicle and looked all around the area. One of them spoke into a mobile phone.

"You getting this?"

"Yep," Morrison confirmed. He keyed his personal radio and spoke to the two on the floor below. "Something's going down. Wake up."

"Cheeky bastard," Jarvis muttered as they scanned their arcs.

A Mercedes saloon came from the south and pulled into the station, parking close to the two pick-ups. Edge formed himself into the human component of his rifle, the Mercedes' door rested on the dagger of his telescopic site. The reticules of the scope framed the car.

The driver's door opened and a man got out. He was wearing a lightweight linen suit and sunglasses. As he turned sideways, Edge scrutinised his profile.

"That's our man," Edge muttered, his mouth barely moving.

"Confirm positive ID."

Edge chambered a round. He had kept the bolt open to avoid condensation building up in the chamber and barrel. By now, he was framing the target within the environment. A flag on the petrol station's canopy fluttered. In the distance, a pile of tyres burned, sending a long plume that Edge used to estimate wind direction and speed. He did the calculation in his head.

"Four-eight mils, five knots," Morrison estimated.

The bomb maker walked unhurriedly across to the pick-ups and shook the three men's hands.

The rifle was an L115A3 and the round was a .338 Lapua Magnum. The scope was a Schmidt & Bender 5-25×56 PM II LP telescopic sight, and Edge concentrated on the man's head and shoulders.

The target looked into the back of the pick-up and one of the men dragged aside a tarpaulin. He looked in and grinned then laughed, obviously pleased with what he saw.

Edge let his breath out slowly and the rifle rose imperceptivity. The man had a large mole on his forehead that his doctor should really have had a look at. He took up first pressure on the trigger.

At the end of the rifle barrel was a long tubular addition that looked like a silencer. It was a recoil suppressor and flash eliminator. Edge went into second pressure, knowing when the sweet spot would come. The rifle bucked hard against his shoulder. Morrison inhaled the rank nitrocellulose and watched the shimmering of the round disturbing the air as it went down range. Edge had already chambered a second round.

One of the men turned round. He couldn't have heard anything because the round was travelling faster than sound, and after 600 metres, the distinctive crack of a high velocity round disappears. The bomb maker's head from his mandible upwards disappeared in a pink cloud. The lifeless corpse remained on its feet for several seconds before folding up behind the pick-up. The three men scattered to cover.

"Move!"

They went down the stairwell and out into the evening air. Cooper and Jarvis were already out, covering the flanks. Edge and Morrison moved quickly, their bodies running with sweat inside the ghillie suits. Five hundred metres out from the flats they heard the first rattle of automatic fire, very fast, a C8 carbine. Cooper and Jarvis were busy.

After one and a half kilometres of a fast jog, they arrived at the main rendezvous point, one of Al Amarah's crash gates, which was open, the Land Rover waiting with its engine running. Their force protection in the forms of Cooper and Jarvis arrived ten minutes later.

"One of the pick-ups decided to get a bit lairy and have a look at the flats. I had to dissuade them," Jarvis explained.

Edge chugged down bottle after bottle of water. While they were waiting for the helicopter and nature took its natural course, he was doubled up with agony as he tried to get rid of it before the flight back to Basra.

## Chapter 18

# THE RAF LOADMASTER'S STORY

———

The loadmaster leaned forward as far out into the slipstream as he dared and drank in the heady aromas of a helicopter travelling at 130 knots at 500 feet. Sergeant Giles (Gary) Gilmore was inundated by the scream of the engines and the hot winds from their passage across the desert. The oily reek of AVTUR was unmistakable and compulsive. He avoided looking directly at the sodium lights of the GOSPs through his night vision goggles (NVGs), but instead looked down between his boots at a lonely pick-up parked below, showing no lights. Two men looked up trying to spot the helicopter passing above them. Gilmore thought about the helicopter attack sequence in *Apocalypse Now*. He hummed the opening bars of the *Ride of the Valkyries* and said to himself: *I'm being paid to bloody do this. Thank you, God.*

Gilmore didn't know the names of his passengers. He didn't know their cap badges and he wouldn't dream of asking. They were the peculiar ones who didn't do a full tour; they just came and went, plying their trade, whatever it was. But he could tell by the sniper rifle that they would be ruining someone's day. He was grateful to them, because this whole stinking operation in Iraq was falling apart. Sergeant Gilmore turned round and tapped one of the passengers on the leg, extending two digits from his fist. Two minutes. The team became alert and started to check their equipment. They didn't have NVGs, just their night vision.

While essential for pilots, NVGs tend to give the wearer a sense of tunnel vision that overrides all the other, equally vital, senses. They would need all of them once they were on the ground. The pilot headed for a pool of darkness on the outskirts of the district and flared to lose speed. By now, the loadmaster was flat on his belly, hanging out of the door and calling out the height.

"Twenty metres, fifteen, ten…"

The dust came up to meet them and the four men were crouched behind him in the door.

"Five, four, three, two, one…" He thrust his arm out, pointing.

The four-man team disappeared into the dust thrown up by the rotor blades. Gilmore broke a cyalume stick and shook it, sweeping the floor of the helicopter to make sure no kit had been left behind.

"They're clear."

The Puma's pilot applied collective and cyclic control and the helicopter pitched forward, accelerated and gained height, before turning left and heading towards the base at Al Amarah. The wheels hadn't even touched the ground. The Puma landed at the Al Amarah base and the ground handling party of UK Mobile Air Movements Squadron and the refuelling party from Tactical Supply Wing (TSW) were waiting. It would be a hot refuelling with the engines still turning, and while the pilot and co-pilot stayed in the cockpit, Gilmore jumped down and went over to the movers.

"There's been a change of flight plans. Instead of going back to Basra with equipment, you've got six pax. Five have appointments and referrals at the field hospital in Shaibah and the last one has a repatriation flight arranged. His mother's sick."

"Okay, Gilmore shouted above the din of the helicopter. "Five to Shaibah and one for BAS. Anything else we can take?"

"We've got three lacon boxes of out-of-date medical supplies you can dump off at the field hospital."

The loadmaster went back to the Puma and pushed his head into the cockpit. The TSW team had started refuelling and no lights were showing on the apron.

"Change of plans, Skipper," he said to the pilot in the right-hand seat. "Six pax. Five to Shaibah and one to BAS."

Flight Lieutenant Mount nodded and turned to the co-pilot. "Change the ATO please, Louise. Shortest transit to Shaibah and back to BAS, avoiding the bad guys."

Flying Officer Skelton licked her thumb and wiped away the Chinagraph line on the laminated map on her knee. To Gilmore, it was strangely erotic, but then again, Louise had that effect on men and women. She drew in the new course and checked it with a Silva compass for bearings, then imputed the data into the inertial navigation. Gilmore smiled in the darkness. He just loved watching her being so precise and conscientious. She was new to the job. The bad habits would come later.

The lacon boxes went on first while the fuelling was still underway, and he strapped and frapped them to hard points on the floor of the aircraft. The TSW boys pulled the hose away and he waved in the passengers. Al Amarah was in the heart of bandit country, and a Puma helicopter refuelling and loading would make a tempting target for rockets and mortars. Gilmore made sure the passengers were strapped in, checked his safety tether, took up position behind the GPMG and then went on the intercom.

"All secure in the back."

The Puma's engines ramped up the power and the helicopter rose then pitched forward sharply to gain the angle of attack for thrust. The passengers hung on to the seat frames while Gilmore grabbed the GPMG's mounting to stop himself sliding out of the door. Once it reached cruise and safety height, the Puma banked sharply to the left and Gilmore had to use a great deal of effort to lean forward and maintain observation out of the door at the rear of the aircraft. Amaraha's lights pivoted below the Puma's tail and they headed south-east to Basra. Over the desert, a hose of tracer reached up for them. Lazy and inaccurate. Nonetheless, Gilmore triggered the Defensive Aid Suite and he looked away from the chaff and flare to protect his night vision.

"Tracers, Skipper."

"Serious?"

"Well…"

"Stop playing and posing, Gary," the pilot gently admonished. "The armourers will have to replace that."

*It'll give them something to do*, he thought to himself. It was 02:30 local. Gilmore had a gritty tiredness behind his eyes and he realised that he should have had a piss at Al Amarah. But nothing could detract from the joy he felt flying in a military helicopter at low level across the desert. *I fucking love my job!* The bottoms of his trousers flapped in the slipstream and the Glock was hard against his thigh. If only Lorna was here with him, he could unload his bollocks, get rid of the frustration, and it would be perfect. But she was three time zones away in a dank, autumnal Oxfordshire. She once told him that he looked like Jean-Jacques Burnel from the Stranglers. He didn't know who Jean-Jacques Burnel was, so he asked Mr Google and was delighted that he had to agree with her. Lorna had such exceptional taste, he concluded, and adopted the Burnel disinterested pout. It lasted until the other guys on the squadron realised his strange affectation and mercilessly took the piss. Ground crew would start singing *No More Heroes* every time he walked past. Gilmore quietly parked his Jean-Jacques Burnel persona.

On the flare into Shaibah, it was clear that there were a few more pax lurking behind the ground handling party, waiting for a trip to BAS. The helicopter landing point commander guided the Puma in with two cyalume sticks held aloft. With NVGs, it was all rather unnecessary, but hey, that was the way the Army did things. Once on the ground, all the passengers in the helicopter started to dismount.

"Hoy, where are you going?" Gilmore said to the lad who was for the onward trip to BAS. The youngster blinked uncertainly and Gilmore remembered that he was probably worried sick about his mother.

"This is Shaibah. Your stop's Basra. Sit back down. We'll be off again in no time. Can I get you anything?" the loadmaster asked the bewildered-looking youngster, realising just how hopelessly lost he looked.

"I could do with a drink, Sarge."

Gilmore jumped down and met the ground handlers. "How many?"

"Three, including the Colonel."

A senior officer was pacing impatiently next to the ISO containers, arrogantly smoking on the landing point.

"Fine. He gets on last after the other pax and any cargo. Can you give the lad in the back of the cab a bottle of water?"

The handlers grinned.

"And I need a piss."

"Behind the ISOs as good as anywhere, Sarge."

Gilmore studiously ignored the colonel when he clambered on board after the mail sacks and had pressing business in the cockpit. He gave Flight Lieutenant Mount a report on their passengers and cargo, then tried to ascertain whether Louise Skelton was wearing a bra under her body armour. She had cut the sleeves off her top (very naughty given the fire risk), and as she reached up to adjust an overhead instrument, she gave him a good view of her armpit and right-side boob. She wasn't. Oh, Louise. You naughty junior officer, you. It never occurred to him to think if he could see so much of the co-pilot's side and nether regions, just how shit the body armour was that they had been issued with.

Back in the air, the Puma headed north to BAS, keeping well clear of the city and the town of Zubyar, because the locals had a tendency to do a full magazine download at anything flying over them. The helicopter landed on the main aircraft servicing platform, a few metres away from the overhead cover. It meant the ground crews could wheel the Puma under cover to service and rearm the chaff and flare Defensive Aid Suite (DAS) in the shade. Andy Mount shut down the engines and as he was unclipping his safety harness, Gilmore was annoyed to see the colonel get off the aircraft without a word or glance, strutting off to find his transport. *Wanker,* Gilmore thought to himself, *I hope his next shit is a pineapple.*

He supervised the pax getting off and was pleased to see that the young Tom had a member of the A1 admin team waiting for him. From now and until he arrived at the hospital where his mother lay in intensive care classed as very seriously ill, the young soldier was in the hands of the Joint Services Repatriation Team. Once the movers unloaded the lacons, the crew disembarked and gathered by the aircraft's nose.

"Another successful one," Mount observed, patting the cockpit door. It was his little ritual. They walked towards the ops room to file the report and get a brew before turning in. Gilmore felt good as he sniffed the cool early morning air.

"Hey, Louise, my roomie is back in the UK on R&R, if you fancy a nightcap in my Corimec."

She pulled off her flying helmet, stuck her flying gloves inside the helmet and undid the bun at the back of her head, shaking her long hair loose. She fixed the loadmaster with a contemptuous stare. "This may come as a complete surprise to you, Sergeant Gilmore, but once you've tried a bit of girl-on-girl action, anything with a cock, particularly one as small as yours, just doesn't measure up."

Andy Mount laughed and pushed Gilmore away. The loadmaster pretended to be crestfallen, slouched and dragged his feet like a stroppy teenager. "So I suppose doing my ironing is out of the question?"

"Do fuck off, Gary," she said good-naturedly.

The ops building was largely empty except for the duty officer and the Immediate Response Team (IRT) medics and aircrew who were sleeping in any comfortable nook and cranny they could find. Gilmore asked the ops officer if he could use one of the computers, and he nodded to one in the corner. Gilmore logged in with his MoD account and accessed his email account.

"Come on, come on, come on," he muttered, waiting for it to open. There was a load of dross about fitness testing times, signing his FMT 600; otherwise, he wouldn't be able to drive the squadron vehicles, and an unpaid mess bill from the sergeants' mess back in the UK. Finally, he saw the email and it was as though something warm was wrapping itself around his heart. Feeling as though he was sixteen again, he clicked on it.

**From:** *Lornagg1976@hotmail.co.uk*
**Sent:** 26 October 2005 at 22:07
**To:** Giles.Gilmore@jhc644Sqn.mod.uk
**Subject:** The bed's too big without you

Giles, my love,

I hope that you're OK and you're getting enough to eat and enough sleep. I'm also hoping that you're staying away from the laydeez, coz I've bloody heard about detachment rules applying. No, they bloody well don't.

There have been lots of Wokkas flying around with underslung loads. The kids love it but the locals don't seem too pleased when they transit over Wallingford. Probably think it will affect the house prices. Why are they here? I thought they were tucked up in Odiham. They're not coming out to where you lot are, are they? I love seeing them. They make the house shake. One of the loadies waved at me from the rear ramp as I got out of the car at the post office. It went over at about fifty feet. Cheeky sod! Still, they must be a lot cleverer than you, coz their helicopters have two lots of spinning thingies.

I've got a bit of bad news. Danny posted some toast and marmite in the drawer of the DVD player and I'm afraid that it's stopped working. Really sorry, Giles, but I can't watch him every minute of the day. I'll be glad when the little sod's old enough to go to play school and I can get back to work.

OC Admin Wing has been badgering all the wives to attend a meet and greet in the Station Social Club, so we can all share stories about how we're coping with our hubbies being away. I know he means well, but this isn't the bloody Army. This morning, we all trotted off like good little girls and stood around sipping tea and pretending to be united. There was even one poor sod who was a bloke, married to one of the female engineers and boy did he look uncomfortable. I wouldn't have gone had it been me.

At this point, Gilmore grinned. He knew the female engineer. Louise also knew her... Very well. He wondered if the bloke would have been angry, or just want to watch.

Personally, I found it all rather patronising and contrived. This is the 21st century and us ladies' lives don't revolve around the one- and two-winged master race. Sorry to disappoint you.

There followed a detailed account of just how much Gilmore's wife was missing him and what she was going to do when he came home. He rubbed his eyes and groaned.

So that's it as far as my life goes. Boring, isn't it? Not like your exciting life. Just stay safe and don't come back with any bits missing.

Love you, Giles xxx

PS: Danny sends you a big, dribbly kiss.

He started typing:

**From:** Giles.Gilmore@jhc644Sqn.mod.uk
**Sent:** 27 October 2005 at 03:20
**To:** Lornagg1976@hotmail.co.uk
**Subject:** RE: The bed's too big without you

Hello Lorna, love,

Your arrangements regarding my homecoming are to my liking and I will dwell on them, during the lonely, empty hours in my Corimec. The problem is that by the time I get home I will have to wheel my bollocks off the Tristar in a wheelbarrow.

The Chinooks may be heading further east to that other well-known shithole. Don't know why they're flying round our gaff. Probably doing some pre-deployment training with the pongoes over at Abingdon. That loadie couldn't have been waving at you, because it's a well-known fact that they are all gayer than a Christmas tree.

Don't worry too much about the DVD player. Just tell Danny if he does it again he'll be sent to a medical research laboratory. Give him a manly hug from me.

I'm fine and eating well, too well. Andy is looking after us. He's good and steady and doesn't take unnecessary risks. Louise is coming on in leaps and bounds now that she's been licked into shape and is popular throughout the Det. Don't worry. I wouldn't get a look-in and I don't want to.

Most of the time we do the shuttle runs around the Div area, boring really, but tonight we dropped off some tough hombres who were probably going to do some bad things. It pays not to be too curious. Tomorrow we go on stag for the IRT.

That's pretty much it for me for now, as I'm off to bed. Really miss you, babe.

All my love,

G xxx

He pressed send then leaned back from the screen, suddenly feeling really tired.

"See you tomorrow, Gary," Mount called to him as he and Louise opened the door to leave.

"The offer still stands, Louise," Gilmore said with a grin.

"Which I've heard is more than your cock does. Goodnight, Gary."

Chapter 19

# THE LOADMASTER'S STORY

———

Gilmore woke up around 12:00 because he was too hot and the continual aircraft movements made sleep impossible. He went to the ablutions Corimec and pampered himself with an enormous piss followed by a Basra shower. Water was a premium in this part of the world, expensive and time-consuming to desalinate then ship into the base by tanker. So the British military had a standard operating procedure for taking a shower:

Enter shower cubicle and turn on the water. The water will run for no more than 20 seconds. During this time you must ensure all bodily parts are thoroughly wet. Do not ingest water.

Turn off the water. Select shower gel, soap or myrrh-scented oils of choice and thoroughly lather the entire body. Avoid contact with the eyes.

Turn on the water and rinse off cleansing agents for a maximum of 40 seconds ensuring all residues are removed, to prevent chemical irritation.

At this point, male personnel are to shave. This stage is optional for female personnel.

Ensure all sensitive body areas are well moisturised because the highly chlorinated water is likely to irritate sensitive skin to buggery.

The combined messing facility was getting busy when he piled his body armour and helmet by the door. If the rocket and mortar alarm were to go off, a stampede of around 200 people would rush to find their kit among the piles of identically camouflaged personal protective equipment. Some tube had made a decree that body armour was not to be worn in the combined messing facility, so that was it. Gilmore elected to have a freshly cooked ham and tomato omelette with French beans and found a quiet corner of the mess hall to sit. There was no sign of Flight Lieutenant Mount or Flying Officer Skelton.

Surrounded by people, Gilmore had never felt so lonely. Aircrew did three months in theatre rather than the usual four months for other RAF personnel. The Army did six months, but helicopter aircrew were rotated every six months, so it was three on six off. Specifically included in the six months off were specific to role and pre-deployment training. This was Gilmore's third tour in Iraq. It was quite bad for the medics as well, particularly those with acute care or trauma specialisations. He was beginning to feel maudlin when he felt someone brush past his back, go round the end of the table and sit opposite him.

"Hi, Gary. I didn't see you at the gym this morning."

She was one of the MT drivers on the squadron. Very fit, very vivacious and very pretty. For some reason he couldn't fathom (well, actually he could, because she was only human), she had something of a 'thing' for Sergeant Air Loadmaster Gilmore. But dalliances with junior airwomen by senior NCOs was likely to have the squadron commander beating him over the head with a copy of *Air Publication No 1: Ethos, Core Values and Standards*. This all seemed rather unfair to Gilmore, given that his co-pilot was carpet-munching her way through her operational tour.

"We didn't land 'till just before three this morning. Been in bed."

"You poor thing," she said, her limpid brown eyes melting his soul. "When are you flying again?"

"Fourteen hundred hours, twelve hours IRT stag."

"Do you want a lift to the flight line? I've got a wagon."

"Thanks, but I need to collect my kit."

"No worries, I'll wait," she said brightly. "Tell me where your Corimec is and I'll bring the Land Rover round."

\*

They were watching *Team America* on a DVD in the crew room. Well, the men were. Most of the women thought it was silly, with puppets and stupid accents.

Gilmore would have enjoyed it even more if Louise hadn't been sleeping with her head on Andy Mount's shoulder. She was wearing her cut-off jacket, but at least her arms were decorously folded on her lap. She had once again forgone undergarments and as one of the gunners had pointed out earlier, she looked like a dead heat in a Zeppelin race.

Louise presented to the world the façade of a worldly-wise tough cookie. A young woman who was confident in her own abilities. She was easily beautiful, a true pin-up for the Armed Forces careers office, and she appeared in several recruiting pictures, complete with grow bag, flying helmet tucked under her arm so that you could see her auburn hair, not done up in a bun, but cascading over her shoulders, because she was so photogenic.

Parts of Louise's life were a façade. She was nearly thirty but still didn't command her own aircraft. She had struggled through officer training at Cranwell and the Joint Helicopter Flying Training School. Their squadron commander was desperate to help her, which is why she had been partnered with Andy Mount, one of the most experienced pilots on the squadron. Louise also struggled with her own sexuality, as if anyone else could give a toss. Everybody loved Louise; the pity of it was she could barely love herself.

The medical team consisted of a flight nursing officer (FNO), a flight nurse (FN) and a male flight nursing attendant medic (FNA). He was chortling away to the film. The two nurses were reading. The two RAF regiment gunners of the force protection detail were enjoying the film so much, they kept repeating lines:

"Hans Blix, you break my balls. Durka, durka. I promise," Etc.

Time passes very slowly during an extremely boring shift. Coffee, even good coffee, becomes dry and tasteless. It was stiflingly hot in the crew room and the air conditioning seemed to be working as well as most systems seemed to work at BAS. The next highlight would be the delivery of the packed dinners. Probably a cheese pasty, still frozen in the middle, packet of crisps, tasteless apple and a melted chocolate bar, Gilmore thought gloomily. He looked at the clock and sighed.

It started as do all these things, a series of random, sometimes innocuous, seemingly unrelated events that stoked the volcano. It was the theory of synchronicity in action to cause the perfect storm.

During Op TELIC One in 2003, during the initial invasion of Iraq, the British forces couldn't move for television and newspaper journalists. But once the warfighting was over and the coalition forces moved on to the more difficult phase of peace-making and nation building, they got bored and packed up their cameras and satellite dishes, leaving the only people who would give a shit about the 12,500 British personnel in theatre, their families. What some commentators would describe as a warmongering prime minister with a Messiah complex and his propaganda minister had assured the military planners that the relief agencies and NGOs would flood into the country. The problem was that the NGOs were reluctant to put their name to an enterprise that many regarded as an illegal act of war on a sovereign state. And a hostile chancellor wouldn't finance it anyway.

The long-suffering Shia Muslims of Iraq's second largest city were prepared to give the British a chance, but it soon became apparent that the occupying British forces could barely sustain themselves, let alone provide reconstruction and development for a population of over 375,000. The willingness to see what would happen didn't take long to slide into anger and insurrection.

On 1st May 2004, the repugnant editor and wannabe celeb of a national red-top rag of a newspaper published a set of photographs purporting to show British troops abusing Iraqi internees. Despite boasting that he had a brother in the Army and how he admired the British military, the editor ran these pictures, which were so obviously faked a Boys' Brigade cadet could have pointed out they were a hoax. Given the global nature of news, the Iraqi population was less than impressed and rioting around the isolated British bases ensued. It's a shame that he didn't show his brother the photographs before he published them. And if he did, it's a shame his brother was so ignorant of the type of vehicles used on Op TELIC.

Around this time, a Shia paramilitary force, likely backed by Iran and headed by a cleric, the Jaysh Al-Mahdi (JAM), became a focus for the anti-British insurgency in Southern Iraq. The JAM were well armed, well organised and well trained, probably by Iran's Revolutionary Guard. RPG attacks on British bases, sniper fire and roadside IEDs continued throughout 2004/2005 and the British casualty numbers began to climb towards one hundred deaths. As a rule of thumb used by medical planners, for every death there will be one very seriously injured, one seriously injured and four minor to significant casualties. All of a sudden, the media became interested in Iraq again and they wanted to be there to get a scoop when the one hundredth British serviceman or woman was killed.

A BBC team that had recently flown into theatre and demanded priority over other news networks, had so far done a few pieces to camera outside the old airport fire station, pretending they were downtown Basra. They were fully kitted up with body armour and helmets, and the lead presenter, a darling of the television morning news programme, didn't like it when passing Toms on the way to work laughed at them. Probably stung that their professional integrity was being questioned by what they perceived as uneducated cannon fodder, the BBC team went to their corporate comms civil servant minder (yes, you even get the parasites on operations) and demanded free passage and military escort into Basra City. They spun it as showing what a good job the military was doing under difficult circumstances, but back in the UK it would be edited to show what a clusterfuck they were making of Iraq.

It's impossible to fathom the degree of obsequiousness and general fawning that senior military officers show the media, and the lengths they would go to, to enable the media to portray the military as a bunch of incompetent arseholes, but ho hum. The BBC team got their way and a two-vehicle convoy left BAS and headed into the city. All went well until they took a wrong turn, missing the turn-off to uptown Basra with the stores, hotels and coffee houses, and carried on towards the slums and narrow streets of the Al Mishraq district. The BBC vehicle didn't have a radio, so the escort Snatch Land Rover couldn't communicate with them and thought this was all part of the plan. The driver of the BBC vehicle realised they had made a mistake and turned up a narrower road with a watercourse running along the right. Two children dashed out of an alley on the left. The elder, a boy, made it. The Toyota Land Cruiser hit the little girl, who didn't, and her body was thrown into the air like a ragdoll.

*

It was *Sean of the Dead* on the DVD player, and Louise, Andy Mount and the FNA were playing Risk. The gunners were chuckling like Bevis and Butt-Head as Simon Pegg threw records at a girl zombie. Gilmore was trying to read *Angels and Demons* and look down Louise's top as she bent forward to throw the die. The nurses were knitting. The ops phone rang and the duty bod answered it.

"Methane!" he said loudly and started to write in the log, relaying the information to everyone in the room. Andy Mount and Louise pulled on their body armour and went out to the helicopter. On the pan, the ground crew were pulling off the Day-Glo red protective and warning tabs. The starter generator was plugged into the aircraft. The medics were putting on their kit and shouldering the medical bergens. Gilmore opened his notebook and went over to the ops table with its map.

"Callsign: Babysitter Three-Zero. Grid reference: three, zero, zero, niner, four, five delta. Incident is a road traffic collision involving a vehicle and civilian personnel. Hazards at scene include large and unfriendly crowd, with as yet no enemy fire. Landing point is problematic as insufficient space on road in a built-up area. Nearest possible landing site is the opposite side of the waterway, accessible by a footbridge, approximately 200 plus metres from the incident. We will mark with florescent square. Casualties are numbers one, a female child of approximately eight to ten years of age. Suspect skeletal trauma and internal injuries. GCS of eleven. The casualty is in a great deal of pain and very frightened. Conscious and responding to pain and speech. Require medical team and additional force protection as situation is deteriorating."

Gilmore had marked the position on the map and was the last one on the Puma, which by now was burning and turning. He checked the Pax and that the medical equipment was netted down. The RAF gunners were grinning, eyes shining with excitement. He put on his harness then pushed his head in the cockpit with the map.

""That's where it is. The landing site is the wrong side of the canal or whatever it is. The medics will have to go in on foot. I suggest we take off as soon as they're out and loiter. The helicopter could exacerbate the situation."

"Agreed," the pilot said. Louise took the map and went on the radio. She was calm, as though ordering a pizza over the phone.

"Bravo, Alpha, Sierra, this is Damp Duster One Zero requesting clearance and transit to three, zero, zero, niner, four, five delta. Eight souls on board, for immediate priority clearance. Thank you."

"Roger, Damp Duster, One Zero, you are cleared for transit. You have priority, over."

"Thank you, Bravo, Alpha, Sierra, Damp Duster One Zero listening, out."

The Puma's engines ramped up and she rose then tipped forward so that the rotor blades could gain purchase and thrust in the hot, thin afternoon air.

\*

In the Divisional Headquarters in the partially finished and abandoned Basra Airport Hotel, the SO3 med ops was running through the options with his head on fire. The first constraint was that all he had to go on was the initial

Methane report, but the fact that the casualty was a child was a complicating factor. The British field hospital at Shaibah had no paediatric capability, and while the casualty could be stabilised at Shaibah, they would have to be moved elsewhere for further care. The coalition was now morally bound to make sure the casualty received the best treatment, and they, indirectly, had caused the accident. Politically, it would have been disastrous to dump the little girl off at a civilian hospital.

The second was the range of the helicopter. He looked at a map on the wall showing the maximum combat radii for each helicopter type. The American hospitals in the Baghdad area were excellent and had all disciplines. The Americans also had a can-do attitude, but Baghdad was beyond the Puma's range. There was a modern, well-equipped teaching hospital in Kuwait City, but there were cultural difficulties in moving what was probably a Shiite little girl to a Sunni country.

Thirdly, although technically all medical assets in the Divisional area were Divisional assets, this was often far from the case. There were different countries who had very different national caveats on who they could and wouldn't treat. He also knew from the Methane report that the medical team was going into a potentially explosive situation. He updated his log and wrote: *IRT wheels up 1725 L and estimated wheels down at incident around 1740.* He then started to make phone calls. He had fifteen minutes.

\*

The Puma swept over the Al Kadhim Grand Mosque, Gilmore in his favourite position behind the GPMG, legs dangling in the slipstream. The helicopter began its flare with a watercourse to port. Louise spotted the footbridge and pointed out the florescent fabric square of material pinned out in the dust. She didn't need to point out the crowd and the lines of people joining it from all directions.

"Bugger," she said, somewhat unnecessarily.

The two RAF regiment gunners were ready in the port door. They would be first out.

"Remember, lads. Discreet, low profile," Gilmore yelled.

They nodded and the Puma slowed, then they were out into the dust. A few moments later, the three medics followed, the FNA carrying a folding stretcher as well as a medical bergen. The helicopter lifted away and side slipped to starboard, the nose swinging round so that Gary could cover a hot withdrawal with the GPMG.

The FNO had her own radio and now she could talk directly to the SO3 med ops in the Joint Operations Cell (JOC) at Div HQ. She kept it brief: "This is Medic Zero-One. Wheels down 1737 and we're going on to the casualty."

Gilmore and Louise took stock of the situation, as the incident was on their side. Mount concentrated on keeping the Puma in a stable hover. The two vehicles were surrounded by a crowd. One was instantly recognisable as a Snatch Land Rover; the other was a white SUV. It seemed to be a camera team, with military minders.

"The cheeky bastards are filming the medics," Louise said, craning past the pilot to get a good view.

"She's right, Skipper."

"Go down and sort it out, Gary. That's just fucking outrageous."

Mount dropped the Puma while Gilmore undid his harness and unplugged the intercom. He jumped down and ran across the footbridge, seeking out the senior member of the military minders. It was a second lieutenant. He ignored the medics doing their job, working on an immobile, fragile, little body and looked at the crowd, a sea of hostile faces.

"Sir, you have to get these civilians out of here."

"We've tried but they want a story."

"Who's in charge of them?"

"The sound recordist, the prick with a furry dildo on a stick. The fragrant presenter is in the car getting ready to do a piece to camera."

Gilmore stalked towards the two who were filming. "Sir, would you please stop filming and get in your vehicle. The Iraqis don't like being filmed and this is medical in confidence."

The camera moved up from the medical team for a new angle on the story. "Listen, matey, we're just doing our job. Piss off and do yours. We can edit that out, can't we?" he said to the soundman.

Gilmore put his hand on the lens of the camera and rammed it back into the cameraman's face. The last piece on the film was the well-worn palm of his Glove, Flying, Desert, NATO Stock Number: 8415-01-040-1453.

"You bastard!" the cameraman yelled, holding his eye.

Gilmore went face-to-face with the sound recordist. "If you don't get in your fucking car, and fuck off out of here while you still can, I'm going to ram that fucking furry microphone right up your fucking arse. Do I make myself fucking clear?"

He went back to the lieutenant. "Sir, I think they've decided they've got enough for *Panorama*. Get them out of here."

Gilmore went to go back to the helicopter but noticed an Iraqi woman wearing a hijab. She was looking down at the little girl and was inconsolable with grief. He was struck with a thought. "Do you have an interpreter?"

The lieutenant pointed to a worried-looking Iraqi in civilian clothes with a blue covered flak jacket. "We have Mr Sharifa."

"Can we borrow him? We'll make sure that he gets back in one piece."

"Wellll, okay, seeing as how you were so nice to the media. And of course, if he'll go."

"Cheers, sir."

Gilmore went up to the interpreter and made the traditional Arab greeting: "*As-salāmu 'alaykum.* Mr Sharifa, would you please ask that woman if she is the little girl's mother."

He did and she was. Gilmore bent down next to the FNO who was on the radio, speaking with the JOC. "They want us to take her to the Japanese Field Hospital at Di Qar Province in Nasiriya."

"I'll let the skipper know. This is Mr Sharifa and he is an interpreter. That lady is the little girl's mother. I'm not telling you your job, ma'am, but I suggest she goes with us on the helicopter."

"It's your call, Gary."

The FNO stood up and held the mother's hand and looked at the interpreter. "Please tell the lady that her daughter has a broken hip and she is probably also hurt inside her body. We will need to take her to a hospital for them to X-ray her and fix whatever is wrong inside her body. She can go with her little girl, but she must come in the helicopter with us. Also tell her that although her little girl's eyes are closed, she can still hear, so ask her mother to talk to her daughter and not be frightened."

Gilmore made his way back to the helicopter and was relieved to see one of the gunners was keeping the bridge and their exfiltration route open. The Puma came down and he jumped on board and poked his head in the cockpit.

"The casualty is a little girl and we have two extra pax, the mother and an interpreter. But the best bit is, we have to fly her to the Japanese Field Hospital at Nasiriya.

"Do we have enough fuel, Louise?"

She made a few calculations that accounted for the extra payload. "Yes."

Gilmore saw that the medical team had got the little body onto the stretcher with a spinal board. The Land Rover and Land Cruiser were retracing their route, hopefully back to BAS. The medics were just lifting the stretcher when the first rock was thrown. Even from the helicopter he could sense the change in the mood of the crowd as the casualty was moved towards the aircraft. One rock became a fusillade, which became a shower, which became a storm. The medics were running with the stretcher across the footbridge, trying to shield the casualty, while the interpreter protected the mother.

"It's kicking off."

"I know, Gary. Just get them in, away from the doors. I'll get away and then we'll worry about strapping them in. You may have to help the civvies."

The stretcher was first in, followed by the mother and the interpreter. Gilmore helped them with the seatbelts while the medics hurried on board and just hung on. The gunners were last, and rocks were thudding into the ground and clanging off the rotor blades. The crowd surged forward.

"They're all aboard," he yelled.

The Puma surged upwards like an express lift and pivoted to head west out of the city, before heading north. Gilmore slammed the port door shut and finally remembered to put on his harness and plug in the intercom. The medics were working on and around the child on the stretcher, kneeling on the floor. She was wailing in pain and terror while the FNO began to put in a central line. Her mother was rocking with grief. Gilmore looked away, his eyes burning, and sat on the other side of the aircraft with the gunners.

"This is the bit that kills me."

The two gunners looked at each other and one raised his eyes.

Half the medical complement of the Field Hospital at Nasiriya seemed to be waiting for the Puma when it landed. The FNO handed the patient over and the last they saw was the stretcher on a trolley and the mother disappearing into the trauma unit.

The flight back was quiet and uneventful. The medics and gunners slept, the interpreter read the Koran and appeared to be praying. Gary stared out at the passing desert, an unfamiliar emptiness in his soul. When they landed, he bagged the medical waste and rubbish with the FNA, then wandered off to stare at the crimson sky and the setting sun. He squatted down and put his head in his hands.

Louise went out to smoke a cigarette; she was smoking too many, because her fingers were becoming stained with nicotine. Not good. She saw Gilmore crouched down, just beyond the pool of lights from the ops building, and her heart seemed to lurch. Of one thing she was certain. Despite his Jack-the-Lad bullshit, Louise loved Giles Gilmore more than he would ever know.

But Giles was married. She had seen his wife and little boy on the camp. Louise envied her and part of her even hated her. And she was an officer and Gilmore was a sergeant. Those little details still mattered to some people, people who had never felt the loving comradeship of those who had shared the grinding monotony and danger of operations. She threw the cigarette away and walked towards him.

He felt a hand on his shoulder.

"Are you all right, Gary?"

He stood up guiltily and pretended his eyes were tired.

"I know it's a bastard when it's kids," Louise said gently, "especially for you in the cheap seats. Come on, I'll get you a coffee."

Chapter 20

# THE LOADMASTER'S STORY

———

The aircraft movements woke him again, specifically a Nimrod MR4A blasting off at 10:00 hrs to commence its eighteen-hour patrol, hoovering up electronic intelligence with its ninety antennae. The Nimrod turned north and began the long cyclic patrol above Iraq, data pouring in from the sensors like Wiltshire Police Service's monitoring of sixteen-year-olds' Twitter accounts.

Gilmore knew that further sleep was impossible, so he chugged half a bottle of water and headed for the gym. It was a large, well-appointed and air-conditioned luxury, and one of the few benefits of being on ops, along with the food. He plugged himself into an MP3 player and listened to the Lightning Seeds' upbeat and cheerful ditties. He had run 5 miles and was halfway through a forty-minute stint on the cross trainer, when he became aware of someone lurking just behind his right shoulder, so he paused and turned round. It was his little friend, the MT driver.

She smiled. "Hello, Gary."

"Oh, hello, errr."

"Faye, I did tell you."

"Yes, you did. Sorry, Faye. What is it?"

"The SWO wants to see you and asked me specifically to come and get you. He said: 'Don't let the wriggling bastard get away and tell him it's a hat's on, no coffee type of meeting. And no, he hasn't been awarded the Air Force Medal.' Have you been up to something naughty, Gary?"

Gilmore mopped his brow with a green hand towel and wondered why the hell the station warrant officer wanted to see him.

"I'll need a shower first."

"He said: 'Once you've found him, don't let him out of your sight.'"

"Well, you can't come in the bloody shower with me. It would appear that I'm in enough trouble as it is."

Faye made a pretend pouty face.

*Fuck me, she really is a gorgeous little thing.* "You can wait in my Corimec and I promise I won't do a runner."

"Okay, Gary," she said brightly.

While Gilmore was in the ablution block, Faye discreetly went through his things. His pistol and holster were hanging over the end of the bed. Very naughty, as all weapons were supposed to go in the armoury when not in use. Typical bloody aircrew, a law unto themselves. There were bluies on the top shelf of his locker with a woman's writing on the address label. She definitely didn't want to look at those. His clothes and t-shirts were hanging up, just the smell of fresh laundry. A picture of a little boy of about two stuck on the inside of the locker door. That made her feel sad and empty. But she consoled herself with the thought that there was always a chance of detachment rules applying.

He came back with a towel wrapped round him and she was sitting on his bed.

"Err, Faye. You'll have to go out while I get changed."

"Oh yes, sorry. I'll wait in the Land Rover."

As they drove to the headquarters of the RAF contingent about ten minutes later, Gilmore asked if she knew why the SWO wanted to see him.

"No idea, but he said he wanted to speak to you before you spoke to anyone else."

The RAF admin cell was inside blast walls of Hesco bastions, and none of the Corimecs were air conditioned. As fitting for the most senior non-commissioned officer on the base, the SWO had his own office. Gilmore was wearing a beret rather than a floppy desert hat. He knocked and went in. The SWO was sitting behind a desk; a shaven, bullet-headed man with the RAF regiment mudguards on his shoulders. Gilmore came to attention, realising he was probably in the shit.

"Good morning, Mr Gilmore. I'll cut to the chase. Why did you twat a BBC cameraman and threaten to physically assault a sound recordist by inserting a large microphone up his rectum?"

Gilmore grinned. "So that's what this is about."

"It's no laughing matter, sunshine. The complaint against you has gone straight up to Multidivisional Headquarters and the general is involved. This is now an RMP matter and you are under investigation."

"That's complete bollocks, sir! I didn't twat anyone. I may have shouted at them because they were filming a medical incident in front of a hostile crowd, even when I asked them to stop. The situation was getting dangerous and in my opinion, by continuing to film an injured child, they were inflaming the crowd. I asked the cameraman to stop filming. He told me to piss off, so I pushed the camera down. It may have accidently caught him in the face."

The SWO nodded. "Did anyone else witness the incident?"

"The medics must have seen it."

"All right. Relax, Sergeant. I thought as much. The Army hate the fact the RAF run BAS and they are always making mischief. The fact one of the one-winged master race is involved is grist to their mill. You're caught up in a turf war and you'd think they would have more to worry about than who has the biggest willie on Basra Air Station.

"So here's what you are going to do. Stick to the story as you've told me. Play up them telling you to piss off. If there is any film, insist that they show all of it from at least thirty seconds prior to the incident. If they won't, tell them we have film from the medics' helmet cameras and this will show them refusing to obey a reasonable order in potentially a combat situation. I know your crew will back you up because the squadron commander has already spoken with them. You'll probably be interviewed by the red death tomorrow. Go in hard, Mr Gilmore."

Gilmore was stunned but grateful to the SWO. He came to attention and turned to leave when the SWO stopped him.

"A couple more things. Why, in the heat of the Babylonian desert, do you sport a hairstyle that makes you look like an ageing punk rocker?"

"Why, thank you, sir."

"And for God's sake, ask Flying Officer Skelton to wear some supporting undergarments. I find it extremely distracting to have to look at what amounts to two little boys fighting in a sack.

"I quite like it, sir."

"Get out!"

In the crew room, Gilmore's so-called colleagues had been busy decorating his flying helmet with black arrows cut from duct tape.

"Very fucking amusing," he told them.

"Gary, wouldn't it have been easier to just stop paying your television licence, rather than beating up BBC employees?" Mount said to him as they walked out to the aircraft at the beginning of their shift.

"Oh, not you as well, Skipper."

That afternoon, they moved cargo and people around the Basra area. The Puma was jam-packed full of the necessities a modern army needs to maintain a battle group in a city the size of Newcastle. Endless pallets of water and rations. Steel boxes of ammunition, replacement clothing and kit. Mail sacks. Army publication amendments that some poor bloody clerk would have to go through page by page.

They went into the Old State Building complex with an underslung load of ammunition and water in cargo netting. Gilmore hated flying into the Old State Building (OSB) because it was in the heart of bandit country, like Moss Side in Manchester crossed with Swilly in Plymouth. They came out at night… Mostly. RPG attacks were *de rigueur* around OSB, as were AK-47 unloads. Mount came in deftly over the RPG screens, the underslung load rock steady. The ground handlers were waiting to unhook it, stripped to the waist but wearing body armour and helmets with goggles, like a scene from a war fifty years earlier and a continent away. Gilmore noticed that the soldier who would unhook the lifting shackle didn't have a static hook.

The passage of carbon fibre rotor blades moving rapidly through the air tends to generate a great deal of static. This isn't usually a problem, as the helicopter earths itself while on the ground. However, while in the hover, the earthing point is usually through whoever touches the aircraft's hard points, such as undoing an underslung load. Gilmore was hanging out of the starboard door, calling out the height. The dust came up as the Tom went towards the shackle underneath the Puma. The load was down and the straps relaxed.

"Earthing hook!" he yelled at the Tom. The two troops behind him waved at the loadmaster, telling him to shut up.

"For fuck's sake!"

There was an audible whop, and the Tom screamed as he earthed the helicopter. His 'mates' were rolling on the floor laughing. He picked himself up and dragged the straps away.

"You evil bastards," Gilmore said, trying not to laugh himself.

"What was that, Gary?"

"The endlessly hilarious no earthing hook trick on some gullible idiot, Skipper."

"Oh, the oldies are the best," Mount said as the Puma climbed away.

*

It was getting dark and the air was full of unburned hydrocarbons from the GOSPs in the desert. He was drinking a coffee outside the Ops building with Louise, who was decorously smoking a cigarette. The welcome breeze was a cool nipple stiffener after the heat of the afternoon.

"These are the best times we will ever have, Gary," she said with a certainty he found surprising.

"Oh yeah? My life's just peachy at the moment, Louise."

She ground the cigarette out under her desert boot and sighed. "We're alive. People would pay good money to do what we do. I'm getting laid. You could be as well if you weren't getting laid somewhere else." She touched his arm in an intimate way, like they were a band of brothers, which of course they were, "because despite your testosterone-fuelled bullshit, you're a decent man, Gary. In twenty years, I'll have stretch marks, some kids and a nice, safe hubby. You'll have a gut and prostate problems. We'll remember standing outside an Ops building in Iraq and wonder what the hell we did with our lives. Andy Mount will of course be the Chief of the Air Staff, because everything he does seems to come so easily."

She lit another cigarette. "Faye's nice. I don't know how you can keep your hands off her."

And neither did he. "It's because of my barbed wire garter and the cold showers."

She laughed. "I've got corned beef sandwiches in my butty box. What about you?"

"Bloody tuna."

"I'll swap you."

"Done."

Three hours later, their empty Puma was rattling north towards Al Amarah. No cargo, no pax, just instructions to pick up four personnel and return them with all haste to BAS. They flared into the base at Al Amarah and their four passengers were waiting. It was the same four that they had dropped off on the outskirts of the city, less than forty-eight hours previously. They were dirtier and stank of stale sweat and nitrocellulose. Their faces were drawn and unshaven, but they still cuddled their weapons like they were the most important things in their lives. The hard-faced bastard with the sniper rifle sat down towards the back of the aircraft as though he were in a great deal of pain. Less than twenty minutes later, 500 feet above the Euphrates, it became obvious that he was.

One of them unbuckled and tapped Gilmore on the shoulder. "My oppo's in a bad way. He needs a piss."

"This isn't a rugby tour bus. We can't just pull into a lay-by," he yelled in the soldier's ear.

"He's got something wrong with his bladder. He has to go."

Gilmore looked at the man who was sweating with pain.

"Either you land and let him have a piss, or it's all over your deck."

Gilmore ran through the options. Landing? Out of the question. Sick bag? Recipe for disaster. He delved into his daysack and pulled out a flask. He emptied the tepid coffee out into the slipstream. Most of it went over his glove and up his arm.

"He can piss in that."

"You sure?"

It was a particularly nice flask, the type beloved by aircrew that doubled as a large insulated mug.

"Needs must."

They all turned away while the deed was done. The soldier handed back the flask. Gilmore suspected it would be slightly warm and damp to the touch.

"It's okay. He can keep it as a souvenir of the time when a Crab didn't take the piss."

The soldier laughed and emptied the flask out of the door. Rather irritatingly, none of it blew back in the slipstream.

# Chapter 21

# SERE

———

The following morning at 07:45 local, as Louise nestled closer to an engineering technician and cupped her warm breast with her hand, Gilmore was dreaming of flying pissoires that were full of holes, and hard-faced attendants that demanded a flask as conditions of entry.

A Mercedes saloon was sitting by a junction in the Al Jameea area of Basra City. The two men inside the vehicle were wearing Arab clothing and headdress. A few street kids were playing football before school and one of them mis-kicked the ball towards the Mercedes. The ball bounced off the passenger door and the man turned towards the boy as he ran up to retrieve the ball. He stared at the boy with cold, bright green eyes. Green eyes are not uncommon in Basra's Shia community. However, ginger hair is. The boy ran back and told his friends what he had seen. His friend told his brother. His brother told his friend. His friend was a mover and shaker in the JAM.

\*

Gilmore's ops phone went off an hour later.

"You awake, Gary?"

"Skipper, it's not nine yet."

"We're on the battle order. Now. Everyone is. The shit has well and truly hit the fan. Get your arse in now, Gary. No shave, shower or shit. Ten minutes. Grab Louise. I can't get her on the phone."

"She can't hear it because someone's thighs are wrapped round her ears."

"What?"

"Doesn't matter. I'll get her."

Fifty minutes later, they were hard turning above a seething and burning city of Basra. The Puma jinked around tracers and the smoke trails of RPGs reaching up for them. Gary was firing off the chaff and flares like confetti. The radar warning was going off every time they climbed above the skyline. Twelve Toms in the back of the cab were tooled up with full fighting order and extra ammunition. War faces were applied and locked in. No more hearts-and-minds bullshit. No more patrolling in soft headdress because some stupid senior officer thought it was a good idea and would look less threatening on the news. These boys were going to fight the JAM on their terms and they were fucking looking forward to it. They were going to kick arse and get the undercover team being held in the police station by the JAM. Gilmore was fairly certain he was going to get to fire the GPMG today. He was terrified.

"Gary, I'm putting them down on the cloverleaf junction. No fucking around if it's too hot. If anyone comes close, hose them down with the General."

*Be careful what you wish for*, Gilmore thought, and held up two fingers to the stick leader. They made ready while still in the aircraft. He did the same with the GPMG. He looked at the columns of smoke rising from the buildings. The sky seemed full of helicopters, and every road was choked with vehicles.

"It's the Al Markazi junction according to the map, two blocks from the police station and the first objective for the Warriors," Louise said, watching the roads and buildings ahead.

The Puma followed a descending, weaving course, and Mount aimed for a stretch of open ground just east of the junction with plenty of walls and buildings for cover. The helicopter flared in the dust and the troops were out and rapidly deploying while Gilmore covered them with the GPMG.

"They're clear."

The Puma rose and bowed forward, Mount making a rapid transit out of the area. Two hundred meters on their ten o'clock, a much faster Lynx rose up from between buildings heading to cross their path.

"Aircraft on ten o'clock, crossing our course."

"Seen."

Mount banked hard right and switched on the strobe light. The change of course was taking them towards the river at Arvand Rood and across Sinbad Island. Because the helicopter was hard banked to the right, Gilmore's body weight pressed him against the GPMG mount. The aircraft was at about 50 feet above the Shat al Arab waterway, when Gilmore to his horror saw the smoke and fiery rocket trails of two RPGs rise from the vicinity of the Fayhaa Mosque. At first, they moved slowly, but soon closed like an express train.

The first one hit the top of the pilot's cockpit door; the high-explosive anti-tank warhead sent shards of the projectile's casing into the cockpit, killing Flight Lieutenant Mount instantly. A large fragment entered Flying Officer Skelton's side just below her rib cage. It ploughed through her liver and lodged against her spinal cord in the vicinity of vertebrae T12. The hollow charge sent a supersonic jet of molten metal upwards, completely removing one rotor blade and damaging a second. The Puma's rotor head screamed and vibrated the gearbox to destruction. The second projectile hit the aircraft's tail just below the intermediate gearbox. The tail rotor shuddered to a standstill. By any accounts, it was an exceptionally good piece of shooting.

Louise Skelton tried to keep the helicopter stable, but she had no function or feeling below the waist. The shattered main rotor pitched the helicopter into a nose-up attitude and it immediately started to spin. She was so calm as she fought through her agony to save them. The gearbox warning was screeching, the rate of descent warning klaxon was bellowing, the ground proximity radar was yelling *Pull Up, Pull Up!*

"Mayday, Mayday, Argus Three-zero. I am hit and going down in vicinity of Sinbad Island, east of waterway."

Gilmore kicked away from the gun and grabbed the edge of the cockpit bulkhead as the spinning became nausea-inducing. The Puma slammed down in the reeds and soft mud on the eastern bank of the waterway. This may have absorbed some of the impact, but the front of the helicopter crushed backwards and was inundated with muddy water. Gilmore's rib cage rammed against the bulkhead; he felt ribs break and he screamed and screamed…

**From:** Lornagg1976@hotmail.co.uk
**Sent:** 30 October 2005 at 02:23
**To:** Giles.Gilmore@jhc644Sqn.mod.uk
**Subject:** Where are you, Giles?

Giles, my love,

I know that you'll never read this, because in my heart of hearts, I just know that you've gone on to wherever it is you were destined to go. This day started out so normally. I did some shopping and treated myself to a trip to Bicester Village and the garden centre. Danny slept most of the afternoon and I was preparing tea for us, when I saw the Station Commander, OC Admin and the Padre coming down the path. My heart stopped and I just wanted them to fuck off somewhere else, because they must have made a mistake.

But they hadn't. I think they were shocked that I barely said anything. I just wished they would go and leave me. They were nice and OC Admin sounded positive in as much that you were missing and not dead. But you are, aren't you? Something's gone from inside me.

Your mum phoned in hysterics. She heard about it on the fucking BBC. I can't be strong for all of us, Giles, not for me, Danny and your mother as well. I'll never meet anyone like you ever again. I'm just glad I had you when I did. I hope you didn't suffer, because I would rather that you were dead than wearing an orange boiler suit while those bastards cut your head off. I'll love you always. I can't write any more.

Lorna

*

The Nimrod MR4A had been replaced by a USAF Rivet Joint flying out of Incirlik in Turkey. The updated Boeing 707 was in a gentle holding pattern, 35,000 feet above Falluja. It was monitoring cell phone traffic and tens of thousands of bytes of data could be processed every few seconds, the sensors' electronic brains programmed to detect certain key words and phrases. CIA-trained interpreters would listen in to calls of interest.

Three consoles down towards the less glamorous rear of the aircraft, signals from two personal locator beacons (PLBs) suddenly appeared and were beamed back to the aircraft from a geostationary satellite over the Persian Gulf, one of many. The USAF master sergeant zoomed in her console to show Basra City and the surrounding waterways. She notified her supervisor.

"Captain, I think we've got a bird down in Basra."

"Really?" He looked over her shoulder at the city map and saw the two signals, so close together it looked like a single trace apart from the datum labels. "Let's get a real-time view from Cyclops."

The master sergeant manipulated the display via computer programme and the image of the city appeared on her console. They were viewing a real-time picture with a delay allowing for satellite links of a few seconds.

"It was by that island, down from the bridge. Can you superimpose the readout from the PLBs onto the real-time satellite telemetry?"

She shook her head. "No, but I can run the two displays in parallel."

She zoomed in and they saw the wreck of a helicopter, very badly mangled and partially obscured by reeds and vegetation at the side of the river.

"One of ours?"

"Don't think so," he said. "Brit, probably a Puma, certainly not a CH 47."

"One of them is on the move."

They watched the red dot marking the last known ping move south along the river, leaving a trail of green dots marking the progress.

"I can't see him. Can you zoom in?"

"They must be in the undergrowth, as I'm at max magnification. How do you know it's a he?"

"Sorry, sexist assumption."

## Survive

*Ladies and gentlemen, your survival will be the most catastrophic event of your lives. You are alive, but you are at your weakest and most vulnerable. The decisions that you make in the next ten minutes will ultimately decide whether you have grandchildren, or come home in a flag-draped coffin. The problems you will face at the beginning of the ordeal are exactly the same faced by the crew of a Lancaster bomber who have bailed out, or a paratrooper who has been accidently dropped in the wrong area behind enemy lines.*

*At this point, your duty is to continue the fight by other means. It is time to repay the taxpayer for your training and for you, members of the one- and two-winged master race, it's no longer about poncing around in your growbags, looking cool. Your sworn duty is to survive, evade, resist and extract.*

The interior of the Puma was a shambles, the aircraft lying partially on its port side. Half of the interior was full of stinking, muddy water. Gilmore groaned and pulled himself into the cockpit, having to push the pilot's body out of the way. The instrument panel had come forward and seemed to be pinning Louise's bloody legs. He went in further until his back was resting on the panel and he twisted to get to her face. There was a searing bolt of agony in the side of his chest and he contemplated passing out again.

"Louise, you okay?"

She wasn't breathing so Gilmore wriggled his fingers into each side of her helmet and felt for the angles of the jaw, hooking his index and middle fingers behind the angle of the mandible. He put his thumbs on her cheekbones and gently pulled her jaw forward. Louise gasped, coughed and showered his face with bright red frothy blood.

"Is that you, Gary? I can't see."

"It's all right, Lou, I'm here. You've got blood in your eyes, only a bit. I'll get you out."

She felt for his face and caressed it. "You'd better get out of here, Gary."

"I'm not leaving you!"

"Gary, I'm going to die. There's something inside me and it's done terrible damage. I can't feel anything below my chest and my legs are smashed to fuck."

"Oh, Louise," he sobbed.

"Stop grizzling, Gary, and go."

Despite his pain, he hugged her. "Oh, Louise."

"I always loved you, Gary. Does that surprise you?"

"Yes." He was weeping openly now.

"Fuck off, Gary, while you still can."


## Evade

*It is vital that you have a plan. Something to work towards; otherwise, events will overwhelm you. Be sure of what you are doing, your goal and how to achieve it. But at this point, your overwhelming consideration must be to put as much distance between you and your ejection, crash site or landing point as possible.*

He headed south, following the course of the river, which was too wide to swim across. There was a pontoon bridge by the zoological gardens and he might be able to cross it in the water, moving from one pontoon to another. He was aiming for the British base that was at Basra Palace. He could hear helicopters but none of them came close enough for him to show himself. It was very boggy underfoot in the reeds and his progress was slow. He could hear shouting and vehicles from his left. Someone was obviously looking for him.

In the distance behind him, he heard men shouting *Allahu Akbar* and firing in the air. They had found the helicopter. He tried not to think of Louise, part of him hoping she had died quickly. The injury to his chest was slowing him down and he was gasping for breath. He would have to go to ground.

*You should keep moving unless injury or the enemy's physical presence demands that you hide up. If a location is obvious to you, it will be obvious to those who are searching for you.*

In a creek joining the river from the north, he came across a pipe, or conduit, and it was just big enough for him to wriggle into. It was a sewage pipe, but he was beyond caring.

\*

"I think he's stopped moving. And let's not get bogged down with the PC bullshit. I'm assuming it's a he, which is reasonable."

There was a sizable group huddled round the console. "There's a group of bad guys following him on the road above the riverbank. They must have others in the undergrowth. They're good."

The immobile dot at the crash site disappeared off the screen.

"They've found the bird," the master sergeant observed.

The group on the road moved down towards the riverbank, heading towards the immobile red dot. It didn't move, and ten minutes later, it too disappeared.

"They've got him."

## Resist

*This is not going to be pleasant hearing for many of you. With all respect for the brave lads of Bomber Command, you won't have the luxury of a roughing-up in Dulag Luft, where a frightfully civilized German officer offers you a cigarette. There will be no Stalag Luft III where you can dig tunnels, forge documents and sing Christmas carols.*

*Ladies. You are going to be raped many times and continually by many different men. Gentlemen, you will be forced to watch your female comrades abused and beaten, then it will be your turn. The filth who have you don't care what sort of orifice it is. It's just another way of stamping their authority, barbarity and control over you.*

*And one day, sooner or later, they will drag you in front of a camera and very slowly, they will cut your head off. Reflect on that and decide on which way you want to die.*

They dragged Gilmore out of the conduit and stripped him of his body armour, smock, boots and trousers. His Glock was waved in front of his face, and he cursed, because like the unmilitary PONTI that he was, he had forgotten all about it. They found the PLB and smashed it up, before dragging him to a waiting people carrier where he was hooded and thrown inside. The men with him reeked of filth and tobacco. In the back of the vehicle, Gilmore received the first of many beatings. There was no hardbody bitch wearing just skimpy bra and pants, laughing at the size of his cock and blowing cigarette smoke in his face. He wasn't forced to stand in stress positions against a wall. The fists, boots and rifle butts were very hard and very real and very painful.

He could tell despite the stinking hood that the vehicle was going across a bridge back into the city. He even knew that he was heading west because of that innate sense of direction that aircrew develop. He also knew that he was a high-value catch and he was deeply in the shit. They dragged him out of the vehicle and dragged him down two flights of stairs to some kind of basement. Judging by the smell of oil and fuel, it was a garage of some kind. He was thrown against the wall and the hood was dragged off. It was an underground car park. Then there followed the inevitable ritual of a few kicks and slaps, some random and pointless spitting in his face and some nice selfies where various assorted Iraqis gurned to mobile phone cameras, holding Gilmore's hair, which he had allowed to grow to a convenient length. Then someone pissed on him and how they laughed. In fact, they all thought it such a good idea they were queuing up to empty their bladders on one of the Royal Air Force's finest, in between the odd random twatting with an AK-47 butt.

Then they left, leaving Gilmore to be guarded with a lad who couldn't have been much older than sixteen. His AK was real enough, though. Gilmore looked at the lad and smiled. He looked away, scowling with a certain self-importance. He was in charge. Gilmore studied him. It soon became obvious that this lad was simple. To describe him with a word that Gilmore hated, the boy was a retard. His eyes burned with self-importance, but he was a gap-toothed simpleton, a few chromosomes short of a picnic.

*Your first few minutes after capture are crucial. The longer that you are held by the enemy, the deeper into their system you will go. The more difficult it will be for us to find you and for you to escape. You must take your chance as and when it arises.*

"Do you want to see a trick?"

The boy stepped back and shouted something in Arabic. Nobody came to see what was going on. Okay, might be promising.

"I can pull my thumb off."

The boy spat at him.

"Seriously, I can."

Gilmore showed him the timeless trick of pulling his thumb off by deftly manipulating his hands. The boy's eyes widened and he leaned in, then realised what an important job he had been given and stepped back, unslinging the AK.

"Can I have a cigarette, please?" Gilmore asked, and made a pretence of smoking with his hand.

The boy grinned. His teeth were manky. "Fuk yoo," he said, and laughed.

Gilmore smiled and held up his thumb again. The boy leaned closer.

"I'll show you how, for a cigarette."

The thumb came away from the rest of the hand, yet again. Gilmore showed him his open hand.

"No thumb here. See?"

The lad grinned and leaned further forward. Gilmore rammed his index and middle fingers into the boy's eyes. He felt an eyeball burst and was nauseated and disgusted with himself. The boy screamed and clutched his face as vitreous humor trickled past his fingers down his face. Gilmore forced himself to remember a dying Louise and he rammed the butt of the AK into the boy's face. He was screaming with the high-pitched wail of a child. He was up and trying to drag the rifle away from the boy, but the sling was twisted round his neck. Gilmore was on his feet and he was stamping hard down with his heel. He felt the boy's nasal cartilage break under his foot and the screaming stopped.

Out of here. Which way? Stairs? No, they'll be having a fag at the top. Up the ramps. The coarse concrete hurt his feet but soon he was out in an alley, blinking in the harsh midday sunlight. He ran down the alley, the rubbish shredding the soles of his feet.

*I'm out, I'm fucking well out!*

The car hit him from the side and he thudded up the bonnet and over the roof. Something went inside. There were at least four that arrived and proceeded to beat him to a pulp. This was the mother of all beatings and he went under gratefully, through a pink mist of his own blood.

\*

He didn't know how long he had been awake. His head felt twice its normal size. His back and kidneys ached. His liver was burning and he could barely see out of his swollen eyeballs. The man in the suit spoke to him; Gilmore's head lolled forward and he puked bloody bile. The man in the suit started screaming at the other men with guns, incandescent with rage. He slapped one of them around the head, gesticulating to the bloody body in the corner, sitting in its own blood, piss and vomit.

That evening, they moved him. Very gently this time. Gilmore drew back into himself. He knew he was going to die, but he conserved enough strength and moral fibre to be sure he would take the man wielding the knife with him.


**Extract**


*Never give up hope. If we can find you, we will come and get you. All the assets we have at our disposal will be applied to come and save your arse. When we come, do everything we tell you to. It will be sudden, very noisy and very violent.*


\*


Satellites had scoured the city in all modes. Tornado GR4s flew endless sorties above the city with their RAPTOR Pods, but it was an Mk I eyeball that found him. An eyeball belonging to a young woman who had grown up in Derby, had failed her GCSEs and whose dad had the sense to insist that she went to college and pass English and Maths. A daughter who joined the army at eighteen as a supplier, who saw a notice in *Daily Orders* for volunteers for duties of an arduous and unusual nature.

Now she was just another woman in an Arab city. Shrouded from head to foot in a chador, from which her beautiful eyes peered. The car hooted angrily at her and she dropped the washing she had been carrying. As she picked up the folded clothes and dusted them off, she watched the car grind to a halt and three men drag out a body wearing Service issue boxers and a brown t-shirt. Because she was just another, shrouded and oppressed, worthless woman in an Arab city, nobody took the slightest notice of her. This piece of chattel had a Glock under her chador and a Fairbairn Sykes fighting knife tucked into her knickers. She also had a VHF radio, throat mike and earpiece, and she clicked her jaw to activate the radio.

"I've got him. Position as follows…"

\*

Gilmore could tell it was dark because the air smelled differently. They had carried camera, sound and lighting equipment into the room next to where he lay chained to a radiator. Tomorrow, they were going to decapitate him. Tonight, they would give him a drink, heavily laced with drugs to make him dopey and compliant. He would stare at the camera, glaze-eyed, while they sawed through his neck. Well, fuck them! He was going to go down fighting. He would make himself sick rather than ingest the tranquilisers. He thought about how he was going to kill the knifeman. It was difficult with arms tied behind the back. Perhaps smashing his head, thick frontal bone first into the nose and maxilla area. With any luck, he would knock himself out. Anyway, a knifeman with blood pissing down his face wouldn't look too good on Al Jazeera. Gilmore smiled grimly.

"Fuk yoo, Tommy. Tomorrow choppy-chop," his guard said, seeing him smile.

"Fuck you, you inbred piece of Mohammed shit. The best part of you dribbled out of your dad's camel's arse. Your mother fucked goats coz they are better at fucking than your…"

The door blew in off its hinges and Gilmore instinctively went down. Three stun grenades went off in quick succession and Gilmore's eardrums went with them. Four men piled into the room and the guard disappeared in a red mist.

"GILMORE, STAY DOWN!" someone yelled. He knew what would happen next, and he went lower than a snake's genitalia.

Chapter 22

# THE WOMAN FROM
# THE 'DET'

---

*The Special Reconnaissance Regiment, or SRR, is a special reconnaissance unit of the British Army. It was established on 6 April 2005 and is part of the United Kingdom Special Forces (UKSF) under the command of Director Special Forces, alongside the Special Air Service (SAS), Special Boat Service (SBS) and the Special Forces Support Group (SFSG).*

*The regiment conducts a wide range of classified activities related to covert surveillance and reconnaissance. The SRR draws its personnel from existing units and can recruit male and female volunteers from any branch of the British Armed Forces. (Wikipedia)*

It is very difficult to get a poor post-operational report unless you clash severely with someone in your command chain or you are a complete tube. SAC Khan's post-operational report was by any measure absolutely exceptional and it was signed off by the Director of UK Special Forces. She was interviewed by the station commander of RAF Marham and congratulated. Two days later, a man in a dark civilian suit interviewed her in the station's conference and briefing facility. He was well-spoken and his eyes never left hers, which she found disconcerting.

"Ms Khan, have you ever heard of a unit known as the Special Reconnaissance Regiment?"

"No."

"I have some literature that I would like you to read. It is of a rather sensitive nature and you should not let it out of your sight. When you have read and thoroughly understood it, please give it to the chief clerk or station duty officer for safekeeping. I would like you to consider the offer we are making on the final page."

That was it; he gave her a card with just his name and a military telephone number, shook her hand and left. She read it and reread it several times that late morning and afternoon, then made her way to the station headquarters and the chief clerk.

"I was given this paperwork this morning, Flight. I would like to formally apply for special duties."

"Are you sure? This will be for years, not just a few months on an operational tour."

It was as though he had been expecting her. He had.

"Honestly, I've thought it through and made my mind up."

"He sighed. "All right, but think it through again tonight and if you're sure, come back in the morning and we'll start the ball rolling as far as the paperwork goes. You'll need to go for a briefing at Command HQ and from now on, everything to do with this is classed a Secret UK Eyes Only. That includes everything you say. For what it's worth, I think you're incredibly brave. You've proved that, but the next few years if you're successful will be grinding and gruelling. You may not come out of it at the other end the person you were when you went into it. You may not come out of it at all. Think on that, SAC Khan."

*

It started with medicals and aptitude tests. They became progressively harder as did the physical training. Five-mile runs became ten, then fifteen. Then carrying weight. One-hour circuit training followed by a swim and then a run. She would be woken in the early hours and made to do aptitude tests. She was taught how to memorise things by word association, then made to run to checkpoints and memorise the contents of cached ammunition boxes. She would have to run to a certain place, reconnoitre it then run back and produce a scale tactical map.

The training became progressively harder. She was kept awake and given no food and water for what seemed like days. She was stripped and hosed down in a cell with a fire hose, while men would laugh at her as she tried to cover herself. She was interrogated, beaten and hurt in extremely cunning ways that left no marks. And all the time there were less and less of them. She lost count of the number of times she wanted to jack it in, but some perverse attitude kept saying *fuck them*.

She spent endless hours on a range firing various hand guns and machine pistols. Never stationary. She fired out through the windscreens of cars and learned to drive defensively and aggressively with police drivers, clocking up speeds of over 100mph through country lanes. Then she learned how to fight with knives, everyday objects and knees, elbows and hands, never fists and always in defence. Makeup artists from London theatres showed them how to change their appearance and gender with theatrical makeup and wigs. Members of the Magic Circle showed them how to perform sleight of hand tricks and conceal objects around and in their bodies. She was taught how not to walk and run like a girl.

The culmination of their training consisted of her syndicate being given a target of strategic importance. A nuclear power station; a high security prison; a prominent, well-guarded person; an airport or a crucial military establishment. The syndicate would research and reconnoitre their given objective. Produce detailed models and plans of the target and fully understand its everyday routine and workings. Then they would separately plan a means of infiltration and carry out their given task. There followed a Character Assassination Group (CAG), where the syndicate members would forensically tear the plan to pieces and pick holes. The person whose plan they all thought had the best chance of success was elected team leader.

Afarin's plan was voted as being the second worst, and using the best plan, her syndicate infiltrated an RAF airfield in Scotland. In broad daylight, they placed a teddy bear wearing a fake explosive belt in the cockpit of a Tornado F3 in the Quick Reaction Alert Hardened Aircraft Shelter. They also left a bright red oil drum marked *Bomb* in the cellar area of the officers' mess bar, and stole the station commander's car from outside SHQ. The station commander, who was also AOC Scotland, was in it at the time.

She had done it. She had taken the exhaustion, abuse, physical and mental pain and self-doubt and got through. The little girl from Derby was now a member of the 'Det'.

*

It was always the kids that provided the signpost. Follow the gutter rats to find out where the action is. This area of Basra was a ghastly sprawl of poorly constructed, single-storey buildings, set in a filthy, rubbish-strewn district north of the Abu Mustafa markets. She glanced across at the other side of the street where her shadow was keeping sight of her. Malik was dressed as a poor workman; his beard was unkempt and his dish-dash filthy from the engines and vehicles he was supposed to be working on. She was shrouded in a chador, the all-covering garb favoured by Shia Muslim women in the predominantly Shia city of Basra. She was a washer woman, a basket of washing balanced on her head. She even shimmied her arse like the Shia women, because she had been taught to walk like them.

She was the eyes. Malik was her backstop, her protection in the febrile atmosphere of a city in the midst of insurrection. Two hundred metres behind them was a Toyota pick-up, their Q-car with the heavy artillery should the shit really hit the fan. The Jaysh al-Mahdi (JAM) had already taken two SAS undercover operatives who should have known better that morning, and the insurgents were not in the mood for finding more on their doorstep. They were following the trickles of the street urchins northwards, and more heavily armed men, wearing the black of the JAM, were apparent, lurking on roofs and in alleyways. Ahead was the only substantial building in this slum district, the brutalist two-storey architecture of the Muwafaqiya Police Station.

She made a close observation as she approached, noting the aerials and satellite dishes on the roof, along with the myriad of black-garbed JAM armed with assorted rocket propelled grenades (RPGs) and AK-47s. The British were reaping the fruits of their inability and unwillingness to occupy and police Iraq's second largest city. The JAM had poured into the vacuum and they now effectively ran the city. The building was surrounded by RPG screens, a throwback to a time before the British Army handed it back to the criminally corrupt Shia police force. She made an unobvious circuit of the building, remembering doorways, windows, loading bays and all ways in and out of the complex. On the last quarter, a member of the JAM came up to her and shouted in accented Arabic:

"Get out of here, you disgusting split-arse. Why are you not with a chaperone?"

"I am a widow, and I must make a living collecting washing. My children have to eat," she replied in Arabic, avoiding eye contact. She suspected this man was Iranian, possibly Revolutionary Guard.

He kicked her. "Get away. You disgust me."

She hurried back down the street while her shadow watched the JAM militiaman. Bored with his misogyny, he went back into the police station. Two blocks away, the Toyota pick-up was waiting. Malik got in the cab with the other two men. Afarin naturally got in the back because she was a woman. The rear glass window was slid open and as they headed back to the safe house, Afarin told them what she had observed.

"You take too many risks," Malik told her in a mixture of annoyance and concern.

"At least we now know where the JAM are holding them. They'll need to move fast."

*

Their safe house was in Al Quiba in the south of the city, a nondescript house that was in turn kept under observation from another safe house of the second team. When the Toyota arrived, the men went straight into the building, leaving Afarin to struggle out of the back of the pick-up with her washing. To have done otherwise would have invited suspicion. Two men were already inside waiting for them to return. Although they were both wearing Arab headdress and clothing, one was an intelligence officer, the second a captain in the SAS.

"Give us ten minutes while we produce some drawings and maps."

While Malik drew a tactical map with ranges and datum points, Afarin drew a plan, elevation and three-dimensional view of the police station. It was draughtsman's quality and would be used for briefing the assault teams. Because she had been the 'eyes', Afarin briefed their two visitors.

"Could we have a team rappel down from a helicopter onto the roof?"

She shook her head. "Too many obstructions on the roof to tangle your rappel ropes, plus there's a sangar of sandbags which is manned. The chopper would be a sitting duck."

"Okay then," the SAS officer said, looking at the drawing of the police station, "what's the best way in?"

"Through the eastern side of the building where the loading bay is. You'll need to go through the wire with some big vehicle, such as a tank, while you distract the JAM round the other side."

They rolled up the map and drawing and shook the hands of the team. They seemed almost humbled by the level of risk taken and the commitment.

"Gents, lady, you are truly remarkable and brave people," the SAS captain said without a flicker of bullshit, because he knew when his teams went in, they had all the firepower they could handle. That evening, they would get their men out.

The special reconnaissance team had done their job and thought that they would get the rest of the day to clean weapons and see to personal admin. Afarin was desperate for a long soak in a bath, a proper bath, but it wasn't to be. The team leader's sat phone went off just before 11:00 hours. He listened and then his face became grim.

"A Puma has gone down east of the Arvan Rood waterway, near Sinbad Island. No word on casualties but the CSAR team needs to pinpoint it. And we're it again. We'll take both the Toyota and the Passat. Afarin and Malik in the Toyota, me and Percy in the Passat. Fully tooled up. Fuck subtlety, just find them."

"What do we know about the crew?" asked Afarin as she put on a shoulder holster and then the chador.

"Three. Male pilot, flight lieutenant; female co-pilot, flying officer; and a sergeant loadie, male. No names as yet."

Afarin got in the cab of the Toyota this time, and in the footwell, within easy reach, was a Remington 870 shotgun with a folding stock and an H&K MP5A3. They headed north-west towards Dur el Naft and turned right to follow Dinar Street, which runs parallel to the Shat al Arab waterway. They kept the Passat in sight as it turned to cross the huge bridge that crossed both the waterway and Sinbad Island. The sky was full of helicopters and the air was rank with burning tyres. They turned off the main highway once across the waterway, past the Al Jazeera building and were in the heart of bandit country, Firuziyah District. "Follow the kids," Afarin told Malik and as they drove past the Fayhaa Mosque, they saw a large and gathering crowd ahead of them.

The Passat was ahead of them and it pulled in when it became obvious the crowd was too dense. They saw Percy get out of the car and look back at them.

"Stop here, I'll go in on foot. You'll have to stay here with the wagon and the artillery."

She got out of the Toyota and did a quick radio check to establish contact with all of the team members. She headed towards the crowd while Percy hung back to cover her. The atmosphere was febrile with much shouting of *Allahu Akbar* with associated firing in the air. The crowd were mainly civilians with, as yet, few black-clad members of the JAM in sight. She pushed into the heart of the throng and saw what looked like two bodies being carried by men in old tarpaulins. A member of the clergy seemed to be directing operations and she pushed in closer. The bodies were dressed in desert flying coveralls. One had a ruin of a head and upper body and he, she assumed it had been a he, was quite obviously dead.

The second tarp contained the body of a woman. They had removed her flying helmet and a shock of auburn hair hung over the edge of the tarp. Her eyes were closed and she looked almost serene until Afarin saw the mangled lower limbs. She looked at the striking, peaceful face and remembered a vibrant young RAF helicopter pilot on an Armed Forces recruitment stand, in a Derby college. She turned away, tears prickling in her eyes.

Afarin keyed her throat mike. "Positive ID numbers two bodies. Repeat two only. Co-pilot definitely, possibly the pilot as well. Mobile one, suggest recce of possible landing site for CSAR."

After a few minutes, it became clear that there was a definite rift within the crowd. The civilian contingent carried the bodies towards the precincts of the mosque, and the members of the JAM wanted to take the bodies. Even corpses can be bargaining chips. There was a heated stand-off until two Merlin helicopters swept low across the buildings and landed in a sports stadium close to the mosque. The undercover team, which had marked the landing site, watched; the Merlins disgorged around fifty troops of the CSAR recovery teams. They were very heavily armed and while half fanned out to secure the landing site, the others headed for the mosque. There was a brief exchange of fire until the outnumbered JAM melted away. The undercover team waited for the crowd to dissipate and then headed back to the safe houses for updated orders.

"So where's the third one, the loadie?" Afarin asked rhetorically. They knew they wouldn't be getting much sleep over the next forty-eight hours.

*

"Right, let's look at what we know. According to the USAF Rivet Joint, at around 12:00 today, the signal from Gilmore's PLB went off air in this area where the Hassan River meets the Shat al Arab," the team leader said, pointing at the location on the map. "From that, we have to assume he was captured by the JAM. Now what would you do if you had him? Malik?"

"Into Iran quickly, before we set up border surveillance at the crossings."

"Percy?"

"Up to Amarah then across the border into Iran at Chaddabeh."

"Afi?"

"I don't think the Iranians would want him on their soil. Politically too controversial. I think he's back in the city in one of their strongholds and they'll keep moving him… until…"

"Until when?"

"They're going to kill him and film it, like they did with those American security operatives and hung the bodies on the bridge in Fallujah. They're not interested in exchanging him for some bottom feeders in the JAM. They want to show the world and more importantly, the Iraqi Sunni population, how powerful they are. The Shia, that is."

There was a shaken silence in the room.

"And there's two undercover teams, eight people to cover an entire city."

"Not quite," Malik pointed out. "We can discard certain areas, such as downtown, the ministries and close to our bases. And there are the Special Forces covert teams."

"One of which has just had to be rescued from a police station, so that just leaves sixty percent of the city," Afarin observed quietly, looking at the map.

\*

They knew they were facing an impossible task, even with the satellites and Tornado GR4s that made constant passes over the city with their RAPTOR pods. Less than thirty undercover people were looking for one person in a city the size of Newcastle. The regular Army patrols were predictable and it was impossible to search every house, garage or industrial building, had they known where to look in the first place.

It was 16:30 when Afarin made her eighth sweep of a city area on foot. She was in the Al Hayyaniyah district having been dropped off with her basket of washing. Their vehicles had to keep moving because occupied parked cars were immediately suspicious, and unoccupied strange vehicles had the tendency to be regarded as a bomb. She was beginning to feel despondent as the enormity of their task struck home. They had been passed a photograph of the man they were looking for and she had memorised his impossibly handsome face with his just-long-enough-to-get-away-with-it hair. *You poor bastard*, she thought.

It was an unlovely slum of mainly single-storey houses, chaotic shops and garages and storage buildings. A seething mass of humanity with endless places a person could be hidden. Fate plays a hand in all the endeavours of mankind. Napoleon recognised this when he said to his marshals, "Yes, I know you're good, but are you lucky?" Perhaps God had other plans for an insignificant dot of humanity called Giles 'Gary' Gilmore.

As Afarin shimmied across a road junction, just another bint in an Arab city carrying a basket of washing, a car turning right nearly hit her. The driver hooted angrily and she jumped back, dropping the basket. She looked into the car as it swept past imperiously. Two men in the front, dark glasses. She couldn't see into the back because of the tinted windows, but she felt something in her guts. Morrison used to call it his spidey senses and she smiled to herself at the memory. She made a show of carefully picking up and dusting off the washing and watched the car covertly but carefully. It pulled in halfway down the street and the two men got out of the front and one man from the rear-left side. He went round to the other rear door and pulled out a body. Hooded and slumped, but Afarin recognised the bloody brown issue t-shirt and soiled black issue boxer shorts. The man could barely walk and was in a bad way. She clicked her jaw to activate the throat mike. "I've got him. Position as follows…"

She waited until they disappeared inside a building and went down the street on the opposite side to the car. For the next half-hour, she conducted a close recce of the building front and back, getting in as close as she dared, memorising everything, air con boxes, drainpipes, windows, mainly barred, doors and what she could see of the roof. She was glad when the second team was in place to relieve them and she finally extracted back to the Toyota. She clambered in the cab and Malik was beaming at her.

"Fucking good effort, Afarin. Time is as they say of the essence. We're to go straight back to BAS. Percy took some photos of the surrounding area where they can get a chopper in. The assault team is going in tonight. You're a bloody star!"

"We got lucky, Malik. Or rather Mr Gilmore got lucky. Let's hope we're in time."

*

She had borrowed a T-shirt and trousers that were far too big for her, because she had been wearing nothing apart from pants under her chador. She felt dirty and dishevelled. She was still wearing sandals when she went in front of the assembled bad-arses to brief them. Afarin loathed speaking in public and blinked nervously in front of the thirty-odd members assembled in the Divisional Headquarters briefing room. There was the main four-man assault team and four more back-ups. The force protection who would secure the area, the drivers, helicopter crews and medics. The ground teams were all armed, faces and hands blackened, and looked at her expectantly as she was introduced by J2 Int as 'the eyes'.

Afarin started off by outlining the ground area, routes in and out, helicopter landing points and RV points. The Int boys and girls had been busy putting a PowerPoint presentation together, which included images taken from the Tornado RAPTOR pods. Her precise drawings had been scanned and included in the presentation. As she spoke, her glance swept across the audience and she faltered when she looked at the assault team at the front of the audience. Henry Morrison was looking at her coolly and Jarvis was giving her a broad grin.

*Oh fuck!*

Stumbling over her words, she kept going, but she could feel her face burning. Henry looked away, a strange expression on his face. She was glad to finish the scripted bit, but the questions were endless. The helicopter crews wanted to know about power lines and obstructions in and out of the LZ. The state of the ground on the LZ regarding FOD. Rotor clearances. Dust state on the ground. Bright lights in the area that could glare out the NVGs. The assault teams wanted to know how many were in the building, the state of the windows, obstructions inside the walled complex. Afarin felt like telling the hard-faced bastard with the broken nose that she hadn't exactly been able to knock on the door and invite herself in. Jarvis just smiled dreamily at her. Henry studiously avoided eye contact.

Once they had wrung all of the information out of her like a dishcloth, Afarin gratefully sat down and swigged water while the assault and back-up teams conducted some very quick and dirty planning. She was exhausted and listened to brief snatches of their conversations.

"Go in with unmarked vehicles. Frame charge for the main door. In through the roof too risky. Bars on back windows. Spare frame charges for locked internal doors. Cooper, you carry the frame charges. Jarvis, you place 'em. One way in. No time to secure houses either side. Flash-bangs, shitloads of them. No CS. Clear entire house once Gilmore's extracted. No NVGs, too constraining and they're always going tits-up. Take anything like phones, papers, laptops, flash drives. Go in with unmarked vehicles, out on the Merlin once the Chinook, Gilmore and the medics have fucked off to Shaibah. Booby trap the door? No, danger of civilian casualties, you know what the fucking kids are like. Don't want 'em getting a gob full of Mr Claymore's finest. Right, that's the plan, vote. For? Against? Fuck's sake, why, Cooper? I can't carry three fucking frame charges. I'll take two. Jarvis, the first one for the main door. Okay, agreed."

"We have a plan, Stan. Let's go and get our Crab friend."

And then they were gone. Afarin went for a shower and went back to the briefing room, to hang around with the Int team and the Det teams. They all felt like Barnes Wallis waiting for the signal to come back from the Ruhr Dams.

*

The night smelled of thick, heady tobacco smoke, hydrocarbons from the GOSPs and the stench of raw sewage coming off the Tigris. No dogs were barking, unlike in other cities. The only sounds were snatches of wailing, caterwauling Jinglie music from a distant radio. Edge was crouched in the deep shadows between two parked cars. His personal radio was turned down low, its earpiece taped in his ear, throat mike in position. He was wearing SBAV sentinel body armour with groin protection, as he would be going in first. Morrison was just behind him, talking very softly on the radio.

"Red team in position. Radio check."

"Two," said Edge.

"Three," came Jarvis's voice.

"Four," Cooper affirmed.

"Blue team ready," came over the net. Edge recognised the voice as Moose.

"Go, go, go!"

There was an explosion from the roof of the building. The external lights went out and Jarvis scurried along the wall, carrying a large elliptical object, which was effectively a plastic frame holding a circle of C3 explosive. He went through the gap in the wall and Edge and Morrison waited either side of the gap and were joined by Cooper, carrying more frame charges. Edge was armed with his standard C8 Carbine while Morrison carried a Remington 870 shotgun, loaded with Hatton breaching rounds, solid shot to blow off door hinges and locks. A Hatton or Breaching round is 12 Gauge and weighs 1.4 ounces. It is composed of powdered steel or copper with a wax binder. It is designed to destroy locks, deadlocks or hinges, without harming anyone within the room beyond. However, in an enclosed space up to twenty feet it is lethal. Like Cooper and Jarvis, his C8 was rear slung. Assault operations was one of the few occasions SF troops used slings. They were all carrying respirator haversacks packed with stun grenades, and wearing ski masks.

Moving quickly, Jarvis placed the frame charge against the main door, clamping it in place on the upright jambs. He pulled the fuse toggle and turned to move back out into cover. The fuse may have been faulty and the frame charge went off prematurely, catching Jarvis in the blast. He was blown off his feet, his smock and trousers burning. He was beating out the embers when Edge and Morrison went over him, followed by Cooper. There was no time to go to assist their comrade, who was for the moment on his own.

Edge went through the doorway, the torch taped to his C8 sweeping the hallway, which was full of choking smoke. At the end was a door. Edge pointed the torch at the handle and Morrison blew off the lock. They each threw a stun grenade into the room, then they both hammered through the door, Edge going left, Morrison right. A man in a long robe was standing over a body cowering on the floor. Edge fired a three-round burst at the standing man's centre of mass and he slid down his own blood on the wall. Somebody appeared from a doorway on the right and Morrison blew in the man's chest with a Hatton round.

Somebody yelled: "GILMORE, STAY DOWN!" Edge looked at the cowering body and realised that it was chained to the radiator. "Gilmore?"

"Urgh."

Edge was horrified. The RAF crewman's head seemed twice its original size and his body was smeared with blood and his own filth.

"The fucking bastards!"

Jarvis came in, slightly unsteady on his feet and a trouser leg and sleeve partially burned away, while Cooper cleared the room off where they had forced entry. Cooper threw a phosphorous grenade into what resembled a well-appointed film studio, complete with backscreen, a setup camera, sound and lighting. They knew who was going to be the star of the show, and the long knife on the black flag confirmed it. A man staggered out screaming, the phosphorous burning through his suit and into his flesh. Both Jarvis and Cooper fired at him, nearly cutting the man in half.

"It's Gilmore!" Edge yelled above the gunfire as Morrison was being a bit feisty with somebody on the stairs. He placed his hand gently on Gilmore's head and Jarvis used bolt cutters to cut the chain.

"Wait until we've cleared upstairs, then get him to the chopper."

Edge bypassed Morrison, who had finished sweeping the empty kitchen area. He went up the stairs first, stepping over a body, Morrison following. As he turned on the landing, a round hit him on the front trauma plate of his body armour, hurling him against the wall and winding him. He swung the carbine and a torch illuminated a woman with a pistol. She obviously wasn't used to firing it, as she raised it again. Morrison fired from below and the Hatton round shattered her pelvis. She went down screaming and Edge finished her with a short burst to the head. They cleared the rooms with stun grenades, firing at wardrobes and throwing stun grenades under beds. In the second room, a man fell out of the riddled wardrobe.

Edge changed magazines and burst through the door of the last room after the boom and high-pitched screech of the flash-bangs. He fired at a cupboard's twin doors and swung his carbine to the bed. Two terrified and screaming children looked into the torchlight. He thought about the loadmaster's battered and degraded body.

"Leave them, Edge!"

They both went downstairs and Morrison went on the radio. "Red team. Target clear, we have our man."

Cooper had been trying to do some rudimentary first aid on Gilmore, but it was difficult to know where to start. Morrison produced a folding canvas bag and with Edge, they went through the building lifting every electronic communication device or papers they could find, including searching the bodies. They heard the wop-wop of the Chinook, and trying to be as gentle as he could, Cooper lifted Gilmore, who screamed in agony.

"Sorry, mate. We'll get you outside and the medics will look after you. You're gonna be okay," but Gilmore had passed out with the pain of his broken ribs.

Once the Chinook had taken off for the field hospital, a Merlin landed and the assault, cover and force protection teams got on board quickly. As it lifted off, the dust of the wretched city swirled in its wake, and Edge felt sick for what he had contemplated doing.

*

Twelve thousand feet above Basra, a Tornado GR4's weapon systems operator (WSO) released a Brimstone missile. Its solid fuel rocket boosted the little missile to supersonic speed, while the WSO maintained sight of the target with the laser designator. The missile's modest HEAT warhead would avoid collateral damage in the streets and buildings around the target. The Brimstone impacted with the building's flat roof, and the crush fuse activated the warhead a few milliseconds later, after it had punched through into the room below. Everything within the top floor was vaporised, causing the upper storey to pancake down onto the ground floor, crushing everything below. It was like Edge had said:

*"They show precision-guided bombs going down ventilation shafts on the news, but they never tell you that there are people at the bottom of that shaft."*

At 03:30, they heard the helicopters returning and a few minutes later the bad-arses burst into the room, reeking of firearm residue, explosives and blood, mixed with testosterone.

"We got him," Morrison said. "I need a drink!"

Afarin, who had expended a great deal of emotional energy on Giles Gilmore, asked him softly: "Will he make it?"

Morrison looked at her as though noticing her for the first time. "He's not good. The bastards gave him a right old kicking, but the medics think he'll get through it."

"And what about the—"

"Dead. Every last fucking one of them. *Pour encourager les autres.*"

\*

The station commander of BAS authorised the opening of the All Ranks Club, the 'Camel's Toe' despite it being the early hours. The party was tinged with sadness because although Gilmore was safe in the field hospital, the bodies of Andy Mount and Louise Skelton lay still as eternity in the refrigerated reefer behind the medical centre, waiting for their repatriation flight. Afarin was exhausted but smiled at Jarvis, glad of his company. He was shouting at her because he had been temporarily deafened by the frame charge going off prematurely.

"Look at you now," he yelled and guffawed, "the Gash with the 'Tache."

Later, the sergeant with the hard face and twisted nose from the assault team came across to speak with her. To her surprise, he put his hand on her shoulder and smiled at her. It seemed to light up his soul through eyes that had been grey and cold.

"You are an incredibly brave woman. A man owes his life to you, not to me or everyone else here, because I'm just a trigger man. She who saves one life saves the entire world. Thank you."

And then he was gone.

Afarin didn't feel even slightly brave, just tired and lonely. She went outside craving a cigarette and stared up at the stars and the lightening sky to the east.

"I tried to find you for two years," said a voice from the shadows.

She went to him.

Morrison watched her getting dressed, first the shoulder holster and then the chador over the top of her head.

"Don't the straps chafe?"

"You get used to it," she said, slipping on the sandals.

"So that's it for another two years."

He was still in bed. She went and sat next to him and bent down to kiss him. The chador made it almost impossible.

"You've sacrificed everything to serve your country. Is it worth it? Do you think your country gives a flying fuck about you? Like me, you'll probably end up dead in some fly-blown shithole."

"Oh, Henry, I thought that of almost everyone, you would have understood. There's nothing for me, no home or family."

"I waited for you."

"Could you ever see the two of us living together in multicultural nirvana?"

"Yes."

She ruffled his hair. "Bloody liar."

She opened the door of his Corimec.

"See you in two years."

He could tell she was smiling because her beautiful eyes shone like the sun breaking through a sad, wintery sky.

*

It was difficult to sleep in the evacuation ward of the Role 2 at Basra Air Station. Faye had gone, sobbing, meaning well but really not helping at all. It was difficult for him not to feel sorry for himself. For someone as vain as

Giles Gilmore, it was a shock when he saw his smashed and ruined face in a mirror. He was due to go home on the Tristar that night. In a way, Gilmore was lucky. There was a Czech general surgeon with a specialisation in oral and maxilla facial surgery in the field hospital at Shaibah. His jaws were wired to stabilise them and wire cutters were tie-wrapped to his wrist. If he was going to vomit, he would have to cut the wire cleats holding his shattered mandible and maxilla together, rather than choke to death. It would take several operations to rectify his crushed cheekbones and the orbital floor of his left eye. Gilmore felt sorry for himself, then he thought of Louise and he cried. His hot, salty and futile tears seemed to put it all in perspective.

The RAF nursing sister was talking to the young MT driver. "I know he looks a right old mess now, but he will get better."

Faye looked at her with forlorn hope.

"All that swelling will go down and his face is a bit lopsided because they broke some of the bones in his face. They'll do some operations and in six months he'll be fine and as handsome and vain as ever."

The young girl cried her heart out while the older woman cuddled her, trying hard not to think that all men were bastards.

"But the problem is, you mean well, but you're not really helping. He's been through an awful lot and is probably now at the guilt stage, because he survived and the others didn't. You remind him of what has happened, and I know you don't want to. Just let him go for a bit. Let him get it out of his system. He's going home tonight, but you're staying here, so you need to think about you. Get it?"

Faye smiled gratefully. "Thanks, ma'am. I didn't think of it like that. I'm here for a few more months."

"Yes, dear, you are. And so am I. There will be many more Mr Gilmores to take care of."

The duty nurse went into the area behind the medical facility where they parked the ambulances and enjoyed a cigarette. On the evening of the next day, someone else wanted to see Sergeant Giles 'Gary' Gilmore. He was the sort of person who wouldn't take no for an answer.

"I'd like to visit Sergeant Gilmore."

"Out of the question, Pocket Magnum PI. He's due to fly out tonight and he's been through enough."

"I have a present for him."

"I'll give it to him."

"Would it help if I said I was one of the team who rescued him?"

The RAF nursing sister had qualified as a state registered nurse fifteen years previously. She had seen a lot of life… and death. The man in front of her was fairly typical fare that she had met on operations. She could smell clean hair and a freshly showered body, but the clothes always gave it away. There was the faint but fetid aroma of vehicle and gun oil, gun residue, stale sweat. And fear. He was slightly below average height, wiry and very hard. His face may have once been handsome, but now it looked like someone had set it on fire and put it out with a shovel.

His eyes were cold and grey. Part of her was uneasy, but she knew this man was capable of kindness as well as violence, and she knew that the patient on her ward owed his life to this man and other men like him.

"Please."

His eyes softened, so she did as well.

"Ten minutes, max!" she said.

"Don't worry. It won't take that long."

Gilmore opened his eyes and saw a hard-faced man scrutinising him.

"I know you," Gilmore mumbled through immobile jaws.

"Probably," the man agreed.

"You came to get me."

"Me and a few more blokes. And ladies too. Aren't you lucky?"

"I don't feel very lucky."

"Well, dry your eyes, coz I've got a present for you."

The man held up a black cylindrical object. It was a particularly nice flask, the type beloved by aircrew that doubled as a large insulated mug.

Gilmore laughed with difficulty. It was the first time he had felt good for a long time. The man tossed the flask onto the bed and smiled, but the warmth didn't quite seem to reach his eyes.

"Seeing as how you saved my life, I would like to thank you…"

"Edge, my name is Edge."

He turned and left.

"Bye, Edge." Gilmore closed his eyes and slept.

## Chapter 23

# POOR LIFE CHOICES

———

The Warrant Officer and Sergeants' Mess at Torres Vedras Barracks on the edge of Salisbury Plain was a hideous 1960s structure, thrown up when the MoD embraced 'progressive' architecture. Like most buildings knocked up in the '60s, it was ugly, poorly ventilated, impossible to heat and riddled with concrete cancer. It had been condemned fifteen years before, but because only soldiers were living in it, it would do for them. Despite starting with a sow's ear, the mess members made the best of their building, because for many of them it was their home. The mess silver glittered in their cabinets in the foyer, and the public rooms were adorned with large and often very good oil paintings of battles past, a pictorial representation of the Regiment's prior glories and disasters. It had a comfortable, slightly old-fashioned ostentatiousness of all messes, and that night it was a hubbub of noise, loud conversations and laughter.

The Regiment was dining out three mess members. One was being medically discharged after a medical board concluded he was unfit for further military duties. IEDs tended to have that effect on soldiers who were too close to them when they went off. Two had reached their twenty-two year point. One had been offered further Service and declined. The other hadn't. Edge had returned for resettlement in his old regiment, or rather what was left of the amalgamation of two regiments. It would be better for resettlement purposes and was closer to home. Edge had had enough of killing and the constant strain of Special Forces operations, but in the few months he had been with his new regiment, he realised he had nothing in common with them.

A few people spoke with Edge, but it was out of politeness rather than genuine friendship. Staff Sergeant Edge had that effect on his fellow SNCOs. He was like Marmite. A staunch comrade on operations, but rather difficult to get on with during the crushing routine of peacetime home postings. Their company commanders, the colonel and the quartermaster had been guests of honour and had made speeches about comradeship and service. Some gave anecdotes of past misdemeanours or memorable moments. The speeches concerning Edge were slightly stilted, despite the enormous mother lode of his transgressions from which they had to choose.

It was just before midnight and Edge decided he'd had enough. He headed out of the anteroom and decided to go for a piss before going up to his room. In the gents, he was relieving himself, still painful after the years, and he barely acknowledged the person in mess dress who came in, using the urinal a few spaces away.

"Evening, Edgie. Good turnout. But not for you, eh?"

It was the Regimental Sergeant Major (RSM).

*Fuck.* "Evening, sir."

Edge finished and hurriedly washed his hands. The RSM made a show of zipping himself up, as though he were stuffing an anaconda into his trousers.

"Don't rush away. I'd like a quick word if you'll indulge me, Edgie." The RSM washed his hands slowly, like a surgeon. "Food's getting worse since they got in this contract, don't you think?"

Edge followed the RSM into the empty snooker room where the table was showing an unfinished game. Someone had left his cue on the green baize, practically a hanging offence. The RSM opened the window and lit a cigar and sat on the window sill. Well, he was the RSM. Edge fidgeted with the balls on the table.

"What is it you want, sir?"

"I wanted to say goodbye. I wanted to thank you for your time served and I wanted to say what a pleasure it's been having you in the Regiment. Well, I can do the first two, but I can't in all honesty do the last. You're a bloody good soldier, Edgie. Your report from Two-Two stated that you were courageous, steady in the firefight and a role model for the youngsters. Sometimes."

The RSM inhaled deeply on his cigar and blew the smoke out of the window. "But for most of the time when we're not on ops or on exercise, you're a fucking liability. Think about it. After twenty-two years, you're still a staff sergeant. Your contemporaries are warrant officer ones or twos."

Edge rolled the white ball into a pocket off the cushion. Angles and deflection was his bread and butter.

"And look at that lapel full of medals. More than me, eh, Edgie. A lifetime of service, but there's one you don't have, isn't there? The one that a civilian employer who knows his stuff would damn you for. No Long Service and Good Conduct. Because you couldn't hold your temper and decided to deck a German copper. Three months at Colchester. Was it honestly worth it?"

Edge picked the cue off the table, inspected the tip and put it in the rack on the wall. "It was actually twenty-eight days, sir."

The RSM smiled sadly and flicked ash off the cigar. "You'd probably like to wrap that cue round my neck, wouldn't you? I've had too much to drink, but I'm in *vino veritas*, Staff Edge. I want you to know that I had to bribe your company commander to attend your dining-out, because he hates your fucking guts."

Edge tried to pot the black off a red and two cushions.

"I believe that you've lined up a job with your wife's father?"

Edge nodded without looking up.

"I'm glad, but I have a feeling that you'll fuck it up. The only reason you haven't totally fucked up your Service career is because the Army is a family and we look after our own. And as I've already said, you're a good soldier, Edgie."

Edge picked up the blue ball and tried to crush it.

"I'll give you one piece of advice that's really important for your life outside the Army and it's totally free and unbiased. It doesn't matter how much you've been through, or whatever you've done in the Army. It doesn't matter if you've won the VC, because the civvies won't give a fucking toss. And why should they? Don't waste your time with the 'you don't know coz you weren't there' routine. They couldn't even begin to understand, and their eyes will have glazed over before you even tell them about getting on the trooper flight. The only way they can judge you is by the way you get on with them, and if you think barrack life is boring, wait until you're a civvie. I have a horrible feeling that one way or another, being a civvie will kill you."

He threw the cigar out of the window and went to the door.

"Must go. Fucking Ruperts to entertain. Good luck, Edgie. It doesn't matter what my opinion of you is. You now have the sole responsibility for your family. You're leaving the Army, so you have to look after them. It won't be easy."

Edge waited for several minutes then shut the sash window. He sat on the window sill and sighed long and hard because twenty-two years had gone in the blink of an eye. He would never get them back.

*

In 2010, Edge had conducted his last mission for the UKSF in Belgrade and this time it was personal. He flew home from Bucharest and after debriefing, went on leave prior to his return to his donor unit for resettlement, although his old regiment no longer existed. When he arrived home in Devon, the news was breaking that a former Serbian Warlord, Jakovljević Milorad had been abducted from a Belgrade street and flown to The Hague to stand trial for war crimes. Moira listened to the television news and looked at Edge, who was finishing a bottle of Nuits-Saint-Georges.

"Mark, you know that I've never asked you about what you do or have done, but you were involved in that, weren't you? Don't ask me how, but I just know."

Edge closed his eyes and relived another of those bad dreams…

*

In Belgrade, the evening had been warm, and a gentle breeze was coming from the Danube. Opposite the park, the Salon 5 restaurant was gaily lit and a hubbub of cheerful noise. A drunk was lying, passed out, amid some large wheelie bins, a spattering of vomit coating the front of his coat. A prostitute slunk out of the light and stared at the drunk with contempt, as though his being there was bad for business.

The doors of the Salon 5 opened and a thick-set man in a suit looked up and down the street, before waving for a car. The black BMW pulled up outside the restaurant and the man hurried over to open the BMW's rear door. The restaurant's doors opened again and two men came out. One watched the street, staying close to the other man, well dressed in a bespoke suit and Italian shoes. Jakovljević Milorad felt better than James Brown that evening. He had eaten well and pulled off a deal with a German lumber firm for bio-fuel. He even smiled at the prostitute, who sluttishly thrust her hips forward and delved in her handbag. Milorad smiled indulgently at her and then his eyes widened as she produced a

Sig with a silencer and double-tapped the nearest bodyguard in the head. The bodyguard holding the car door open went for his gun, but the drunk double-tapped him with a silenced Glock and in an easy action, slammed into Jakovljević Milorad, hurling him to the ground. There was a crack of a high velocity rifle from the park, and the BMW driver's brains were all over the plush interior.

A metallic grey van came up the street, while the drunk and the prostitute cable-tied his arms and legs, ball gagged him and dragged a black hood over Milorad's head. The drunk peeled the plastic vomit off the front of his shirt. The van doors opened and the drunk and the prostitute rammed him through the side door, 'accidently' bashing his head off the door stanchion. They were joined with a man with a rifle, who got in the front.

"Come on, Gloria, let me help you in. Beauty before age."

"Fuck off!" said the prettiest trooper in 22 SAS.

The van headed north, preceded by a car that joined them from a side street. The van flashed its lights to show all had gone well. They headed north-west to the Romanian border and a remote airfield, where a Falcon executive jet was waiting to transport Jakovljević Milorad to The Hague and his war crimes trials. Once they had crossed the border, the 'drunk' sat on the floor next to the hooded and tied man.

"Good evening, Mr Milorad. I trust you had a fine meal?"

There were muffled protests from behind the gag and hood.

"Now you probably won't remember me, and why on earth should you? But I have made a point of never forgetting you."

He bent down close to the hooded ear and hissed: "You took something that was so very precious to me. You destroyed my future happiness because of a fucking dog. And now you're going to die in prison. You said to me a long time ago: 'I will remember your name, Edge.' Well, here I am, you bastard, and this is for a woman called Jozica Marić."

Edge reached for Milorad's testicles and crushed them. He screamed and was still groaning with agony as he was dragged onto the aircraft. Captain Gardner had never told Edge about the note crammed in Jozica's mouth. If he had, Edge would have killed him.

*

Edge sighed and reluctantly told her about a callow young corporal, who had fallen in passionate and intense love with an older woman called Jozica Marić

233

and how a stupid and thoughtless act by him had resulted in her being tortured to death. He told Moira that she was the first woman he had ever loved and that he would always love her. And yes, he did love Moira, but you can still love somebody from beyond the grave. He told her it had been one of his life's driving precepts to track down Jakovljević Milorad to make him pay for what he had done. Edge told his wife that he would have preferred to have made him suffer for a long time, like he had made Jozica suffer, but if he was ever released, that option remained open.

Moira went very quiet. She remained very quiet for two days, and cold disapproval poured off her like the breeze from a glacier. And Edge just couldn't understand why his wife would seem to disapprove of an affair that happened twelve years previously, two years before he even met Moira. Edge would never understand the jealous stupidity of women, and he became annoyed that his wife was drifting round the house like an undertaker's assistant. Three mornings later, he could stand it no more.

"For fuck's sake, give yourself a shake, Moira! Jozica is dead. She's cold in the ground and her earthly remains are lying in a municipal cemetery in Zagreb. On the other hand, your former bit of rough, for clarity, Mr Daz Copeland, is still very much alive and fucking kicking, isn't he?"

For some reason, this didn't seem to help calm the situation, and the first point of the wedge had been driven into the fissure in their marriage. His date for leaving the Army was looming and he still didn't have a civilian job. In truth, he didn't need to work. He had made some very useful and lucrative contacts in America, and Horace Cutler, with whom he regularly corresponded, gave him some very useful tips on investments, but he knew he would go mad if he had to stay in Weare Giffard for the rest of his life. Having only an estranged family, Edge could not understand why his wife was so wrapped up and dependent on her parents.

"I will never understand women," Edge told his reflection as he shaved one morning. "Why can't they see life the way we do?"

Both Edge and Moira knew that if he worked away from home after a career in the Army, their marriage would be over, and Edge still loved his wife and children. Despite being another cat that walks on its own, he didn't want to be alone in the world. He started to confide in Monty, who would stare at him unblinking as though he understood. Monty would stare at his Edge father and wonder why it was that humans made their relationships so complicated and were incapable of seeing what was obvious to him, a cat.

Monty's attitude to life was simple. The thing he had loved most in the world, Snowflake, was dead. Moira mother looked after him, fed him and took him to the horrible place of pain and suffering every year or when he got into scrapes. He loved Moira mother and would and almost did give his little life for her. Sara and Francis he also loved, but Francis could be annoying when he teased him with a ping-pong ball. But Edge father he loved the most, although he was probably the most stupid of all of them. Edge father used to come home smelling of killing, which Monty found interesting, because cats would never kill each other. They would communicate on a similar level, although his human father was mostly too stupid to fully understand.

Against both of their better judgements, Edge took a menial job in Moira's father's firm. His *bête noire* was now his line manager, and it was as though Moira's father had arranged this situation to deliberately humiliate him, which he had. Edge was no fool and he suspected that a long trip down to St Ives, dropping off some tractor bits and pieces and animal feed, plus the overnight stay, was to keep him out of the way. On his return, Edge's suspicions were confirmed when he saw some bruising on Moira's breast and inner thigh.

"Been walking into doors, Moira?" Her panicked look was all the confirmation he needed. With the absolute certainty of someone who couldn't be more wrong, Edge was on the slippery slope that would lead to his family leaving him, a criminal conviction for actual bodily harm and his illegally possessing a firearm, namely a .308 Ruger hunting rifle. It was a toss-up what would do for him first: the vast quantities of alcohol he was consuming or a shoot-out with the police. Edge would have preferred both options running concurrently.

*

It had been a terrible first year after leaving the Army for Edge. On the 2nd of January, he was arrested in his house at 06:00 for causing an affray and actual bodily harm. The arrest related to an incident that had taken place in the Hoops Inn and Country Hotel just outside Bideford in North Devon. It was during a New Year's Eve party that Moira's father had been involved in arranging for all of the firm's workers, a bolt-on to another event that was already taking place at the venue. It had been quite a boisterous affair and the drink had been freely flowing. Edge had made an early start at lunchtime in the pub and needed little in the way of encouragement to take advantage of the delights of the Hoops Inn.

It started as all these things do, innocuously enough. Edge wasn't a Devonian but Moira was, and even when they married she had refused to follow him on his postings "like some baggage or chattel," as she had put it. "My family lives here and here I want to stay." So they had bought a house on the river, south of Bideford, before the house prices started to go through the roof. Edge had spent ten years of unaccompanied tours, commuting from places like Germany, the Midlands, Scotland and Wiltshire, paying a mortgage and living in the block and then the mess. They had two children, a boy and a girl, but how they had managed to find the time was a miracle.

*

Since leaving the Army, life had been relatively easy. Too easy, but monstrously difficult. It was impossible to know where the lines were, because they seemed to change all the time, constantly shifting like Goodwin Sands. He would say something one week and people would laugh, but the next week there would be a complaint. Never to him, but to a line manager, a union rep or a 'good friend'. And on a long, boozy New Year's Eve, he crossed the start line in the Hoops Inn and Country Hotel. There would be no going back.

And the problem was, Moira was still gorgeous and she had been there, stayed there, while he had been in assorted shitholes around the world. And Daz, who had been in North Devon, stayed there. Stupid name. Daz the line manager and Moira's dad's right-hand man. The same Daz who had his left arm lightly draped around Moira's neck, his index and middle finger neatly tucked in that interesting little depression on her upper sternum, the xiphoid process, just before the plunging valley between her still amazingly pert tits. And he had a knife, an agricultural knife with a rubber handle, and Daz was going to kill Mark Edge that night, for the humiliation in the forest and Edge's mate who had attacked him at the wedding, but most of all, for taking Moira away from him, and she was his.

"All right, Daz?"

He looked up and gave a smile, or was it a sneer? "All right, Mark?"

"I was wondering, Daz, if I could sit next to my wife."

"Plenty of room either side, Mark."

Moira gave him that: *Oh, don't make a fuss* look. *It's just Daz being Daz.* But in reality Daz had showed her the knife and she had a pretty good idea regarding what he was going to do with it. He would take her later at a time of his choosing.

Edge nodded almost thoughtfully. "Oh, I see. All right then, Daz. Let me put this another way. If you don't stop feeling my wife's tits, I'm going to rip your fucking face off," Edge said in a low, almost pleasant voice.

It was that walk into the saloon, through the swing doors moment. That moment when the piano stops playing and the boy runs to get the sheriff. All conversation round the table stopped.

"Mark, for God's sake, stop it," Moira hissed up at him. Across the room, her father looked up as though this were predestination.

"Look, mate, you've obviously been having a stressful week. You're not in the Army now. See, all those years in the Army have made you paranoid."

Edge put his glass down slowly on the table. "I tell you what, Daz, why don't we step outside so that I can show you just how fucked up the Army's made me?"

Daz was a big man in his prime, slightly running to fat. Edge was small, stocky and well past his fighting fitness. Daz was at least eight inches taller than Edge. Daz was going to fuck Moira Edge, nee Tremain, tonight, after a little heave-ho in the hotel car park with her drunk of a husband. He undraped his arm and grinned up at Edge. "Lead the way, dickhead. I'll see you in a minute, Moira."

Edge had no intention of having an unseemly brawl outside with this swaggering piece of shit. Edge had learned over twenty years ago that those who play by the rules end up hurt or dead. As Daz stood up, he was level with Edge, but pinned by a table in front and the seat behind. Edge drove his head and neck forward with such violence and force that he split his forehead open on Daz's nasal septum. He felt it shatter like an eggshell. Edge would have a headache for two days and have to stitch his forehead in front of the mirror with sutures from his survival first aid kit the next day, after dousing the wound the previous night with white vinegar. But it wouldn't stop oozing blood. Daz would wake up in the North Devon District Hospital the following evening. The criminal compensation pay-out would pay for the extensive bridgework on his upper front teeth, but he would never breathe through his nose again. He never got to fuck Moira again until much later, but then again, neither did Edge.

Predictably, he lost his job; hardly surprising as Edge suspected that Moira's father had been angling to get rid of him for months. The thing that hurt him the most was Moira's coldness towards him, and her siding with the man who had been attempting to seduce her for the past fourteen years. What kept him awake in their now permanently separate beds, or in his case a sofa bed, was the terrible nagging doubt that this was no New Year's Eve silliness; this had been happening all those years while he had been serving in assorted shitholes.

Things became worse when the story made the front page of the *North Devon Gazette*, and the details of a short, albeit severely violent, fracas in a hotel bar were given spin and polish by an otherwise bored shitless journalist. He had hit the jackpot. No more red diesel shenanigans, no more farm health and safety breaches. A Mr Mark Edge, former, disgraced, soldier (somehow the hack had found out about his time in Colchester, and Edge suspected Moira's father), had uncharacteristically (or maybe not, ran the backstory) erupted violently at a family function on New Year's Eve. Mr Daniel Copeland had suffered life-changing injuries as a result of the assault. There was even a nice picture of Daz looking wan and helpless in a hospital bed.

Edge was taken in for questioning. During his two days and nights in Barnstaple Police Station, Edge said only eleven words:

"I will make no comment to you. I want a brief."

The duty solicitor quickly became exasperated with Edge and his stubborn silence. "You have to meet them halfway, Mr Edge. You are facing a serious charge of assault."

Edge, who had successfully completed the full Conduct After Capture Course, or SERE as it is now called in the Forces, said absolutely nothing to the two detectives. He just continued to stare at them in a detached, contemptuous manner. He was released on bail paid out of his Service gratuity and appeared in Barnstaple Magistrates' Court two weeks later. Edge wore his regimental tie and medals and was reprimanded by the female magistrate that despite his service to his country, no one was above the law. He pleaded provocation, was fined and given a community service.

He managed to get jobs as a deckhand on the crabbers sailing out of Bideford. The pay was dependent on catch, and most of the pond life in the area wouldn't have got out of bed for the money he earned. But he liked the hard work in the open air and became friendly with the skippers who didn't give a toss about his predilection for ultraviolence. He did his job and became stronger and fitter, but he was drinking astonishing amounts on his days off. Once, in a supermarket car park, two associates of Daniel Copeland attempted to even the score, regarding Daz's nasally snuffle. Edge broke one of his erstwhile assailant's thumbs, sprung a rib with his boot and displaced the right kneecap of the other. The police were either uninterested this time or more likely uninformed. Probably because Edge explained to one of the men on the floor that he should return to Daz and tell him that if anything like this were attempted again, Daz would be strung up by his bollocks from the rafters of a remote, desolate farmhouse they both knew.

Just before Easter, Moira wanted to have a 'long chat' with him regarding their future. Edge was drinking enough and yet not enough to know that they had no future.

"Mark, I don't know who you are anymore. You're not the person I married."

And that was the problem in a nutshell. He was exactly the person she had married. But she wasn't. She was older, perhaps wiser, and had moved on with children. He hadn't. His children seemed to skirt round him, as though he were a stranger in his own house.

"It's not me, it's you, Mark."

Well, that was a novel take on things.

"We can't go on like this. Dad was really good to you and you just threw it back in his face."

Edge tried to remember just how good Mr Tremain had been to him while he had been driving his poorly serviced, clocked delivery lorries.

"And I feel for the safety of the children, after your violent escapade. Do you know they've been saying to them at school that their dad's a nutter?"

"Is that because their nutter of a father stopped their mother making a fool and a trollop of herself?"

There was silence. He heard a jet fighter rumble overhead, a distraction in their court of misery.

"You're a bastard, Mark. You always have been. There's something missing in your head. Poor Daz can't…"

"Fuck him! If I ever see him again, I'll kill him. Fuck Daz, fuck your father and fuck your entire family."

He'd wanted to say those things for about fourteen years and now he had said them, he could never take them back. She was gone in less than thirty minutes. When he returned the next afternoon, well oiled (the boat had docked at 11:00), all her clothes and possessions had gone. The children's bedrooms were gutted. It was like his life had been wiped off the slate. He lit the wood burner and cried a few dry Merlot tears that were as salty as the wounds in his hands and just as wretched. Self-pity did not sit comfortably with Edge.

\*

Edge's father died in August on a hot, stormy day when the swallows were dipping over the wheat, twisting like fighters in the warm afternoon. His sister phoned him to tell him, sounding just as disinterested in life and him as she always was.

"Thing is, Mark, we're so busy and it's not as though you have a proper job now, is it? Ronnie and I can't get the time off and you're the male heir, so you'll have power of attorney. We've already been to the house, when he went into the hospice. There's nothing really left that we want."

"Why didn't you tell me he was dying, Anne?"

"Well, because he didn't want to see you. Sorry, Mark, but that's how he felt. You never really got on. I've got the address of his solicitor. The housing association want the house cleared as soon as possible."

"So you've grubbed through it and taken what you wanted and now I'm supposed to clear up?"

"You always resented me, Mark. It's about time you did something. You were away for years, swanning around in the Army while I had to pick up the pieces when Mum died. It took you all your time to be bothered to turn up for the funeral."

"The RAF flew me back from Belize in a specially arranged repatriation flight. If I was late, it was because I'd spent twelve hours flogging across the Atlantic and into Coventry Airport."

"I'll post everything to you. Stuff from the solicitor."

"When is the funeral?"

"It was last week, Mark."

He stared at a watercolour above the hall table. It was a kingfisher, nicely executed, its bright blue plumage reflected in the water. The seconds drew out.

"We thought that it would be for the best, as we didn't want a scene."

The kingfisher was Edge's work, which was probably why Moira hadn't taken it.

"Anne, I've never really told you this before and I really should have done a long time ago. Your husband is a mincing caricature of a man and he's been having homosexual liaisons with men in public lavatories throughout Warwickshire. This is supposedly while he has been away on business. You however are what you have always been. A mean-spirited, grasping, heartless bitch."

She hung up. He smiled grimly to himself. As unlikely as it was, Anne was such a twisted person that she would believe it, and tonight, she and her husband would begin their transit through hell.

A large brown envelope was waiting for him a couple of days later. It contained legal papers, as it would appear that he was the executor of the will, and a set of house keys. As it was a housing association property, they wanted it cleared as quickly as possible. Edge decided to drive up to the Midlands the following Monday.

He had decided not to stay in his father's house and booked a cheap hotel nearby on the internet. He also phoned a couple of house-clearance companies in the area for the cheapest quote. He set off from Weare Giffard at 04:00 on the Monday morning, and within a few miles, just after crossing the Torridge Bridge, he was stopped by a police car that had been following him since Bideford. It was the thirteenth time he had been stopped by the police since January.

"Good morning, Officer. What's the excuse this time?"

"This time, sir? Excuse? I have stopped you because I have been following you for the past three miles, and in my professional opinion, you were driving erratically and did not come to a full stop at a stop sign."

Edge chuckled. "Okay, so the same reason for which you personally stopped me on Friday May 24th."

"I don't believe that I've made your acquaintance before, sir."

"Well, Officer, I have made yours, not only in May but also twice in April, twice in March but not in January or February. Spot of leave, was it? Well, not to worry, your other three colleagues more than adequately took up the slack. In fact, Officer, since the 14th of March, I have made your acquaintance on nine occasions. Five when you've been on duty and the four times I've noted you while you were off duty, or at least not in uniform. You see, Officer, I'm extremely observant and sometimes you may not notice me, but I notice you. Shall we get this charade over with?"

It almost sounded threatening because it was, and the copper contemplated arresting him. It was as though Edge could read his mind.

"You had better have very good grounds, Officer. And who knows, my PTSD may kick in and I may resist arrest. Do you really want to start with all the paperwork so close to going off shift?"

The copper breathalysed him to save face, but Edge wasn't stupid enough to have been drinking the night before. The constable decided to try once more to establish moral authority: "Before I let you go, would you mind telling me where you're going this time of the morning?"

"Well, Officer, as this country isn't quite a police state yet, yes, I would mind telling you. But you better get on the blower to your pals in the West

Midlands and let them know a shockingly bad driver is heading up to their manor."

The copper watched him drive off and bagged the breathalyser in an evidence bag for his report. "We will get you, you bastard."

It had been a large village when Edge had left it in 1984. Now it was more or less a suburb of Nuneaton and Coventry. The house had the same carpets, wallpaper and paintwork as it had when he was at school. The garden was overgrown, the entire neighbourhood was shabby and run-down and women shrouded in black scurried past with their entourages of assorted offspring. Inside, the house was a shambles. It was as though it had been visited by burglars who had decided to wreck it, because everything inside was so shabby. His father's clothes were scattered across an unmade bed. A picture of his mother had been kicked under the bed. Edge went downstairs, sat at the kitchen table and put his head in his hands.

He was angry, not just at his appalling sister, but with his father as well. His dad had worked all his life in the car industry at a time this neighbourhood had been prosperous. His father was prosperous. He smoked big Castella cigars and they went on holiday twice a year; Spain and Wales. Car manufacturing earned some people a lot of money, until the shop stewards like the Red Robbos and superior Japanese cars destroyed the industry. They got greedy at the wrong time and his father had been too stupid to buy the house. Whatever had been half-decent in this house, his sister had taken it.

It took him most of the day to speak to the solicitor, a clearance company and a gardener and to realise that his legacy amounted to some old *Shoot* annuals that had been his and a shoe box full of correspondence and paperwork from his now also dead uncle. He kept these on a whim. His uncle had never been close to their family, but he had a soft spot for young Mark. Edge knew that like him, his uncle had been in the Army and was one of the main reasons he hadn't followed his father into the factories as an apprentice, but joined the Army instead as a boy entrant. His father had despised that decision. Uncle Jack left the Army and became a gamekeeper in Norfolk and a ghillie up near Perth. Edge had last met him at his mum's funeral, a frail man and old before his time. He died two years later.

In the afternoon, Edge handed over the keys and money to the house clearance cowboys and went to the solicitors to sign some paperwork, before heading to the hotel, via a supermarket to buy food, cider and wine. He had two shoe boxes of papers, a few books and some football annuals to show for forty-three years. On the way out of the Tesco car park, he spotted a minaret between the dilapidated houses. To him, it seemed like a symbol of decay and oppression.

That night, rather than watch televisual gaga, Edge made inroads into the cider and wine, reading through his uncle's paperwork. Letters to Dad when Mum had been ill, but more interesting, about a hundred pages of typed A4, with lots of corrections. It related to the time when Jack Edge had been a corporal in the Support Company of the 1st Battalion of the Royal Leicestershire Regiment from 1951 to 1952, during the Korean War. Uncle Jack had been in the sniper platoon.

"Well, bugger me," he said out loud. "So that's why you became a ghillie."

Edge became engrossed with Uncle Jack's account of the Korean War. The story was in places rambling, incoherently written, but was the honest reflection of a man whose life seemed to mirror his own. Jack had been disenfranchised by the 1950s. *Never had it so good*. Well, he certainly had in a more honest time. *The Swinging Sixties*. Poofs in flamboyant clothes, a million miles from the woods of Norfolk and the Southern Highlands of Scotland. Edge was chorizo and cheesed out, not to say pissed by the time he came across the OS map number, the eight-figure grid reference, plus the intricate, hand-drawn tactical map. It showed a distance in pacing from the corner of a wood and a back-bearing in Mils to a high-tension electricity pylon. There was a position marked with a simple annotation: *Cache*.

Edge laughed. "Arrr," he said in his best pirate accent, "X marks the spot, eh, Uncle Jack? You and me both, eh?"

He put the papers back in the shoe box, finished the second bottle of Merlot, fell asleep and forgot most of what he had read. By the next morning, he had a thumping headache and had to wait until the afternoon before he was in a fit state to drive. By the time he reached the M5, his childhood, school days and family had gone. He was alone in the universe.

Chapter 24

# WAR CRIMES

———

By October, the trees along the Torridge were a beautiful sweep of yellows and oranges. The recent heavy rains had swollen the river, which tumbled over the weirs and fallen trees in the race to the sea. The woods that glowered above the river valley were still dark. The air smelled strongly of the coming winter. It was the 16th and there were two remarkable events that day. Edge was chopping last year's logs for his wood burner and piling them up in the lean-to. It was 10:00, so he hadn't started drinking yet. The boat was going in for the end-of-season overhaul and the only work available was on the tourist fishing boats. He hated those pricks from London with all the gear but no idea. His pension continued to pay the small mortgage and the CSA's legalised extortion. He hadn't seen his wife and children since March. What worried him the most was that he didn't care.

Edge felt relatively upbeat. He had recently sold two paintings: A study of Appledore from across the Torridge and a portrait of an old fisherman, smoking a pipe outside a pub. The photographs had been taken from the other side of the river with one of his ridiculously large telephoto lenses. Edge was a voyeur and had taken the photograph of the fisherman at 900 metres from the cover of a wood above East-the-Water, just to keep his hand in. The exposure was perfect. He was a talented artist but an exceptional photographer. The Army had trained him well.

His back was beginning to stiffen from swinging the axe when he saw the

Vauxhall Insignia turn off the road and head up the track. It was a big car and a small, muddy track. Edge would never associate with anyone who drove black Vauxhall Insignias. This could be trouble, so he tucked the axe in the lean-to, but it was still within easy reach. He watched the car stop at the end of his drive, well, more of an opening into the property.

Edge slipped into another, earlier, iteration of himself. *There are two men in the car. Driver fifties. Passenger thirties. Driver suit. Too small for him now. Tight across the chest. Fucking Plod. Old Plod. Passenger, not Plod. Reaching behind to get something from the back seat. Gun? Do I need to go in now, fast and hard? No, not a gun, a camera. Press? Plod and press in collusion? Not really likely. Stand down from murderous intent.*

"Can I help you?" asked Edge.

The man was in his fifties. He was used to having some authority, but the mud in Edge's drive rather robbed him of any dignity and decorum whatever position he held may have given him. He stepped gingerly across the firmer ground to avoid the puddles. He was holding a brown envelope.

"Are you Mark Edge, formerly Staff Sergeant Edge?"

"And you are..?"

"Detective Sergeant Warberton."

"Let's see your warrant card, pal."

"I'm retired, but I represent the—"

"I don't care who you represent. Get your arse off my property."

"…The Iraq Historical Abuse Tribunal."

"The what?"

"IHAT. We are investigating historical cases of war crimes, committed by British Service personnel, between 2003 and 2011 in Iraq during Operation Telic."

"Are you taking the piss, Mr Warberton?"

"I have hereby served notification on you," he tapped Edge on the shoulder with the envelope and tried to thrust it into his hands, "Staff Sergeant Edge, you do not have to say anything, but it may harm your defence if—"

"And it may harm your bollocks if you don't get back into your big, flashy car and fuck off back under the stone from which you have crawled." Edge purposely glanced at the axe in the lean-to.

"Please don't threaten me, Staff Sergeant Edge. I have a warrant that I will issue once you have read the documents and the allegations against you. My colleague over by the car is filming you, so I would strongly advise against physical violence. I will return tomorrow to interview you under caution. I advise you to make a point of being in."

The retired copper slipped and squelched his way back to the car. "I'd bring some wellies with you next time, Mr Warberton," Edge suggested helpfully.

"I will be back tomorrow, Edge. You can count on it."

Edge shook his head and picked up the envelope, which was with assorted papers. He went into the kitchen and filled a tumbler with the dregs of last night's Merlot. Edge opened the envelope and swiftly went through the top papers, resplendent with the IHAT's governmental logo. In the paperwork below, he came across the specific allegations against him, compiled by a legal company that had its own headed paper: Community Legal Notaries.

*Staff Sergeant M Edge (complete with Service number) is accused of unlawfully killing a Mr Muhammad Al Jazari on the 28th of October 2005 in Amarah in Maysan Province Amarah. Staff Sergeant Edge did unlawfully open fire on Mr Al Jazari without issuing a verbal warning, in contravention of then current Rules of Engagement outlined on Card Alpha.*

*Mr Al Jazari was unarmed at the time of the shooting and at no time during the event did he engage in any violent action towards Staff Sergeant Edge or any British troops. Given these circumstances, it is deemed that Staff Sergeant Edge's actions transgressed any definition of the use of reasonable force. In addition, Mr Anah Ahamad and Mr Jamail Hamdani are seeking recompense from the Ministry of Defence (MoD) for mental trauma, caused when Mr Al Jazari was unlawfully killed in front of them.*

Edge read the documents a second time with a sense of growing disbelief. He drained the tumbler and opened a second bottle of wine. As he went through the documents more thoroughly, it became clear to Edge that all of his personal details had been passed on to Community Legal Notaries by civil servants in the MoD, including details concerning an operation he thought was Secret UK/US Eyes Only.

The second remarkable event was heralded by the kitchen door opening slightly behind him. Edge felt the hair on the back of his neck rise in fear, and then, bold as brass, Bernard Law Montgomery, 1st Viscount Montgomery of Alamein, strolled into the kitchen and jumped up on the table. He sat down opposite Edge and said: "Meow!"

Monty was a tabby cat of around seven human years of age. He was supposed to be the kids' cat but the little looking-after he required, they didn't do. Edge was convinced he had gone with Moira and the kids, but the lure of his own territory must have overcome his dislike of Edge.

"Bloody hell, Monty. You look like shit."

The cat was thin, his fur matted, and he walked with a pronounced limp. There was a tear in his right ear, crusty with blood, and a partially healed scar ran from his right eye to his nose. He had made the ten-mile journey back to his home, and judging by the state of him, the journey had not been uneventful. Edge cleaned the cat's wounds with white vinegar and removed a large thorn from a front paw. This was accompanied by much yowling, hissing, biting and scratching. He also cleaned the wounds on his own hands with the vinegar. He found a basket and stuffed an old blanket in it, lit the wood burner and opened a tin of tuna, which Monty turned his nose up at.

"It's all I've got, so you'd better bloody eat it."

Nevertheless, Edge walked into Bideford and came back with cat food. That evening, they both sat in the kitchen in front of a very hot wood burner. Edge told him the facts of life.

"I don't know why you came back, Monty. I'm a cuckold, a drunk and a fucking war criminal."

"Meow," the cat agreed.

*

Warberton and his sidekick returned the following morning, as promised. Edge watched the car come up the lane from his observation post in the hedge. It turned in and it was the same routine as yesterday; Warberton got out and made his way to the cottage's door while the wingman came out of the car and laid the camera on its roof. Edge was amused to see they were both wearing country jackets and Bekina wellies, brand new on expenses from the outdoor shop in Barnstaple. Edge slipped out of cover and came up silently behind the cameraman, reaching over and grabbing the digital SLR. He opened the flap on the camera's base and removed the battery pack. The sheer speed and commitment of Edge's move left the cameraman powerless and speechless.

"I'll give this to your boss when you leave."

Warberton watched Edge approach him. "You shouldn't have done that."

"And you know very well that you shouldn't be filming me. I spent a long time on the IHAT website, so I'm absolutely up to speed as to what you can and can't do or say. Now, would you like to come in and have a cup of tea? I'll even take one out to your pal, or he can come in if he wants."

Warberton seemed taken aback but waved to his companion to come in with him. The inside of the kitchen had been tidied and cleared of bottles. There was the smell of coffee and baking bread in the oven. Monty's basket had been moved into the utility room and the cat was outside somewhere, murdering smaller furry creatures.

"Please sit down, Mr Warberton." Edge gestured to the kitchen table.

"Actually, it's…" he began but decided it wasn't worth it. He did sit down. His colleague came in, still angry and confused.

"Aren't you going to introduce us, Mr Warberton?"

"This is Aspinall."

"Ex-police?"

"No, civil investigator," Aspinall said rather resentfully.

Edge nodded sagely. "So you pair are what IHAT calls a 'pod'?"

"Yes."

"Right, gentlemen, let's start with the basics. I am no longer a staff sergeant. You are no longer a detective sergeant. We will conduct this meeting as Edge, Mr Warberton and Mr Aspinall."

"Now wait a minute—"

"Sorry, where are my manners? What would you like? Tea or coffee."

"Err, coffee, please," Aspinall said, "no milk or sugar."

"Oh, for fuck's sake!" Warberton said in frustration.

"I take it you want tea, milk and two sugars? If you'd only come a bit later we could have some bread rolls and jam, but they've only been in the oven ten minutes."

"Can we please stop messing around?"

Edge raised his eyebrows, ever the attentive host.

"Oh, for God's sake. Tea, milk, two sugars."

"Standard NATO. Good choice."

He gave out the drinks and sat down at the head of the table, facing the door.

"Now before we start, we'll be taking notes and we may ask you for clarification over certain details," Warberton said, opening a black notebook.

"Absolutely fine. And just to let you know that I'm making an audio and visual recording of this meeting," Edge told them, indicating with his head where the camera was located on top of the Welsh dresser.

"Now wait a bloody minute!" Warberton said angrily, you can't—"

"I'm in my own property. I can do what I like within reason. Now before we start, I wonder if you can explain to me how a civilian firm of lawyers has information regarding a military operation that I may or may not have been involved in. An operation that was classified as Secret UK/US Eyes Only. Can you explain to me how you and your associate are party to this information?"

"Don't be bloody ridiculous!"

Edge looked at Aspinall, who was looking sharply at his boss with a concerned expression, he was gratified to note, and he decided to press home the advantage.

"In fact, it isn't a case of what I do or don't say, because I have no intention of saying anything to you without legal representation. Furthermore, I believe that you have identified a major security breach, for which I will have to inform the Serious Organised Crime Agency."

Edge knew that he was kicking the arse out of it with the last statement, but he knew it would be enough to stall these two clowns for the time being. Warberton rose up to leave, Aspinall following his boss.

"We'll be back, with an arrest warrant next time."

"Was the tea and coffee not to your liking? By the way, shouldn't you have given me a pack-up, Warberton, the one with all the Service charities and NHS mental health providers I can go to for help and advice? Don't forget this, Aspinall." Edge threw the battery pack and Aspinall made a fumbling catch.

He heard the car start up and reverse out of the property. He put his feet on the table and grinned up at the camera. It had been a textbook piece of conditioning: disorientate, keep moving, use surprise, keep them off balance and never allow the enemy to regroup. His instructors would have been proud of him. Edge reached in his pocket. He had given up drinking but needed something to replace it. The old standby he used on operations. He lit a cigarette, inhaled deeply and coughed. The cat sauntered in and registered his disapproval with a stare.

"Oh, do fuck off, Monty."

The throbbing headache he developed took some of the shine off the rest of the day and it kept him awake until he fell asleep exhausted in the early hours.

Edge did contact the various organisations and Service charities, and while they were sympathetic and could provide advice on representation and financial hardship, they were unable to influence or even approach IHAT while an investigation was ongoing, and Edge's was one of the more serious, as it involved an actual killing.

*

The police arrived at 05:30 on a Monday at the end of October, in two police cars and a riot van. They searched his property for six hours and took away a standalone computer, an old digital bridge camera, assorted CDs and DVDs, an MP3 player and an old Nokia phone. The unmarked police car conducting surveillance on him and his property promptly fucked off when Edge took out two mugs of cocoa on a tray to the occupants. He waited three days and went down to the river at night to check if his laptop, cameras and other equipment was still safe under the overhanging tree root system. The Torridge was still in full flow, but they were out of the water, well secured and tucked back into the bank in waterproof diving bags he used when on the boats. He retrieved some paperwork with a view to going through it. Some of it was the stuff from his uncle.

The work on boats was drying up as winter approached and Edge was feeling bored, and withdrawal symptoms and smoking made him edgy and caused stomach cramps and upsets. He was interviewed under caution by a different 'pod', much more polite and professional this time, but said absolutely nothing. He revisited the journal from the Korean War, sober this time, and became fascinated with the map of his Uncle's 'Cache'. He took a trip to Barnstaple and purchased a 1:25,000 scale map of the Central Highlands of Scotland. He spent hours poring over it with an anglepoise lamp on the kitchen table. After endless coffees and cigarettes, plus irritating cat's paw prints on the map, he had pinpointed the position of the corner of the wood and the high tension line. He cross-referenced the area from Google Maps, accessed from the local library in Bideford. In the finest traditions of a *Blue Peter* presenter, Edge cut out the area of the map he would need and covered it with sticky back plastic, the same for a photocopy of his uncle's map.

During the next week, Edge visited Exeter, Truro and Plymouth. He made a large number of unremarkable cash withdrawals from various savings accounts and purchased a list of outdoor clothing and equipment, paid for by cash. Back at home, he put these newly acquired items in the river cache under the tree roots. By November he was ready. He was pondering what to do about Monty as he hedged the treeline area of his property by the lane. Edge felt better, but he still wasn't sleeping brilliantly. At least the shakes and stomach cramps had gone. As he swung on a hazel to pull it into the hedge line, he became aware of an elderly lady watching him from the lane. She lived about four properties away. She had keen little eyes and twisted grey hair sticking out from under a waxed bonnet. Edge wondered how long she had been watching him.

"Morning," he said.

"Morning," she replied, watching him keenly.

"Err, can I help you…?"

"No. I see they haven't arrested you yet."

"Sorry?"

"The pigs. They've been keeping a rare old eye on you. You being a bit of a lad an' all."

Edge dropped the billhook and stared at the old lady with a sense of reality spinning away from him.

"It was in the papers. But I don't take any notice of the bollocks they print in the rags."

Edge had been conditioned, disorientated and kept off balance by an elderly lady. He was hooked. "Would you like a cup of tea?"

She seemed to think about it. "All right."

In his kitchen, they both lit up while the kettle boiled. Edge coughed more than she did.

"You were in the Army, weren't you? You're wife's gone and taken your kids."

"That's pretty much it," Edge agreed.

"You were a silly boy last Christmas, weren't you?"

"It was the New Year, actually."

She inhaled deeply and blew out a thin blue plume of smoke. "And the police are being bastards to you. Because they don't care what you've done or where you've served. That's because you worry them."

Edge poured the teas. "Milk and sugar?"

"No thanks, watching my weight. Well, go on then, three."

They stared at one another over the rims of tea mugs.

"I see your cat came back."

"Well, he isn't really mine. He was the ch…"

"He's yours now. But he comes into my house."

"I'm so sorry."

"It's all right. I feed him. I like him. He brings me mice. Mostly they're dead."

"Actually, Mrs…" She declined to help him. "…I was wondering if…"

"Look after him while you go away for a few days."

Edge put down his mug and stared at her. "Look, Mrs whatever your name is. I know I've seen you around many times, but this is the first time you've spoken to me. Why?"

"Because I feel sorry for you. Because the bottom has fallen out of your life and at the moment the only company you have is a tabby cat."

Edge began to feel annoyed. "I'm sure I don't need an old lady to feel sorry for me!"

Yes, I know, you can manage that perfectly well yourself."

"I think you should go now. I'll find a cattery."

"How old do you think I am, Mr Edge?"

"Look, I don't bloody know."

"I'm probably about fifteen years older than you, if that."

"Well, that's what I thought."

"Don't bloody lie to me. I look like this because it's my own fault. It's called heroin chic." She grinned and showed a mouthful of missing teeth. "I was an 'It' girl. A topless dancer in London clubs during the very late sixties and most of the seventies. At least that was how I started out. The clubs became seedier and then they wanted me to give 'extras'. There came a time when I wouldn't give a shit what I did as long as it involved getting the next fix. We've met before, you know," she told him.

"I don't recall that."

"It was April 1977."

Edge scoffed. "Don't be so bloody daft, I was only seven and I lived in Nuneaton with my mum and dad."

She sucked on the cigarette. "You looked exactly like you do now. Hair a bit longer, more suntanned, but you had that bloody big scar on your forehead. That's how I recognised you. It frightened me. You frightened me, but you saved my life. I could have loved you, you know."

"You're off your head, with respect."

"Right, now listen! The rifle fires one or two more rounds, then stops again. Come on! Cock, hook and look. No, for fuck's sake, that's the IA drill for the SLR. We're on the L85. The clue is one or two more rounds then stops again. It's a fucking gas stoppage. What are you going to do?"

Edge put his mug down on the table, his hands shaking slightly. "How do you know that?"

"Because you told it to me in 1977, to keep me awake and stop me falling into a junkie coma. There are many things in heaven and on earth that we don't understand. Just accept that they are." She pushed her chair away from the table. "It's been nice talking to you, Mark Edge, former Staff Sergeant 22 SAS. Let me know when you want me to look after your cat."

After she had gone, Edge sat at the table in stunned silence. Despite the fact she hadn't introduced herself, he knew with absolute clarity that her name was Cynthia Penrith.

*

Edge left the next morning at 04:00, kicking out an indignant Monty and putting his basket, food and water in the lean-to. He headed south-east on the side roads to Tiverton to avoid Devon and Cornwall's finest. It added at least an hour to his journey, but the first police car he spotted was near Bristol. His first refuelling stop was north of Birmingham on the M6, the second south of Glasgow. He arrived in Perth at 15:00 and managed to get a room in the second hotel he tried, paying for three nights by cash. He slept for five hours and got up, slipping out of the hotel unnoticed.

He drove north-east and picked up the A822, heading north until the road branched off to the left, following the River Almond up the valley towards Auchnafree and the estate. Predictably, it was raining when he pulled the car into the cover of dank evergreen trees. Edge shouldered a small rucksack that held a poncho, para-cord, sleeping bag, bivvy bag, a folded and rolled carry bag, a Coleman stove, puritabs and food and two litre canteens of water. Perhaps the most important tool was a lightweight, folding entrenching tool, strapped to the pack. He had three layers on the top, a wicking undershirt, a Buffalo jacket and Gortex shell. His boots were Haix's finest, and Berghaus gaiters. A hat for warmth but ears uncovered. (Please note, there are other brands of outdoor clothing available.) He headed north, following a surging burn tumbling down from the hills, and a harsh, slippery climb lay ahead.

As part of his training, Edge had spent a week with an RAF mountain rescue team in Scotland. "You'll love it. A nice easy-osy week with the Crabs. Decent accommodation and food, and with their levels of fitness you'll be lucky to break a sweat."

The food and accommodation were first rate, at least on the first night and the last night before he returned to his unit. The six days between were spent in the mountains, well above the snow line. They slept out in blizzards, covering over twenty miles a day. A cocky little ginger Scouse corporal was the team leader, and it was interesting to watch him yelling obscenities at an officer who had recently joined the team and had made a mess of tying off some ropes. The RAF certainly did things differently. By the end of the week, he was physically exhausted but understood the mountains and his limitations. He was grateful to see the huge yellow Sea King flare and hover in a rotor blizzard to pluck them off the mountain.

After two hours and at a height of 500 metres, he was almost at the crest onto the plateau, but he had discovered that starting smoking to stop drinking wasn't the smartest of moves. He stopped briefly, soaked through with sweat rather than rain and got half the water bottle down. In cover, he was steaming. It was very dark and he followed the path by keen night vision alone, remembering to look off-centre to give his eyes' rods and cones the best chance. Finally on the plateau, Edge checked his map and marching compass with a cyalume tucked inside his Gortex. (He preferred to do things the good old-fashioned way.) Aiming off, he hit the plantation of trees beyond the stone wall, then turned right, following the wall to the corner of the wood. There was no sign of the power cables. Edge crouched in the relative safety of the wall and consulted the tactical map with the cyalume. He looked at the bearing on the compass, but there were no reference points in the darkness.

"Bugger," said Edge. He decided to set up the poncho as shelter, cook a meal and wait until it got lighter. Once again, he had developed a throbbing headache and he rubbed his eyes. Once out of the wind and rain, he cranked up the Coleman stove and heated some soup. He snatched some sleep, tucked into the Gortex bivvy bag, and a few hours later, there was a greyish tinge below the solid overcast. Forming out of the gloom was the dark upright structure. As dawn came closer, it was obvious that the structure was the leg of a pylon.

Edge clambered stiffly out of the bivvy bag, took the map's compass bearing on a tussock about 100 metres away and paced out the distance. After the requisite number of paces, he placed down a water bottle. He moved to the south-easterly leg of the pylon and paced the requisite amount on a different bearing, taken from the tactical map, and put down the second water bottle. The two bottles were about three metres apart, not a bad margin of error given pace length and magnetic variation. Then he started to do a two-metre, ten-metre search, spreading out from a point equidistant between the water bottles. He found the flat stone covered with heather after ten minutes and marked it. Expanding the search showed no other obvious feature, so he went back to the stone, unfolded the entrenching tool and started to dig.

The stone was large but broad and shallow, so he was digging underneath it and beginning to feel rather foolish. Still, the exercise was good for him. It was almost fully light by the time the blade of the entrenching tool hit something solid. Edge dug more carefully and revealed something that was wrapped in heavy duty plastic. It took him a further hour to free it and pull it from under the stone. He instinctively knew what it was, but continued to excavate the hole to find a smaller package, again wrapped in plastic. The second package rattled and again he was pretty certain as to what it was. He continued to dig but found nothing else. He backfilled the hole and tried to leave no trace of his having dug the site, then put the two packages in the carry bag and strapped it to the side of the rucksack.

By the time Edge had broken his camp and made his way back to the car, it was after 10:00. He drove into Perth and had breakfast at a supermarket and went back to the hotel. His wet, bedraggled appearance raised no comments as the staff were used to serious hillwalkers staying with them. Edge left the carry bag in the car but took the rucksack up to his room. While most of the staff were dealing with the lunch orders, he retrieved it and opened the packages in the bath, having to cut them open with his Leathermans.

Edge was looking at a hunting rifle; the stock and butt had been unscrewed from the barrel and working parts and a telescopic sight. The second package contained two boxes of .308 Winchester ammunition.

"What the fuck, Uncle Jack?"

He cleaned and assembled the rifle that afternoon. The barrel was slightly rusty and there was a small amount of corrosion on the face of the bolt. The optics of the telescopic sight were beyond repair. After dinner and checking that the coast was clear, he put the rifle and ammunition in the boot of the car, knowing from this point on, he was committing a serious offence.

The next morning, Edge purchased some items from the B&Q store in Perth, including Scotch-brite, two types of oil, lint-free cloth, a two-part epoxy resin and some heavy-duty twine. At an outdoor pursuit and gun shop, he bought a Leupold 9x40 telescopic sight for £250 cash and an A1 flipboard pad and marker pens from an office and stationery outlet. From WHSmith he purchased a 1:2500 walking map of the Cairngorms National Park and noted a likely spot. Edge picked up the A9 and headed north, turning into the heart of the park at Braemar. Half an hour later, he pulled off the road, cleaned and assembled the rifle and telescopic sight with the help of his trusty Leatherman. Using the twine twisted and small pads of cut Scotch-brite to pull through, he cleaned the barrel. Satisfied the rust had gone, he pulled through some cloth and oil. Edge put one box of ammunition, the pad and pens and the rifle in the carry bag and fashioned a rucksack arrangement out of some straps.

By the afternoon, he was in the heart of the Cairngorms and hadn't seen another soul since Braemar. It was late in the season and unseasonably cold for November. There wasn't much wind, and the heavy, glowering sky threatened snow. He was in a wide valley following a large stream that ran straight for some 500 metres before twisting sharp right. The outcurve of the river had cut a deep bank, and this area would be ideal for what he wanted. The stream was out of what little wind there was. Edge took out the flipchart pad and coloured in a black 4" square in the centre of the sheet. He put it on the bank weighted by stones so that the sheet of paper hung down. He paced out 100 metres from the paper along the bank and found a position where he could lie with the rifle fully supported. Edge cleaned and wiped six rounds of the Winchester ammunition and took up a firing position.

The first shot was hard against his shoulder, the .308 round kicking like a mule. Through the sight he could see the hole in the top right corner of the paper. He didn't need a check shot and adjusted the sights. The second round was touching the top edge of the black square, dead centre. Edge paced out a further 100 metres and fired two shots. This time, he had to jog back to the target and was gratified to see both were in the black square. He jogged back to the rifle and moved back a further 200 metres so he was firing at a range of 400 metres. He fired two rounds, putting the cross-hairs just above the black square. Back at the target, the rounds were level with, but slightly to the right of, the square. Edge knew that he would have to aim off slightly at 400 metres. He moved quickly, burning the paper and wrapping the rifle and putting it in the carry bag. He jogged away, wanting to clear the area before anyone came to investigate, and to avoid the impending snow. Back at the car, he covered the telescopic sight's adjustment screws with epoxy resin, locking the settings.

The next day and night, Edge drove home, briefly stopping at Manchester, Leeds and Birmingham during the night. He stole three sets of number plates from cars of the same type and colour. He chose the older style of plates that wouldn't break up while being removed, but even so he was very careful.

The rifle was wired and cable-tied in the car's engine compartment, wrapped in silver foil and insulation. It would escape a cursory search of his car, the types of searches the police undertake when they have to be seen to be doing something, or just as a weapon of general harassment. The number plates joined it. The following night, all of the items joined the cache under the tree roots that overhung the river.

# Chapter 25

# A FAR-RIGHT
# TERRORIST HATE CRIME

———

For the next few months throughout the winter, Edge spent a great deal of time in the public library conducting research. He had exhausted and largely met a dead end with IHAT. Their ongoing investigation on him was progressing with glacial slowness. He was interviewed again by the Investigation 'Pod' and once again refused to make any comment.

"You're going to have to say something sooner or later, Staff Edge." He stubbornly maintained silence, saving it for his court appearance, whenever that would be. But it was as though the investigator had read his mind.

"You do realise that you're not going to have your day in court. It will be a closed hearing, no press, no public. You don't even have to attend. Whichever way you look at it, you're fucked."

So Edge moved his research on to the law firm that had initiated the claims against him, Community Legal Notaries. The organisation had a flashy website and he spent hours trawling through the organisation and its purpose, or rather its Common Purpose. Community Legal Notaries (CLN) operated under the umbrella of the Human Rights Act and was acting on behalf of 'victims' of the Iraq War, Afghanistan and the Occupied Palestinian Territories. What was strikingly absent were any investigations into socialist regimes such as Venezuela, China, Zimbabwe and an unending list of National Socialist failed states. CLN, the website proudly boasted …*acts in several cases arising out of the alleged unlawful actions of the UK armed forces in Afghanistan. These cases cover a wide range of issues and are presently being litigated in the Administrative Court. CLN also has cases arising out of the alleged unlawful actions of multinational companies in Africa.*

The organisation stated that it did these things by actively seeking out the victims and the oppressed in whichever countries these acts had taken place. The CLN was soliciting for 'victims' in Iraq and Afghanistan, flying them to the UK, accommodating them in London hotels and charging this to the MoD or more specifically, the English taxpayer.

"Bastards!" Edge said from his corner of the library. An elderly lady doing research into tarot cards glanced sharply at him from over her computer screen.

"Sorry."

Edge looked into the history of CLN and found out that the company had been set up in 1999 during the Blair reign of terror by a Mr Ron Gleam, a lawyer who specialises in employment and human rights law. Mr Gleam was a darling of the *Guardian* and the Left, and there were many images of him hobnobbing with the Labour leader, the ubiquitous head of Freedom and La Liberté International. Ron Gleam was also a donor to the Labour Party.

"Naturally," Edge agreed.

Ron Gleam was an unlikely champion of freedom. He had an owlish face, extremely trendy spectacles with a pink tint, an Armani suit and a ponytail. In the next few days, Edged decided on what he was going to do. He made a new will with a local solicitor, who if she was surprised, hid it well. Edge visited the former heroin addict up the lane and had a cup of tea with her.

"I'm going away again," he told her.

"Oh, how long this time?"

"Permanently."

She stared at him. "What about your house?"

"It's all taken care of, in due course."

"And you want me to look after your cat."

"I can take him to a refuge."

"No. I've grown rather attached to him." They said their goodbyes, but he couldn't bear to see the cat's disapproving stare as he looked into Edge's soul.

"I hope you're not going to do anything silly, Mr Edge."

He smiled sadly. "I already have. Bye, Monty. I'll miss you in my own way."

\*

Moira continued to remain in contact with Edge, but there was always anger and suspicion on his part and bitter sadness on hers. She wanted them to be a family again, but apart from their own problems, there were too many external influences from her own extended family, but at least Daz kept away.

One afternoon, they met over coffee. She told him about what she and the children had been doing while he remained non-committal.

"The children, particularly Francis, are upset because Monty has gone missing."

"He's with me. He came home in a right old state." He chuckled like the old Edge. "You can take him back, but he'll just run away again. It's not me he wants, it's his territory."

"Please let us get back together, Mark."

"Are you prepared to move away from here, away from your fucking parents?"

She shook her head and her eyes welled up.

"Then you know what the answer is."

*

In the New Year of 2013, Moira decided that she had had enough of trying to bring up a family in an annex above garages and workshops. It had been a turgid Christmas spent in the company of her family, and she had come to the decision that a flawed husband was better than living with controlling parents. She had analysed her life with Edge and had come to the rather startling conclusion that he had never once raised his hand in anger against her, or the children. Then she started to pick apart her parents' arguments and accepted wisdom. None of it stacked up. But the biggest shock was when she realised that her father had actually put her in harm's way regarding Daz Copeland. He had to have known, and she suspected her father had grown frightened of his right-hand man. His killing of Edge would have removed both problems, and Moira was acceptable collateral damage. She screwed up her fists and hammered them down on the table to punctuate her anger.

"YOU... FUCKING... BASTARD!"

Moira drove to the cottage at Weare Giffard and saw an empty and depressingly uncared-for building that had been her home. She tried her key in the lock, which didn't work. Then she toured the building, peering in windows. It was still furnished but empty. Their little cottage on the river was cold, damp and derelict. It was like a nail through her heart.

"Hello, can I help you?" an old lady asked from the gate. "Oh, sorry, it's you, Mrs Edge."

"Hello, Miss Penrith. I'm looking for Mark. Do you know where he is?"

The old lady looked at Moira with kindly eyes. Being no stranger to heartache and misery herself, she put her hand on Moira's shoulder. "Come up to my place and I'll tell you what I know."

She made a pot of tea and a cat sauntered into the kitchen.

"Monty. Hello, boy."

The cat raised his tail in greeting, recognising his old mum.

"I'm looking after him now. You can take him if you want."

"Mark said he would just run away again. He loves his territory more than humans. He seems happy. Poor boy with that scar. He has been in the wars."

They sipped tea and Miss Penrith shook her head sadly. "Your husband has gone away."

"For how long?"

"For ever."

Moira started crying. "Where's he gone?"

"I don't know, honestly. He left before Christmas and said everything was in the hands of the solicitor. Here's their card. He even changed the locks."

"God, he really must hate me," Moira said miserably.

The lady put her liver-spotted hand on Moira's. "He hated everything, including life. You're not to blame. There's something wrong with him. There's nothing I can say to ease your pain. I'm so sorry, dear."

"Did you ever like him?"

The old lady's reply puzzled Moira. "With all my heart. He saved my life a long time ago and he never even knew it. I could easily have loved him if we had shared the same time for more than a few hours."

Moira walked back to her car in tears, but then a new resolve overcame her, tempered by a new hatred for her father and contempt for her mother. She did drive back to Barnstaple, but not to her parents' house. She went into several letting agencies in the town and asked for information on three-bedroom properties to let in Bideford, Appledore, Northam and Torrington.

Within a month, she had moved into a three-bedroom flat in Okehampton, still drivable to her work at the glass factory, and the children had a new school. Before she left, she took her father's prized golf clubs to the workshop and ground off the heads with an angle grinder. She contemplated filling his MG A with concrete but realised she would need too many of the small post hole sacks. She consoled herself with pouring some paint stripper over the bonnet, boot and wings. For the icing on the cake, she went into the kitchen, found a potato and rammed it up the exhaust.

Angela helped her move with a couple of male friends. "What the bloody hell took you so long?"

*

Money was no problem for Edge, thanks to contacts he had made in America while working with their Special Forces, and some very lucrative investments Horace Cutler had prudently suggested. Edge had several foreign bank accounts under other identities and his Service pension paid for the maintenance of his children. Unlike many marriages that are in difficulties, Moira badly wanted back the Edge she had married and not the violent, alcohol-dependent version. In truth, she could hardly blame him for the violence on Daz Copeland, who had provoked both of them beyond measure. Moira didn't want revenge on Edge, she didn't want to financially ruin him, she just wanted him back and she was prepared to wait. It took eight years.

Around 500 people go missing in the UK every single day. Edge became one of those who chose to. Because he had operated within the darker regions of the deep state, he knew just how much the state despised and distrusted its own citizens. He knew the levels of state surveillance and how it was conducted and more importantly, he knew how to avoid it and disappear. He knew the limitations of surveillance cameras and how the state hated the cash economy. Cash gives people freedom. Cash prevents the state from making an individual a non-person. An individual who uses cash has freedom from state surveillance and can purchase what the hell they like, without being under the interfering gaze of the state and some of its disreputable employees.

The Annual Local Area Labour Force Survey, 2001/02, Office for National Statistics noted that by ethnicity, the unemployment rate for males was 20% for Bangladeshi immigrants, 16% for Pakistani, 15% and 14% for Black Africans and Black Caribbeans respectively. The statistic for indigenous White Males was 5%. What do you think those figures are likely to be now, fifteen years later? The statistic for homelessness was that 37% of those declared homeless were White British and the rate for Bangladeshi males was 1%. You may wonder why the most unproductive sector of society has the lowest homelessness rate by ethnicity.

In a country that professes to care for 'Our Boys', one in four of the homeless are former members of the Armed Forces. Some might speculate that councils and the government are prioritising homing those who offer the least to society at the expense of the most productive and people who have risked their lives and freedom for their country. Some councils give ex-prisoners a higher priority for finding accommodation than former Service personnel. I'm sure there is no correlation, but just remember that the next time your local councillor comes touting for your vote.

He stole three very popular types of Ford cars of the same make and colour from London, Southampton and Birmingham. He changed the number plates and stashed the cars in different southern cities, choosing areas of high immigration that he knew were virtual no-go areas for the police.

That spring, Edge was operating with the absolute basics of kit to support and sustain survival. He maintained personal hygiene by slipping into swimming pools and leisure centres at busy times. He paid particular attention to foot and oral hygiene. Unfortunately, he continued to be plagued with cluster headaches and was existing on a steady flow of painkillers. Only codeine-based painkillers seemed to give him respite. In the world of the homeless, the drug takers were the worst; desperate and with no sense of morality. One night, two, driven by desperation, tried to rob him. They came to wish they hadn't. He could slip in and out of various personas simply by changing clothes and walking with a different gait or deportment.

Edge had met a virtuous, unselfish woman who volunteered in one of the soup kitchens and hostel he frequented. She was caring and vivacious in an easy way. Despite his circumstances, Edge called them do-gooders, but her demeanour lacked what he regarded as that nauseating, virtue-signalling persona in which do-gooders seemed to wrap themselves. Edge's cynicism as well as his anger was consuming the kindliness he had once had. The fifteen-year-old boy who had helped the Non-conventionals with their homework had long gone. She would talk to any of them. The alcoholics with the shakes, who sometimes pissed themselves in the dining hall. Or the toothless addicts who had run out of veins to inject; it didn't seem to matter to her. She would get a mop, bucket and disinfectant and get on with it.

But to Edge she maintained a cold aloofness that seemed to match his disdain for life in general. He was convinced that she didn't like him, and he convinced himself that he cared not one jot. One evening, he arrived too late for dinner and most of the other punters were bedding down for the night.

She was emptying and tidying containers on the bain-marie and glanced up as Edge came in.

"Oh, too late, sorry." He turned to leave.

"Just sit down and I'll get you something. It will be a bit of a mish-mash, I'm afraid."

She came over with a plate, cutlery and two slices of stale bread, and much to his surprise, she sat opposite him.

"Err, thanks." Edge tucked into some corned beef stew with a few potatoes. The carrots were overdone and it wasn't particularly hot, but welcome nonetheless. Her presence was disconcerting as she watched him eat. When he had finished, he smiled awkwardly at her, but there was no warmth in his eyes.

"What's your name?"

"Brink, Maarten Brink."

"Brink?"

"Yes, my father was from the Netherlands."

She stared at him coolly, a wry little smile playing at the corners of her mouth. "Well, Maarten Brink, I've got a question for you."

He pushed his plate away.

"Why are you playing at being homeless?"

Edge looked at her coldly. "I didn't realise it's a game."

"It isn't for most of the poor souls who traipse in and out of this hostel. Circumstance and their own failings have put most of the people you see in here. But you're not like them, are you? I just wondered if you're doing research or just want to see how the other half lives."

"I'm looking for someone," Edge told her reluctantly.

She pulled a little pad out of her apron pocket and scribbled something on it, ripped out the page and pushed it across the table.

"What's this?"

"My mobile number. Let me know when you've decided that you want help, but I don't think you'll ever find what you're looking for."

Edge decided to give the hostel near Waterloo a miss for some time to come. One morning in late February, he caught sight of Gleam in the back of a taxi, but it swung round Lincoln's Inn Fields and headed for the barrier-controlled mews to the rear of Serle Street. Edge went to buy some fast-setting epoxy resin and some wire cutters from a hardware shop.

That lunchtime, the security guard in his booth was both disgusted and astonished to see a drunk lurching towards the security barrier. The man was filthy and bounced off walls, staggering into an alcove to presumably urinate. Edge was frantically mixing the epoxy resin and when he lurched back into view, seemed to bypass the barriers with one step forward and two back. He hit the barrier stanchion and swore at it, offered to fight it then fell over it. The security guard had seen enough and moved quickly out of his booth, but not quickly enough. The card and optical readers were liberally smeared and jammed with the epoxy resin. He couldn't find any wires to cut, unfortunately. He tripped and sprawled over, giggling at the security guard, who hauled him up and rammed him against the wall.

"Shhorry, seem to losht my way." Edge sniggered drunkenly and wiped his hand on the security guard's jacket.

The guard punched him in the stomach and Edge doubled up and fell over. The guard started to kick him, then remembered the security cameras at each end of the mews. He hauled the drunk up and threw him out onto the road. A van hooted angrily and swerved to avoid the body. Edge picked himself up and ran unsteadily into Lincoln's Inn Fields. Out of sight, he composed himself.

"Bastard!" he exclaimed angrily, debating whether to go back and cause the security guard some serious damage, but he calmed down and decided to remain on mission. That afternoon, Edge stole a bicycle and stashed it by the railings on Serle Street. He went to the left luggage locker at Liverpool Street Station and changed into a cycle courier's uniform of Lycra with a document bag. It started to rain so Edge took cover and waited. At 17:50, he saw Ron Gleam leave the offices and hail a taxi. Edge followed the taxi through the rush-hour traffic to Paddington Station. It was exhausting and he alienated a large number of drivers in the 3.5 mile frenetic pedal through London to Paddington Station.

He lost the lawyer in the scrum inside the station but decided to move his area of operations to West London. Five days later, he clocked Gleam and followed him to Platform 5 for the train to Oxford. He purchased a first-class ticket and got in the same carriage as Gleam, slightly underdressed, much like a wealthy musician who didn't need to care what people thought. Gleam changed at Twyford and he didn't notice the scruffy individual who walked with the confidence of a man who deserved to travel first class to Henley-on-Thames. It was pointless trying to follow Gleam from the station, but Edge now knew the type of Bentley that Gleam drove. He moved very much upmarket in his area of operations, and he would have to work very hard to remain unnoticed. It was time for him to stop playing at being homeless.

Over the next week, he would conduct such a thorough reconnaissance of the Thames town that he would know how many people lived in each of the fabulous houses, their level of security, their routines, but more importantly the best positions and angles to take a shot.

However, the woman at the hostel's remark had rankled him. It was like an annoying itch that needed to be scratched, and before he moved on, he pulled the crumpled piece of paper out of his pocket and his cheap pay-as-you-go mobile phone and scratched it. They met in a coffee bar, a suitable and safe public area, and Edge drank green tea, a taste he had developed in assorted Middle-Eastern shitholes. Tea is made with boiling water, so whichever hand had been used to make it wasn't so imperative. She looked good. The apron had gone, but there was still the faint, greasy aroma of the hostel kitchens about her. Edge wondered if she was playing at being a kindly charity worker as much as he had being a homeless down-and-out. He realised that it was an unkind thought and he cringed inwardly. There were parts of him that even he hated.

"Well, Mr Brink. Have you finally decided that you need some help?" Her cappuccino was still too hot to drink.

"No. I've come to say goodbye."

She stirred the chocolate sprinkles on top of the cup thoughtfully. "So you've found who you were looking for. Now what?"

"You'll probably read about it in the papers. Most of it will be a bloody lie."

She looked at him and smiled sadly. "You know, I once knew someone like you."

*Oh God, here we go*, he thought.

"He was a pilot. Nothing glamorous, but he used to fly the routes into the Western Isles. Mostly clapped-out Islanders, or the mail runs in a Twin Cessna into Barra and Benbecula. Sometimes it was to take the islanders to hospital appointments in Glasgow."

Edge thought he could detect a slight Scottish accent.

"He loved it. But it was terribly stressful. The approach and landing to Barra was a right bastard. At least that's what he said. Flying in the Western Isles is so dependent on the weather, and in the case of Barra, the tides. But it was a service the islanders could rely on. Unfortunately, the stress was killing him, the long hours in little planes like that, no second pilot. Alone with the weather."

Edge was genuinely interested in someone apart from himself. "What happened?"

"Two years ago, it was during the cluster of bad storms, he tried to get into Benbecula to pick up a pregnant woman who was having complications. Some bloody idiot hit and damaged the Navy Sea King at Prestwick with a low loader, so they asked him to try. Even in the storm he agreed and made three aborted approaches, but just couldn't get in. Unfortunately, both the woman and her baby died."

"What's your name?" Edge asked quietly.

"Kimberly. You've probably heard them call me Kim at the hostel, but that's all you're getting, Maarten Brink, and at least it's my real name."

"I'm going to hate this, aren't I, Kimberly?"

"Do you know Perth, Maarten, specifically Kinnoull Hill?" He did but shook his head. "It's a beautiful spot where you can see the River Tay meandering through the valley, high above Perth. Well, you see, this pilot was distraught and felt that he had failed at his duty. The trouble was, his wife was too much of a pisshead to notice how much pain her husband was in. As long as she had the vodka and her vacuous friends, she didn't really care. This chap, poor sod, had nowhere to turn, so he walked up Kinnoull Hill. They found him three days later on a ledge a hundred and fifty feet down from the top. Dead, obviously."

Edge looked at her and felt his mouth was dry. "I am so very sorry. Is that why you came to London?"

"To make amends? Atonement?" She laughed bitterly. "No. Initially, it was to drink and fuck myself to death. The other stuff came later. If I hadn't been such a useless lush, I could have seen that he was being consumed, much like you are now."

To Edge's surprise, she reached across the table and grabbed his hand. "I'm like that little boy in *The Sixth Sense*. I see dead people. You might be living, but you're dead inside. I bet you've made friends with the bottle, haven't you, Maarten?"

"The bottle and I have been on intimate terms many times in the past," he agreed.

"I'm going to do something that is probably incredibly stupid. I may well end up as just another statistic, a stupid woman who trusted too much. You may well be the last thing that I see, but I'm prepared to take the risk. Are you?"

*

She looked at him as he came out of the shower. Firstly at the obvious part and then at the puckered and ragged scar above his left hip.

"My God! What happened to you?"

"It's what you call an occupational injury. I got too close to a parting wire hawser on a fishing trawler." The lie seemed to come more easily than the truth.

"I've hidden your knife while you were in the shower, not that I suppose it matters. You wouldn't need anything to kill me, would you?"

Edge towelled himself vigorously. The hot shower had been wonderful.

"You must know that we all carry a weapon of some form or another in order to survive. And you must know that I mean you no harm."

She walked up to him and they embraced. Edge was hit by many conflicting emotions. He thought of Moira, then he thought about Daz Copeland. And he thought about the scent of a woman, how long it had been. He could bury himself in that moment, and he did.

*

When she woke up, he was sitting on the edge of the bed, his head in his hands, rocking gently.

"Maarten, whatever's wrong?"

"Bloody headaches. They keep coming and going. Too much emotion, I suppose."

She put her arm round him gently. "Lie down while I get you something for it."

*An intracranial hematoma is a collection of blood within the skull, most commonly caused by rupture of a blood vessel within the brain or from trauma such as a car accident or fall. The blood collection can be within the brain tissue or underneath the skull, pressing on the brain.*

*Although some head injuries – such as one that causes only a brief lapse of consciousness (concussion) – can be minor, an intracranial hematoma is potentially life-threatening. It usually requires immediate treatment, often surgery to remove the blood.*

*The sufferer might develop signs and symptoms of an intracranial hematoma right after a blow to the head, or they may take weeks or even months to appear. They might seem fine after a head injury, a period called the lucid interval.*

Edge was fast approaching the end of his long lucid interval.

*

Once Edge had traced Gleam to his large, walled and gated house that backed onto the Thames, he conducted a thorough recce of the property, its security and the area. Edge concluded that the best security was offered by the house's area and exclusivity. Now he knew where Gleam lived. He knew all about his family, his associates and fellow travellers. He understood his influence and the protection with which the establishment and the deep state provided the lawyer. He worked out angles, hides, infiltration and exfiltration routes. He timed and recorded the position and angles of the sun. He filled multiple exercise books with notes and tactical maps. That December, Edge retrieved and activated one of his three identities he had constructed in a previous life, because he knew that surveillance over the winter would be impossible. He grew and dyed his hair and beard grey, and rented an apartment in the Algarve for four months.

## Chapter 26

# DEATH IN THE ALGARVE

———

The Transavia flight from Charles de Gaulle Airport touched down at Lisbon thirty minutes behind schedule. The passenger who had been sitting in the starboard isle seat by the overwing exit waited for the usual scrum of baggage collection to finish. He wasn't in any particular hurry, and once he had collected his hire car, he thought it would take him roughly three hours to drive down to Portimão, all being well.

He exited the aircraft and headed for the Hertz desk to pick up the hire car, which had been booked in his real name. He would be using another identity when he flew back to the UK, via Germany. But that was a while away yet. The mid-afternoon traffic was light as he followed the A5 motorway, turning off onto the A2 south and the 25 de Abril bridge across the Tagus. The weather was like a cooler English summer's day, a welcome change from the cold February in London and the Oxfordshire Thames. Kimberly had been distraught when he left, but he promised to come back in around six months' time. Part of him had even meant it.

He had let an apartment in Portimão on a long-term lease for around €500 per month. It would be more than adequate until the end of April, beginning of May, when he would return to England and kill Ron Gleam. Firstly, he needed the quiet of Portugal out of season to prepare himself physically and mentally. What was going to happen after he took the shot, he wasn't sure. He had prepared an exfiltration plan, but whether he would use it was another unknown. Part of him preferred the option to take as many police with him as he could. There was a bomb inside his head and the setting on the fuse delay had been forgotten.

It was early evening when Edge picked up the keys to the apartment from a nearby hotel. It was still very warm and he had a mind to drop off his kit and drive to the sea. He let himself into the apartment, which was comfortable, minimalistic and well appointed. On the small table was a note. Edge opened the envelope.

*Hello, Mr Edge,*

*I hope you had a good journey and now that you are here, everything is to your satisfaction. Please make yourself at home and enjoy your stay for as long as you wish to sojourn in our beautiful part of the world.*

*There is a get-you-in pack of bread, cheese and meats in the fridge and of course a selection of wine and beer. There are several restaurants, bars and brasseries within walking distance, which I have annotated on the enclosed map. Seafood is of course the speciality in this part of the world.*

*I will be around at 10 am tomorrow to greet you and show you how everything works; my apologies for not being able to greet you in person this evening. The instructions for the TV and WIFI are also enclosed. You mentioned if it would be possible to have a part-time housekeeper. I have been recommended a nice lady by the name of Bia Vargas, who is looking for extra work. My current cleaner has moved away from the area, so this arrangement may suit both of us. The typical rates of pay are noted below, but I'm sure she would be grateful for your employment and whatever you feel like giving. I will tell you about her tomorrow and she will be in touch within the week. Bia is keen to improve on her English, which is already quite passable.*

*So once again, welcome, and please treat this place like your home.*

*Sincerely,*

*Clément Béringer*

Edge smiled and explored the apartment. Owned by a Frenchman who had decided to take the better life south. Why were Europeans so much more at home assimilating into other countries than the Brits? An enduring mystery to Edge. Later, he took a beer onto the balcony and watched the boats on the Arade and the Caspian gulls wheeling and diving on the unsuspecting, like

Stukas strafing a refugee column. That night, he fired up his laptop and started to do some research. Later, he suddenly became tired and went to bed early.

After he met Béringer, Edge went into Portimão and the out-of-town retail parks to do some serious shopping. As well as food and drink, he bought clothes and running shoes, a lightweight wetsuit, a sea kayak and a mountain bike. The kayak and bicycle would be delivered in a few days, and in the meantime, Edge purchased a roof rack and a large-scale map of the area to work out training routes. All of the transactions were conducted in cash. He intended to complete each day a run of around 15 kilometres, a cycle ride of 45 kilometres and a paddle of some 10 kilometres. He knew he would have to work up to those distances. He also vowed to read a couple of the classics and do some painting. However, he was unnerved to discover that for some reason, he just couldn't get the preliminary sketches right, and his photography also seemed to be below par. In a fit of frustration, he hurled the sketchpad across the room.

Three days after he arrived, Edge was coming out of the shower when he heard the apartment doorbell ring twice. Assuming it was Béringer, Edge wrapped a towel around himself and answered the door. A woman was staring at him with an intensity borne out of nervousness. She stood side-on. Like an anxious fighter. She was quite tall, mid-thirties, dark with short hair and captivating shyness that seemed to border on fear.

"Hello. Can I help you?"

"Mister Adje? I am Bia Vargas. Monsieur Béringer said I should come. You seek a housekeeper?" The way she pronounced his name, it was like she was describing a weapon.

"Oh, of course, please come in. Sit down while I slip into something more appropriate. Excuse me."

Edge slipped on a pair of shorts and a t-shirt in the bedroom, marvelling to himself. Béringer had said she was a spinster, like it was a physical affliction. He chuckled because he had imagined a kindly old crone, not this fit and willowy young woman who had turned up at the apartment door. He went into the living area. She was sitting looking out of the apartment window and turned to face him. He was smiling and despite everything, he felt the smile freeze.

*Oh Christ!* "Good morning, Senhorita Vargas. Can I get you anything?"

The entire left-hand side of her face was covered with a capillary malformation that had affected the epidermis and in places, her facial skin was puckered. It was as though someone had thrown acid in her face. It was the most severe port wine birthmark he had ever seen. Edge was disgusted. He was revolted with himself and a deep shame burned in his head.

"No thank you, Mister Adje. Do you still require a housekeeper?"

The choice of words wasn't lost on him. "It depends."

"Depends on which?" she asked. Was her face combative?

"It depends on what," he corrected her gently. "Can you teach me to speak Portuguese in a month?"

"No. Can you teach me to read and understand English books in a month?"

"Perhaps not," he agreed. "Can you cook me one meal a day to eat when I get in and tidy up after me?"

"It depends... On how bad you live."

Edge smiled at her eyes and this time there was warmth. She looked down shyly.

"Have you just employed me, Senhorita Vargas?" he asked.

"I will come back tomorrow morning same time. If you agree, I can get a spare key from Monsieur Béringer. We can discuss how much you want to give me and my duties."

"They will be promulgated in Daily Orders."

"Mister Adje?"

"Never mind. See you tomorrow."

\*

Bia Vargas would arrive every other morning, usually after Edge had left on his punishing physical schedule, and spent about two hours tidying, cleaning and preparing a meal. They would have an hour or so time together where he struggled to learn Portuguese, a language he found counter-intuitive compared to Spanish. Then they would discuss the book she was currently reading. He had found a second-hand book shop for the English tourists, and bought a few he thought she would find interesting and would help with her English comprehension. They were the usual bodice-rippers and a couple of the classics, one being Mary Shelley's *Frankenstein*. She seemed to devour them. In time, he barely noticed her face and they settled into a companionable, symbiotic relationship.

"Mister Adje, why did Captain Corelli not get back together with Pelagia after the war had finished? He did go back to Cephalonia and saw her."

Edge struggled to remember *Captain Corelli's Mandolin*. Where had he been when he read it? *Ah yes, Kabul 2007, clearing the airport after the Taliban attack. Shit tour.*

"Because he saw Pelagia with the little girl who had been abandoned as a baby and thought the child had been hers with another man."

"So? It was wartime. These things happen. Are men really so stupid to throw away love and happiness for things that always happen in a war? She could have been taken against her will."

Edge thought about the question, which was uncomfortably close to home. "Some men are, I suppose, yes."

"Then you are fools!"

"I think the book uses an unlikely love affair between two people from different backgrounds and in fact enemies as a metaphor." She wrinkled her nose, clearly not understanding what a metaphor was. "Their love affair is really a way the author shows us, the reader, the stupidity of two such closely entwined cultures as Italy and Greece going to war with each other."

Bia sniffed. "Still, I wish they had got back together as soon as the Germans left."

"There's also the contrast between passion and lust and enduring love. Pelagia feels passion and lust for the fisherman, Mandras, but she feels a more enduring and deeper love for Corelli."

"And by that time, she's too old to enjoy it, stupid man. Have you ever felt enduring love, Adje?"

By now, he was feeling very uncomfortable under her interrogative stare. "Err, yes, I suppose so."

"What is it like?"

"It's a comfortable complacency, and you don't know what you've got till it's gone. I think we should call it a day now, Bia. I need to do some shopping, so I can run you home."

The next time he came back to the apartment on one of the days she worked, she was cleaning the bathroom, singing to a song from a radio station on the cable TV. It was James Blunt and Edge winced, feeling like his soul had been run through with a stiletto. Unselfconsciously, she was harmonising with James Blunt's *You're Beautiful,* turning a dreadfully mawkish song into something quite moving.

"Thank God he was with us in Kosovo, though," Edge said, and Bia jumped guiltily as if she had been going through his things.

"Sorry to startle you. I need to go back out and get something."

Edge went out and drove to a flower shop. He bought a large and ornate bouquet and went back to the apartment.

"Mister Adje, these are lovely. I'll find a vase."

"No need, Bia. They are for you to take home."

She looked at him and to his surprise and infinite sadness, she burst into tears.

\*

Edge's Portuguese was slowly improving, with the help of some schoolbooks she brought in for him to read. Bia was having trouble understanding the meaning of the two different stories in the *Life of Pi*.

"Why is there this second horrible story about cannibalism and the murder of the sailor and Pi's mother on the lifeboat? I think the one with the tiger is much nicer."

"You are meant to. The story is all about struggling to believe. But on a different level, it's a wonderful story about a boy's struggle through adversity. I wish it had been written when I was a boy like Pi. Life is a story and you can choose your own version. But above all, in the story with Richard Parker, the tiger is trying to tell us that a story with God is a better story."

"Do you believe in God, Mister Adje?"

Edge sipped his beer and thought about it. He knew that one of his foul headaches was on the way. "I've spent most of my life wanting to prove that the existence of a higher being is a primitive superstition. A throwback to the Dark Ages. But my life became so fucked-up, oh, I'm so sorry, became so complicated, that the effort I was expending was pointless. Besides, I was a soldier. It seemed rather hypocritical to beseech God's help one minute and try and disprove his existence when I was no longer in danger."

He looked at Bia for an opinion and she self-consciously touched the side of her face with the birthmark. "I think he is a cruel god. To allow children to suffer and for people to fight wars in his name. What god would allow that to happen?"

Edge reached out and gently touched her face. "Apart from you, most of our woes are self-inflicted and caused by our own stupidity. Like my face. Just think how awful the world would be if everyone thought there were no consequences to our actions. It would be hell on earth. We'll have to start looking for more books for you. I can't believe how quickly you read them.

Now, Bia, you'll have to excuse me. I have the mother of all headaches and I'll have to go and lie down in a darkened room for a while. Let yourself out and I'll see you in a couple of days."

*

When Edge woke briefly, it was still light outside, although the sun was going down behind the blinds. His headache had diminished and he felt rested. She was curled up behind him, knees tucked up behind his, her arm over his chest, hand spread to feel his slow heartbeat. He could feel her breath on the nape of his neck and her breasts warm on his back. Edge closed his eyes and slept peacefully. Later, they would share an easy, passionate intimacy that Bia wished would last forever, while Edge knew that it couldn't.

*The function of the frontal lobe involves the ability to project future consequences resulting from current actions, the choice between good and bad (or better and best) actions (also known as conscience), the override and suppression of socially unacceptable responses, and the determination of similarities and differences between things or events.*

*The frontal lobe also plays an important part in integrating longer non-task based memories stored across the brain. These are often memories associated with emotions derived from input from the brain's limbic system. The frontal lobe modifies those emotions to generally fit socially acceptable norms.*

*

He was cutting through the water with easy strokes; the paddle seemed to be dripping with molten silver as he powered the kayak through the swell. Edged loved the simple monotony of paddling and knew that this time he was really pushing it. He thought of Bia and how she approached sex with the same all-consuming quest for knowledge as her reading. Edge couldn't wait to get back to the apartment.

He thought about killing and his discussion with Bia about God. Everything he could ever want was here, and he could fade into gentle and blissful obscurity with someone who took him for what he was. And for his part, Edge loved perfect beauty, but he could see beyond it to the perfection of the whole person. He thought about that James Blunt song, particularly the bittersweet last few lines.

276

"But make the most of it, Edge!" he said out loud, and chuckled.

The kayak rounded the breakwater and he felt the full force of the swell from the open sea. Edge headed for the shore to run parallel to it, just out from the hardy paddlers and swimmers. The water was Baltic. He would leave his kayak at the water sports club at Praia Três Irmãos and transfer to his bike for the final leg back to the apartment, to enjoy a shower, a meal and a great deal of Bia Vargas.

Edge both smelled and tasted a sudden acrid tang at the back of his throat and in his head. It was like saltpetre on a medieval battlefield, with the coppery taste of blood. He rested his paddle on the cockpit, suddenly feeling disorientated and dizzy. Without warning, he vomited.

*Shit, must have overdone it today.* He gently paddled towards the shore and when he reached the shallow water, the headache hit him like a brick on the front of his head. He ripped off the spray deck and half fell out of the kayak. Edge stumbled back onto his feet and tried to pull the kayak onto the beach. The sun had a peculiar halo around it and people were looking at him strangely. A bomb went off in his head and he was enveloped in the brightest light he had ever seen.

*

"I thought you said the Algarve would be hot."

"Well, it is bloody hot compared to Southport." They were sitting on the beach, the woman wrapped in a cardigan, watching the boats. "Besides, I needed a holiday away from bloody Lancashire Care NHS Foundation Trust and the sodding North West Ambulance Service."

His wife of twenty years shaded her eyes with the *Puzzler* magazine and watched a man staggering as he tried to drag a canoe to the shore. "You'd think that people would have more sense than to play about in the water when they're pissed."

"I'm not sure he is." The man stood up just as the figure struggling with the canoe fell face down into the water. He threw his mobile phone at his wife. "Phone 112 and ask for someone who speaks English! Tell them someone has collapsed at Praia da Rocha. Tell them it's serious."

He ran down the beach as two children tried to heave the body's head out of the water. He yelled for help at two men by the breakwater and the three of them dragged the body out of the water and up the beach. They fetched a towel and he put it behind the unconscious man's shoulders to open the airway. He was fairly sure there was no C-spine injury. He checked for at least ten seconds for breathing but there was nothing. He frantically waved to his wife to come over, then he checked for a carotid pulse, which was faint and ragged. He opened both of the man's eyes and saw that the left pupil was blown.

"Is there an English speaker yet?" His wife handed him the phone. "I have an adult male of approximately forty years. He is not breathing and the pulse is weak and irregular and he has tachycardia. He has a fixed and dilated left pupil and I suspect a head injury or a cerebral haemorrhage. We are on Praia da Rocha, two hundred metres west of the breakwater. I am commencing CPR."

*

Edge watched the off-duty paramedic working on him and felt an irrational surge of national pride. *Good lad, but you're wasting your time. I'm toast.* A child ran up to the body on the sand to get a good look, actually running through Edge. He must have felt the chill of death, because he turned in shocked surprise and looked round, although he saw nothing.

He concluded that his body was a pretty unedifying sight as the paramedic pumped his chest to *Nellie the Elephant*. Shouldn't that be *Staying Alive*? Edge was pretty sure that's what he had been taught. And he had even remembered to carry his own Guedel mask for the inflations. This chap was a man after his own heart, but the collection of flesh and bones down on the sand seemed to have outlived its usefulness. He heard the siren in the distance and moved away towards the sea. A bright sphere of light opened up about ten metres from the shore and Edge went into it.

## Chapter 27

# EDGE, THE LONG FIGHT BACK TO HUMANITY

———

He came out of the water at the side of a lake, near where a small river joined the main body of water. The air was cool and fresh with the scent of the pine forest, and the surrounding mountains were dusted with snow. It felt like early spring. Edge thought he could hear a woman's voice calling in the distance, so he followed the left bank of the river through the trees.

"Hedge."

In this section, the side of the river opened up to a small meadow, which was flecked with spring flowers such as bluebells and snowdrops. The beauty of it all was sublime.

"Hedge, you came."

She emanated out of the trees like a spirit of the forest, a long, diaphanous garment hiding the movement of her feet in the long grass. But it didn't look like she was walking. She was exactly as he remembered her, but more serenely beautiful. He felt like weeping.

"Jozica. I thought I would meet you once before, but…"

"But Minty stopped you. I know. He is here as well."

Edge turned away in anguish. "Jozica, I'm so sorry I killed you."

"You didn't, Hedge. He was going to kill me anyway. But as long as he lives, I torture him during his sleepless nights, driving him mad in that small but luxurious cell of his." She looked at him and smiled. "All that guilt, bitterness, fear and anger that you carry. Get rid of it. Don't carry it for me."

They both looked at two swans on the lake, their necks entwined in courtship. A gentle and sudden breeze ruffled the still water.

"Jozica, am I dead?"

She sighed softly. "Well, you're here with me. What do you think?"

"Good. I can be with you."

"It is not that simple, Hedge. Your wife Moira is beautiful and despite your unkindness to her, she wants you back. You have caused much unhappiness and yet you are capable of such random kindly acts. Please be kind to Bia Vargas and don't let her love you too much."

"Where's my mum?"

"Waiting for you. But there's something you must understand, Hedge. This isn't your time. There are things for you still to do. There is somebody you must save because your lives are interconnected. You must go back."

"I don't want to!"

"You must. If you don't go back, you will have died alone in that cottage by the river. The woman you are about to see will be the continuation of your earthly existence and you must save her life to save yours. There is no element of freedom involved." She embraced him. "I will always love you, Hedge, and I'll be here when it is your time. I'm sorry, but the rest of your mortal life will be one of difficulty and some pain, but bear it for us."

She gently placed her hand on his forehead and the bomb went off inside his brain again and he was screaming with pain.

\*

He was looking over the shoulder of a surgeon who was performing a craniotomy on his skull. Skin flaps had been opened and the surgeon was now drilling out a bone flap on his frontal bone.

*Well, thanks a bunch, Doc. That's going to look a right old fucking mess now, isn't it?*

The surgeon finished cutting with the high-speed cranial saw and stepped back through Edge to allow the theatre nurse to aspirate the wound. He felt the sudden chill and shivered.

*Don't worry, Doc. I have that effect on people.*

The anaesthetist was monitoring the blood pressure, O2 sats and heart rate, like an anxious parent. They had already lost Edge twice, once in the ambulance and once in the ER. The out-of-body Edge felt himself being drawn backwards towards a tunnel in the corner of the room. There was somewhere else to go and somebody who needed his help.

*Catch up with you later, perhaps…*

He came out of the light in a confused state. He had been looking down at himself being worked on by the crash team, but now he seemed to be sitting on the top of a cheap wardrobe in an insalubrious bedsit. He was looking at a girl slumped across a bed…

*

Edge finally woke up fifteen days after they had put him in the medically induced coma. Every day they would check his intracranial pressure and drain the fluid from inside his skill with an intraventricular catheter. They were also constantly monitoring for signs of bacterial meningitis, but although the NHS was the envy of the world, hospital-acquired infections were much lower in Portugal, and the Hospital Particular do Algarve was a very good hospital. Most nights, Bia would sleep just outside the HDU suite on a camp bed and Edge would watch her in his ethereal state, both humbled and saddened by her devotion to him. It would have been much easier for him if she had just left.

He was bored, endlessly wandering through the hospital corridors, desperately trying to find the route back to the meadow beside the river. He suspected that as long as the machines were keeping him alive, that route was barred to him. The day of his awakening, the out-of-body Edge was dragged back to his flesh, blood and bone version, and the pain was back. The nurse doing the 15:00 obs saw him looking at her. She smiled in genuine joy and surprise and went to page the neurosurgeon. She came back and gently wiped the dribbles away from the tubes. As he regained full consciousness, Edge started to gag and with the help of a senior nurse, they removed the airway tubes. The neurosurgeon came in with some sheets of paper and sat on the bed next to him.

"Good afternoon, Mr Edge. We are so glad to have you back. How do you feel?"

"Rough," he whispered hoarsely.

The surgeon checked his pupils and their reaction to light. "Do you know what day it is?"

"It's a Friday because I can smell fish."

"And what is this?" the surgeon asked, holding up a picture.

"It's a car."

"What colour is it?"

"It's blue."

"No, it's red, but don't worry. You will probably get a few things mixed up until your brain rewires itself. Of course, some things you may never get back. Mr Edge, you are a tough man. You will need to be on your long road to recovery. God has given you a second chance."

"No, actually it was the spirit of a Croatian forensic anthropologist called Jozica Marić, whom I killed with my stupidity."

The surgeon smiled uncertainly. "You are bound to feel confused for some time. I will be back later this evening to see how you are."

"Did you operate on me?" Edge asked, grabbing the surgeon's sleeve.

"I was part of the team which saved you, yes."

"Thank you, sir. I'm sorry I made you shiver when you stepped back in the operating theatre."

The neurosurgeon looked at Edge uncertainly. On the way back out, he spoke with the senior nurse. "Keep a close eye on the English patient and make a note of what he says. You do speak English?"

"Not very well."

"All right, ask one of your colleagues who does. He seems to be over the worst, but some things he said are a little worrying. We will need to know how well his higher faculties are working after his brain injury."

That evening, Bia visited him and hugged him to death and cried on him. "Oh, Adje, we thought you were dead."

"I bloody well will be if you don't let me breathe." She held his hand and he smiled lopsidedly. "Tonight, I want you to sleep in a proper bed, not a camp bed. Got that?"

"How did you know?"

"My guardian angel told me. Thank you, Bia, for staying with me, but I'm getting better, so a good night's sleep for you. Keep the bed warm for when I get out. Can you do me a favour, please? Bring my laptop, and inside my bag in the bedroom there is an internal pocket on the side away from the straps. Inside it, there's another cell phone and a notebook. Could you please bring them tomorrow with the laptop?"

She nodded but seemed reluctant to leave. "Go on, Bia. Sleep well and don't forget to bring the stuff I asked for. How did you get here?"

"I drove your car."

Bia finally let go of his hand and went to leave. "Night, love. By the way, the story with Richard Parker the tiger is much nicer."

The following day, Edge put the phone on charge from the laptop with a USB cable. There was only one telephone number in the phone's number log. Edge called it and left a message. He switched on the laptop and sent a short email.

**From:** In.kspot02@hotmail.co.uk
**Sent:** 24 March 2013 at 18:54
**To:** Ink.spotsps@hotmail.co.uk
Subject: Stand-to

FAO Inkspot01. I am in extremis Portugal Hospital Particular do Algarve, Faro, Portugal. Please join me with all haste.

Edge asked if it would be possible to see the hospital's dermatologist, and a small, darkly intense man visited him and he explained his problem through an English-speaking nurse.

"Sir, this is a photograph of my housekeeper." The nurse smiled knowingly at that before translating. "She is dear to me and I would like to repay the kindness she has shown me. I have considerable financial assets, and I am asking you if the lady's birthmark can be treated. I don't care about it at all, but she is very self-conscious."

The dermatologist looked at the photograph Edge had taken, unknown to her. He looked at him and smiled sympathetically. "I'm afraid, Mr Edge, that there is no guarantee that any procedure could make the unfortunate lady's facial blemish less noticeable. Laser treatment will have very limited success, as I believe that the epidermis is affected. Surgery could well make the disfigurement much worse and I would caution against it. I'm sorry that this isn't the answer you wanted but I have to be fair to you and her. On the other hand, I could perform a skin graft on your head to disguise the wound to your forehead."

He gave Edge his card and left. The nurse patted Edge's arm. "God bless you, Mr Edge."

\*

The receptionist looked at the impossibly handsome man, who for some reason wanted to visit the English patient.

"Ha yes, Meester Hedge." The lady made a telephone call and a nurse clip-clopped into the reception. He was grateful she looked like a nurse, wearing white clothing that was clean, rather than scrubs.

"Come, please."

He followed her into the bowels of the hospital to the high dependency unit. In the HDU, Edge was still connected to many machines that went beep.

"Ten minutes," the nurse said sternly, and left.

He was shocked at his state. It was like half of his face was slumped, with a rheumy, half-closed eye that looked red and sore. Edge opened his good eye and looked at him.

"What have you done, Edgie?"

"Thanks for coming," he whispered hoarsely.

Edge told him everything that had happened from his leaving the Army to the discovery of the rifle and the war crimes investigation. He told him about living rough in London and following Ron Gleam. He also told him about Bia and how they had formed an unlikely relationship. Morrison told him about his life.

"Edgie, we've both been done up like a couple of kippers," Morrison concluded.

"Who do you reckon it was?"

"Don't know, but when I find the bastards, I'll kill them."

Edge gave him a flash drive with his good hand. "It's all in there. Where the rifle's hidden. Where that bastard Gleam lives, his family and movements. Photographs and plans, maps of the area. Ways in and out."

"I'll take the shot for you," Morrison said, looking at Edge's lopsided face, and tried to stop himself from bursting into tears.

"Did she ever come back, Henry?"

"Who?"

"The Persian princess with those lovely eyes."

"No, mate. She never did. I'll be back to see you before I go and then to let you know how it went."

On the way out, Morrison saw a young woman heading for the HDU ward. She turned away from him, looking down at the floor. Morrison stopped and looked at her.

"Excuse me, are you Bia Vargas?"

She turned side-on to him, with a hunted look. "Yes."

Morrison hugged her. "Thank you, Bia. He isn't the easiest person in the world to like. He can be a bastard, but there's always something else. You've probably discovered it."

When Bia went in to see Edge, she was furious. "How did you describe me to him?"

Edge sang, in a cracked and croaky voice, a verse from *You're Beautiful.*

"He said you could be *um bastardo*, Adje," but she hugged him nonetheless.

# Chapter 28

# MORRISON'S STORY

———

**"People sleep peaceably in their beds at night only because rough men stand ready to do violence on their behalf."**

Morrison came down to breakfast and looked at the offerings the Pacific Plaza hotel had laid out for their delectation. He baulked at the fried rice and eggs and knew that misery would follow the consumption of the freshly peeled fruit on ice. He settled for white rolls and conserve. Even with the air conditioning, it was getting hot and immensely humid and it had rained for most of the night. He saw Mitchell dressed similarly to himself in a dark suit. Opel Canyon Securities insisted that all of its operatives dressed in dark suits for city business and airport runs, a lightweight linen suit for work in the field. Smart professionalism at all times. He joined Mitchell at the table and ordered coffee from the Filipino waitress, slightly puzzled.

"Morning, Harry. I thought you were supposed to be up watching the rooms 'till I take over at nine."

Mitchell shrugged. "They told me to piss off, more or less. Said they had business to discuss and the hotel security was just fine." His accent was Kiwi to the core, a tawse of a man with a number one cut. This was the third time they had partnered up on a job. They were a good team, known as the M&Ms in Opel Canyon.

"Business?"

"I suspect that it's the kind of business that involves burying the mutton dagger prior to a shower and the airport run to get out of this shithole."

Morrison tried to visualise the two Americans making the beast with two backs, but found it difficult. The two oil company executives were not exactly ugly; they just seemed very different and sewn up. An unlikely coupling. Morrison thanked the waitress as she left the coffee, and looked around the hotel's dining room. Middle-aged German and British sex tourists. Adventurous young Australians. Two American oil executives who had just cut a deal with the main Philippine petroleum company, and their close protection.

"This place gives me the creeps."

"Why's that, mate?" Mitchell asked, pushing his plate away.

"Because I've done this job in places where the danger is clear and present. Obvious. Expected. But here the threat can come from nowhere."

"I know what you mean. Like Bali. A paradise full of Islamic nutjobs who smile as they give you your bourbon on the rocks and then blow you to pieces."

Morrison looked across at Mitchell and guessed that he was ex-New Zealand SAS. They never asked those kinds of questions.

Morrison pondered the email he had received the previous evening, the one that had kept him awake most of the night. "Do you mind if I ask you a question, because I reckon that you and I have walked in the same cuds, probably on different occasions."

"As long as it isn't 'Do you find me attractive in this suit?' then ask away."

Morrison was very astute. Mitchell had been part of the SAS team, which had cleared Taliban insurgents from the diplomatic quarter in Kabul.

"I've had an email from an old comrade. He's in some bother and wants me to do something for him."

Mitchell drained his coffee, then asked: "Legal or not?"

"Not."

"How well do you get on with this guy?"

"I hate his fucking guts."

"Do you have a bond, an agreement?"

"Yes."

Mitchell pondered this for a while. "Mate, you're damned if you do and damned if you don't. Sorry, I can't help you. Anyway, let's get down to practicalities. Who gets Elmer Fudd and who gets the Ice Maiden?"

They tossed a coin and Morrison called.

"Bollocks," said Mitchell. "I've got Elmer in the front. You've got the Ice Maiden, but don't worry. She'll be nicely warmed up for you."

*

The cars were pulled round to the front of the hotel at 10.30 am, two Toyota Land Cruisers with Kevlar padding and armour. The doorman did the niceties of opening the doors while Morrison and Mitchell politely hustled them down to the cars while watching the roofs. Both of them carried briefcases and if you were to press a button on the handle, the case would drop away and they would have access to the Heckler & Koch .45 ACPs. Both carried Glocks in shoulder holsters and Morrison had a Fairbairn Sykes knife in a sheath attached to his leg. Mitchell preferred the KA-BAR. Both of them had personal radios with an earpiece and throat mike. All of the luggage had been put in the vehicle, supervised by Mitchell.

Morrison got in the rear Land Cruiser after the Ice Maiden and sat on a fold-down seat so he could watch the road behind. Neither of them noticed the doorman move round the side of the hotel and make a call on his mobile.

"Morning, ma'am. Did you sleep well?"

"Good morning, Mr Morrison. I found it rather hot and oppressive if I'm honest."

She was professional and polite. Nobody wants to piss off their close protection team, and she did love his quaint British accent. He could have sworn her face had a healthy glow and she seemed less buttoned-up. She was wearing a linen trouser suit, very wise for the flight to Manila and then onward to the States. The next day, Morrison and Mitchell would go their separate ways for some leave, their jobs done until the next time.

She started reading some notes taken out of a folder as the mini convoy left the hotel. Soon, the modern multi-storey buildings of Cotabato City became a single-storey jumble of shanty buildings, heaving with humanity on scooters and tuk-tuks. Children yelled and ran after the Land Cruisers, screaming and holding up their wares. After crossing the Tarbeng Creek Bridge, the buildings seemed to be more random and dilapidated. Ahead was the Tamontaka Bridge, low on piles with each-way traffic, a water pipeline running parallel with the bridge. The Tamontaka River was turgid, muddy and populated by a few boats going with the flow.

The Land Cruisers were about 50 metres apart when the lead hit the bridge. A truck pulled out from the right after them, cutting up the traffic and slowing any vehicle that had been following. The traffic on the bridge was light as they headed south to the airport. Too light. Morrison's spidey senses were tingling. He glanced at the truck behind.

"Err, Harry, we seem to be making good time."

It was their code word for possible trouble, so as not to alarm the passengers.

"Roger that," Mitchell replied in his earpiece.

Morrison looked over his shoulder at the lead vehicle and caught the glance of the driver, who had also been briefed. There was very little in the way of opposite traffic on the bridge. Just then a van suddenly veered across the central demarcation line and ploughed into the lead Land Cruiser. The explosion swung Morrison's vehicle around; the windscreen became an opaque mass of splinters, but it held and the Toyota hit the crash barrier on the nearside of the bridge. Morrison dragged the American woman onto the floor and pressed her head down.

"Stay down, ma'am, and stay in the vehicle!" he yelled.

The case was gone and the Heckler & Koch was cocked. His driver was slumped over the wheel, blood coming from his ears. He rolled out of the door and looked ahead. What was left of the van and lead Land Cruiser were entwined, both vehicles burning furiously. Mitchell was crawling out as the pick-up roared up the bridge from the south. It slewed across the road, blocking it, and four armed men poured out of the back. Behind him, the truck allowed a pick-up to come past from the north then veered across the road. They were trapped on the bridge and the first rattles of the AK-47s came from both directions.

Morrison concentrated on the pick-up that had passed the truck, leaving Mitchell to cover the threat from his end. A song popped into his head unbidden in the terror and he started to hum loudly as he laid down short bursts at the windscreen of the approaching pick-up.

The windscreen went and the pick-up fishtailed to a halt, four men jumping out. Eight against two. Not good. Morrison dropped one and the others scurried into cover behind the pick-up. He turned round to see how Mitchell was doing, and the New Zealander was changing magazines when the 7.62mm round blew off his mandible. He remained on his feet and rammed in another magazine, firing frantically, no more controlled bursts. His bloody tongue lolled down the front of his neck like a grotesque tie and he must have been in agony. A second round hit Mitchell in the groin and he went down still firing until a man ran up with a grenade and tossed it into the burning Land

Cruiser. He was wearing the white of a martyr and Morrison duly obliged. But the grenade went off, destroying the wreck of the Toyota and shredding what was left of Mitchell. Elmer Fudd and the driver were out of the equation.

He turned back to his arc and the three were out of cover and running up the bridge. He heard the dead man's click of the empty chamber and frantically changed magazines. He dropped a second, but the rest were closer now, taking cover in the steelwork of the bridge.

"Mr Morrison," the Ice Maiden yelled at him from the back of the second Toyota. She was covered with glass and her face was cut. "I do not want to have my head sawn off for the entertainment of these fucking savages!"

"Me neither, Treacle. Can you swim?"

"You've got to be fucking kidding me."

He fired two long bursts in either direction, then grabbed her by the collar of her lovely linen trouser suit. Rounds were cracking past them as they went over the crash barrier, Morrison holding on grimly to the woman, hoping she had taken a deep breath. He clouted his shoulder off the water pipeline and they went into the muddy water. He had an arm over her chest, dragging her deeper with powerful breaststroke kicks. Ribbons of bubbles followed them down where the insurgents were firing at them from the bridge until he found the current and went with it. She started to struggle but he held her down for as long as he dared, then they broke surface and he gasped for air.

"Sonofabitch!" she gasped, panting.

"Save it! Ready, down."

In the brief moments they had been on the surface, Morrison saw the men on the bridge firing down at the river and a second party following them along the southern bank. This time, he held her down longer and she had stopped fighting him, allowing the current to take them. The Heckler & Koch had gone but he still had the Glock and fumbled it out of his jacket. When they surfaced a second time, he fired at the men on the bank, those on the bridge being out of range. They scattered into the trees. He saw something about 30 metres away, going on the same course with the current. When they went down again, he kicked towards it, guessing where it would be because the water visibility was so bad. They surfaced just short of the raft of tree debris and rubbish, a brief gasp then down again. This time, they surfaced within the mat of debris, next to the corpse of an animal, so decomposed and full of putrid gas, it was impossible to tell what it had once been.

"Not a sound," he whispered to her.

The stench of dead animal was so bad she started to gag.

"Breathe through your mouth."

"I can fucking taste it!"

The party on the bank were unable to keep up with the current and they were soon out of sight of the bridge around the bend in the river, but they could still see smoke rising from the structure. He felt bad for his oppo and the drivers, but his duty had been to protect the woman. Thirty minutes later, they swam for the north bank of the Tamontaka River in a spot that was protected from sight by Punul Island. They walked the 3 kilometres back to Cotabato City and flagged down the first police car they saw. In the back of the car on the way to the main police station, she started to shake with delayed shock.

"I'm sorry about Mr Ridges," he said, but was thinking about Mitchell and his lolling tongue. He shuddered and she grabbed on to him. *I'm alive because of the toss of a bloody coin.*

"Morrison, you saved my life. I can never thank you and you don't know how grateful I am not to die in this awful place."

The American Embassy had both of them flown to Manila that afternoon after being questioned by the police. She was accommodated in the best hotel in the capital. Morrison's was slightly less plush, but she upgraded him to her hotel out of her personal account. That night and for most of the next day, Morrison discovered just how grateful she was.

*

Back in Oxfordshire, Morrison made an inventory of his barn conversion near Bledlow. While the shell was safe and secure, there was still much work to be done inside. He had a functioning kitchen, bathroom and living area, but extensive work was needed on the guest rooms, dining area and outbuildings. Mick the builder looked after the place while he was away and helped with the work while he was there. Morrison had never married, something he rather regretted, but he reckoned he would have made a terrible husband and even worse father. Mick had left him a note:

*A couple of blokes were round asking after you yesterday. I think they were Old Bill. They asked when you were coming back, but I said I wasn't sure. I can make it next Friday if you want.*

Morrison assumed they were wanting to question him about his Philippine adventure, so he had a few drinks with a meal and went to bed. The next day, he didn't feel like working so caught up with his mail. He didn't notice the Vauxhall Insignia pull up in front of the barn, so he got a shock when there was a loud, purposeful knock on his door. When he answered it, two men in suits stood on his doorstep. He didn't think they were Plods for some reason. Spooks?

"Mr Morrison, formerly Warrant Officer One Morrison?"

"Yes, you being?"

"Retired Chief Petty Officer Regulator Hooper and Civilian Investigator Clements. We represent the Iraq Historic Abuse Tribunal and we are serving you with these documents."

He tapped Morrison on the shoulder with the envelope and handed it over over. "Would you please read the documents we have served you with and be available for an interview under caution tomorrow, here at eleven am. You may have representation if you so wish. In fact, we would advise that you do."

"Is this some kind of a joke?"

"I'm afraid not, sir. Please be in when we return."

They were gone and he stood blinking in a state of shock. He carried the envelope into the kitchen and put on the kettle, made a strong coffee and started to read.

*Warrant Officer One D Morrison (complete with Service number) is accused of being party to the unlawful killing of a Mr Muhammad Al Jazari on the 28th of October 2005 in Amarah in Maysan Province Amarah. Warrant Officer Morrison was a member of a team which did unlawfully open fire on Mr Al Jazari without issuing a verbal warning, in contravention of then current Rules of Engagement outlined on Card Alpha.*

*Mr Al Jazari was unarmed at the time of the shooting and at no time during the event did he engage in any violent action towards any British troops. Given these circumstances, it is deemed that Warrant Officer Morrison's actions transgressed any definition of the use of reasonable force. While it is acknowledged that Warrant Officer Morrison did not personally open fire on Mr Muhammad Al Jazari, as the senior non-commissioned present, he bares ultimate responsibility for the conduct of the operation. In addition, Mr Anah Ahamad and Mr Jamail Hamdani are seeking recompense from the Ministry of Defence (MoD) for mental trauma, caused when Mr Al Jazari was unlawfully killed in front of them.*

Morrison was sorely tempted to have a drink but knew he had to keep a clear head. He thought again about the email he had received and had not as yet responded to. He left a long note to Mick the builder and once it was dark, drove six miles south-east into the Chiltern Hills. He was very close to Air Chief Marshall 'Bomber' Harris's old stomping grounds when he parked the car and went into the beech woods.

He found the tree and the hollow in the bole and dug. He came across the ammunition box, retrieved the money and documents, put the steel box back and backfilled. Like most of the men and women in their former teams, they had decided that people with their knowledge were a danger to the deep state, and she was a fickle mistress.

Two days later, Morrison was a different person with a different look and identity. He booked an early holiday in the sun with a travel agent. "To get away from the awful British weather." The nice young lady in the travel agent's had smiled her understanding.

"You lucky thing," she said.

*

The Hospital Particular do Algarve was close to Praia da Rocha in Portugal and it boasted that it was equipped with modern facilities and the latest technology. The hospital certainly looked the part, and the white building hurt his eyes in the bright sunlight. At the reception, he tried his passable Spanish, but for some reason, the two ladies chose not to understand him, so he gave up and reverted to Pidgin English.

"Ha yes, Meester Hedge." The lady made a telephone call and a nurse clip-clopped into the reception. He was grateful she looked like a nurse, wearing white clothing that was clean, rather than scrubs.

"Come, please."

He followed her into the bowels of the hospital to the high dependency unit. In the HDU, Edge was still connected to many machines that went beep.

"Ten minutes," the nurse said sternly, and left.

He was shocked at his state. It was like half of his face was slumped, with a rheumy, half-closed eye that looked red and sore. Edge opened his good eye and looked at him.

"What have you done, Edgie?"

"Thanks for coming," he whispered hoarsely.

"I'll take the shot for you," Morrison said, and tried to stop himself from bursting into tears...

*

It was an unseasonably warm and balmy May bank holiday, late morning in the Thames Valley. A gentle but firm breeze swayed the willows on the riverbanks and in the water meadows. The matriarchal moorhens were taking their broods up and down and across the river. Their passage was marked by gentle wakes as the fluffy, little birds followed Mum like gunboats following a destroyer. The ducks had lost most of their early offspring due to bad parenting and voracious predators. Their second and third broods would fare better.

A keen pair of rowers in a skiff pulled hard up-current and nodded to the man on a sit-on lawnmower, who was giving his sloping paddock down to the river its second cut of the year. The man with the tinted glasses and the ponytail avoided the soft ground near the bank, just up from the boathouse. The mower chugged back up the gentle slope, the driver ducking to avoid the bright green willow fronds.

The boom of the rifle made the lead oarswoman of the skiff miss her stroke. The flattening .308 round hit the mower driver in the centre of the parietal bone, slightly left of the tied ponytail, and exited out of the right eye. Ron Gleam's skull split open like a melon, and brain matter spread up the sloping lawn in a pinkish-grey fan. His body slumped forward and the Yamaha mower assumed a gently turning course, heading back down to the river. The mower tipped into the water and the body pitched into the river, a dark stain moving down-current from the ruined head. The body and accompanying stain rotated and headed inexorably towards the weir. The screaming from the house started a few minutes later.

He moved position immediately after the shot, a slower moving bush against the hedge on the flood meadow. His green coverall purchased from a market stall selling military clothing was festooned with jute and hessian strips, cut from bags purchased at a garden centre. And just like Just William, his face was streaked with burned cork and slimy mud. The burned cork was aromatic and kept the midges at bay. He munched on some fruit and nut chocolate to help the tablets go down, and waited. He had the beginnings of a headache, probably caused by mild dehydration because he had been waiting for days, mainly immobile, and moving position at night. Twenty minutes later, he heard the sirens.

Here was his chance. By the time Thames Valley Police had conducted their safety assessment and moved in, he could have dumped his rifle, clothes and ammunition in the deepest part of the river and have been in Reading, waiting for a train back to Devon. But his anger was burning out his soul, so he waited. Florescent jackets started to move in the properties on the other side of the river. An hour later, a fallow deer and calf approached to within twelve feet of where he was hiding, the mother sniffing the air cautiously. Their simple beauty made him screw his eyes shut. He watched the pair sadly, until the helicopter caused them to disappear into the undergrowth, their white tails bobbing insolently.

There were three crew inside the Eurocopter that swept in from the east, its rotor downwash shaking the trees and dappling the surface of the river. It flew slowly north to south above the river, the infrared camera in the pod under the fuselage scanning the cover in the water meadows. The helicopter was a force multiplier, which was a primary threat. He wouldn't stand a chance while the helicopter remained over the combat area, because he now considered himself to be at war.

The observer in the left-hand seat glanced over the trees and hedges with a pair of powerful binoculars. There was a loud bang from the bottom of the door and his left thigh exploded in a welter of blood and debris. The cockpit was filled with gore and screaming; the pilot snatched on the cyclic and the nose went down as the helicopter clawed for safety behind the houses. The operator in the rear cabin glanced into the scene from hell that was the cockpit.

"Get him straight to hospital!" he yelled at the pilot, and had the presence of mind and discipline to attempt to tie a tourniquet fashioned from the strap of his daysack around the screaming observer's thigh.

The man in the meadows didn't bother to watch the retreating helicopter. He was on the move down to the river. He waded into the strong flow, holding the camouflaged rifle above his head, his powerful legs kicking him towards the opposite bank. In five minutes, he was in his secondary position, where he could watch the water meadows and most of the westerly bank. He could hear vehicles and movement behind him from the houses, but knew that the threat wouldn't be from this direction for some time. An hour later, he saw the riot van moving off the road behind the hedges. A few minutes later, the four police marksmen and their spotters pushed through the hedge, spread in a line, about 10 metres apart. They were wearing dark blue boiler suits, baseball caps and high-quality body armour.

He grinned to himself. Obviously, they had missed the lesson on why things are seen. Shape, shine, silhouette, spacing, movement pattern and thermal IR signature. He needed to tie as many up as possible. He thought about the humiliation and laughter in the police station, of someone trying to have a piss, the difficulty, the pain and the hand pushing into the back, against the urinal in mid-flow. The first round at these new targets blew off the man's kneecap second from the right, and the second round fired less than a second later hit the marksman third from the left, dead centre of the front ceramic plate of his body armour. The first policeman folded; the second flew backwards as though he was attached to a speeding car. The energy of the disintegrating round spalled upwards, but the ceramic plate dissipated the energy of the flattening round and kept the policeman alive. The purple bruise on the centre of his chest lasted for eight weeks. But one of them was switched on, and the cracks of rapidly fired rounds passed dangerously close to his position.

He broke cover and headed for the dense beech hedge that surrounded a property, wriggling through the thick roots at the base of the hedge. Two more rounds cracked past, merely worryingly close. As he tracked up the hedge, a policeman in a florescent jacket appeared round the corner of the very nice house. He fired from the hip and a chunk of brickwork atomised the brickwork close to the copper's shoulder. The florescent jacket disappeared back round the corner and he risked a look.

They hadn't pushed the cordon that far back yet, and behind the blue and white tape closing the road, he saw a film crew hiding behind their van, the camera and sound equipment abandoned in the process of being set up. Coppers were one thing; so-called journalists from the BBC were another. He destroyed the camera with one shot and the windscreen of the van with the second. As he sprinted for the next property, he rammed in a clip on the run.

The adrenalin was surging through his system and he realised he was enjoying himself too much. The leylandii was hard work through to the next property. As he skirted another extremely nice house, a yummy mummy came out of the French doors onto the patio. They both stared at each other and she opened her mouth to scream.

"Sssssshhhhhh," he said, putting a finger to his lips. "Go back inside. There's a bit of an incident going on."

She needed no second bidding, scooping the child as she fled indoors. He transited three more properties heading north with the river on his right. He could clearly hear sounds of pursuit coming from behind and sirens and flashing blue lights from the other side of the river. Soon there was the sound of a second helicopter, and he was glad to reach the cool shade and the mud under the boathouse.

He reached for the air tank, buoyancy compensation device and weight belt from where he had stashed them three nights before. He kitted up, checked the regulator and gently pushed out into the middle of the river. The current caught him, and with judicious juggling of the buoyancy setting, he drifted with the current, about 4 feet below the surface. Sadly, he let Father Thames claim the rifle plus remaining ammunition and readjusted buoyancy. The coolness became coldness as he swept on his way towards the sea.

He left the river in the woods south of Medmenham. He stripped off the ghillie suit and the dry suit and placed all of it, including the scuba kit, in the dry suit then slipped it back into the river. He had an enormous piss against a tree bole. It hurt. He was wearing lightweight trousers and jacket and put his wet boots back on with a dry pair of socks. By the time he'd reached the car parked in Marlow, it was as though the entire Thames Valley Police Service had been called up. He was glad to reach the M4 and headed towards London.

*

Very heavily armed units of Devon and Cornwall Police raided a property south of Bideford three days later. The cottage was empty, but a police spokeswoman said they were searching for a Mr Mark Edge, a former soldier with a history of violent offences, who was also being investigated for war crimes committed in Iraq, specifically the murder of an unarmed man. They showed the mug shot of Edge taken following his arrest for assault the previous New Year. The split forehead, crudely sutured, made him look totally thuggish, like a typical neo-Nazi. Both the BBC and Sky News covered the police statement as lead news item.

*"Following additional information from Devon and Cornwall Police, Thames Valley Police have announced that the shooting incident at Ruger-on-Thames on May 3rd is now being treated as terrorism.*

*I'd like to thank the police officers at the scene for the heroic and professional way they responded to this incident – as we have seen on a number of occasions in recent years – unfortunately, the prominent human rights lawyer, Ron Gleam, was murdered with a high velocity rifle. Despite an extensive gun battle, no other members of the public were injured.*

*My thoughts are with the two officers who have sustained life-changing injuries.*

*As the police have said, this is a timely reminder that the threat from far-right terrorism in the UK remains severe. The perpetrator is still at large. However, the police, together with the security services, are doing everything they can to protect the public, and they already have an enhanced policing plan to keep the public safe, including a crackdown on hate crime on the internet.*

*It is important we are all alert but not alarmed. Please report anything suspicious to police confidentially on the information hotline. The number is at the bottom of the screen. In an emergency, always call 999.*

*Terrorists who seek to harm us and destroy our way of life will never succeed. This country stands more united than ever and far-right hatred will never sow division in our society."*

Mr Edge, the spokeswoman went on to say, also had a history of right-wing extremist views and an obsession with the Nazi Party. They came to this conclusion because of the 765 books and magazines found in the property; they came across *Das Reich* by Max Hastings and *Fighter Aces of the Luftwaffe in World War 2* by Philip Kaplan. Mr Edge was extremely dangerous and without morality, as he had murdered prominent lawyer Ron Gleam and shot and maimed two police officers, during a desperate shoot-out. There was speculation that Mr Edge had drowned in the River Thames, although no body had as yet been found.

\*

It was early evening and the crickets were revving up to full chorus before the night. The breeze from the sea was cool, blowing away the oppressive afternoon. The man sat down on the bench next to Edge.

"Thanks for taking the shot for me."

To the man's horror and sadness, he saw a lazy tear roll down the slanting face. "No worries. The bastard had nailed me as well. Besides, I'm a better shot than you ever were."

"Bollocks! What you doing now?"

"I've been working for a couple of American firms. Protecting oil workers mostly. Bunch of fucking cowboys. Are you going to get better, Edgie?"

"Physio reckons so. The doctors think it was caused, or started, when I head-butted that bastard who was shagging Moira."

"See that fucking temper of yours." He stood up to leave.

"Come back, please. Sometime, eh, Morrison?"

"I'll come back once it's done and at Christmas. Promise. That's if the fucking Septics haven't got me killed. You got someone looking after you, haven't you?"

"Yes, Bia is less complicated than British women. More realistic in her outlook."

"Then make sure you don't fuck it up this time, Edgie."

Chapter 29

# GOODBYE, MARK EDGE

———

In April, Edge was discharged from the hospital in Faro and referred to a local hospital for ongoing physiotherapy. He made a remarkable recovery due to his fitness, determination and cussedness, but more importantly with the love and support of Bia Vargas. But his progress was not as quick and complete as he would have liked and he was on occasions sharp and bad-tempered.

He could not walk far to begin with and there was a general weakness in his left-hand side. The physio slowly improved his strength, as did swimming, much as he found it tedious and boring. Despite the wetsuit, he seemed to be a jellyfish magnet and his hair was bleached a light grey by the saltwater and the sun.

His artistic flair seemed to have left him, something that Edge bitterly regretted and although his sketching improved, he would never get back his subtle use of colour and the ability to lay down the gentle washes he used to build up his watercolours. But in one aspect, his senses seemed to have become hyper-enhanced. Since his cranial bleed, Edge's libido seemed boundless. While initially delighted, Bia became worn out with his constant appetite for all matters carnal. She worked part time as a sous chef in one of Portimão's better restaurants and had done cleaning jobs until she met Edge. The head chef was an alcoholic and to all intents and purposes, she ran the kitchen and the management knew it. Unfortunately, the head chef was a family member. After a stint in the kitchens, Bia was too exhausted for another stint in Edge's bed, so she went back to her own little flat and slept soundly to recharge her batteries.

On her days away, Edge missed Bia and realised that without really trying, they had fallen in step with one another, two of life's walking wounded. She had become more confident and no longer turned her face away from strangers, while he was grateful to her for giving him an excuse to stay alive. He would drive down to one of the beaches and indulge in simple pleasures, such as eating an ice cream and looking out as the sun dipped down towards the Atlantic. It seemed obvious as to why the Portuguese in their little country had looked out to their future beyond the horizon, much as the English had done. They were two kindred nations with a shared history that dated back to the Anglo-Portuguese Alliance of 1373.

As he had promised, Morrison visited Edge after carrying out the murder. Bia made herself scarce. It wasn't that she didn't like Morrison; in fact, she would never tire of looking at his handsome face. She was just suspicious that he was from Edge's other life, a life she was pretty sure she wanted no part of.

Morrison and Edge were sitting on a bench underneath some trees. The Atlantic was a deep blue, dotted with brilliant white fishing boats. "Now to business. Your name has gone straight in the frame for this. You do realise that, don't you?"

Edge nodded.

"Even if your alibi of being here recovering from a brain fart is accepted, they will constantly hound you. Okay, so you have to die and your death must be connected with the shooting. You have your alter-ego ready to go?"

"Yes, plus air tickets booked in his name. I had to cancel the flights since my mishap, but I can easily book some more."

"Right, I'll need your Edge passport and some cash, preferably in a money belt. There will be no going back. You realise that, don't you?"

"Go back to what?" Edge said bitterly.

"I'll let you know what happens, but be ready to move. Does Bia know?"

"No. I think it may be easier if she doesn't."

*But easier for whom?*

"Right, I'll be going. See you once the deed's done. How do you fancy Helsinki? We'll both need a holiday. Keep monitoring the Inkspot comms for details."

"Bloody gorgeous women in Finland. Did I tell you what's happened to me since my head exploded…?"

\*

Bia came back that afternoon with two pieces of veal and some mushrooms.

"I thought I might cook some veal tonight. You are probably tired of fish. How is your friend, Mister Morrison?" she asked cautiously.

"Henry is fine. He has once again asked me to thank you for looking after me."

"He is very handsome, but there is something about you, when you get together."

Edge sighed. "Sit down, Bia, my love."

He held her hands across the table. "Bia, you have known me for less than two months. I am over forty. I was a soldier for more than twenty years. I have known Henry Morrison for more than ten years, although I have never slept with him in the biblical sense and I do not wish to have his babies. Henry has saved my life on at least three occasions and I have saved his at least twice. Britain has been constantly at war, somewhere or other, since God knows when. As far as I'm aware, the last time Portugal fought anyone was in the 1970s, and bloody good for you, because war and killing people is horrible.

"We are not nice people. Our government didn't want us to be nice people and now we just want to be like everyone else, and become sort of nice, or at least manageable. But people just won't let us. So we have to look after each other. Not like you look after me, but to keep ourselves alive."

"You are nice to me, Adje. You tell me about books and you don't turn away from my face."

"Bia, people turn away from the scar on my head. They turn away from a disabled child. They are just disturbed by what is presented to them. A superficial…" She frowned. "They just see a face and it is a deep-set reaction to something they are unused to. Do the people who work in your kitchen turn away from you?"

"No."

"Of course not, because they accept you for what you are. They respect you because you keep the kitchen running while the pisshead chef can't do a simple roux." *Whatever one of those is.* "So people are shallow and the first thing they react to is how someone looks. But once they know you, they remember how you speak to them. The way you laugh. How you listen to them and how nice your *peitos* look in that top."

"Do you think so, Adje?" she asked, looking down.

"Yes, Bia. I really do."

"We could have the veal later."

*

It was a cooler day at the beach of Armação de Pêra, the trailing edge of a tropical cyclone having briefly kissed the Algarve. Bia was working in the restaurant and Edge was sitting on a low wall, feeding a scrawny and greedy little tabby cat with the last half of an ice cream cornet. He shooed the cat away, who went and collected her kittens.

"Bloody kids having kids," he observed out loud, picked up his stick and walked along the front with his slightly awkward gait. Up ahead there were a couple of kiosks and he bought a small beer and a copy of the *Daily Mail* newspaper that was two days old. There was only the *Mail* and the *Mirror* left and Edge still had a modicum of his strength left. Feeling sullied, he sat at a table, sipped his beer and looked at the front page.

Osborne told 'austerity isn't working' ahead of IMF visit as Britain's economy revealed to be close to weakest in the G7

He started to hum OOOOhhh the *Hokey-Cokey* and turned the page.

Benghazi witness: Army commander said commando rescue was scrapped because State Department officials had 'bigger balls' than military chiefs

This story Edge read.

*The Obama administration denied Special Forces commandos permission to board a military flight to help defend the US Consulate in Benghazi while it was under attack, according to State Department career officer Gregory Hicks, a former second-in-command in the North African country.*

He knew that Henry had been up to some very black operations in Libya two years previously.

*Recalling the words of a Lt. Col. Gibson, then the military commander at Special Operations Command Africa (SOCAFRICA), Hicks said during a House Oversight Committee hearing Wednesday that Gibson said the armed forces should have made the decision about its own soldiers.*
*"This is the first time in my career," Gibson said, according to Hicks, "that a diplomat has more balls than somebody in the military."*

Edge's lip curled in disgust as he read on.

*The Special Forces team was organised and about to drive to a C-130 aircraft with their gear, Hicks testified, when Gibson's superiors ordered him to tell them to stand down.*

*"He got a phone call from SOCAFRICA which said, 'You can't go now, you don't have authority to go now,'" Hicks recalled. "They were told not to board the flight, so they missed it."*

Bastards! He angrily turned the page.

***Pregnant and proud! Kim Kardashian shows off her blossoming baby bump in a bikini as she proves fat critics wrong***

*Oh, for fuck's sake!* The next page was like someone had poured iced water down his spine:

### *Prominent Human Rights Lawyer Shot Dead at his Own Home*
### *Police Seek Disgraced Former Soldier*

*A leading human rights lawyer has been murdered in his Oxfordshire home during the May Bank Holiday. Mr Ronald Gleam was shot and killed by what is believed to be a high powered rifle, while he tended his garden over the weekend. Mr Gleam was a recent winner of the Lawyer of the Year and his legal firm, Community Legal Notaries, specialises in bringing cases against alleged British Government malpractice, as well as investigating war crimes allegedly committed by former members of the Armed Forces.*

*Never afraid of courting controversy, Ron Gleam has represented former Mau-Mau members in cases against the British Government, for alleged brutality in Kenya during uprisings in the 1950s. Community Legal Notaries has also attempted to bring prosecutions against the Israeli Government for alleged atrocities committed by the IDF in Gaza.*

### *War Crimes Committed in Iraq*

*However, it is Mr Gleam's pursuit of serving and former members of the Armed Forces which has caused the most controversy and outraged Armed Forces Ministers and veterans' groups. These allegations against British military personnel have been described as: 'vexatious, trumped-up and wholly without foundation', by the Secretary of State for Defence, but he added that: "No Service man or woman is above the law and all allegations are taken seriously and must be investigated. However, we owe a great debt to these brave men and women, who regularly put their lives on the line for us."*

*There has been criticism of Mr Gleam's conduct and it has been alleged that representatives of Community Legal Notaries actively solicit in Iraq for cases and that the Iraq Historic Abuse Tribunal (IHAT) fail to conduct rigorous tests on the validity of these claims. IHAT teams have been accused of door stepping Service personnel in their own homes and while off duty and questioning them with no legal representation.*

### Violent Former Soldier

*The murder is currently being investigated by Thames Valley Police with specialist support from the Counter Terrorism Command. It is believed that a Mr Mark Edge is being sought, as he was one of the more prominent alleged war crimes cases, passed to IHAT by Community Legal Notaries. Mr Edge, a former soldier, has a criminal record for violence and it is believed that he has links with far-right extremist organisations.*

*When Mr Edge's property in North Devon was searched, police found Nazi paraphernalia and a number of books and publications linked to the WW2 Nazis. Mr Edge was convicted of the assault of a local man in North Devon and a violent assault on a German police officer, during a drunken rugby tour.*

### Shoot-out with the Police

*Mr Edge is understood to have fled abroad, but the police believe that he could return at any time, as he still has family ties in North Devon. Detective Chief Inspector Tanner of the Counter Terrorism Command issued a warning to the public. "Mr Edge is an extremely violent individual who is believed to have committed murders both at home and abroad. Under no circumstances should he be approached by members of the public, who if they believe they have seen him should notify the police immediately."*

*During his getaway, Mr Edge is believed to have opened fire on a police helicopter and members of a specialist firearms support team. A number of officers were injured during the shoot-out, some seriously. It was believed that the shooter remained in the area, but an extensive police search failed to find his whereabouts or any trace of the weapons used.*

### Tributes

*Mr Gleam's murder has been met with profound sadness by the human rights legal community. Tributes have been paid by the head of Liberty and the Law Society. The Leader of the Opposition was moved to state: "Ron Gleam was a paragon of virtue and a fearless seeker of truth and justice. His courageous stance ensured that the politicians and importantly the MoD and generals are held accountable for their conduct on military operations." Mr Gleam was a significant donor to the Labour Party and regularly attended Labour meetings and the annual conference.*

Edge ripped out the page and dumped the paper in the bin, ripping the story into shreds, which he deposited in several bins on the way back to his car. Back in the apartment, he switched on his laptop and sent a short message to the Inkspots' email account:

*Operation Quorn Mince*

\*

On the 25th of May, a small hired sailboat was found adrift, 5 kilometres off the coast of the Algarve. The boat had been hired by an Englishman for four hours, but by the evening neither the Englishman nor the boat had returned to Faro. Three days later, a money belt and document pouch washed ashore near Huelva in Spain. The local police were called and made a cursory search of the items, where a passport and other documentation were found. The Spanish authorities notified the British Embassy, who in turn notified the Foreign and Commonwealth Office.

The British police have a penchant for mounting investigations in the Portuguese Algarve, and obscene numbers of the Thames Valley Service and the Counter Terrorism Command descended on the area around Faro and the south coastal region. They interviewed Bia Vargas, Monsieur Béringer and staff from the Hospital Particular do Algarve, who told them in no uncertain terms that they were delusional if they thought that Mr Edge had murdered someone in England, when he had been seen most days in Portugal.

"So where the hell is he, then?" they asked.

Bia was in no doubt. "He is dead and you coming here killed him. He was getting better until you came. *Bastardos!* He drowned himself because you named him in the English newspapers. He left me a note."

The police took the note until the Portuguese police made them return it to them. They copied it and the already strained relations between the Portuguese and British police took a nosedive. Still, the Algarve was a nice place for some off-duty R&R, and the English police filled their boots.

Predictably, Edge broke Bia's heart. He had touched her life, given her confidence, hope and a simple love, and left his legacy; a clump of cells in the wall of her uterus that was rapidly dividing and subdividing. He would never see his son, but he did hear that Bia had given birth and later married a local businessman who had recently been made a widower. Every month from the following February, an amount of €1,000 would be deposited in Bia's bank account. The amount steadily rose with inflation, but apart from originating from a bank account in Brunei-Darussalam, nothing could be found about this account and why money was being sent to Portugal. When the euro collapsed and Portugal returned to the escudo, the deposits changed to match the new/old currency. Bia wisely used the money to educate her son, and lived with her loss, sadness and new life. On rare occasions, she thought she saw someone she knew watching her from afar, but this was obviously just silly wish fulfilment. She knew she wasn't Pelagia and that she would never see her Captain Corelli again.

\*

In the October of the year he drowned, Edge walked up Steep Hill from the railway station and by the time he got to the top he was blowing out of his arse. He passed Lincoln's beautiful Gothic cathedral on his right and went into the Ball Gate and the maze of narrow streets to the north. On St Paul's Lane, he stopped with the castle walls behind him and regarded the two-storey building that looked not unlike an old workshop or blacksmith's forge. To the right of the door was a brass sign:

**Horace Cutler QC and Associates**

Edge had come to visit the nearest living person he had to a father, and he was expecting the mother of all bollockings.

*

Almost eight years to the day that she had accosted Edge in the middle of doing some hedging around his property, the prematurely old lady noticed a flashy car driving up the lane towards her property, the last one on the right. The car stopped and a well-dressed, professional-looking woman stepped out. She glanced at the mud disdainfully and walked towards the front door. The old woman opened it before the woman tried to ring the bell, which didn't work anyway.

"Are you Ms Cynthia Penrith?"

"Yes."

The woman held up a briefcase. "In which case I have some news that may surprise you. I represent a firm of solicitors in Barnstaple. Here is my card. May I come in?"

Well over three hours later, the solicitor had left and the old lady was reading some documents and a letter that had been in an envelope with a wax seal. It was the last will and testament of Mr Mark Edge, together with a letter. Actually, it was more like a synopsis of his life, why he did what he had done and why he had left all his worldly goods to an ex-junkie whose name he hadn't even known when they first met… Or was it the second time they'd met?

Mr Mark Edge had been well-off in his own right and an estimate put his property at over 250K. The will had been contested unsuccessfully by his widow, Moira, at her father's insistence. She would later receive a separate settlement. The house and savings were for Cynthia to do with as she wished, provided she looked after Monty, the Edges' cat, until either one of them died. On Miss Penrith's death, both hers and the Edges' properties would pass to Moira, or if she were deceased, her children. Cynthia had been well aware of the contents of the will, because Edge had discussed it with her before he disappeared. But it was the last lines that made her dab her eyes:

*I didn't want to take my own life, but if I went into the British prison system, I would have been conveniently dead in a matter of weeks. If I had killed myself in Britain, I would have been cremated and erased from history. I've decided to commit myself to the ocean so that the British State could not delete me, like an old Soviet photograph. To be honest, I just couldn't stand the headaches any longer.*

*Use the money wisely, but enjoy it. Don't waste it all on a bloody cats' home or spoil Monty. He's a selfish, furry little shit, but he does like you putting your hand under his chin and rubbing his jowls. It makes him dribble.*

*My old RSM said that I would make a fuck-up of my life. He was right, wasn't he? Spend the money on you. Have a good rest of your life and stay away from heroin. You should be able to have a good retirement. And for fuck's sake, get some dental implants and do something with your fucking hair.*

"Oh God, Monty," she said to the tabby that had perched his arse on her kitchen table. The cat was older, distinguished, with a grey beard and jowls. Now he walked slightly stiffly, but the white scar still ran from his right eye to his nose. "He was such a bloody silly boy."

She bent forward, trying not to cry on the documents. The cat moved forward and gently head-butted her forehead.

Chapter 30

# THE DETECTIVE'S STORY

———

Detective Inspector Charles Hope made his way up to the Major Investigation Team's offices, on the second floor of the headquarters of Thames Valley Police at Kidlington in Oxford. He was fifty-three, overweight and was currently suffering from an infected ingrowing toenail and gout. He took the stairs rather than the lift, because his doctor told him he needed to take more exercise. It wasn't couched in advisory terms, but a clear directive. *You are to take more exercise, improve your diet and importantly, most importantly, you will stop smoking.*

DI Hope had served in the police force for thirty-two years. He had started in the City of London Police, then the Met and finally, Thames Valley Police. He had applied to leave the Met because he found himself policing a capital city he no longer understood, identified with, and which felt like a foreign country to him. He had been staving off the inevitable. Parts of the Thames Valley area had more in common with the Indian sub-continent than the leafy shires. Hope was enduring the few remaining years for his pension. He loathed his job, the majority of his peers and virtually all of his superiors. The mild exertion of two flights of stairs had caused acid reflux, not helped by the nicotine gum he now habitually chewed.

It was 08:45 and he was late. The traffic from Chinnor, where Hope lived with his wife and recently estranged son, had been its usual, horrendously gridlocked self. It was the slow crawl towards the Headington roundabout on the A40 that caused him the deepest joy. He was convinced that he would have done a Michael Douglas, à la *Falling Down*, if it hadn't been for audio books. Hope was currently enjoying *RAF Police: The 'Great Escape' Murders* by Stephen R Davies. As he stared at the exhausts of assorted 4 x 4s, he was lost in the story of how the RAF police had hunted down members of the Gestapo and SS who had murdered fifty of the Stalag Luft III escapees. To him, that had been proper policing. A single-minded determination to bring criminals to justice and see them paying for their crimes by having their t-vertebrae twisted and broken at the end of Albert Pierrepoint's nooses. As opposed to the tedious and ultimately futile social work that was modern policing.

How times had changed from his nick at Harlesden back in the mid-eighties. There had been swing doors with heavy, interior paned glass. Brass lock plates that were polished by cleaners who actually gave a toss. If people in custody soiled their cells, they were given a mop, bucket and disinfectant and told to clean it up. Now a bodily fluids hazmat would isolate the area, clean it and bill the station for thousands. Coppers had been generally polite to non-form members of the general public, whom they policed by consent. Policing was by the needs of the local area, rather than tick-box directives from the Home Office. Hope jarred his right foot on the top stair and his big toe shrieked in protest.

"Fukit!"

The Major Investigation Team was already assembled and coming to the end of the morning briefing, when Hope rolled into the room. He raised his hand in apology to the female DCI who was heading up the case. She briefly glowered at him, being put off her stride. Hope went to ground at the back of the room and listened to her oh-so-well-enunciated morning prayers. He had to admit, DCI Parry was beautifully well spoken, and the youngsters on the team were hanging on her every word. She had a BA in politics and sociology, was destined for the top, and good luck to her.

One thing Hope did like about modern policing was the enormous power of the IT systems. They had a huge interactive whiteboard for doing something called 'brain dumps', and the results of their diagrams could be printed off. Apparently 'brainstorming' was deemed to be possibly offensive to persons suffering from epilepsy and it was vitally important to avoid offending anyone, as he was to find out. Databases were much quicker than the old cardex systems he had cut his detecting police work teeth on. But he did sense that computer-based policing did make the teams overly reliant on technology and he was constantly losing his nine-letter randomly generated passwords, which he wrote on scraps of paper despite knowing that was not good data protection.

It was clear to Hope as the morning prayers drew to a close that despite all the technology, databases and interactive Smart Boards, they were no closer to finding out who had blown apart Mr Ronald Gleam's head with a one-hundred-and-forty-five grain .308 round. But what angered the police the most was the fact that whoever had murdered Mr Gleam had also severely wounded two members of their tactical firearm unit and a member of the air support unit. Not to mention the damage to the Thames Valley Service's Eurocopter and a BBC outside broadcast van.

They had a list of suspects as long as all of their arms put together, and they were all members of Her Majesty's Armed Forces who were being investigated for war crimes by Mr Gleam's firm Community Legal Notaries. Therefore, most of them possessed the means and motive to kill Mr Gleam and quite frankly, he wouldn't have blamed them. However, shooting at coppers was a different matter altogether.

Another complication was they had absolutely no forensic evidence, despite scouring the meadows and gardens around the shooting incidents. No DNA, no empty rounds and not even a footprint. A few days previously, they had a witness who had seen the shooter at close quarters in her back garden. The police sent a team of detectives and a police artist round to the lady's lovely house on the river. It soon became clear to them that this lovely mummy was a bit of a trophy wife for some young city thruster.

"I never really got a good look at his face, but I'll never forget that evil stare," she told them.

The detectives questioned her for over an hour and left, hoping that the police artist could make some headway. Diligently, he returned the very lifelike drawing to DCI Parry in the incident room. She looked at it and then at the artist.

"This is exactly how that lady described him to me."

"Is this some kind of bloody joke?" she choked.

"I'm quite pleased with it and the lady said it was very accurate. She said he looked just like that."

"Oh dear God," DCI Parry said, and put her head in her hands.

The artist's impression of the shooter was put up on the wall of the incident room and still continued to cause chortles from visitors.

Hope had helpfully suggested that he might decide to pop out for takeaway or nip down the supermarket dressed like that and then they would have him bang to rights. It was comments like that that didn't endear him to his more ambitious colleagues. And the day wore on, trying to track down a list of over thirty suspects out of the 200 who had no alibi and then arrange to interview them.

"Have you ever considered it may have been the Israelis who did away with Gleam?" Hope said at tea break.

They looked at him with incredulity.

"Think about it. Old Ron Gleam had fingered the Israelis for war crimes committed in Gaza. And the way the hit was carried out. Professional, no forensic, no gun, no empty cases and in the end he just disappears into thin air."

"For God's sake, Charles."

"Well, he wasn't exactly popular, our Ron, was he?" Hope observed, chewing on yet another piece of nicotine gum. He picked up a file and began to thumb through it. "Unless you're a subscriber to the *Guardian*. Could it have been the RAF Harrier pilot who killed the newly married couple who just happened to be travelling in the back of the Taliban tour bus? Or the Royal Marine who shot the child, who was actually seventeen, who just happened to be wearing a suicide vest? Or this walking horseman of the apocalypse who shot a totally innocent bomb maker from half a mile and monstrously failed to issue a verbal warning?"

"I think it is him. It's Edge. He has form," a female DS opined. "And what's wrong with the *Guardian*?"

"Reading the *Guardian* is one of the more popular ways to show everyone in your nice suburban development that you are really a rebel at heart, while talking on your new iPhone at Starbucks, wearing a Che Guevara shirt. Call me cynical, but I seriously doubt that those advertising their allegiance to 'Che' know much about the sadistic Argentine Marxist revolutionary and what a truly awful shit he was. And there's just one little flaw in your theory. Just one snag. Former Staff Sergeant Edge hasn't been seen since December last year."

"Well, who do you think it was?" the deeply offended DS demanded of him, because she did talk on her iPhone in Starbucks.

"Two people on our suspect list have disappeared, both known to each other and serving on the same unit, the SAS. Sniper teams operate in pairs. This guy Edge could have pulled the trigger, but I'll bet that former Warrant Officer Morrison had something to do with it."

He headed for the door.

"Where the hell are you going?"

"I'm making a conscious effort to kill myself with a real cigarette, after all this nicotine gum."

"We should be so lucky," someone muttered.

*

Superintendent Allen looked at the official complaint file on his desk and sighed. He spun his chair round and looked across at the Elsevier building in the landscaped grounds. Allen wished he had a more dynamic name, like Chisholm, Gideon, or even Regan. Allen had seen enough reruns of *The Sweeny* to know that it bore as much resemblance to modern policing as *Thunderbirds* did to space travel. He contemplated his latest *bête noire* encapsulated in the file in front of him.

Detective Inspector Charles Hope was an anachronism from a time of simpler policing by consent. He probably thought *The Sweeny* was a documentary, and still called his DCI 'Guv', an expression Amanda Parry hated. Once, Hope had been a good, promising copper, but he had failed to move with the times. He was technophobic, had an attitude that could on occasions be described as 'challenging', and he was widely held in contempt by some of his colleagues, who referred to him as 'Forlorn Hope'. His 'hunches', of which he was quite proud, would seldom fly, and the DPP required more than a hunch from an anachronistic copper from the eighties to successfully complete a prosecution. Superintendent Allen thought long and hard then decided. He sent an email before he realised that Hope would probably not read it. He phoned the Major Investigation Team's offices and left a message.

*

There was a Post-it note waiting on his computer screen when Hope returned. The computer may have been on but it wasn't logged in. Puzzled, Hope made his way to the sainted top floor and smiled nervously at Allen's personal assistant.

"I think Super wants to see me."

"Just go straight in, DI Hope."

Superintendent Allen smiled as Hope came in, a smile that was somewhat lacking in warmth. "Hello, Charles. Please sit down. Can I get you anything?"

"No thanks, sir."

"Charles, I don't believe in beating around the bush with an old sweat such as yourself."

Hope felt reflux burn the bottom of his oesophagus and wished he hadn't cadged that cigarette from the delivery driver in the smoking shelter. He knew this wouldn't be good and wondered what he had done wrong this time. Where to start?

"Charles, I'm sorry to say that I have received an official complaint, regarding something you said last week…"

"Sir, that toerag was being arsey. I know their law firm is going tits-up, but that guy was just being obstructive and—"

"Just stop there, Charles. This is nothing to do with what you may or may not have said to a member of Community Legal Notaries. This complaint comes from one of your colleagues based here."

Hope sighed. "Here we go."

"DI Hope, I have to ask you this question. When asked by a colleague whether you will be attending the Oxford Pride Parade in June, did you say, 'Only when the Chief Constable attends, wearing a pair of arseless chaps?'"

"I may have done, but I said it to Terry Rawlings. There's no way he would have put in a complaint against me."

"Charles, that's not how it works, as you well know. Even if someone overhears what you say and finds it to be offensive, then that is grounds for a complaint. Your ill-advised comment to DI Rawlings was deemed to be homophobic, hence the complaint."

"Sir, that is just bloody pathetic."

"Please just listen, DI Hope. In addition, did you call DS Parkin 'a pathetic bloody snowflake' this Monday in the Major Incident Team Room? Under guidance issued last year in a departmental memo, the terms 'Snowflake' and 'Millennial' are deemed to be offensive."

"Sir, this is complete trivial nonsense."

"I'm afraid that it isn't, DI Hope. An official complaint has been made by one person, and while she is unhappy at being called a 'Snowflake', DS Parkin is happy for me to deal with the matter unofficially. Nevertheless, the official complaint stands and will need to be investigated."

Superintendent Allen looked at the crestfallen Hope and felt torn. It was probably too late for him to ever make a good, modern copper, and with the number of years he had left and with an official complaint against him, promotion was out of the question. Allen did have a soft spot for poor old DI Hope. He was like a dinosaur that couldn't adapt to the Common Purpose and PC comet that thundered down into the Home Office. He happened to think that official police participation in Gay Pride events was a criminal waste of police resources and had chuckled out loud when he read the complaint. He happened to think that DS Parkin was a waste of bloody space, but DCI Parry really liked her, so she had a golden ticket.

Poor old blundering, blunt and tactless Charles Hope had no idea of the forces of right-on righteous indignation fielded against him. It was now up to Allen to do the right thing and save Hope's job and pension. He had to be moved somewhere while the investigation was conducted, receive his reprimand and move away from this nest of vipers.

"Okay, Charles. This is what we're going to do. The current investigation you're on is stalled until we can properly interview all the Service personnel on Gleam's list. We're going to have to liaise with the MoD and Service police, but that's well in the future. We're going to move you to Banbury to help with the investigation of those two murdered taxi drivers. They're a bit short of manpower over at Banbury nick, so we've offered you up to help them. It'll bring a fresh approach to another stalled investigation."

"You're getting me out of the way," Hope said bitterly.

"Yes, Charles, frankly I am. You may not see it, but I'm doing you a favour, because you've upset members of your investigation team and you have lost DCI Parry's confidence." He didn't actually spell out that they were trying to stitch him up and hated his guts. "Clear your desk this afternoon and take the rest of the week off. Report to DCI Reid at Bicester nick on Monday morning. And remember, Reid is heading up the investigation, so play nicely and be tactful. His DI is off sick with stress, so you'll be a godsend. He'll bring you up to speed when you get there."

"Ok, sir." Hope got up to leave.

"Charles, before you go, how about one of your hunches? Who killed Ron Gleam and shot the coppers?"

Hope had no hesitation. "Staff Sergeant Edge set it up and Warrant Officer Morrison pulled the trigger, because Edge was out of it in a Portuguese hospital, but they both did it. They are both cheeks of the same arse."

"So why did they shoot our officers?"

"To get away. To stop us getting them."

"They could have killed them."

Hope shook his head. "A shooter who puts a bullet through Ron Gleam's brain at four hundred metres isn't going to miss coppers if they meant to kill them. They shot at the helicopter to get rid of it and at our firearms team to suppress them while they got away."

Allen thought about it. "Interesting theory, Charles, but how did they get away?"

"They had a hide and holed up for days, or used the river. They are a pair of cunning bastards and the fragrant DCI Parry will never make her arrests. These aren't small-time villains who won't be able to help boasting about what they've done. They're probably in another country now. They have been trained to do what they did by the Government and you and me as taxpayers."

"Charles. Keep shtum please while I deal with the investigation. I won't be able to help you if you keep making waves."

"All right, sir. Thanks."

Superintendent Allen watched him leave and sighed.

"Forlorn Hope indeed."

Chapter 31

# THE DETECTIVE'S STORY

———

Detective Inspector Hope couldn't park at Banbury Police Station and had to leave his car in a nearby multi-storey car park. The police station was a modern 1980s building on the same side of Warwick Road as the magistrates' court. He was directed to the major incident team's room and was introduced to DCI Reid, who was polite but not exactly hail-fellow-well-met. It would appear that Hope's reputation had preceded him. Which indeed, it had. The previous Wednesday afternoon phone call had gone along the lines of:

"Look, sir, I know we're a bit thin on the ground here, but I don't want Forlorn Hope, just because he said something a bit naughty to DCI Parry's little friend."

"You said to your Super that you need help, so we're giving it to you. Hope has years of experience, and you need good coppers to do the donkey work."

"Except he isn't a very good copper, is he, sir?"

"He can be. He's more or less solved the Ruger-on-Thames shootings, except he can't prove it and DCI Parry is too arrogant to let him."

"Then take her off the bloody case."

"You know as well as I do that you don't take anyone with ovaries off a case."

DCI Reid could see he had been presented with a *fait accompli*. "All right then, sir. We'll have him, but if he pisses off any members of my team, then his feet won't touch."

However, Andy Reid had made sure a space had been cleared for Hope in the team room and had arranged all the logistical niceties such as computer log-ins and a parking space. He introduced Hope to the rest of the team; as well as the two DIs, there were two DSs and two DCs with a probationer. They was a 75/25 split male/female and all were under thirty-five. They looked at their new colleague with a mixture of curiosity and bemusement.

"Okay, Charles. That's the team. Come into my office and I'll bring you up to speed."

Over a coffee, Hope was given the case files to read, and stark reading it made. Two local taxi drivers had been killed on the outskirts of Banbury within a week of each other. A Mr Abuukar Warsime was found dead in the driving seat of his taxi pulled off Wykham Lane in a wood, just off the A361. Mr Warsime had been garrotted from the rear passenger seat, with a device that the pathologist regarded to be something made from thin piano wire. The garrotte had torn through the internal and external carotid arteries and the larynx. Mr Warsime had been slumped in a pool of his own blood. There were a number of photographs of the body, which were not for the faint-hearted.

Three days later, Mr Ilyaas Koshin was found dead in the driving seat of his taxi in a lane near Cherwell Edge Golf Club. He had been killed with a single stab wound to his left ear, which had penetrated his brain, killing him instantly. The pathologist estimated that the wound could have been caused by a marlin spike, a tent peg or a stiletto.

In both cases, money was untouched but no trace of the victims' mobile phones were found. On the passenger seat of each vehicle, there was a brown envelope full of good-quality monochrome photographs. These showed taxis picking up young girls, and despite having been taken at night, the exposure and clarity was perfect. There were photographs of a hotel belonging to a well-known budget hotel chain, and the girls being led into the building. Each envelope contained the number plates of various cars in a car park. There was a single printed piece of paper in the envelope, written in Ariel 20 point:

## DO YOUR FUCKING JOB YOU USELESS BASTARDS!

"The hotel's in Bristol in case you're wondering."

Hope put the files down and looked at Reid. "Jesus Christ."

He had so many questions that he didn't know where to start. Reid poured them another coffee from the machine on the filing cabinet.

"Not so easy now, is it?" he said to Hope.

"Right, so these two murders have been categorised as a 'hate crime', I take it?"

"Right from the start. That was a directive that came from the Chief's office."

Hope stirred a sachet of sugar into his coffee. He had managed to wean himself from three down to one sugar under his new health drive.

"These murders don't feel like the stunts that knuckle-draggers from *England Free Corps* would pull," Hope observed thoughtfully.

"Plus, the goading of us with those printed messages."

Hope thought about it but decided to keep quiet, because he wasn't convinced that whoever had left the photographs was inviting the police to catch *them*.

"Do you know much about Banbury, Charles?"

"Not really, Guv. I've not been here since they built the M40. I come from the Aylesbury Wycombe area, and Oxford of course."

Reid pointed at a wall of his office, which was covered in OS maps; one area that was current and the other covered with a number of Cassini reproductions of OS maps from the beginning of the 20th century.

"I've got a bit of a thing for maps," he told Hope, "and I think you can learn a lot about a town and its area from studying old maps. Banbury used to be a market town with connections to the railways. In the past hundred years, the town has almost tripled in size and it is spreading. Now we have some high-tech industries and we used to have very low unemployment levels. But the town is becoming an overspill for London and Oxford, and with that comes its own problems.

"We have a sizable immigrant community in the town and tensions have been rising. The very last thing that we need is some right-wing nutter going around murdering members of the Asian community."

"I thought the victims' names sounded more African to me, Guv. Somalian perhaps?"

"You know what I mean."

Yes, Hope knew perfectly well what he meant. They were Muslims, regardless of from whence they came, and the Thames Valley Police Service had difficulty in articulating that. As did every other police service in the country.

"So what leads have we got? Regarding right-wing nutters, that is?"

Reid frowned irritably. "Precious few, I'm afraid, Charles. The counter-terrorism people give us names and addresses of internet warriors they get from GCHQ every month or so. Most of our resident wannabe Einsatzgruppen are as thick as mince and incapable of stringing a sentence together, let alone conducting a violent and bloody murder without leaving any forensic of any kind. In the main, they spout off on social media. The really dangerous ones leave rashers of bacon in the back of taxis."

"Why would they do that, Guv?"

Reid looked at him sharply. "Come on, Charles. I'm told you can be quite sharp sometimes."

Hope smiled faintly, knowing quite well when he was being damned with faint praise. "Sorry, but I don't know this town. I'm tying a frame to the crimes to understand their context."

"We've had all our known Nazi agitators in and interviewed them. Some just make comments on Twatter or attend England Free Corps rallies in Birmingham, where there's plenty of our cameras to keep tabs on them. There is a worrying rise in tension between the white, what is laughably referred to as 'working class' community, and people from different ethnic backgrounds. We have been able to find absolutely nothing tied to the murders. Like most sizable towns, Asians mainly run the taxi firms."

"Hence the bacon?"

"Yes, Charles, hence the bacon."

"So who sent the photographs?"

"I'm just guessing here, but perhaps it could have been the person who killed the two… er…"

"Somalians?" Hope offered helpfully. "Perhaps we should be looking for an Ethiopian?"

Reid looked at Hope with annoyance. "This isn't a cause for levity, Charles."

"Sorry, Guv. It wasn't my intention to sound flippant," but like most things he said when trying to 'think outside the box', Hope's comments were often taken the wrong way with added extra offence.

"And the annoying thing is that we've heard nothing. The kind of people who go around killing innocent taxi drivers just wouldn't be able to keep quiet about it. Not a peep on social media. No talk from the local touts."

"But you do have the photographs, Guv."

"Yeah, useless. A list of car number plates that we've traced to vehicles belonging to local and prominent businessmen."

Hope decided that this probably wouldn't be a good time to enquire as to the ethnicity of these local businessmen, these pillars of the community. Hope was beginning to wonder if Reid was being wilfully stupid or if he was being leaned on by his superiors. What did they call it? Maintaining social cohesion.

"So what is it you want me to do? Where do you want me to start?"

"I'd like you to partner up with Alice Warboys and start to go through the numbers that have called into the taxi firms. Start with *Joe's the Taxi*, because both the murdered men worked for that outfit. See what you can find. Obviously, most will be from mobile numbers, so we can discount landlines. Even our resident knuckle-draggers wouldn't be stupid enough to use a landline."

"Alice being the probationer," Hope observed noncommittally.

"Yeah, that's right, Charles. She would benefit enormously from your experience and it would be a great opportunity for her. She's a bright kid."

Hope smiled. He knew when bullshit was being heaped upon him. If he had any doubts about the veracity of this investigation, they had been dispelled. "Okay, Guv. I'd like to get to know the area. Do you mind if Alice shows me round the local area before we talk to *Joe's the Taxi*?"

"No, it's a good idea. You can get to know each other."

Later that afternoon, they were in a car while Alice Warboys showed him around Banbury, which to all intents and purposes was a relatively affluent market town... in the main. Areas around the railway station were quite rundown, and one of the estates that sprawled to the south seemed to be indicative of expansion estates the country over. It could have been Blackbird Leys, Chalgrove, or Southcourt. Areas of so-called deprivation where a small minority made life a living hell for the majority.

"I'm sorry that you've been lumbered with me, Alice. If you're as keen as mustard, perhaps partnering up with me for a bit could do you some good. I could be a role model for how not to do modern policing."

She was driving and glanced at him sharply. She saw that he was smiling and she grinned ruefully. Hope was pleased. "Let's not have any pretentions. You know I'm under investigation. You've been told I'm crap and because you're the most junior, you're going to have to put up with me. I ask only two favours of you, Alice."

"What's that, sir?"

"One: you will call me 'Charles' or 'Guv', when DCI Reid is not present. Two: if I say anything that affects your delicate sensitivities, should you have them, please tell me in as blunt and as forthright terms as possible. I would prefer that you didn't go running to DCI Reid with tittle-tattle, because frankly, I'm in enough trouble as it is."

Alice kept looking ahead, but she was grinning. "Well then, you'll just have to behave yourself, Charles."

"Could you take me to where Mr Warsime's body and taxi was discovered, and I'd like to go via the town centre where the taxi company is. Then I'd like to do the same for the site on the golf course where Mr Koshin's body was found."

At Wykham Lane, they both got out of the car and went into the woods where the car had been found.

"It was just over there."

Hope looked around and noted the tyre tracks of the taxi and the heavier tracks of the recovery vehicle.

"I notice the ground is quite soft. Any decent footprints?"

"Just a single one of the sole of a cleated boot. Like a walking boot. Very common pattern, the second most popular in the country."

"No blood? The driver must have been spurting the stuff after he had been garrotted."

"Not a trace. Somebody had forensically swept the area before we pitched up. SOCO found traces of latex and fuller's earth on the door handles. Whoever killed Mr Warsime probably wore surgical gloves."

Hope stared at her. "Mr Reid didn't tell me that."

"I can show you the forensic reports for the two murders when we get back, if you like, si... Guv."

"Does that sound like the MO of a right-wing Twatter warrior to you, Alice?"

"No."

"Do you have confidence in the direction of travel of this investigation?"

"Mr Hope, that's not fair," she said, and bit her lip.

"Sorry, Alice. You're right. It was meant to be a rhetorical question, but it put you in an awkward position. Right, take me to the golf course and then we'll get some late lunch, my treat."

There was little to be gained at the golf club site, either.

"The taxi was half on the road and the two nearside wheels were on the grass verge. No additional tyre tracks. Again, there were traces of latex and fuller's earth inside the vehicle and on the left-hand side passengers' doors. No murder weapons, no prints, no DNA, nothing."

"Okay, thank you for showing me around, Alice. Where's the best pub to get a late lunch round here?"

She shook her head. "Sorry, Guv. I live in Bicester."

And that encapsulated one of the problems of the police service. They had no local ownership of the district that they were supposed to be policing. In the end, they had a light meal at the George and Dragon pub, and very good it was too. Hope had a half of bitter while Alice stuck to Coke. Hope was in no hurry to get back to the police station.

"Why do you want to be a detective, Alice?"

She smiled at the blunt directness of his question. "Because I'm sick and tired of being puked on and abused by drunks on Friday and Saturday nights. Because I'm sick of having to stand in for lazy bastards who have thrown a sickie because they're scared of doing their jobs. Because I get no support from my team or my boss and I'm sick to the back teeth of being a social worker for the people of Banbury who have the intellectual capacity of a toddler."

"Tell me about the photographs found in the envelopes in the two taxis. Were they identical?"

She nodded. "Traces of latex on the envelope, no DNA. Photos printed on good-quality paper, probably a Canon printer. Same with the 'do your fucking job you useless bastards' note."

"Who were the girls in the pictures?"

"Mainly local, most of them known to social services. Some being fostered, some supposed to be in care, some are just feral."

Hope finished his cheese and ham panini. "Now tell me about the photos of the number plates. I'm guessing here, but I reckon that you had to check them out, being the most junior."

"That's right," she agreed. "Mainly local, some from Northampton and the Midlands."

"Now, Alice, where do you think the photos of the number plates were taken?"

She shrugged and nibbled a few of the crisps that had come with her sandwiches.

"Could have been the car park of that hotel in Bristol?"

Alice thought about it. "It's possible. There was a bit of hedge on some of the pictures like the one at the side of the hotel. Privet, I would say."

"Okay, Alice. Now comes the difficult bit, but please be professional and remember that the note told us to do our fucking job. What is the ethnicity of the owners of those number plates?"

He saw her eyes flinch imperceptibly and knew beyond any certainty that she was afraid. "You don't have to answer that. You've told me everything I need to know."

As they got up to leave, he hit her with a supplementary question: "Is the reason your team's DI has gone off sick with stress because he asked the same questions that I have?"

Alice Warboys declined to answer. She was very quiet as they drove back to Banbury, so he didn't pressurise her.

"Thanks for the lunch, Guv. Please don't take this the wrong way, but I really desperately want to be a detective and I have to work here and DCI Reid will be doing my reports. You're coming to the—"

Hope held up his hand to silence her. "I'm coming to the end of my career. I can't go any further and I've already pissed a lot of people off. So you don't want me to drag you down when I go. Does that sound about right?"

"I wouldn't have put it quite as bluntly as that, but yes. Sorry, Mr Hope."

"I understand, Alice, and I hope that you will understand that I intend to do my job without fear or favour, because I'm thick, pig-headed and don't know when to shut up, and because I remember how policing in this country used to be. And I will keep you out of the beaten zone if I can, but I intend to find out who killed those men in the taxis, and more importantly, why. I would be grateful if DCI Reid is not party to what we have discussed."

*Joe's the Taxi* was run from a Portakabin on the edge of a car dealership. When Alice pulled up, a couple of East African guys were outside smoking. Hope got out of the car and showed them his warrant card, instantly recognising them as Somalis.

"Good afternoon. Could I speak with the owner if he's around?"

One of the men went into the Portakabin and returned with a middle-aged Asian man of Pakistani heritage. He was wearing a suit and smiled at Hope.

"Police again. I have told you all that I know, but come inside, both of you."

"Are you Mr Mahtam?" Hope asked inside the overly warm interior of the Portakabin.

"Indeed. How may I help you? As I have said, I've already told your colleagues everything they need to know."

Hope thought that was rather an interesting way of putting it.

"Mr Mahtam, I'm so sorry to bother you but I'm new to the case. I have visited the crime scenes, but I'd like a bit more background on the nights of the murders. Do you keep recordings of people who ring in for a taxi?"

"Alas, no. There was nothing remarkable that my controller reported on any of the two nights. And there is no certainty the killer phoned in. He may have asked the driver directly for a trip during the nights of the murders."

"Would the driver not have reported that to the control room?" Hope asked.

"Not necessarily. Most of my drivers are Somali, not necessarily the sharpest tools in the box. It takes me all my time to stop them chewing khat."

Hope wondered how long it would be before he received a diversity course if he opined such a view, but then it was established police policy that only white men are racist.

"So it would be fair to say, and please don't let me put words in your mouth, that some of your drivers can be a little difficult to keep tabs on?"

"Indeed, but most of them are hard-working."

*And cheap*, Hope thought. He produced a photograph from his jacket pocket that he had lifted from one of the files. Alice stared at him with a mixture of surprise and annoyance.

"Could that be why one of your drivers was photographed outside a hotel in Bristol? The number plate is quite readable. It is one of your cars, isn't it, Mr Mahtam?"

Mahtam shrugged. "It may be one of my cars, or at least one of my drivers. Many are freelance and use their own vehicles."

"And there would be no reason why one of your drivers would be in Bristol on company business?"

"No, not possible. Too far, and we don't do airport runs."

"I thought that was the case," Hope said, but he couldn't help but notice how uncomfortable the taxi company owner seemed. "So I won't take up any more of your time. Thank you for your cooperation, Mr Mahtam."

Back in Alice's car, she rounded on him. "You took that bloody photo from the file. You know it isn't allowed!"

Hope smiled. "It was loose and I picked it up from the floor. I'll put it back in the file back at the nick. Did you see that whiteboard in his office, the one with the drivers' names and number plates?"

She nodded.

"Would you run a check on the owner of this vehicle?" He wrote the number plate on a piece of scrap paper and handed it to her. "See if the registered owner has any connection with, or reason to visit, Bristol."

He could tell that Alice Warboys was cross with him, and part of Hope's cussed nature found it rather amusing. He decided to break the silence.

"Joe's the Taxi. Quite clever, don't you think?"

She stared at him with annoyance.

"*Joe Le Taxi.* She was fourteen when she recorded that song."

"Who was?"

"Vanessa Paradis. I wonder if there's a subliminal connection."

\*

Hope spent the rest of the afternoon going through the case files and surreptitiously copying details from folders and photographing some of the images with his mobile phone. He left with everyone else at 17:30 and Reid had a quick chat with him in the car park.

"Don't envy you on the Oxford ring road this evening, Charles."

"It's okay, Guv. I'm staying locally tonight to get in early tomorrow. Just until I know how long the commute is going to take."

"Thanks, Charles. I appreciate that. Could you let me have the number of your mobile in case I need to keep in touch?"

Hope wrote down the number and handed it to him.

"I'll send you a text so you'll have mine."

Hope reached his car and was getting in when Alice Warboys ran up to him.

"Mr Hope, I traced that car. It belongs to a Mr Musse Hussen, a local man. He works in a fast food chicken shop, and also part time for Joe's the Taxi. He has a caution for exposing himself to young women in Bristol and assaulting a man who tried to apprehend him at Temple Meads railway station. He moved from Bristol to Banbury the year before last."

"Interesting. Thank you, Alice. See you tomorrow. By the way, why wasn't the number plate traced earlier?"

She shrugged. "Night, Mr Hope."

\*

"Who is she?" asked Edge. They were sitting in a car outside a closed garden centre, just off the A41 near Bicester.

"She's Charlie Dorking's niece. She's a uniformed copper who wants to be a detective, so she's a probationer. It didn't take her long to become disillusioned, and Dorking reckons she's as pissed off as we are."

"Why is she pissed off, Henry?"

"Because she's found out there's a conspiracy involving the police, social services and local politicians to keep the incidents of child rape out of the public spotlight. For the sake of 'social cohesion'. They are very worried."

Edge craved a cigarette. "So would I be if someone started slotting Muslim taxi drivers on my patch."

"Manor, it's my manor, you slaaaaaag," Morrison said in his best Ray Winstone voice.

"We're the Sweeny, son. And we haven't had our dinner," Edge agreed.

They were quiet for a while, wishing for a police force like that portrayed by DI Regan and DS Carter that had never existed.

Edge broke the companionable silence. "But this is a rare form of madness. Why are we doing this, Henry? Wayne isn't even an Inkspot."

"I did a tour with Wayne in Afghanistan, back in 2002. We were in a team that cleared the Tora Bora caves. Wayne was a natural fighting underground, while I was scared shitless. He was an inspiration and kept us going. He should have got the MC."

"He can have mine," Edge said, with more than a trace of rancour. "For all the fucking good it did me."

"Nevertheless, Wayne is a comrade and we have to do our best to stop him making a mistake. I hope he gets sick of the whole thing, because you just can't kill everyone. I don't have kids, but how would you feel if it were your daughter?"

Edge was silent for a while. "I'd find out who had done it to her and post pieces of the bastard back to his family."

"But the problem is there are just so many of them. It's like a pandemic. It's the way they subjugate us in our own country, by targeting our children. And it's all done with the consent of the ruling elite and the very people who are supposed to protect us. For the sake of social fucking cohesion."

A car approached from the north, taking the slip road off to the garden centre and retail outlet. Henry switched on the lights briefly and the car pulled up close by. Edge got out and checked that the car hadn't been followed. A young woman got out of the vehicle and walked over to where they were parked, getting into the passenger seat. Edge joined them after a short time, getting in the back.

"Evening, gentlemen."

"Hello, Alice. Good day at the office?" Morrison asked.

"Interesting. We've got a new member of the team. He arrived this morning, a DI called Hope. He's been sent to us because he pissed off his DCI at the Kidlington HQ and he's facing a disciplinary investigation. He was on the team investigating the shooting of that lawyer. His name's Hope and everyone calls him 'Forlorn Hope', because they reckon he's useless. So naturally, they have partnered him up with me. I heard Reid call it 'damage limitation' on the phone, because an old, fat and useless DI and a stupid little probationer can't do much damage."

"Should we be concerned, Alice?"

She delved in her bag for a tube of mints, offering them around. Edge took one. Henry shook his head.

"Yes, I think you should," she told them. "He comes across as an unfit, bumbling buffoon who couldn't catch a cold. I've found out in less than a day that he's as sharp as a dagger and doesn't miss a trick. I think he already knows that Reid is making no effort to find out why Muslim taxi drivers are being murdered. He has spotted the connection between the girls being trafficked out to the cities from children's homes and the local taxi firm. He knows the murder sites were sanitised by someone with forensic knowledge and he's been copying stuff from the files."

"What did he do to get suspended, Alice?"

"When asked if he would attend the Oxford Gay Pride event, he said, "Only when the Chief Constable attends, wearing a pair of arseless chaps.'"

The two men laughed. Alice didn't join them. "You don't realise just how seriously a comment like that is viewed in the police service," and because she wasn't a fool, either, she added, "and he reckons he knows who shot that lawyer. It was either an ex-SAS guy called Edge, but as he was in hospital in Portugal when the shot was taken, he said it was another ex-SAS guy called Morrison."

Edge and Morrison went quiet.

"Plus, he called a junior detective 'a pathetic bloody snowflake'," Alice said as though this was a heinous crime.

"Clearly, we are dealing with an extremely dangerous individual," Edge said light-heartedly.

"I need to protect myself, gentlemen. I know that British policing has become somewhat of a joke shop, but I am still young and idealistic enough to believe in having a career and perhaps making a difference. I don't want to be caught in any crossfire."

"It's okay, Alice. We promised your uncle to keep you safe," Morrison told her. "You should build a cover story and perhaps start tipping off your DCI about what Hope's up to."

Alice Warboys bit her lip, unseen in the darkness. "It's not easy. I really like Mr Hope and I think he's a bloody good copper. Reid is the useless one."

"Sometimes you have to do unpalatable things to stay safe. Hope sounds like he's big enough and ugly enough to look after himself."

"Do you know where Hope lives, Alice?" asked Edge.

"Chinnor, but he's staying in the Premier Inn out near the M40 for a few nights. You're not going to do something bad to him, are you?"

"Of course not! Just the opposite, in fact. Tell us what he looks like." Alice did. "All right. Thank you, Alice. Play it nice and easy. Let's make it 18:30 in two evenings' time, Wednesday night. Make it Bicester Business Centre next time. Look after yourself."

They watched her get out, go to her own car and drive off. Nobody was following her.

"This rather complicates matters," Morrison said thoughtfully, "Wayne's going to slot Hussen tonight, or rather the early hours of tomorrow."

"Who's Hussen?"

"The bastard who drove his daughter to Bristol where she was raped, injected with heroin and threatened with being burned alive. She went under the train two days later."

"When will all of this stop, Henry?"

Morrison leaned on the steering wheel. "Fuck knows, mate. I can clean up on my own if necessary. You'd better keep an eye on Mr Hope, forlorn or not."

"I bet the thick fucking plods don't even know what a forlorn hope is."

\*

Hope had decided to stay in a budget hotel on the outskirts of Banbury rather than risk the commute, until he found out what the battle rhythm of the department was. He had a shower and phoned his wife. She unloaded the latest saga of his son's divorce proceedings and he ground his teeth as he listened to how his son's ex-wife, Cafcass, and the courts were conspiring to destroy his life. But he was just one of many men whom the state destroys and impoverishes every year.

"Yes, dear, I will get a proper meal tonight. No, I haven't smoked anything," *yet,* "and I will get an early night. No, I haven't upset anyone, at least not yet."

That evening, Hope decided to walk into the town centre and get a meal in conjunction with some exercise. He had a meal of grilled chicken in a Bangladeshi restaurant, which was rather good. He decided to look round before going back to the hotel, as it was getting late. The change in atmosphere and demographics was totally different to that of a daytime market town. Taxis with clumps of youngsters round them seemed to dominate the town centre. Groups of louche taxi drivers picked up giggling and clearly underage girls from near the park on the fringes of the fast food joints and seedy pubs.

Hope couldn't help speculating that it was a pity that DS Reid didn't spent a little less time naval-gazing at old OS maps and a little more time actually walking the streets he was supposed to be policing. On the way back to the hotel, he noticed a single police van well north of the town centre, its occupants ensconced with portable electronic devices. He photographed the van with his phone, and none of the occupants paid the slightest attention to him.

Back in the hotel, he decided to get a drink at the bar before turning in. As he walked towards the doors, he didn't notice the car that had been following him all night, from the time he left the hotel. He failed to notice the vehicle's passenger photographing him through a large zoom lens as he went into the hotel. He may have seen but not registered the nondescript man with the longish hair, tinted glasses and *Viva Zapata* moustache who slipped in after him and sat reading a paper in the foyer, where he could watch the bar. By the time Hope went up to his room, he had gone.

# Chapter 32

# THE DETECTIVE'S STORY

———

Detective Inspector Hope's mobile phone woke him up. It was still dark outside the hotel room's partially open curtains. He groped for the phone and noticed the time was 06:15.

"Hullo?" he murmured sleepily.

"Charles, it's me, Andy Reid."

"Christ, Guv, you're early."

"Charles, can you get into central Banbury ASAP, please. Bath Road to the west of People's Park. There's been another murder. Another bloody taxi driver. The pathologist is on his way and we've got the first of the SOCOs here. There's SOC tape around the taxi but the body is actually in the park."

"Okay, Guv, ten to fifteen minutes max."

Hope eventually found Bath Road and the taxi surrounded by blue and white tape, its engine still running. There was a clump of SOCOs around a bed of shrubs, surrounded on two sides by a footpath. Officers in blue coveralls were photographing the area around a body that seemed to have been tossed into the undergrowth. The pathologist was crouched next to the body, examining the head and neck.

"Morning, Charles," Reid said to him, his hands thrust into the pockets of his overcoat. Hope only had his jacket and it was a cold morning, their breath misting in the cool air. "Different MO this time. Killed outside of his cab."

"Any idea who it is?"

"According to the permit and paperwork in the taxi, he is, or rather was, a Mr Musse Hussen."

Hope gave an imperceptible start. *Well, I'll be damned. What a small world.*

"*Joe's the Taxi* again?"

"Reid nodded bitterly. "This is getting beyond a fucking joke, Charles."

Hope wisely kept his mouth shut. The pathologist had finished his primary observations, stood up and peeled off his rubber gloves. He bagged the gloves and walked towards where the two detectives were standing.

"Mr Cartwright, this is DI Hope. I know you don't like speculating this early on, but do we have a cause of death?"

The pathologist picked up his medical bag after straightening his coat. "*Au contraire*, DCI Reid. I'm ninety-five percent certain that the cause of death is a broken neck."

"Christ, the murderer must be a big, strong lad to break someone's neck just like that," Hope speculated. "Can't be many out there capable of that."

"Sorry, Andy, but I'm afraid it's not that simple. The victim's neck wasn't broken with brute force. The victim had a contusion to the chin and extensive bruising to the back and left-hand side of the neck. An absolutely classic example of the commando neck-break manoeuvre. A technique developed by the commando forces during the Second World War.

"The assailant approaches the victim from behind, such a sentry. He or she, because as I've said, it's technique and not force, places the forearm against the back or side of the victim's neck. They reach forward to cup the victim's chin and then jerk the head backwards while twisting to the side. The forearm is thrust forward to act as the fulcrum."

Both of the detectives went through the motions with their arms, to work out the technique.

"So we're looking for someone who has military training and is right-handed?" Reid asked.

"Alas, not that simple, chaps. The technique is easily performed left- or right-handed, and the technique is taught in advanced martial arts training."

"A man with military or martial arts training?"

"Or indeed a woman," the pathologist reminded them. "Right, gentlemen. I'll need to tee up a slab in the John Radcliffe, so I'll give you a bell, Andy.

Probably early afternoon. I assume there's little to be gained by your watching me saw up that unfortunate gentleman?"

Reid nodded.

"You can move the body as soon as you have all the crime scene evidence. Slightly unfortunate this being a park, as there's a plethora of footprints. I shouldn't hold out too much hope of there being any DNA, but I'll swab the body when it's in the mortuary. You never know."

They watched the pathologist leave and then Reid went to chat with the senior SOCO. Hope went to take a look at the taxi, whose engine by now someone had turned off.

"Anything interesting?" he asked the young woman in the blue coverall, who was photographing the interior of the taxi.

"A bloody forensic nightmare, sir. So much DNA on this back seat, you could start a new species." She put her head on one side in thought. "In fact, if my Saturday nights are anything to go by, they already have."

Hope grinned and popped a square of nicotine gum into his mouth. He waited for Reid to finish his brief to the SOCOs. Hope was hungry and decided to go back to the hotel for breakfast. Reid returned a few minutes later.

"Right, Charles, we've got a bit of a steer. I'd like you and Alice to do some delving into the backgrounds of our resident Nazis. Military experience, even the TA. Nunchaku nutters from the Bruce Lee appreciation societies, sad enactment SS Panzer Grenadiers and *Combat* and *Survival* subscribers."

"How far out, Guv?"

"The whole of the Thames Valley area."

"We're not far from Coventry."

"Later. Let's concentrate on our home-grown saddos first."

Hope sighed. He couldn't help himself. "Guv, have you ever considered why someone is killing off 'Asian' taxi drivers, with the single-minded efficiency of a Spetznaz hit squad?"

"Racists. Radicalised right-wing nutters. Whoever it is fits the profile perfectly. Oh, and as my two IC, would you come with me to the JR this afternoon? Take notes and that sort of thing?"

Hope immediately knew why Reid wanted him to go to the autopsy as well. He wanted to keep him under observation and away from the team. Reid's team of useless no-hopers. He had realised that Alice Warboys was as much use as an ejector seat on a mobility scooter.

"Okay, Guv."

"See you back at the station."

Hope decided that he wasn't going to hurry. If he was going to get his time wasted, it would be on a full stomach.

\*

There was very little smell, as the body hadn't gone so far down the stage of decomposition, although rigor mortis had set in. Doctor Cartwright was a lot friendlier than he had been that morning, probably because he hadn't just been dragged out of bed. The body was on the slab, covered with a rubberised shroud, and samples of its internal organs lay in jars full of formaldehyde.

"Afternoon, gentlemen. No real surprises from this morning. The deceased was a male of East African heritage of around thirty years of age. Judging by the state of rigor mortis, I would estimate the time of death at around one am this morning, with an hour's leeway either way. I believe you have confirmed that he was a Mr Musse Hussen?"

"That's correct, Doctor Cartwright," confirmed DCI Reid.

"As I suspected, the cause of death was a torsion fracture of the upper vertebrae in the T2, T3 region. Death would have occurred within seconds. There were two wounds consistent with the method of killing I outlined this morning, a small bruise to the right-hand side of the mandible, consistent with fingertip pressure, and a much larger bruising and pooling of blood to the distal aspect of the vertebrae. A classic example of the commando neck-break.

"Two other points of note, the deceased had pre-cancerous lesions of the buccal cavity of the mouth, consistent with chewing khat, and untreated gonorrhoea. The chin provided traces of latex, so it is highly likely the assailant wore medical gloves. There was no other forensic evidence on the body, I'm afraid, gentlemen."

"And nothing at the crime scene, either. It was as though it had been swept, and there was no trace of a mobile phone on the body or in the taxi."

"Just like the others," Doctor Cartwright observed. "Makes it kind of difficult for you."

As they left the mortuary facilities, Hope turned to his boss. "Guv, I need to drop some paperwork off with the Super at Kidlington. It's about my ongoing investigation. Shouldn't take long and I'll see you back at Banbury nick."

"All right, Charles. Do you think you'll get off?"

Hope shrugged. "I reckon it'll be a reprimand. It'll go on my file but won't make that much difference in the greater scheme of things."

Hope headed to the Oxford ring road and while he was heading for the headquarters at Kidlington, he had no intention of meeting with Superintendent Allen or anyone else to do with his investigation. He had already phoned that morning and arranged a meeting with DI Terry Rawlings. They met in the gym changing rooms where it was quiet this time of the afternoon. Rawlings grinned ruefully.

"I hope you're not going to slip into your arseless chaps, Charlie."

Hope grimaced but took it in good humour. Terry Rawlings was the nearest thing he had to a friend in the headquarters.

"Have you heard anything, Terry?" Hope asked.

"Not a dicky bird. I reckon they've kicked it into the long grass to keep you out of the way. Now why do you want to see me, and why the subterfuge?"

"You're working on an investigation into serious sexual offences against children, aren't you?"

"Err, yes. Operation Bullfinch, but it's a bit hush-hush and you just wouldn't believe the amount of grief and panic it's causing."

"I might be able to help you and me at the same time," Hope explained. "I know it's a huge ask, but can you look at a list of names, number plates and photographs of men and young girls that's on this flash drive?"

Hope held it up. He could sense Rawlings' unease.

"Charlie, we could be in fathoms of shit for this."

"Do you know what I'm working on over at Banbury?"

"Yeah, the taxi murders."

Hope grabbed Rawlings' arm to show how serious this was. "Terry, I'm afraid that Andy Reid who's heading up the case is a fucking Woodentop. He is process-driven and has an irrational conviction that the murderer is a right-wing nutter. There was another killing last night and I believe that the two investigations are linked. All of the drivers that have been murdered are Muslims of East-African heritage. The murderers are professional, yes, there is definitely more than one and they kill with military precision. The crime scenes have always been swept by people who understand forensic investigations. The murders are efficient in that they use the minimum amount of force and they are using terror as a weapon.

"Why? Because I'm willing to bet that several of the men and registered keepers of the cars on that flash drive are connected with your operation.

The girls in the pictures are the victims. Reid is looking for the killer without understanding the motive. I'm willing to bet that when you look at the pictures and data, you'll provide me with the motive and likely the killers and you with a hell of a lot more paedophile scumbags to finger."

Rawlings leaned back and looked up at the ceiling where a florescent tube was flickering. "Jesus, Charlie, I just don't know. This is so political."

"I'm the one that'll be in the firing line. All I need to know is if there is a crossover between the men on the drive and your investigation, and the information should be on HOLMS. I don't have the permission or access to your investigation on HOLMS. If there is, I can go over Reid's head and stop wasting our time and look for the murderers of the taxi drivers who are not, repeat not, right-wing nutjobs and internet warriors."

"Charlie, if you are right, then whoever is killing these taxi drivers may have a very good reason to do so."

"I don't doubt that, and part of me says good luck to them, but murder is murder and we're not a fascist police state yet. Even scumbags don't deserve to be garrotted."

*

Hope had been late in that morning as he had made several telephone calls before arriving at work. Now he was driving with Alice Warboys and they had taken his car. He had told Reid that they were going to investigate a couple of martial arts centres and a Taekwondo dojo. Reid was told they were going to check membership lists with the internet surveillance information on likely 'right-wing' extremists. Reid seemed pleased with the plan and Alice was chatting and seemed in a better frame of mind than the day before yesterday. Hope smiled grimly. That was going to bloody change.

He had spent a sleepless and restless night in the hotel, after his meeting with Rawlings, digesting everything he had been told. The account of what had been happening to children in Oxfordshire over a number of years was deeply disturbing. The experiences of the girls, and the complete failure of public services including the police to protect them, was appalling. Girls as young as twelve would return to care homes half-naked and bleeding. Cigarettes had been put out on their bodies and some had been injected with heroin. That day, Hope had heard enough and he was going to press the nuclear mutually assured destruction button. The clincher was when Rawlings phoned him that evening and confirmed that at least twenty names on his flash drive were persons of interest in the Operation Bullfinch investigation.

Alice was puzzled when he drove the car towards the town centre and the Spiceball Leisure Centre.

"Err, Mr Hope, I thought we were going to the Taekwondo dojo first."

"You may want to waste your time smelling stale sweat and trawling through lists of names of members, but I'm going to do the job I swore all those years ago to do."

"But this is…"

"That's right, love. Oxfordshire County Council, or more specifically, the Department of Children's Services, the head of which I have an appointment with in fifteen minutes."

"DI Hope, I can't let you do this."

He parked in a named slot in the car park and got out to get a briefcase from the boot.

"You coming in with me, or are you going to phone DCI Reid? I bet you've got him on the top of your call log."

"I will have to—"

"You, your boss and your fucking team who laughably call themselves detectives, may be happy at being complicit with covering up the rape and torture of children, but I am not!"

He stalked off towards the buildings and Alice got out of the car. "Sssshit!" she exclaimed, and delved in her handbag for her mobile.

Hope had a short wait before he gained entry to the Children's Services Department. He was greeted by a middle-aged lady to whom he showed his warrant card, and was shown into an office.

"Good morning, Detective Inspector, how can I help you? You sounded awfully concerned when you spoke with my team this morning."

"I'm investigating three murders and I believe that children are in a great deal of danger. I am going to show you a number of photographs of girls and I require you to tell me if any and how many are known to social services."

She looked evenly at him. "I'm afraid that's quite impossible, Mister Hope. I can't comment on wards in our care."

"In which case, I will arrest you for obstructing a police officer in the lawful execution of his duty, under the Police Act of 1996. I am quite prepared to march you out of this building in handcuffs and take you to Banbury Police Station, where you will be asked the question again under caution."

Her face seemed to drain of colour and her eyes were round with shock. Hope put the photographs on the desk.

"You are to tell me how many of these children are known to you, in your professional capacity. You will furnish me with their names and addresses within twenty-four hours."

"You are exceeding your authority, Detective Inspector."

"Oh really? Let's put it to the test, shall we?"

Reluctantly, she started to go through the photographs and she looked at them for a long time.

"I know that at least half of the girls you have shown me are known to us in a professional capacity. There may be more, but I'd have to check with the safeguarding team."

Hope stood up. "You can keep the photographs for reference. You haven't been doing a very good job on the safeguarding front, have you?"

Back at the car, Alice had gone. He knew what was going to happen back at the station and needed to get his ducks in a row. He would have a snack at a pub and let them stew while he prepared his scheme of manoeuvre. He stopped at a newsagent's for a packet of cigarettes and parked up at a pub. He sat outside, which was cold, sipped a half of beer and chain-smoked while he waited for his beef and mustard sandwiches. To a casual passer-by, it looked as though a tubby, middle-aged man was deep in thought, but inside, Hope was boiling with anger. He knew that he had enough evidence to support him and decided that he would go on the attack. The bastards weren't going to get away with it this time. He made a few notes in his notebook for a running script. He intended to control and dominate the inevitable meeting.

Back at Banbury Police Station, he went straight up to the squad room. Predictably, everyone snubbed him except DCI Reid, who seemed to be hopping with anger.

"We're to go upstairs, now, DI Hope."

Hope ignored him and went over to Alice, who seemed to be ensconced in some paperwork. "I trust you didn't walk all the way back here, Alice?"

"Now, Hope!"

"That will be DI Hope to you, DCI Reid. Two juniors and a probationer are present."

They headed for the stairs and halfway up on a landing, Reid rounded on him. "What the hell are you playing at, Hope? You had strict instructions on which lines the investigation was to take. We are supposed to be catching a triple-murderer and you threaten to arrest the Head of Child Protection Services and show her ludicrous photographs of dirty, little skanks—"

Hope was overweight and an assumed figure of ridicule; nevertheless, Forlorn Hope smashed DCI Reid into the wall. The meaty hand against Reid's throat was very strong.

"Those 'skanks' are children that nonce-enablers like you and social services have allowed to be raped, beaten and abused. You're a fucking useless piece of shit, Reid. You and your team of hopeless pricks couldn't catch a cold! And you know perfectly well why those taxi drivers have been murdered and yet you have refused to follow the most obvious line of investigation."

Reid gasped. "You'll lose your job and pension for this, Hope."

"I may, but I'm going to make sure that you go down for perverting the course of justice."

There was a superintendent and a chief superintendent waiting for them in the top floor office. They didn't ask Hope to sit and went on without preamble: "Detective Inspector Hope, you have committed a serious breach of discipline in that you have wilfully disobeyed a direct order from a superior officer and—"

"Be quiet, sir, and listen very carefully. Detective Chief Inspector Reid has been wilfully negligent in the conduct of his investigation. He has deliberately withheld crucial information, which has had an impact on not only this case, but Operation Bullfinch."

Their faces were priceless.

"He has wasted time investigating so-called right-wing persons whose opinions on social media he doesn't approve of. Because of this, he and his team have allowed the trafficking and abuse of underage girls to continue in epidemic proportions. I believe that there is a culture of cover-up and corruption not only here but within the Force area. I believe that you, as DCI Reid's superiors, are complicit in this cover-up. I intend to find out what hold the Muslim community has over the police service, and whether your lack of action is a misguided attempt to preserve community cohesion at the expense of young white girls. Or whether you are complicit in these crimes.

"There will be no internal disciplinary investigation or action against me. I have contacted a legal firm that investigates police corruption and I intend to hand over all the evidence I have collected. There will be no involvement from the Independent Complaints Commission because they are neither independent nor competent to deal with the magnitude of corruption I have uncovered. If you take any action against me, I will take a counter action through the courts and all of this sordid dishonesty will be in open court. I have prepared a pack-up which I intend to forward to the foreign media, should you try and thwart me through injunction.

"I intend to take paid gardening leave until such time as my period of engagement is concluded, or I am forced down the judiciary route."

Hope left. He collected his coat and few bits and pieces from the squad room but said nothing to them. As he drove back to Chinnor, he thought about what the hell he was going to say to his wife and what the hell she was going to say when she found out he'd started smoking again.

\*

A couple of years later in the summer, during a clement Sunday early afternoon, Charles Hope exited the Phoenix cycle trail and rode into the centre of Thame. He hadn't noticed the man who had been following him, also on a bike, about 300 yards behind. Hope chained his bike, bought a broadsheet newspaper at a newsagent's and went into the Black Horse pub. He chose an unoccupied table under the vines in the conservatory and bought a pint of bitter from the bar. Hope had lost weight and looked healthy and fit.

The other man who had been following Hope wheeled his mountain bike over the road to a car park opposite the pub, near a man with long grey hair sitting on a bench. He leaned the bike against the back of the bench and pretended to fiddle with the gears and chain. He spoke softly without looking at the seated man.

"It's him. Usual Sunday ritual. Bike ride, couple of pints and a read of the paper, then home."

"Anyone follow him, apart from you?"

"No, but his house is being watched."

The man on the bench stood up stiffly. He had a heavy fringe and cold grey eyes. He wore a ranchman's coat despite the warmth of the day and walked towards the pub. His gait was slightly stiff and he leaned on an old-fashioned walking stick. The stick concealed an épée with a 30-inch blade. He went into the pub and saw Hope sitting almost alone in the conservatory. Another couple were a few tables away, but lost in each other's eyes. It was obvious they weren't married, at least not to each other.

"Mr Hope, do you mind if I sit down?"

Hope looked up and felt tendrils of fear wrap around his vitals. The grey-haired man smiled.

"I mean you no harm. But I have information that may well give you, what's that expression? Closure."

Reluctantly, Hope indicated to the chair opposite.

"Thank you. I believe that you are now fully retired from the police and in receipt of your pension. Well done. You fought a hell of a battle. Now, just a few admin points. Could you please put your mobile phone, MP3 or whatever on the table so that I can check you're not recording this."

Hope complied uneasily. "I feel I should know you."

"You know of me. You were bang on with your theory about who shot Gleam. I set everything up, did all the recce, provided the weapon but never took the shot," the man said in a low voice.

"Are you Edge or Morrison?"

"I used to be Edge in a different life, but as you know, he no longer exists. He drowned off the Algarve. Or did he?"

"The case is still open, you know."

The grey haired man laughed softly. "Is that arrogant DCI Parry and her little carpet-munching friend still on the case?"

"No, they have gone on to greater things."

"Which brings me on to another unsolved case, despite all the good work you did on it. You were right about that as well, Mr Hope. The tragedy is nobody listened to you."

"Why? Did you kill those taxi drivers?"

"Oh, I never killed any of them. I was part of the surveillance team and it wasn't just Somalians. There were Bangladeshis, Pakistanis, Afghans, white British guys. Banbury was, as they say, the tip of the iceberg. Bad people have been slotted in Manchester, Birmingham, Leeds, Bradford and Bristol. But there is so much criminality in those unpoliced cities that nobody misses the odd scumbag. There's an ISO container full of rotting paedophiles, child traffickers, slavers and murderers, just waiting to be discovered at Tilbury Docks. Or by now it may have gone on to Indonesia."

"Jesus Christ! What kind of a monster are you?"

"A monster that's prepared to do the work you lot aren't. Have you ever heard of a book called *The Feather Men*?"

Hope nodded.

"Well, it was fiction, but organisations like the Feather Men exit. People who have served their country in certain roles make many powerful enemies. Many who have served in the Regiment still have a price on their heads courtesy of the IRA, Tony Blair and the Good Friday Agreement. The State or the MoD won't look after us, so ex-serving members have formed mutual help and support groups. Its members have sworn a blood oath to come to the aid of a comrade *in extremis* or danger.

"I want to tell you about a comrade of ours, who for the sake of argument we'll call Wayne. Our Wayne was a fine soldier but rather a poor husband and father. His wife grew tired of living effectively as a single parent with a young daughter, so she and Wayne separated. Unfortunately, for whatever reasons, Wayne's daughter became rather wayward and fell in with the wrong crowd, as they say. It's a long story, but Wayne's daughter was made a ward of court and placed in care. She was sent to a care home in Banbury, nearly one hundred miles from her mother. While she was in this care home, she was groomed by Muslim men of Somalian heritage. Her mother desperately tried to get social services and the police to do something, and when she turned up at Banbury social services, she was arrested for obstruction and affray.

"When she was fourteen, Wayne's daughter was raped, infected with sexually transmitted diseases and forced to take drugs. Pleas to the police resulted in her mother being arrested again. This girl was trafficked by taxi to Bristol, Northampton, Nottingham, Leicester and Birmingham. It was estimated that she was raped by over fifty different men of which persuasion? You've guessed it. Still, the problem soon went away when the girl walked in front of a train.

"Her death was the result of the inability, or more likely the unwillingness of your lot to do their jobs, protect the public and uphold the law. This includes, whether you like it or not, young girls from 'difficult' and 'challenging' backgrounds.

"Something went in Wayne's head and he vowed to track down and kill every single person involved with the degradation and death of his daughter. He asked for our help, but we knew it was an impossible task. He would have to kill members of the police service, social services, you name it, so we tried to get him to see sense and avoid getting caught. Yes, we were accessories, only because your useless and compliant colleagues refused to do their jobs. We formed three teams; surveillance of the targets, the solo killer and the clean-up team. Have you ever read a book called: *Operation Wrath of God*? You might know the film version, *Munich*."

"I've seen *Munich*."

"It's an interesting study of how retribution and the single-minded pursuit of revenge corrodes the soul. I'm a classic example of the destructive power of retribution. In my determination to kill Gleam, I lost my wife, my family and my life. Wayne stopped being a human being. In the end, I think he even lost sight of why he was doing this. The realisation that all the people who so badly abused his daughter could never be brought to his version of justice drove him mad. Don't worry, Mr Hope. Five months ago, Wayne ate both barrels of an antique Purdy and spread his brains all over the inside of a Land Rover. Once again, we cleaned up and made sure poor, sad, tortured Wayne got a fitting burial in a place he loved. They used to call you 'Forlorn Hope', didn't they?"

There was a brief flash of anger across Hope's eyes.

"Do you know what a forlorn hope is? It's a band of soldiers or other combatants that have been chosen to take the leading part in a military operation. For example, an assault on a heavily defended position, where the risk of casualties is high. Sums you up to a tee, I would say."

The grey haired man pushed back his chair and stood up. "I hope it is closure for you, Mr Hope. It is for us and I'm truly sorry for what we did, but an oath sworn between brothers in arms is an oath for life. You may see it as twisted loyalty and perhaps you're right. Goodbye and enjoy your retirement. We will be keeping a watchful eye on you from now on, because now you've made powerful enemies as well. You're now a brother in arms, so to speak. Don't follow me out for at least fifteen minutes if you'll be so kind."

Hope watched the man walk out leaning on his stick. He closed his eyes and shuddered.

## Chapter 33

# THE BURNING MAN

———

Daz received news from Moira's father that would drive him mad with jealousy and the awful feelings of rejection. One day in work, he was driving Frank Tremain to a farm to demonstrate a new type of harrow, suited to manoeuvring in the small Devon fields. Frank confided in Daz, wishing this charming and helpful young man could have been the son he never had.

"That bloody daughter of mine has just dumped a piece of news on me that makes me want to spit. She's only gone and informed me that she wants to marry a bloody soldier. A bloody thick infantryman she met at a wedding in Bristol."

Daz's hands grabbed the steering wheel, and seething rage bubbled up inside him.

"It's a crying shame and a waste of her life, on which we've lavished a great deal over the years. I thought you were walking out with her, Daz?"

"We was, Mr Tremain, but I'm afraid I decided that she was too good for the likes of me. It was never to be... sadly," Daz said obsequiously in a shameful display of acting that would have made Kenneth Branagh blush.

"Such a pity, Daniel. You were made for each other. I've already tried telling her we won't pay for the wedding, but she says that she'll just elope."

"What's his name, Mr Tremain?"

"Edge, Mark Edge, and he's only a bloody corporal. Not even an officer."

"It'll fizzle out when he keeps going off to get killed, Mr Tremain. A mug's game."

But it didn't fizzle out and it continued to drive Daz mad with jealousy. His sociopathic tendencies rewrote the truth and it had been the fucking pongo, Mark Edge, who had turned Moira's head and split her up from Daz. They were even planning to get married, until she went to that wedding and Edge stole her off him. If he had been there… well, it would never have happened.

Just before the wedding, Frank Tremain spoke with Daz again. "It's this Saturday, Daniel. I hope you'll come to the evening do at the hotel. I'll need some friends around me, to help me through a day I'm dreading. Bring your mates."

Daz needed no second bidding and had a word with Paulie and Steve, asking if they wanted to tag along.

"There may be some argy-bargy," Daz told them, "coz after all, it wouldn't be a proper wedding without at least one fight."

And Daz and his posse turned up at the hotel, pre-loaded and itching for a fight. But what made him incautiously angry the minute he walked through the door was the sight of a handsome man, totally at ease and chatting with two of Daz's exes, Angela and Moira. He sought out Frank Tremain slightly before Moira did.

"Who's the joker who was sitting with Moira and Angela?"

"Henry Morrison, the best man, although that's a matter of opinion. The bashful groom is over there at the bar."

Daz and the team sauntered over to get some drinks. He looked at Edge and made his acquaintance with a particularly insincere smile.

"So you're the lucky groom, eh?"

"You are?"

"Daz." He didn't offer his hand to shake. Neither did Edge. "Lucky, lucky you. Me and Mo used to be a bit of an item."

"So I believe," Edge said evenly.

"I hear that you and Mo are staying at some place in Weare Gifford." Edge said nothing.

"And that your new wife is staying in it all alone when you go back to the Army. Puts a lot of strain on a marriage, does that."

"Are you Marjorie fucking Proops?"

"Just saying, that's all. Keep your hair on. I'm sure she'll be well looked after."

"I tell you what, Daz. It'll be me giving Moira a good old looking-after tonight and for long, long nights to come. You must excuse me while I mingle."

Daz ordered the beers and the posse took up station at the end of the bar. "Well, lads, we're a bit spoiled for choice tonight, but the groom gets his second. We'll do the best man first. I'll need to rile him up a bit to get the party started."

They bided their time, getting steadily more drunk, and Daz spotted his opportunity when Morrison got up to refill his and Angela's glasses at the bar. He swaggered over to the table and sat down next to Angela.

"Piss off, Daz."

"Now that's not very nice, Ange."

"I've told you, don't call me that. Why did you have to come here?"

"Mo's dad invited me. And I had to come, because after all, he is my boss."

When Morrison went back to the table with the drinks, Daz was sitting next to Angela, who was looking uncomfortable. Daz put his hand on her forearm and she dragged it away sharply.

"I really don't think the lady is appreciating your attention, Mr Copeland."

"Piss off, Pongo. You don't come from here," Daz said, and tried to kiss Angela, who slapped him across the face.

"Bitch!"

Morrison grabbed a fistful of Daz's curly hair and bent down close to his face. He said quietly so the girl couldn't hear, "You and me outside now, you bastard!"

Daz watched him leave the function room and head for the exit corridor. He smiled at Angela and winked.

"This shouldn't take too long. Keep yourself nice and warm for me. Then it'll be Mr Edge's turn, followed by Moira. Fancy a threesome?"

"Pig!"

He collected Paulie and Steve and they headed swiftly down the corridor, past the pool, for the hotel's back door. They caught up just as Morrison went through the closed fire doors ahead of them. Daz was leading and as he went to push through the fire doors, they burst open. A heavy door caught Daz above the eye, a contusion that was white and became rapidly suffused with purple blood.

Daz became entangled with one of his wingmen and went down. Morrison went down on top of him like a cat and smashed the heel of his right hand into Daz's face, three times in quick succession, aiming for the sensitive area under his nose, the philtrum. He had never seen anyone move with such violence and speed before and he felt the roots of his front teeth shatter. His mouth was full of splinters of dentine, enamel and blood, and it felt like a bomb had gone off in his head. He heard but couldn't register the words that Morrison hissed into his face:

"Listen to me, you piece of Pikey shit. If Moira Edge or Angela are touched, hurt or looked at in the wrong way, I'm coming back here and I'm going to kill you very slowly. Do you understand, Daz?"

Eventually, his wingmen dragged him outside and the cold air hit his shattered incisal roots like liquid nitrogen. Daz was crying with pain, they drove him to the North Devon District Hospital, where the fragments of three of his upper incisors were removed under topical anaesthetic. The duty registrar was incapable of performing an injection with local anaesthetic and there's a definite knack in locating the incisal papilla in such a mangled mouth, had he known what he was looking for. After a few months, when the swelling and infection had subsided, Daz was fitted with a cobalt chrome skeleton denture, as he couldn't afford implants. Poor Daz was destined to be a martyr to his anterior maxillary region and his anterior nasal spine, courtesy of his own mental afflictions, his own erratic behaviour and members and former members of the British Army. The oral and maxillo-facial department of the North Devon District Hospital would gain valuable teaching time and case studies. It's an ill wind that blows nobody any good.

\*

Daz was slipping into mental illness. It had been caused by Frank Tremain employing Mark Edge when he left the Army and the fact that Moira was further beyond his grasp than ever, now Edge was home full time. He couldn't actively carry out his toxic fantasies, yet, but he could and did undermine Mark Edge at every available opportunity. As a senior now in the business, he ensured that Edge was allocated the worst jobs, the worst vehicles and the most useless co-workers. If Edge did something right, someone else did it. If anything went wrong, it was Edge's fault. One afternoon after everyone had left, Daz was chatting with Frank Tremain.

"Mr T, I know you had your reasons for employing him, but Mark Edge is bloody useless. He just can't be trusted to do a proper job."

Frank Tremain, who rather liked being called Mr T, sighed. "It's very difficult for me, Daniel, seeing as how he's my son-in-law, although God knows, I wish he wasn't. Why don't we give him until next New Year, see if he's improved and get rid of him then? It'll mean that Moira can't say I never gave him a chance."

That August, almost driven mad with jealous frustration, Daz hatched a plot to make sure Edge was well out of the way, so he could take what was rightfully his: Moira Edge, nee Tremain. Frank Tremain mentioned in passing that Moira was off work and Edge was earmarked for delivering some animal feed and assorted farm machinery spares to St Ives, in a truck that was so dilapidated it would be lucky to get there and back without breaking down. The following afternoon, Daz drove to the Edges' cottage on the Torridge with the sole intention of raping Moira. He wheedled himself into the cottage with the pretence of seeing how she was and asking for a drink.

Once inside, fuelled with lust and hate, Daz pounced. It should have been easy except for a mangy fucking tabby cat, a jar of flour and a breadknife. Moira, he was certain, was going to kill him that hot afternoon. Daz got away, but by now the toxicity of his thoughts were out of his control. He would kill them both, Edge first then Moira, but first he would teach her not to defy him.

On New Year's Eve, Daz had been drinking since lunchtime with his posse in a pub on Bideford's waterfront. Mark Edge had also been drinking, alone with his thoughts, while Moira and her family had a meal with Tremain and Co's senior management. They were all due to meet up in the Hoops Inn and Country Hotel for a work function. Edge was drinking to anaesthetise the anxiety and doubt he had been feeling since August, when he discovered strange bruises on Moira's intimate areas. He was convinced she was having an affair with Daz Copeland. While Daz had his sociopathy, Edge had his anxiety and anger.

Daz also had a fishing knife with an 8" blade with a serrated top edge. It had been honed as sharp as a razor. It was for the Edges, Daz told his posse. They were too drunk to persuade him that it wasn't a good idea in front of so many potential witnesses. He was beyond caring anyway.

In the Hoops Inn, Daz intercepted Moira and steered her to a table, away from the lights and the groups of revellers. He showed Moira the knife and laughed.

"I know you have a liking for knives, Moira. But this one's better than your stupid breadknife and I'm going to shiv a pongo tonight, Moira. And then I'm going to fuck you. Depending on how well behaved you are, I might not cut you up too much."

When Edge arrived and saw his wife sitting alone in a secluded spot with Daz, his heart lurched. His doubts and anxiety had been vindicated, but he wasn't going down without a fight.

"All right, Daz?"

He looked up and gave a smile, or was it a sneer? "All right, Mark?"

"I was wondering, Daz, if I could sit next to my wife."

"Plenty of room either side, Mark."

"Oh, I see. All right then, Daz. Let me put this another way. If you don't stop feeling my wife's tits, I'm going to rip your fucking face off," Edge said in a low, almost pleasant voice.

"Look, mate, you've obviously been having a stressful week. You're not in the Army now. See, all those years in the Army have made you paranoid."

Edge put his glass down slowly on the table. "I tell you what, Daz, why don't we step outside so that I can show you just how fucked up the Army's made me?"

Daz undraped his arm and grinned up at Edge. "Lead the way, dickhead. I'll see you in a minute, Moira."

The vicious knife was concealed under his jacket as he stood up. Moira went to sweep the glasses off the table as a distraction to get away, but Edge moved impossibly fast and smashed his forehead into Daz's nose and mouth as he stood up level. For the second time, a bomb exploded inside Daz's head like JDAM penetrating a cave. Daz had felt nothing more for over forty-eight hours when he woke up in the acute care ward of his favourite hospital. His head was swathed in bandages, from which protruded a drain and a nasal oxygen line.

"Dearie, dearie me, Mr Copeland, we have been in the wars," the maxillo-facial consultant said to Daz sympathetically. "I'm afraid we're going to get to know each other rather well over the next few months."

*

His rage was all-consuming and as soon as he could get his life back on track, he would settle the score with the Edges. Things were falling into place. Edge had been sacked after the court case and Moira had left him, moving back in with her parents. But in the May of that year, Daz had an altercation with a motorhome on one of North Devon's narrow lanes. Frustrated by the crawling tourist vehicle, Daz had forced his way past in his 4x4 and ended up ramming the motorhome into a hedge. In the following road rage incident, Daz beat the driver into a coma in front of the man's wife and disabled daughter. The incident was filmed by a dash camera in the car that had been following. Daz, despite his good character references, was sentenced to eighteen months.

While he was in prison, he missed the disappearance of Mark Edge, his probable involvement in the murder of a human rights lawyer and the theory that Mark Edge had drowned himself off the coast of the Algarve. When he left prison, Daz had lost his job, much to Frank Tremain's regret. Daz maintained an obsession with Moira, and through contacts who still worked at Tremain and Co, he kept tabs on the boss's daughter. Moira had moved into a flat in Okehampton with her kids so it would be impossible to do anything while she was there. He even followed her to and from work and again anything he contemplated would be too risky.

He waited four years after Edge had disappeared, then he heard that Moira had made peace with her parents. While her mother and father took Francis to see a show in London, Moira would stay in her parents' house for the weekend. Sarah was far too old to babysit her mother, which was a pity. At fifteen, she was eminently fuckable in Daz's eyes. Moira would be alone in that large, rambling house. Daz had lost all sense of restraint and his revenge had been a long time coming.

At 17:20 on the Saturday night, the bell rang on her parents' door. Moira opened it and her bowels turned to water.

"Hello, Mo. It's been a long time."

*

Just before midnight that Saturday night, Angela's phone rang in her house in Torrington.

"Hello?"

"Angela, it's me, Moira. You know where my mum and dad live? Please come now. It's very important."

Moira sounded like she was having difficulty speaking

"Moira, are you all right?"

"No, please just come."

*

Moira's left eye was fully closed, her lower lip was split and she had dark bruises around her neck. Her wrists were raw from where he had tied her. He had bitten her breasts and burned her with the many joints he had consumed. She could barely walk. Angela was crying and sobbing with anguish, but Moira was beyond that.

"You have to go to the police," Angela said between sobs.

"No! I'm not going to be violated by them through the courts. He will drag everything out and insist that I'm cross-examined. He'll tell the world that I was his girlfriend and what we used to do. It's beyond that now."

"Have you had a shower, you know, evidence?"

"Course I bloody have. I wanted to wash every trace of that filthy bastard off me."

"Are you sure it was him?"

Moira held up a Zippo lighter. "Daz. See? He dropped it."

"Oh, Moira, I'm so sorry."

"What the bloody hell do you have to be sorry for? Just help me put some vinegar on these bites and burns and then I'll tell you what we're going to do."

"Vinegar?"

"Yes, Edge swears... swore by vinegar." A single tear ran down Moira's cheek. And she did. "You're still bleeding, from—"

"Just get on with it."

Later, they had tea, heavily laced with Frank's best Remy Martin XO cognac. There was a strange look in Moira's eye, the one that was open. She had stopped shaking by now and when she spoke, her voice was icy with determination.

"Angela. I want you to listen to me. Don't palm me off or treat me like an idiot. I'm lucky to still be alive. He lost his nerve when the phone rang, probably my mother worrying about something. He will come back and kill me or one of the kids. He could kill you as well. He is batshit, fucking mental.

"Tell Henry... No, don't fucking start. Tell Henry everything. And get him to speak to Mark. Everything. Don't miss out anything. Give Henry the lighter and get him to tell Mark what he's done to me. Tell Mark that he was right. We should have done it his way a long time ago. Please, Angela, I'm begging you. Just tell them before it's too late."

*

A man whose passport identified him as Andrew Poulsom was woken in the early hours of Sunday morning. He was in Romania providing security consultancy to a Romanian oil company. He recognised the voice and listened to the long one-sided conversation intently. His face betrayed no emotion, but the muscles in the forearm holding the mobile phone writhed like a snake. When he spoke, his voice was expressionless.

"I'll be back on the first flight I can get today, if not, tomorrow," the man calling himself Poulsom said.

"Where will I meet you?"

"The Bear, Devizes. I'll book a room in Calne or Chippenham."

"Do you want me to have the Inkspots stand to?"

"No. You and I should be able to deal with it. I should have dealt with it years ago."

The silence on the other end of the phone was not accusatory. In truth, there was little to say. Poulsom reeled out a list, some items in clear, others coded, to avoid the ever-snooping ears of GCHQ.

"This is what I think we'll need. Add anything you think I've missed."

"See you sometime today or tomorrow."

"God willing."

\*

His paranoia knew no bounds. Daz was expecting the police to come for him at any time, and he was ready for them. He had drunk himself sober, and even the skunk seemed to have no effect. Somehow he knew that it would be tonight, and he gripped the sawn-off shotgun like it was a lucky charm, a talisman.

Did Daz have any regrets? In truth, he was incapable of feeling remorse, but he had plenty of regrets. He should have kept Glen's bike instead of throwing it into the quarry. It had been a good bike. He should have killed Moira Tremain when she first defied him, and he certainly should have finished the job instead of panicking when the phone rang. He should have done Tina's cat in front of her, then Tina. Now even his posse had deserted him, because they said he was out of control, but they were just gutless bastards. And as the shadows grew longer and darkness fell across the wooded valley of the Torridge, Daz thought about all of the people who had let him down over the years, starting with his mother and father.

In the small hours, Daz heard movement outside, imperceptible, like an animal. Fox? Deer? He slowly sat up and pointed the shotgun at the door. The window disintegrated as a gun fired and a green cylinder skittered across the floor. There was a boom and a blinding white light, followed by a deafening high-pitched screaming. Daz ran to the door, wrenched it open and fired blindly into the night with one barrel of the shotgun. He was silhouetted by the light from inside the house and he had still not got his night sight back, when a .32 hollow point round destroyed his right kneecap. He slumped against the doorframe but managed to keep hold of the shotgun.

He saw a figure about 15 yards away in the darkness that seemed to stop his heart and take his breath away. It looked like a cavalry man from the English Civil War, complete with boots, buff coat and some kind of helmet and face covering. Bellowing with pain, Daz raised the shotgun and fired at the figure. He definitely hit it, because he saw it sway under the impact of the birdshot pellets. The figure raised its arm, which seemed to be holding a snub automatic that was inside a strong, clear polythene bag. There was no aiming required; thousands of rounds and hours spent in the Killing House and the twenty fired in Savernake Forest three days before, made aiming superfluous. Daz's left kneecap went the way of the first. With a scream he went down and tried to drag himself back into the house. The figure was unhurried as it slowly walked towards him. Daz looked backwards over his shoulder, whimpering in pain and terror.

"Top tip. Birdshot is only good for birds. You should have used deer shot."

"Who are you?"

The figure removed its helmet and face mask, while the extremely stubby and truncated automatic pistol inside its bag was pointed in the vicinity of Daz's crotch.

"You're dead! You're fucking dead!"

"I'm a ghost. Where are your car keys?"

"Fuck you!"

He put a motorcycle boot on Daz's bloodied right kneecap and applied moderate pressure. He waited for the screaming to stop.

"I won't ask nicely again."

"Kitchen... Hanging up."

He returned, holding the keys up and jingling them, then put the automatic in a pocket of the strange coat and dragged Daz outside by his feet. This was accompanied by much screaming and it took a while because he was a big fellow. He passed out with the pain before they reached the outhouse where the Honda generator was thrumming away. The figure started Daz's

Ute and backed it up to the door of the outhouse. He unscrewed the Ute's petrol cap and put a length of reinforced plastic pipe from the vehicle into the generator's fuel tank. He fetched a jerry can of petrol and waited for Daz to regain consciousness. Eventually, Daz started groaning with pain and fear.

"Why are you doing this?"

"Oh, Daz, I think you know very well why." He held up a Zippo lighter. "Finders keepers?"

He poured petrol over the back of the Ute, inside the outhouse and all over Daz, who was crying and begging for his life.

"You see, what we've got here is one of those unfortunate accidents. A man drunk and out of his brains on skunk, tries to refill his generator while it's still running."

"Please, I'm sorry, I'm so sorry."

"Which, as we all know, is just asking for trouble. I don't really want this lighter. You have it."

He flicked the Zippo open and lit it in a practised action. He tossed it into the outhouse and walked away. The screaming began after the initial whump of the igniting petrol. It took a long time before Daz's larynx was burned away and by that time the heat had contracted the tendons in his arms and legs and drawn his body into the pugilist attitude.

The figure walked away down the track and a motorbike started down by the road. A second figure with a powerful hand-held spotlight appeared out of the darkness by the trees. It was a man dressed like a scene of crime officer, with a blue coverall, hair and boot protection and gloves. He meticulously swept the area on hands and knees, picking up any other scraps of twigs or material. The two empty cases had been caught in the polythene bag. He swept the line in the mud where Daz had been dragged into the outhouse. Inside the house, he picked up the empty shell and the fusing mechanism of the stun grenade and dug out a flattened hollow-point bullet from the hallway wall. Of the other, there was no sign, and he had no intention of seeing if it was still in what was left of Daz, which by now was very little. By the time he'd finished, the outhouse and burning vehicle were like a furnace and the flames had spread to the rest of the house. He walked half a mile to where a car was parked off the road, and in the trees, stripped off the coverall and put them in a holdall in the boot.

Ten miles away, he collected a similar holdall from a lay-by. He drove north to a small town, parked up the car and went to where a small boat was moored next to a slipway. It was a cruiser, about 15 feet with a small wheelhouse. He started the engine and headed for the darkness and the open sea. Two miles out, he put two breezeblocks in each holdall and lugged them over the side. As he motored back, the dawn was beginning to break and he sang tunelessly KC and the Sunshine Bands *That the way I like it*.

A man was waiting for him and helped him moor the boat. He jumped ashore and they headed for two cars parked together. It was still very early and no one was about.

"Is it over?"

"Yes, Frank. He's gone."

"How will I ever be able to look Moira in the face again?"

"She's still your daughter and you're still her father."

"I've been so bloody stupid. How could I have allowed this to happen?"

"It's what they do, Frank. But they can't fool all of the people all of the time."

"Do you think he'll come back? Moira misses him terribly."

He had to think who he was talking about. "He's dead. Remember that, should anyone ask. But one day I'm sure he will, once he's exorcised his own demons."

"What about you, Henry?"

"Henry's dead as well. Remember? But I'm going to go and see Moira's oppo, Angela, and ask her a question I should have asked her years ago."

# Chapter 34

# ANGELA'S AND MOIRA'S STORY

———

She was asleep when her phone started ringing, her mobile, the number of which was known by very few people. Angela groaned and fumbled for her glasses and then the phone and just as she picked up, it stopped ringing. The glowing screen said: *One missed call – K.C. Sunshine*. She immediately called back.

"Where are you?" he asked. She could hear the wind so knew he was outdoors.

"At my own place. I was getting on Moira's nerves and she was glad to see the back of me. She still has the up and under you provided. Has it been done?"

"Yes, she won't need it anymore. I'll explain when I get to you."

"Where are you?"

"Appledore. Just dropped the boat off with her father. I'll be with you in thirty minutes."

"It's just after four. Can't it wait?"

"No. I have something very important that I must tell you."

He rang off and Angela sighed and made herself a cup of tea. Then waited.

\*

357

She watched him come out of the shower and wrap a dressing gown round himself. When he had come in, he was reeking of smoke, petrol and something else. It reminded her of when her mother had burned a pork roast joint, after too many lagers in the club on a Sunday. But now he smelled good, and she would never tire of watching Henry Morrison.

"I'm going to have to burn those clothes," he told her, and sipped a coffee. It was getting light outside. "And those boots, more's the pity. I loved those boots."

"Has he gone? I mean properly gone, forever?"

"There wasn't much left of him after Edge burned him alive. Just a shrunken little pigmy about four foot tall and all shrivelled up."

"Good! I know of at least three women who he terrorised and whose lives he ruined," she said with feeling. "There was Moira, obviously, another girl called Tina from Westward Ho! from a few years back… and me."

Morrison looked at her and Angela looked down like she was ashamed. "I reckon I was the first, at least round here."

"I'm glad you never told me that," he said quietly.

"Why? Am I soiled merchandise, Henry?"

"No, because I would have killed him myself and saved Mark Edge the misery, the bother and probably the guilt."

"Mickie sorted him out for me. He frightened the bastard to death, stripped him and took photographs of him, tied up in the buff in the woods."

"Shame Mickie didn't kill the bastard."

"I asked him not to," Angela said in a small voice. "Bad mistake, but…" she started to giggle, "but he did stick a torch up his arse. A big one."

Morrison chuckled then laughed out loud. God, how she loved him.

She went and sat next to him and he put his arm round her shoulder. They shared a long, companionable silence. Angela reluctantly broke it.

"Henry, when is Mark coming home? Moira knows that he isn't dead."

"When he has fully exorcised his demons."

"Oh for God's sake, Henry."

"He exorcised the last one last night. He has something to do abroad and it'll let the heat die down… If you'll excuse the pun. He's ready to come home."

She detected a sudden reticence come over him. "Angela, there is something I have to say to you. I'm not really good at this and what I say might seem a bit clumsy, but hear me out, I beg you.

"I realise that I haven't been totally honest with you. There is, or rather was, someone that I loved, long before I met you." He felt her stiffen. "I can't tell you who it was, but I met her on operations and we shared, well, we shared a lot. But we could never have shared our lives. There was so much between us, but the kind of stuff that is born in the intensity of operations, not the kind of love and respect you need to build a solid relationship. The sharing of souls, if you wish. But God, was she brave."

Angela was like a statue, leaning away from him. "So although you had this Joan of Arc to keep you nice and warm on operations, you needed a few shags when you came home and I fitted the bill nicely. Is that about the size of it?"

Morrison put his head in his hands. "Bugger! I knew that it would come out wrong. Look, Angela, what I'm trying to say in my ham-fisted way, is that I've come to realise that you are the most important thing in my life and I want to share whatever is left of it with you."

"So rather than just pitching up on-spec for a bit of horizontal gymnastics, you'll book me like a squash court? Give me a bit more notice?"

"I'm asking you to be my wife."

She laughed. "What, like a bergen bride? One on every drop zone, eh?"

"No. We live and make our lives together. Forever."

"A proper marriage? The sort where I have a wee while you're in the bath?"

"Yep. The kind where I fart in the bed and hold your head under the covers," he affirmed.

"I'll need to think about it. All right. You're on."

"You sure you don't need more time?"

"Henry. I've had over fifteen bloody years."

*

In the May of the year Ron Gleam was murdered by a high-powered rifle, Moira was interviewed by two Counter Terrorism Command police officers; a man and a woman. They wanted to know if she had been in contact with her husband and if she knew his whereabouts. This followed the shooting of a high-profile civil rights lawyer at his Oxfordshire home.

"Mrs Edge, did your husband hold Nazi views?"

Moira thought about the question. "No, he was never a socialist."

She had learned a great deal through osmosis over the years.

The female detective sergeant smiled in a slightly patronising way. "No, I think you misunderstand. A Nazi, you know, like Hitler."

"No, I think *you* misunderstand. My husband was never a member of the German National Socialist Workers' Party, or Nazis. He never wore their uniforms or insignia. He doesn't have his blood group tattooed in his armpit and in fact he didn't even like Hugo Boss suits."

The female copper looked at her notes, getting flustered. "Err…"

"I think my colleague is trying to ask you if your husband had right-wing tendencies," the DI said, coming to her aid.

"What do you mean by right-wing?" Moira asked in an irritated way.

"Oh, for goodness' sake, you must know what right-wing means."

"I know what it means to me. What does it mean to you?"

"It's obvious."

"Not to me it isn't. Define right-wing to me."

"Did he hold any extreme views?"

"Well, sometimes he used to buy the *Guardian*. He said it was 'for balance', but I had my doubts. Then he started buying the *Daily Mail*. That's why I left him."

They gave up and once back in their car, compared notes.

"Well, the bitch knows something. Put her under round-the-clock."

Moira had learned a lot from Edge about the police and being followed in the weeks following his arrest. She twigged within a couple of days she was being followed by an unmarked car when she drove to work or picked the kids up from school. She asked for a day's holiday the following day after asking Angela if she would pick up the kids and look after them until she got home.

That morning, Moira drove to a service station on the M5 near Exeter. She ordered a coffee, then made two calls using the public phone booths. One was to a Freephone police charity number, the other to her parents' house. She reversed the charges, her mother accepted, and she left the phone off the hook. She drove to RNAS Yeovilton and took some photographs of helicopters through the wire. Then she drove to St Budeaux in Plymouth and took some photographs of the submarines down in the naval base. She headed north and stopped at a service station at Launceston. She slipped out of a fire escape and headed towards the car that had been following her all day. It was empty, the two occupants inside looking for her. She slipped an envelope under a wiper blade. There was a simple note inside: *If you're going to waste my taxes, then I'm going to waste your time. Get off your arses and catch some real criminals.* She drove home, feeling pleased with herself.

*

One year became two, then three, and Moira was convinced that Edge was still alive. One Monday, she buttonholed Angela.

"Are you still in contact with Henry, our best man?"

Angela looked slightly embarrassed. "Only when we have a mutual itch that needs scratching."

"Please ask him to pass this to Mark," Moira said, giving her an envelope.

"Moira, he's dead. You have to accept that."

"He isn't," Moira said fiercely. "When you give it to him, look into his eyes."

*

Almost eight years to the day since she had walked out of Edge's life and their home, Moira noticed a flashy car park outside her flat in Okehampton. The car stopped and a well-dressed, professional-looking woman stepped out. She glanced up at the flat and walked towards the front door.

"Mrs Edge, Moira Edge?"

"Yes?"

The woman held up a briefcase. "I have some news that may surprise you. I represent a firm of solicitors in Barnstaple. Here is my card. May I come in?"

*

One night, over a year later, Moira slept in a strange, hypersensitive sleep that transcended the two worlds of the conscious and the other world we inhabit for twenty-five percent of our existence. She had enough money and property to ensure her and her children would be comfortable for the rest of their lives. Moira would wake in the early hours and remain awake for ages until she fell into the essential sleep and REM until dawn.

She was awake when she heard a noise from the bathroom, and the hair on her arms and neck bristled. The temperature in the room plummeted. Her breath misted in front of her face. She had one thought that almost loosened her bladder.

*Copeland.*

Moira reached under the pillow for the carving knife.

He came into the room and pulled back the covers and slid in next to her. His heat was burning cold. He gently ran his finger from her forehead, down her nose and across her top lip.

"Moira, I've been so stupid. Please forgive me."

"Mark?"

"Moira, I'm so sorry. I wasted the best years of our lives."

"I knew you were still alive."

He smiled sadly.

"Why, Mark?"

"Because we're human and fallible."

They went into each other and Moira was taken back to a time eighteen years previously. She had no dreams and woke up to an almost-forgotten scent and a bloody imprint on the pillow. When she went to pee, the flow burned, jogging a memory of a Bristol hotel bedroom, so many years ago.

*I snipped that lovely parachute badge off your tunic, Mark, and I've still got it tucked into our book.*

Very early the next morning, they stared at each other. "I'm sore. It's been a long time, Mark. I expect you're a dab hand at pleasuring the ladies by now, aren't you?"

He didn't rise to the bait. She looked at him across the table while their coffees cooled. "Why is your forehead so light?"

"It's a skin graft. They had to cut a hole in my skull to reduce the pressure of a bleed on my brain. I died. Twice apparently. They took the graft from my arse."

"So the wax effigy and the pins did work. I expect your arse has improved your common sense no end." Edge chuckled and Moira looked down as she composed her thoughts. "Mark, this isn't going to be instant happy families, you know. I'm a different person and it took me all my time to let you anywhere near me last night, I mean, this morning. Especially after what happened. Sarah has grown up without you and Francis hates your guts for leaving us and 'dying'. He's at that awkward stage and the last thing he or I need is for you to blunder in and start laying down the returned father law."

"Mark Edge is dead. I'm Andrew Poulsom now. I'm not going to come back straight away, but I'll always tell you where I am. That's if you want me to."

Moira reached across the table and held his hands. "In our own time, carry on."

They talked of different things and Moira told him that she had read in the *North Devon Gazette* that Cynthia Penrith had passed away, and the grisly circumstances of her death. Edge's face was grim. "Did the paper mention if there was a dead cat in the property? She was looking after Monty."

"No. Oh, poor Monty. No, nothing about a cat, and that's the sort of thing they would dwell upon."

Edge looked upset then thought out loud: "Under the reciprocal arrangement we drew up with the solicitor, now that Ms Penrith is dead, both our old cottage and hers belong to you. She had no relatives and she was living off the proceeds of letting our old cottage. Plus, there's the money I left you that came in eight years after I died. Have you been spending it wisely?"

"I haven't touched it. I thought it was dirty money. Did you kill that human rights lawyer, Mark?"

"No. Henry did it for me, because at first I was in an HDU in a Portuguese hospital and then could barely walk. I really wanted to, though. Henry added a nice touch. He got away. I would have stayed and played with the plod."

"Why the bloody hell couldn't I have married someone nice and uncomplicated?"

"Because you were a spoiled little brat and must have been something bad in a previous life. Come on. Let's get our old home back. You'll need to go in and speak to the solicitor and get the keys. Don't take any nonsense from them. Both of those properties are now legally yours."

*

The trees were more overgrown and the hedge line he had worked on was now a tall bocage, overhanging the lane. The state of their empty cottage was dismal. It looked dilapidated and uncared-for. The garden was overgrown and Edge noticed tiles missing from the roof and weeds growing in the gutters. Inside, it smelled of damp and neglect and they were glad to be back outside in the cold, late autumnal air.

"Bloody hell," Moira said, her voice heavy with despondency.

"It looks worse than it is. We'll get the fires up and running to dry out the inside, fix the paint outside and inside and repair the roof. Don't be downhearted, love. The garden can be your project once I've cut back the undergrowth. Cynthia's cottage is in a better state, and with a little work, we can either sell it or let it out."

"It smelled funny."

"I'm afraid that was death. We'll need to air it, obviously."

Moira sighed. "So what's the plan, Stan?"

"I'll move in here and start work. You can move back in with the kids in your own time. And no, I'm not expecting a *Railway Children* ending. Just ask them to try to understand, which won't be easy, as I don't understand myself sometimes."

They were silent for a while, Moira supporting Edge, who was still using a stick. He hadn't bothered to tell her that it was a swordstick. In that close relationship they had refined over the years together and apart, they seemed to have developed identical thought processes and both said the same thing at the same time.

"I wonder what happened to Monty." Moira started to cry and Edge felt the back of his throat closing.

"He probably died years ago, he was getting on," Edge said, but it made neither of them feel any better.

"Miiiaaoow!"

They turned round, startled at the familiar cry. An elderly tabby cat pushed through the undergrowth under the hedge. He was very thin, bedraggled, and limped towards them, meowing a baby cry and yowling indignantly. A jagged white scar ran from his right eye down to the cat's nose, and he had a long-healed tear in his ear.

"Monty? Could it be you?"

Edge picked the cat up and wrapped him in his coat, so only the little head showed. Moira was rubbing him gently between his ears. They had all come home and they were all crying, apart from Edge, who had something in his eye. They went back inside the cottage then Edge found some wood and lit the wood burner. He knew in his heart that they were going to be all right, provided they were left alone.

"I'll go and get some kitten food," Edge said. "It won't be the first time…"

# Chapter 35

# MONTY'S STORY OR THE UNBEARABLE LIGHTNESS OF BEING... A CAT

———

I think you will all agree, that is rather a good portrait of me. It captures the essentials of... well, being me. Of course, it was taken a lot of seasons ago by my human father when I was in my prime. My fur has a lot more grey in it these days and now I have a facial blemish that I got... Well, you'll hear about that later. I hate it because it mars my face, of which I've always been quite proud. When I had to go to the vets for my annual check-up and having that hateful sharp thing stuck in me, the lady vet would say, "Oh, what a handsome boy!" They dragged me out of my basket, which I hated, and plonked me on the examination table to leave sweaty paw prints, and I couldn't wait to get back in the basket. Now they say, "Poor old Monty. You have been in the wars, haven't you?" I do know and it doesn't help, lady.

I have no idea where I was born, but I was weaned on a farm. My birth mother was a farm cat and there were four of us catlets: me, a ginger brother and two tortoiseshell sisters. I have no idea who my birth father was. One of my sisters caught the dreaded leukaemia disease and my mother immediately moved the rest of us to another nest, leaving my sick sister behind. We never spoke of her again, but I often think of her, because she was closest to me when we were in Mother. I sometimes wail in sorrow for her.

There was always plenty to eat on the farm as long as you like rat. I've always considered the flesh of a rat to reflect their corrupt lives, but the pieces my mother brought home were nourishing. At least the remaining three of us made it through to our eye-opening. Later, she would bring us small rats that were still alive. She would encourage us to kill them and rip them open. Now I largely forgo the taste of rat and kill them to satisfy the urge rather than sport or food. It's part of our primeval urge and the reason why humans, apart from lonely ladies, tolerate us. We were once kings and queens and we were embalmed and buried with human kings and queens. The bit about being killed when they died was a bit of a drag. Perhaps sometimes it's better to be tolerated than worshipped.

I was getting to know my surroundings in the barn and used to enjoy play fighting with my brother and sister. One afternoon, a car came into the yard and a human female got out. I'd seen humans before and had come to the conclusion that they were very clumsy and gawky, rolling around on their hind legs. They didn't even have tails, so no wonder they couldn't jump and climb like we did. The female spoke to the farmer.

"I've come about the advertisement. You have some kittens?"

*What are kittens?* I was asked by Sister.

We soon found out when the two humans came into the barn and the farmer scooped all three of us up in his arm.

"Now there's two boys and a girl. The ginger one has a bit of a wonky eye, but he's healthy. The female is the tortoiseshell, nice markings, and this tabby. They've all been weaned."

The woman looked at us and smiled at me. "The tabby's a handsome little thing. Could I have him, please?"

"Now these is farm cats, so they may be a touch feisty."

"We need a ratter," she told him. "We have some outbuildings and some unwanted friends. I don't like poison."

"He'll do the job, just give him a few months. Don't feed him too much, but you must feed him some. If you've got any kids, I'd get his little balls chopped off as soon as you can. Unneutered cats are great for farms, but not when there's small kids. Bit bitey and scratchy, they are. He'll still catch the rats but probably won't eat them."

"Good."

"You may not be saying that when he brings them into your kitchen as a present."

Before I could even say goodbye to my birth mother, the farmer put me in a shoe box and carried me to what I later learned was a car. The woman got in and drove me away from my family, who I would never see again. I yowled all the way until the car stopped. The woman carried me into what would be my new home and I was inundated with unfamiliar smells. Three more humans were waiting for me, an Alpha male and humanlets: an older female and a younger male. They opened the shoe box and I immediately ran behind the sofa and wet myself with fear.

"Willum, come on, Willum."

"No, Sarah," the man said. "His name will be Monty. Come on out, Monty. Come and meet your new family."

And eventually I did. They showed me what I would in due course accept as my bed, my food and water, my litter. Fortunately, they didn't handle me too much, and over the following days, I scented my new home from my cheeks, but they wouldn't let me go out. As the days and weeks passed, I became bored with the inside of the house and yearned to go outside. I became angry and driven by some emotion I didn't understand. Then came a day when I was put in the car and driven to a place of horrible smells, the distress of animals, pain and sickness, even death. They wore nice, clean clothes and they took me away from my mother, my new mother, and put something over my nose. When I woke up, between my back legs hurt and I felt sick and dizzy.

I slept, but every time I woke up, I yowled for my mothers and eventually the human one came for me. I now had a wicker basket for transportation purposes. Its appearance meant trouble and would continue to make trouble every time I got into a spot of bother, and annually for my sweaty paws experience on the examination table. When I got back to my home, they had moved my bed in front of the hot metal box with doors.

"Poor Monty. You'll be unsteady on your legs for a bit, but you'll feel better."

And I did, and a few weeks later they let me leave the house and I explored. I was particularly blessed. I had outhouses that were dry, relatively comfortable and teeming with rats and mice. I had no intention of sharing my summer quarters with the pointy-faced bastards, so I vowed to get rid of them.

Our house was above a field that ran down towards the river. It had nice long grass and sheep occasionally grazed in it. The river was fairly narrow and wound through the flood meadows. There was a busy road on the other side of the river, which I had no intention of crossing. I knew I could be happy here and almost forgot my birth mother and brother and sisters.

There were other cats in the area, and I picked up their trails and territory marking scents. One morning, I came across a white and black female cat. She was much bigger than me, so we went through the ritual of staring at each other, making ourselves look bigger. I caught her eye and looked away to show I meant no harm. We both raised our tails and approached one another to sniff cautiously.

*You must be the new catlet. What do they call you?*

*Bernard Law Montgomery, First Viscount Montgomery of Alamein. Monty for short,* I said, watching her reaction.

*You poor sod. They call me Snowflake.*

I purred loudly.

*Well, I think it's a nice name,* she said indignantly. *Now we need to come to an understanding, as I've been here a lot longer than you. I need to go through your territory at least twice a day.*

I thought about it, because she was bigger than me. *All right, but the sharp faces are mine. And so is inside the buildings.*

*My buildings don't have sharp faces,* she said in a superior manner.

Snowflake and I grew to tolerate each other. She told me about the other cats and which dogs to avoid and where the best places were to ambush the grey, bushy tails. They always got away, but chasing them was fun.

My human family was good to me and looked after me well. My human father wasn't around much and I missed him when he went away. He used to pretend to be indifferent to me, but when we were alone, he would rub me under my chin, which I loved. While we were alone, he would talk to me and it was then that I realised that humans were pretty dumb. They couldn't communicate like us. They made noises and pulled their faces into silly shapes, but while we could understand them, they just couldn't understand us, unless we made a noise or cried like their young. They couldn't even catch things. They couldn't even see their ancestors. They would regularly walk through the walls, as the cottage had been built across an ancient pathway. They were of no substance, but real, nevertheless, and what's more, we could communicate with them, when they decided they wanted to.

"Monty, what are you looking up there at? You give me the creeps sometimes."

They were so stupid. Hundreds passing through the house every week and they didn't even notice the temperature plummet.

"Don't you think it's a bit cold in here tonight, love?" My human father could feel something. He called himself Edge, because he was always on it. I loved him with all my little catty heart. When he came home, he smelled of violence and death. Cats recognise that, but his soul was so gentle. The problem was, his brain wasn't wired to his soul, yet.

One morning, very early, I was down by the river looking for water voles to play with... kill. There was a little boy sitting on the riverbank, the ethereal sort of little boy. He was sitting, holding his knees, looking at the placid surface of the river. It was mid-summer and there hadn't been any rain for a few days. I cautiously went up to him.

*Hello.*

He looked at me with sad, dark eyes. *Hello, Mr Cat.*

I bowed, acknowledging the formal way of his addressing me.

*I've noticed you here on this day for the three summers that I've been here.*

*I died in that river many summers ago.*

*How many?* I asked.

*At least three hundred.*

*You should move on.*

*How?*

I respectably folded my tail around my body and placed the front paws on the tip to stop it twitching. This was serious business. *You should head into the light when it comes.*

*The light frightens me.*

*It frightens all of us, but that is where your ancestors and the higher one is. You can't stay here for eternity.*

*Will you stay with me until the light comes?*

I looked at this lost soul, feeling my own fear at my mortality. *I will.*

I stayed with him, sharing the same space and time, as the sun went down over the trees. The light opened up over the river and we stared at it.

*Go on,* I coaxed.

*I'll drown again.*

*Unlikely,* I told him.

*Goodbye, Mr Cat.*

*Goodbye, Master Rowe.*

He went into the light, and the air he occupied filled in with a slight whoosh. The light folded in on itself and vanished. I stayed looking at the placid river and headed back to my home. Something had been lifted from my being and I felt an unbearable lightness.

*

When I was six winters old, I lost Snowflake, or rather, my lovely friend was killed. My life was filled with sadness from then on. It was a day when the first frost was on the newly fallen leaves and they crunched underpaw as I walked over them. I had just been let out and I was sitting by the woodshed when she pushed through my hedge and came up the hill to where I was sitting. I raised my tail in greeting and we touched noses. She smelled of the night and fresh kill.

*Hello, Snowflake.*

We sat together and stared at the mist over the river.

*They're getting harder to find now,* she told me.

*The winter is coming,* I agreed.

*Time for my bed.*

She headed towards the road and pushed under my gate. A short time later, I heard one of their cars being driven very fast, and a thud. The car didn't even slow down. With a deep dread, I ran towards where I'd heard the noise, under the gate. Snowflake was lying by the side of the road, and she was very still. The fur around her white face was flecked with blood and some trickled out of her nose. Her outer eyelids were still open but the inner ones had closed, and the light had gone from her eyes. I pawed at her, howling with anguish, because my friend was dead.

I ran to get my human mother before she dropped the children at school and went to work. I was very vocal with my distressed cry.

"For goodness' sake, Monty. What's wrong?"

I walked to the door and looked back at her, crying in a high-pitched meow. Fortunately, she seemed to understand and followed me out of the gate and up the lane.

"Oh no! The poor little thing."

Moira Mother found one of Snowflake's human family and they all started crying. Snowflake's human father buried her at the bottom of their garden, under a beech tree. Snowflake's human sisters would lie little bunches of flowers on her grave, until they grew older and forgot. I never did and laid dead mice and shrews on her grave and used to sit trying to remember her how she was and how we would sit together, watching the river. The beech tree grew tall and strong; its roots enriched by my friend's little body and my presents to her.

Edge Father came home for good in my seventh winter. Straight away I could tell he wasn't happy and seemed to be missing something from his life. He and my human mother seemed to argue a lot and he was drinking the stuff humans use to deaden the pain in their souls.

Humans are capable of great kindness, courage, selfishness and thorough stupidity. When they do bad things, it's usually because they haven't thought things through and looked at the likely repercussions of them doing something dumb. We cats call it the law of human unintended consequences. In fact, most bad things are due to human stupidity and their trying to cover it up. However, in the first summer after Edge Father came home, I met someone who was truly evil. Someone whose soul had plumbed the depths of wickedness and depravity and had decided to remain there.

Edge Father was away at a place called St Ives and was staying overnight. Moira Mother said he was dropping off some tractor bits and pieces and animal feed, whatever they were. The children were at school and Moira Mother was not at work, something to do with the furnaces, she told my father. She promised him something nice when he got home. I sighed. Sometimes they're worse than our females are when they are on heat. I was picking up burrs and couch grass in the meadow, when I heard a vehicle go into my yard through the gate from the lane. When I got closer I saw it was like a big car with an open bit on the back.

A man was standing next to the vehicle, looking over my cottage. He was a big man. Hard physical work was stopping him from running to fat and he had very dark, curly hair. As his gaze swept around the property, his eyes fixated on me as I came through the hedge.

"Puss, puss, here, kitty," he said, clicking his tongue, but I knew there was nothing friendly about him. His eyes were empty and he emanated evil. He was the first living, truly evil man that I had ever seen. I backed through the hedge and watched him. He seemed to grow bored with me, went up to the door and hammered on it. I was afraid for Moira Mum and skirted round the house to get in through the window in the scullery that was always kept a little open. I jumped up lightly and slipped through the window, which I'm rather good at. I taught Edge Father everything he knows about getting into buildings, and he makes a lot more noise than me. From my OP behind a flour jar on a shelf, I could see most of the kitchen.

"For God's sake, I'm coming," yelled Moira Mum. She had been upstairs tidying my brother's and sister's bedrooms. They needed a lot of tidying. The hammering at the door was becoming insistent.

She went into the hall and was lost from view when she opened the door.

"Oh, it's you. What do you want, Daz, and what are you doing here?"

"Your old dad asked me to keep an eye on you, seeing as how Mark's away for a couple of days."

"As you can see, I'm fine. How did you know I wasn't at work?"

"Like I said, your dad asked me to make sure you're okay, and here I am, making sure."

"I'm truly grateful to both of you, now if you'll excuse me."

"I've driven all the way from Tiverton and I could murder a drink, Moira."

She hesitated and I could hear the doubt in her voice.

"Well…"

*Don't be so stupid!*

"Just a quick cuppa," he wheedled.

*No!*

"You'll have to make it quick coz I'm very busy, Daz."

"Thanks, it's hot out there and I'm parched."

Moira Mother put the kettle on and dumped a teabag in a mug. I could feel her fear and unease. The evil man made himself comfortable at the kitchen table. He stretched out his legs and looked round the kitchen, a supercilious smile playing on his lips.

"Very nice, Moira. Very Joanna Trollope. I notice you've even got an Aga as well."

"I prefer Kathy Reichs as an author. Much more in tune with the darker side of human nature. How do you take your tea?" she asked as she poured the hot water into the mug.

"Milk and three sugars, just to keep me sweet."

*Get rid of him, Moira Mother! I know what's coming.*

"Thanks, love," Daz said as she dumped down the mug. He sipped it. "Mmm, nice, just how I like it."

"Daz, I need to get on."

"Well, don't let me stop you. You know you could have made the perfect wife for someone. Like me for instance. And now you're home alone. Your no-hoper of a husband is away and that's how we all like him, because he's useless.

It's only a matter of time before your dad gets rid of him. You made a mistake marrying a thick pongo, when you could have had me."

Moira backed against the sink. "Well, at least he's a proper man who does a good job, unlike you, Mr Hair-trigger man. A quick in and out and off you'd go. Not that you'd notice, coz it was so small."

He stood up, the chair legs scraping on the flagstones. "I'm going to have you again, you bitch."

He pinned Moira against the sink, trying to ram his knee between her legs. She tried to hit him and he grabbed one of her breasts and twisted.

When she screamed I went into action like a coiled spring. I jumped from the scullery shelf, knocking over the jar of flour which smashed on the floor. I jumped up on the table and faced the two of them and hissed at him in my especially ferocious way.

The jar smashing startled both of them, and Daz relaxed his hold on Moira as he looked round. He saw the snarling, hissing cat on the table and laughed, but Moira was able to reach for a breadknife next to a board on the work surface. Edge was experimenting with bread making, but his loaves seemed to turn out with the density of composite armour. Moira ate the offerings to be polite and the Edge loaves needed a very sharp and robust knife to cut through them. The knife was now pressing against the skin of Daz's throat.

"Get out of here before I kill you, you fucking bastard!"

He sneered at her, but there was something in her eyes that frightened him and she rammed the knife into his throat, breaking the skin. Blood trickled down his neck and he pulled back, putting his hand to his neck.

"I'll kill you for that."

Moira gave a demented scream and went for him, the knife held straight ahead, thumb on top of the blade, meaning deadly intent. He sidestepped to grab her knife hand, but she was too quick and slashed the flesh over his volar wrist ligaments.

"You're fucking dog meat, Daz," Moira hissed, advancing slowly, her left arm in front in defence, the knife hand tucked into her body, the blade forward and level with his abdomen. "Edge says gut wounds are the worst, you piece of shit!"

At this point, I swung the battle, crabbing sideways, my tail like a fox's brush, jumping up to rake his forearm with my front claws. He swatted me away and Moira slashed at his left upper arm, tearing his shirt, still advancing.

"Fucking bitch! That's my best work shirt. I'll kill you!"

But Moira had the knife and the red mist. She kept coming.

Daz looked at her twisted face and felt real fear. "You'll pay for this."

But he went out and we heard his truck... car... drive down the lane towards the big town on both sides of the river. Moira Mother dropped the knife on the table and she was shaking with fear and unused adrenaline. After she had stopped being sick in the sink, I nuzzled her with my head.

"Oh, Monty. You were so brave. But we must never tell Edge. Otherwise, he will be a murderer. I just know that he'll kill him."

I purred, my little heart bursting with pride, but I knew that Moira Mother was making a mistake. That evil man would come back again sometime. There could only be one way of exorcising him from our lives.

*

Things really went wrong just after mid-winter, and for me, they would never be the same again. The house had been empty and Edge Father came home in the early hours, reeking of alcohol and with a terrible wound to his forehead, the same place that I have my M for Monty mark. He had a skin flap, which he went upstairs to stitch, but he was drunk and concussed and he made a right old mess of it. I watched over him all night while he lay on the sofa, semi-unconscious through drink and a head wound. Moira Mother and the children didn't come home for a number of days and when they did, the atmosphere in my home was poisonous.

Moira Mother wasn't telling Edge Father the whole truth about what had been happening and as a result he filled in the gaps with his own narrative. Things just kept getting worse and the essentials that bound us together as a family unit unravelled. Edge Father got a new job on the sea or near it, because I could smell it on him when he came home.

That spring, there was an especially big row and a few days later, Moira Mother came with a man with a van and loaded lots of stuff from our home into it. I was dumped in my hated wicker basket and put on the back seat of the car. The van and Moira Mother's car following it drove away. She was crying and so was Francis Brother. We headed north and we all found ourselves in a big house at a place they called Bishop's Tawton. The house belonged to the father of Moira Mother and I hated it from the start. I wanted my own territory and to sit under the tree next to Snowflake. I was soon to find out that I was in terrible danger as long as I stayed at that house.

# Chapter 36

# MONTY'S STORY, THE LAND BETWEEN THE RIVERS

———

Right, let's get a few things straight. We all realise that my species isn't overwhelmingly loved by all members of the human race. One hundred percent get that. But it works both ways. Quite a few of my species hate humans with a vengeance. I know that we've only got ourselves to blame, because we do enjoy killing things and humans don't always approve. Particularly when we bring our kills into human homes, simply to gain approval and show humans where they're going wrong. You don't mind us slotting mice and rats but don't really approve of us killing birds. But they are so bloody annoying to us. We are aloof, solitary and difficult to read because we don't readily show emotion. We don't appear to be very affectionate to humans, but you're so used to the overt friendliness shown by dogs, that you miss the subtle signs we cats use to display our fondness of some of you.

But in the Middle Ages and later periods, we were linked with witchcraft, which is a stupid human superstition anyway. More cats were burned alive than lonely old women who happened to upset the wrong person at the wrong time. You would smash our paws with iron hammers and roast us in wicker baskets. So if some of you don't really like or approve of us, then you can all swivel on my extended digit… if I had one. And besides, you kill things to eat. You just lack the guts to do it yourselves. Sorry, rant over, but as you'll understand, this may explain why I did what I did.

Moira Mother's family home was a large house, set in extensive grounds. It had assorted outhouses, one of which we lived in, above garages, and an extensive workshop. It had a paddock, an orchard of fine apple and pear trees and a meadow that swept down to the River Taw. I hated it, but I hated Moira Mother's father even more. It was a mutual loathing, because he associated me with Edge Father, and therefore the deflowerer of his daughter. I associated him with a psychopath who had tried to rape my Moira Mother the previous summer. That evil man was a frequent visitor to the house and he had deflowered Moira Mother long before Edge came into her life. Cats know these things because you constantly tell us, assuming we don't understand a word. We are continually astonished at the selective memory of humans.

One lazy afternoon in the summer, I was prowling through the long grass at the edge of the river, where the motor mower didn't reach because of the uneven ground. I came across a metal tent peg, with a length of chain leading from it into a clump of grass. I followed the chain and came across a mechanical contraption. It was as long as my body, with a set of serrated jaws with a metal plate located between the jaws. On the plate was cat food. Tuna flakes in jelly, my favourite. I moved forward to sniff the plate.

*I wouldn't go anywhere near that, if I were you.*

I looked up and saw a heron standing on a rock in the river. He was a handsome great bird with a streak of black feathers across the top of his head, ending in a plume. His dark eyes were looking straight at me.

*It's called a gin trap. If you touch the plate, those metal jaws will spring shut on your neck. And that would be the end of you, Mr Cat.*

I backed away from it and sat down, bowing my thanks to the fine bird, who if anything was bigger than me.

*Someone means you harm. There is another of those things over by the trees. There's a dead badger in it. But it was meant for you.*

I thought I could smell death in the air and felt sorrow tinged with anger.

*Thank you, sir.*

The heron stretched out his great wings and flew upwards with ungainly flaps, before skimming across to the other side of the river, to his favourite hunting spot under the trees. He had put himself out to warn me and now I suspected that someone was trying to kill me. I didn't have to think too hard as to whom it was.

While Moira Mother was at work and my human brother and sister were at school, her father would come home in his huge car and prowl around the grounds of the house with a shotgun. I soon found out what he was trying to shoot and went into deep cover every time his big car drove into the grounds. He killed several rabbits, an otter, and wounded a stray dog, but the bastard never managed to find me.

The final straw came in the autumn just as the leaves were turning. My bed, food and water were downstairs in the workshop, where it was warm through the night because of the boiler. I came back from my morning patrol after Moira Mother had taken the children to school. Instead of a bowl of food, there was a bowl of a sweet yellowish liquid that smelled incredibly alluring. I bent forward to sniff it and started to lap at the liquid. Suddenly there was a burst of light in my brain and Snowflake shouted in my mind.

*Don't touch it! It will kill you! It is called 'antifreeze' and once you drink it, nothing can stop you dying. Everything inside you will stop working.*

*Snowflake?*

*Your human mother's father put it there and he means to kill you.*

By the afternoon when Moira Mother came home, the antifreeze had gone to be replaced with my normal food bowl. Much as I loved Moira Mother and my brother and sister, that night I decided to go home.

*

I had stuffed myself with food before setting off.

"Goodness me, Monty. You are a hungry boy."

I had no idea how long it would take me to get home, or really which way to go. There was just something in my little walnut-sized brain that lay my world out like a grid. I was very frightened because I would have to cross the Land Between the Two Rivers. It was reputed to be a wilderness full of unknown creatures.

I slipped out of the window when the three-quarter moon was getting higher in the cloudless sky. My heart was heavy, but my wish for survival outweighed the love I felt for my family. I padded south along the road that followed the big river and the railway line, running into cover every time I heard a car. It was getting near dawn when the road turned to cross the railway and river on a double bridge. This was the dangerous part because there was no cover on the bridges. I thought about waiting until the next night before crossing but decided to risk it. I ran across, stopping and crouching as a huge truck passed by. The sky was lightening as I dived into the undergrowth on the other side of the river. I was now in the Land Between the Two Rivers, so I slept.

That evening, I tried to find something to eat, but the water voles were far too clever for me. It started to rain that evening… I hate rain… but I couldn't afford to waste time waiting for it to stop. I was racing against distance and hunger and I was not used to walking such long expanses. The pads on my paws were aching. I skirted some hills to the north at a place they call the Ridge of Ash Trees. It had been a miserable night, sodden underfoot, and my fur was soaked through to my skin. Before it got light, I went into a derelict farm and found I was sharing it with a pair of barn owls.

*Piss off, cat. This is our barn,* the male said from the rafters.

*Piss off, yourselves, you ghost-faced cretins. I'm cold, wet and tired. If you don't like it, come down here and we'll sort it out, cat to bird.*

Rather spitefully, they kept me awake most of the day hooting and screeching at each other. One of them tried to hit me with an owl pellet. I was glad when it was nearly dark and I could be on my way again, and I left with a parting shot.

*I hope the humans turn this barn into a holiday home.*

I had to eat something this night; otherwise, I would never make it home. I turned south, following a broad, open valley of farmland. So humans did live here. There was a broad stream to the west, but no prey. The stream petered out into woodland. I decided to head into the woods to see if there were any mice or grey tails. I was so tired that I fell down a bank towards a depression.

I was face-to-face with a vixen with three big cubs, who immediately scurried down into their earth. The vixen hissed angrily and I backed up, knowing I was in big trouble. Vixens with cubs should be left well alone. She bared her terrifying teeth.

*Please, ma'am, I mean no harm to you or your cubs. I am lost and apologise for disturbing you.*

I turned to run, knowing that I could never outpace her, but she called out: *Wait!*

Terrified, I turned round. She was a beautiful creature with a soft face, now that she wasn't snarling.

*Why are you, a house cat, out here in this land of few humans?*

*I'm trying to get home to my human father. My human family have lost their togetherness and I was forced to choose.*

*Where are you heading?*

*The Fish Weir on the River.*

*At least two days away,* she told me. *You will never get there unless you feed. But you're a house cat, aren't you? The odd mouse and shrew here and there, perhaps a stupid or young rat. But your food comes from the humans, doesn't it?*

I nodded and began to yowl.

*Oh, be quiet. Cats are so bloody hopeless. You're lucky I feel sorry for you. Wait here.*

She disappeared and returned a long time later with a large rabbit in her jaws.

*This is for my young, so you will not touch it.*

The cubs tucked in and when I looked round the vixen had gone again. I was tempted to steal some of the meat off them but realised that would be suicidal, so with a growling belly, I watched them eat. She returned with a small chicken in her mouth and I was shocked.

*The feathers are a nuisance, but you can have some with me.* She ate her fill. Leaving me with the carcass. The chicken's blood was still warm and there was meat on the legs. It was delicious.

I went to groom her in gratitude.

*Steady on, cat. Let's not get too familiar. You're just a human vassal, after all.*

*We all do what we need to in order to survive,* I said huffily.

The vixen laughed. *You cats are so pompous. It's no wonder you spend so much time licking yourselves.*

I decided to change the subject. *Where is your mate?*

*The farmer killed him, which is why I decided to raid the bastard's henhouse.*

*I'm so sorry.*

*Are you?*

*Yes, the humans killed a dear friend of mine, although we could never have been mates.*

We fell asleep and the sun was high in the sky when I woke. The vixen had cleared the surrounds of the den of bones, feathers and fur. She was nowhere to be found, so I whispered to the cubs in the earth, *Please tell your mother that I am grateful to her with all my heart. I will never forget her kindness and I wish you all well. May you all grow and prosper.*

I left and headed south again. I could feel that I was getting closer to home and I had regained my strength. I decided to risk travelling in the daylight, as it had stopped raining and the low sun on my back warmed my bones. The land ahead grew wilder and I could see that a large wooded valley lay ahead of me. In there should be the big stream that led to the river, my river. How did I know that? I don't know, because I had never been there before. I just knew.

I went down towards the stream, that was more of a tributary to the river, and there was a narrow strip of water meadow. The setting sun was turning the trees to golden fire and the tributary was like a ribbon of molten gold running from the crucible of the hills into the sprue of the river and on to the mould of the estuary. Where did I get that from? I don't even know what a crucible is.

The Land Between the Rivers is known as Tarka country, after a book written by a human called Henry Williamson, concerning the life and death of otters. I don't know if it's any good, because I've never read it. I am a cat! I believe that it is one of those stories that engender an *ahhh ohhh, aren't they nice* feeling in humans. I've always regarded otters as rather difficult creatures to get on with, best left alone. Anyway, I needed a drink, so I went down to the water for a few gulps. Some distance upstream, an otter couple were twisting and writhing together in a pool. The male looked at me, droplets of water running off his whiskers. I had my fill and turned away, jumping up the bank and heading towards the setting sun.

The male otter hit me from behind on my right rear quarter. His teeth ripped my right ear open. The sudden ferocity was heart-stopping and instinctively I rolled on my back to rake him with my powerful hind legs. He was twisting between my front legs, his head and upper body squirming to bring his sharp incisors into action on my face. I swiped an eyelid away from his right eye with my claws, which he bit savagely. He was on top of me now, fast and furious, and his incisors tore my face open from the corner of my right eye to my nose.

Blinded with pain and anger, I fastened my jaws on his neck and shook him like a rat, hissing with indignant anger. By now, I was on top of him and tore at his vitals with my hind legs.

*You bastard!* I screamed, and I went to tear out his throat.

*Please don't!* the female otter cried.

I threw the male aside and turned on the female.

*What is wrong with you? What has possessed you to attack me?*

Blood was dripping down my face and into my mouth. I could taste it.

*I don't know. He's never been like this before. I'm so sorry, Mr Cat.*

*You otters are mental!*

To this day, I have no idea why the otter attacked me. I have heard that they can be a rather troubled species because of the humans. Perhaps he associated me with humans, which to my mind is as stupid as associating mice with dogs. Whatever his reason, my gashed face was throbbing and as I pushed through a thicket of hawthorn, I picked up a thorn in the pad of my right front paw. As far as I was concerned, Henry Williamson could get hold of a bumper illustrated copy of *Tarka the Otter* and cram it up his arse. And don't get me started on *Ring of Bright Water*!

I followed the tributary down to where it met the river, but I was moving painfully slowly and my body ached. There were still hours of darkness left, but I decided that I was too exhausted and in too much pain to travel any further. I found a dry patch in old grass under a hedge and slept. I slept throughout the day and well into the following night. I was in so much pain that I decided I was too exhausted to carry on. My life was full of pain, anguish and unbearable loneliness, and I decided as the first frost stiffened the leaves, that I would die here. I curled into myself and closed my eyes forever.

*Wake up!*

*Go away.*

*Wake up, you useless waste of fur!*

I opened my eyes and the countryside was bathed in a silver glow. The near-full moon was close in the night sky and cobwebs sparkled in the hedge. Snowflake hovered above me. Her face was clear, but her body was indistinct and shimmering like the moon on the water. She looked very cross.

*Do you intend to die here?*

*Yes, that's the general idea. Then we can be together.*

*It doesn't work like that.* She scoffed at my stupidity. *We don't have souls.*

*So where are you?*

*Here.*

*I don't understand.*

*Well, understand this, Bernard Law Montgomery, First Viscount Montgomery of Alamein. If you die here, here is where you will stay and it is not your time yet. Get up and start walking. Take the pain, because I will be with you every step of the way. Do not stop until you reach your home. A man is waiting for you, and believe it or not, he needs you.*

I shook off my stiffness and began to follow the river downstream to the sea. The pain was enveloping me and I hobbled through it. Every time I stopped, I could hear Snowflake hissing in my brain:

*Keep going!*

I crossed the meadow in the late afternoon and dragged myself to the cottage's kitchen door. It was slightly open and I pushed it open with my body weight. Edge Father was slumped at the kitchen table, an empty assortment of glasses, bottles and paperwork scattered in front of him. The cottage interior was cold, untidy and lacking Moira Mother's touch. I jumped on the table with a yowl. His slack face focussed on me and a light seemed to come into his eyes. I am convinced that my human father had been in the process of drinking himself to death. I meowed at him to get a grip.

"Bloody hell, Monty. You look like shit."

*Have you had a look at yourself lately!*

The lights went fully on behind his eyes and he regarded my battered little body. He stood up and went into the kitchen then the bathroom upstairs. He came back with kitchen roll, cotton wool buds and balls and white vinegar. I knew that this wasn't going to be good and I was right. He cleaned my wounds with copious amounts of white vinegar, which was misery. He meant well, but it was agony, especially the laceration on my face, so I hissed, growled, tried to slash his face with my claws, and got in a couple of good bites. He took the thorn out of my paw and some pus came out with it.

"We'll have to keep an eye on that, Monty," he told me, pouring vinegar on the pads of my paw, then cleaning up the scratches and bites on his arms.

Edge Father lit the wood burner in the kitchen and set up a blanket in a cardboard box for me, in front of it. He opened a tin of tuna, but it would have hurt too much to eat it. He grumbled but went out and came back with some packs of kitten food, which I could eat. That night as we sat together, soaking up the warmth of the burning wood, he looked at me with a sad expression.

"I don't know why you came back, Monty. I'm a cuckold, a drunk and a fucking war criminal."

I couldn't comment on his committing of war crimes, because I'm a cat. The fact he was a drunk, no one could disagree with. But he had not been cuckolded and I told him so in no uncertain terms.

*Meow!*

The next morning, Edge Father gave up drinking, but he needed something to replace it. The old standby he used when he was away for long periods. He was sitting in the kitchen smoking a cigarette, inhaled deeply and coughed. I happened to come in at that point and registered my disapproval with a stare.

"Oh, do fuck off, Monty."

A change came over Edge Father and he seemed to be more driven and had a focus in his life. It's a pity that he didn't use his new purpose to get his family back. He would go down to the river in the darkness, across the meadow and hide various things in a huge willow root system in a wood, which overhung the riverbank.

An old lady who lived up the lane from us visited the house a couple of times. She was old before her years, but she had a kind disposition and took a shine to me, even when I went into her house on pilfering expeditions. I called her Cyn Grandmother. She liked Edge Father a lot, much more than liked as a matter of fact. They had a bond between them that he seemed totally unaware of, but that old woman felt a deep sense of love and gratitude to him that he would never understand. Humans are so stupid!

One night, my human father was sipping cocoa that I suspected was laced with rum, but I didn't mind because it was late and he hadn't drunk anything all day. He wasn't smoking, either, thank goodness. I have never liked being picked up and mithered by humans, but I did enjoy their company. He was lying on a sofa in the sitting room, the wood burner cranked up, and I was curled up next to him, close enough to reach out a paw and feel his leg. He gently ran a finger down between my ears to make them twitch.

"Monty, I have to do something. People will say it's a bad thing, but I don't think it is. I have to stop a man persecuting my brothers and sisters in arms, just for doing the job their country expected them to do. I'm going to kill a man. I think he is evil. Many people don't, and he thinks he's doing what's right. But nevertheless, I will kill him.

"I will have to go away for a long time. Perhaps forever. The old lady who you like up the lane will take care of everything. She really likes you and will see that you're looked after. I'm so sorry. I'll miss you, Monty."

I raised my head and looked into his soul. To my endless sadness, I saw tears prickling in his eyes so I spoke slow and hard into him.

*Why not expend all this time and effort you're wasting in getting back together with Moira, Sarah and Francis, who love and miss you, you fucking stupid man.*

He looked at me. It was one of the rare times I managed to make direct conscious-to-conscious contact with a human.

"Because it's too late, Monty. I've crossed the start line and there's no going back."

\*

She did look after me, but Cyn Grandmother wasn't my family. I would spend long hours sitting next to Snowflake's tree, but she never provided the reason or solace. For eight years I lived in my new house, as other people had moved into my old house. Cyn Grandmother was pleased because they were paying her to live there. She had suddenly become an affluent old woman, who appreciated life and my company. We were growing old together, which makes what happened next even more tragic and heartbreaking for me.

On a late summer's morning, I woke up in the utility room. It was nice and comfy in there and the water boiler heated the little room when it came on in the morning. I had the run into the kitchen, but the two doors, the first into the pantry and the second into the hall and the rest of the house remained closed. I was slightly confused because the sun was pouring under the crack of the hallway door and normally Cyn Grandmother would wake me up. By late morning, I was getting worried as to why she hadn't come down and fed me, then let me out. I started to cry at the door, but the house remained silent and empty. It was the same the next day after I had a fitful sleep.

By the next morning, I was very thirsty as well as hungry. I tended to get most moisture from the wet food, but because I hadn't been fed, I had to resort to waiting for a drip to form on the kitchen tap, licking off the little sphere of water just as it formed. It was a long, laborious and boring process. I wondered if Cyn Grandmother had gone out and left me, which seemed so unlike her. By the hot afternoon, bluebottles were making their way under the door from the hall, transiting the kitchen to the pantry. There were a lot of them and I knew that I was in the shit.

After five days, the house was stinking of corruption and I started to look for a way out. I tried jumping up to open the kitchen door, but as it was a round door knob, it was a pointless exercise. The kitchen window was locked but the small window in the utility room seemed more promising. It was an old-fashioned bar closure with holes that fitted into a pin. The window hinged at the top and the bar could be put into the peg at any point, depending on how far it needed to be opened. Unfortunately, I lacked the strength in my front paws to pull the bar up off the peg. I couldn't get my stronger hind legs under it, and I suddenly realised that I was going to be the second thing to die alone in this house.

That night, Snowflake came to me again. She jumped up on the kitchen table without seeming to touch it. Her face was concerned but determined.

*You're on the right lines. The little window is your only chance of getting out, but don't waste your time trying to pull the bar up. Look at the little metal plate for the peg. The wood around it is rotten and the screws holding it in place are short and loose. Dig away the wood around the screws, then push it out with your back legs.*

*That's going to take forever.*

*Have anything better to do, or are you happy to become an incubator for maggots?*

*Seeing as how you put it that way. Snowflake?*

But she was gone.

It took me two more days to dig the fastener out of the soft, flaky wood of the window sill. By the end of it, my front claws and paws were worn down and bloody. The fastening came out and the bar clattered onto the window sill. Desperate by now, I flung my body weight against the window and it opened. I went out and landed in the herb garden, the window above shutting behind me. There was no going back into the house, whether I wanted to or not.

The cat that fell out of the utility room window was a different cat to the one that had been bundled into a basket. The first priority was food and water. An obligingly stupid female rat made my acquaintance in the wood shed of my old home. I disposed of her and tracked down her litter of ratlets, which provided a well-needed top-up. Unsatisfying but necessary for survival. For the first few days, I hung around Cyn Grandmother's house, which was ghastly, knowing that she lay dead upstairs. There were no kindly RSPCA ladies to come and collect me, which was just as well. I didn't want to be put down.

Many weeks later, the police broke into the house and discovered the grisly remains of my carer and friend upstairs. By then, I was practically feral anyway and supplemented my food by going into other cats' homes and bullying their food from their dishes. But the winter was upon me and I took stock of my situation. I was sitting by Snowflake's tree, but she never reappeared to offer advice or wise counsel. I was now thirteen winters old, grey and stiff. Some of my molars had rotted away and I felt weary with age. So far, the winter had been mild and kind, but I smelled snow. When the snows came, I would go out and lie down forever.

As I headed back to my now empty first home, I saw a car in the opening by the locked gate. A man and a woman were looking at the cottage. The man was grey haired and favoured a stick as he moved with an awkward gait. The woman held his arm and as she turned towards him to speak, I saw...

*MOIRA MOTHER!* I screamed.

They both turned round and looked at me.

"Monty? Could it be you?" the man said with amazement. He looked different, but the scar was still on his forehead, under his long fringe.

I limped up to them, crying and wailing. Edge Father picked me up and wrapped me in his coat, so only my head showed. Moira Mother was rubbing gently between my ears. They had come home and we were all crying, apart from Edge Father, who had something in his eye...

I don't have many years left, but at last I am truly happy. Sarah Sister is at a place called University and Francis is nearly a man, who is too busy for cats. Most of the time. He still throws a ping pong ball on the flagstones in the kitchen and I'm still imprudent enough to chase it. I don't get out as much now but still pay my respects to Snowflake. I am happy to lie in my basket in front of the wood burner and glower at Edge Father, for all the years he wasted. Really and truly, it's only to be expected, because humans are so incredibly stupid!

Chapter 37

# EPILOGUE ONE

———

*I will instruct my sorrows to be proud;*
*for grief is proud, and makes his owner stoop.*

WILLIAM SHAKESPEARE

The RSM who had told Edge, "I have a feeling that you'll fuck it up. The only reason you haven't totally fucked up your Service career is because the Army is a family and we look after our own," drank himself to death.

"I'll give you one piece of advice that's really important for your life outside the Army and it's totally free and unbiased: It doesn't matter how much you've been through, or whatever you've done in the Army. It doesn't matter if you've won the VC, because the civvies won't give a fucking toss. And why should they? Don't waste your time with the 'you don't know coz you weren't there' routine. They couldn't even begin to understand, and their eyes will have glazed over before you even tell them about getting on the trooper flight. The only way they can judge you is by the way you get on with them, and if you think barrack life is boring, wait until you're a civvie. I have a horrible feeling that one way or another, being a civvie will kill you."

Well, it certainly did for the RSM. With his contacts and experience, he found a good job that paid very well. But he was surrounded by younger workers with a hunger to get on. The RSM didn't feel the need to strive and work all the hours, because of his Service pension. As time went on, he slipped down the sales league. He had his top-of-the-range company car replaced with a runaround, and the travelling killed him. He waved goodbye to his wife eighteen months after he left the Army. He started drinking to function, and then as a reason to get out of bed, and then it became the only reason to live.

On a bitterly cold early morning in Staffordshire in January 2015, a dog walker could no longer stand the whining demands of his Border Collie and took it outside into the still dark, frozen landscape of hoar frost and glistening trees. The stagnant water at the side of the river had frozen and the frost crunched underfoot. The man and his dog walked past the war memorial opposite the church. The yews were white and so was the figure sitting under the cross, slumped against the rack, holding the frozen poppy wreaths.

"Oh dear God!" said the man, and walked towards the memorial. The figure was wearing a blazer complete with medals, and the hoar frost dusted his hair and moustache like icing. In stiff, gnarled fingers, he clutched an almost empty bottle of Chivas Regal, and another empty bottle lay at his feet. His eyes were closed, but a single frozen tear had solidified as it tracked down his cheek.

The man tied the Collie to the memorial gate and fumbled for his mobile phone.

*

Henry Morrison had a few blissful years, living another man's life, a man who had died as an infant and enabled Morrison to obtain a copy of a birth certificate. It could have been perfect, but he and Angela were never blessed with children. They moved to Cumbria and Morrison would often disappear off for a few weeks on some 'job' or other. Angela knew from her brother not to ask too many questions, and she loved Henry beyond measure.

Angela never knew exactly how old Henry was, but she reckoned he was around fifty when he suddenly announced that he was sick of leaving her and that he would get a 'proper job'. The news lightened her heart and even when she found a tender and swollen lymph gland in her armpit while having a shower, it couldn't dampen her spirit.

But then the two of them became engulfed in a whirlwind of doctor and hospital appointments, for scans, biopsies and consultations. Morrison was her constant, her brick and her capable second in her duel with death. He was always optimistic, always positive and he never let her see him weep in his workshop, rocking with grief and hammering his fists on the workbench with frustration, cursing a selfish and capricious god.

The Inkspots provided his support and security at the beautiful church in Hartland, a place where Angela had requested to be laid to rest, because she had come home to die. The primroses were out in a gorgeous early-spring morning, and bumble bees were doing their initial air tests before the gruelling operational tour of summer.

It was Cooper that spotted the dark saloon, a car with a man and a woman in the front seat that should just not have been there. He and Jarvis sauntered over. Cooper got in the back seat while Jarvis reached into his overcoat and rammed the barrels of a sawn-off shotgun through the passenger window, pointing it at the female undercover police officer's face.

"You, get out and get in the back. Now!" Jarvis hissed at her. Terrified, she complied while Jarvis slid into the passenger's seat.

"If you move your hands off the steering wheel, your brains will be all over the inside of this car. I've seen it and it's a bugger to clean up," he told the driver.

Cooper had rammed a silenced automatic into the female copper's side while they frisked the pair, pulling out warrant cards, driving licences and credit cards.

Cooper handed the documents to Jarvis in the front seat and he looked at both sets. "Well, Detective Sergeants Oxlade and Rice. We now know who you are, where you live, some information about your families and we have all your bank and credit cards. It must take a particularly lowlife piece of shit to conduct surveillance on a man who is burying his wife. Let's go for a little drive. Head towards Hartland Quay."

From the church door, Edge saw the saloon car pass and head west. The first hymn was starting as he slipped into a pew towards the back of the church. Moira was up at the front next to Morrison and Mickie and they were all inconsolable. Edge felt the loss as keenly, but preferred to be alone with his thoughts, trying not to look at the coffin in the chancel. He had to try very hard not to weep at the hymn, *O God Our Help in Ages Past*.

Less than 500 metres out of Hartland, Jarvis told the driver to halt near a gate on their right. He got out and opened it and Cooper told the driver to drive through. Jarvis closed the gate behind them and got back in the car.

"Follow the track towards the gorse and the trees ahead of you."

"Are you going to kill us?" Rice, the female DS, asked in panicked horror.

"Right into the gorse and stop when I tell you," Jarvis said, the shotgun never leaving pointing at the driver's head. The car was in a very dense thicket of gorse and trees, stunted and twisted by the Atlantic storms. It was on a steep slope, pointing towards a gully, with a drop of a couple of hundred feet down to the swirling sea and rocks below. Jarvis got out.

"Okay, DS Oxlade. You'd better make sure that handbrake is on nice and tight, then get out."

"You too, love," Cooper said, indicating out with his pistol.

"Please don't kill us," she said, beginning to hyperventilate.

"Does this ring any bells with you pair of bastards?" Jarvis asked, and quoted:

"I do solemnly and sincerely declare and affirm that I will well and truly serve the Queen in the office of constable, with fairness, integrity, diligence and impartiality, upholding fundamental human rights and according equal respect to all people; and that I will, to the best of my power, cause the peace to be kept and preserved and prevent all offences against people and property; and that while I continue to hold the said office, I will to the best of my skill and knowledge discharge all the duties thereof faithfully according to law. Aren't you going to ask me how I know that?

"The problem is that you and your sick, corrupt organisation haven't done any of those things. And now you are the enemy. You probably thought today was going to be a bit of a laugh. Keeping an eye on bad people, ex-military thickies, enemies of the State, thinking you were untouchable. But now you're in Shit Street. We don't play by your rules. We don't do courts or the criminal justice system. We know we're all going to die and we don't fucking care. Most of us have been dead men walking for years, who have seen horrors you couldn't begin to contemplate."

"What, like I've felt the wind in my hair riding test boats off the black galaxies and seen an attack fleet burn like a match and disappear. I've seen it... felt it! You fucking sad pongo bastards are out of your depth!" DS Oxlade sneered at him. Jarvis smashed him in the face with the butt of the shotgun.

"I thought it was starships on fire off the shoulder of Orion," Cooper observed nonchalantly.

"Smartarse, still he knows his *Blade Runner*, sad git. Get undressed, the pair of you. Leave your nose, Oxlade, and drop 'em, blossom."

"Oh God, no," Rice sobbed.

"Just get on with it and put your clothes in a pile, then get into the front seats of the car. You in the driver's seat, Oxlade. MOVE!"

They complied and slid into the car. Rice was shivering with fear as Cooper retrieved two sets of handcuffs from the pile of discarded clothing.

"Okay, Oxlade, right arm through the steering wheel, Rice, put your left arm through the other side."

They did so and Cooper cuffed their hands on the other side of the steering wheel.

"Rice, right hand up to that handle above your head. Oxlade, reach across with your left arm. Come on! You're going to be nice and intimate for the next few hours…" he paused "…or days…"

"Or until the handbrake wears out," Cooper suggested helpfully as he cuffed their other wrists to the suit hanger. "And do try not to bleed on your colleague."

They surveyed their handiwork.

"We should be in time for the third hymn," Cooper observed casually.

Jarvis opened the passenger door and squatted down to speak with DS Oxlade. His tone was even and low and undercut with pure malice. "We now know a great deal about you. By tomorrow, we will know more about you and your family than you know yourselves. If what is laughably referred to as the police service makes any move against any of us, we will kill your families in front of you. There are a lot of us and we have had enough. We will wage a war on you and the State that you would not believe.

"Most of the kids who join the military now do five years or less. They can't hack it. They are weak, feminised and emasculated. We served a lifetime and we learned a lot. And now you will fear us, because we can find you whenever we want. Tell your bosses and political masters that we are coming for them."

"Why are you doing this?" the woman sobbed.

"For the same reason you decided to pitch up at a funeral, because you think the widower is someone else. You came to intimidate and humiliate. It was the worst mistake you and your bosses ever made. Now I'm going to take a photograph of you pair and you have joined our database. If we ever meet again, you will watch your family screaming out their last."

Jarvis stood up. "And I wouldn't wriggle around too much if I were you. The handbrake could be a bit iffy and it's a long way down to the rocks. If any ramblers come across you pair, they'll have a bloody good chortle and assume it's all been a sex game that's gone a bit wrong. I might give the *Western Morning News* a ring. Mind how you go."

They threw the clothes into the thickest, nastiest gorse clump they could find and strolled back towards the road. Cooper stopped and lit a pipe.

"You have to be kidding me," Jarvis said with incredulity.

"I've been told that it makes me look trustworthy and distinguished."

"By who? Mrs Hudson, your housekeeper?"

*

Morrison had lost his reason to live and went back to his old profession to seek a noble death. He was as anachronistic as Brave Horatius, who kept the gate in the brave days of old. But he was looking for a past that had never existed. His fellow mercenaries were neither professional, nor noble. Most of them he decried as 'Walts' or psychopaths. The really good ones, the Kurds, were fighting the resurgent Ottoman Empire in Iraq, Iran and the Stans. The Russians were protecting Mother Russ in the Caucuses, which left – apart from the mentally ill – the brave, the idealistic and hopelessly prepared soldiers of fortune, who needed protection from the environment, let alone the savagery of their Islamic enemies.

He was fifty-five when he ended up in the mercenaries' graveyard of the Congo, fighting against the spreading Islamic terror from the Sudan. It wasn't a 7.62mm full metal jacket, or a roadside IED that killed Henry Morrison. It was a tiny Anopheles mosquito that carried the plasmodium falciparum form of malaria. By the time he realised how sick he was and had managed to get to the Catholic hospital in Kisangani, he was delirious with fever. The doctor and nurses knew there was no hope, and a compassionate Indian nurse from Chennai watched over his final hours. They knew he was a mercenary, but they also knew for which cause he had been fighting. Morrison's fever broke in the small hours, and after hours of delirium, he was lucid and at peace with himself. The Indian nurse tried to get him to drink some water.

"I should have remembered to keep taking the Lariam. Bad drills," Morrison said softly. He looked up at the nurse, who smiled at him sadly. "Do you know, you've got the most beautiful eyes. They are just like someone's I once knew. But by God I loved her."

He closed his eyes and she held his hand while he died.

*

Giles 'Gary' Gilmore never flew operationally again. His rehabilitation road back to fitness was long and painful. The surgeons, nurses, medics and rehabilitation teams at Headly Court put his body back together, but none of them really fixed his mind. Gilmore vomited before the first time he got back in a helicopter and he came to the shocking conclusion he was terrified of flying. Those very things that had given him so much pleasure now frightened him into becoming a cowering wreck. He had developed a morbid phobia about heights and going anywhere near the open doors of the helicopter, strop or not, was enough to close his throat with terror.

He couldn't hide it from his new crew, and the squadron commander discretely took him off flying duties. Gilmore may have lost one pillar of his life but gained another, perhaps more useful to his well-being and salvation. He requested a career break from the RAF and with Lorna's support, both spiritual and financial, he managed to get through the selection board and studied theology in Durham. He was ordained four years later and completed the Commissioned Vicars and Tarts course at the RAFC Cranwell and the padre course at Amport House. Giles Gilmore was as accomplished a military padre as he had been a loadmaster, albeit slightly less cocky.

Every year on a certain date in October, Padre Gilmore would drive to Gloucestershire and leave a single red rose and pray at a simple white gravestone with the RAF crest carved into it. He would then drive to a small village in the Pennines and go into the graveyard of a pretty little church. Fighting to keep his composure, Gilmore would lay a second rose and stand vigil at the second simple headstone, the tears streaming down his face. One year, a woman who had recently lost her husband spotted the distressed man at the military grave. She went over to the dejected chap in his long black overcoat.

"Are you all right, dear?" she asked, and looked at the gravestone. "She must have been special to you. So young."

"She told me she loved me, just before she died."

"Oh, I'm so sorry. Did you love her?"

"Not then. I was in lust with her. We all were."

The woman didn't know what to say.

"She saved my life. They all did." He was weeping openly now.

The woman put her arm round his shoulders. "Sometimes, dear, life can be a reet bugger!"

*

Afarin Khan's luck finally ran out near Liboi, in the border country between Kenya and Somalia. She was travelling in a car with Timothy, a member of Kenya's Army Paratroopers, a cover for a British-trained Special Forces unit. Timothy was a Muslim and Afarin was wearing the traditional Somali woman's garb of a *dirac*, headscarf and shawl. Unlike Somali women, she had forgone traditional underwear and wore her usual assortment of automatic pistol, ammunition and a fighting knife. They had intended to cross into Somalia and recce Bilis Qooqaani, a seething hotbed of Islamic terrorists in the guise of Al-Shabaab.

The billiard table flatness of the arid bush spread for miles every direction, but up ahead was a bus that had been stopped at what looked like an illegal checkpoint. There were armed men with a number of technicals, pick-up trucks which mounted heavy machine guns. The men were wearing black headscarves. It looked like Al-Shabaab had found them.

"No worries," Timothy said calmly. "We can blag our way through this."

And they could have done, because they looked just like any other Somalian couple. Afarin's headscarf denoted that she and Timothy were married. An Al-Shabaab fighter sauntered up to the now stationary car, an AK-47 over his shoulder. He was holding the rifle by its barrel. Up ahead, more of the fighters were moving the passengers off the bus. Afarin looked away to avoid the man's gaze, like the modest wife she was supposed to be.

"*Assalamu alaikum*," said the terrorist, peering into the car.

"*Wa alaikum assalaam*," Timothy replied.

The conversation was conducted in Somali. "Where you going?"

"Home to Jilib. My second wife wanted shopping in Nairobi." Timothy raised his eyes as though in resigned frustration. "Gold and fabric."

"Be sure your first wife is behaving at home."

"My brother has seen to it."

Up ahead, the passengers had been sorted into two groups. Afarin felt a chill of terror.

"Have you seen Kenyan Army?" demanded the terrorist.

"Only in Nairobi. None since."

The first gunshots boomed out as the Al-Shabaab started to kill the non-Muslim passengers. They must not act. They had to keep to their cover story and briefing. Their tasking was more important. Timothy looked at Afarin and they exchanged that look. It said *fuck the mission*.

Timothy shot the terrorist under his jaw and the round exited through the top of his head.

"What the fuck!" he said before his legs folded. Timothy was out and grabbed the AK off the man, who was still twitching on the ground. Afarin was out of the other door, sprinting to the other side of the bus, away from the killing. She didn't remember getting the Glock from the garter holster on her inner thigh. Timothy was laying down short bursts and moving position, from cover to cover. The shooting of the passengers was forgotten now.

"Run. Run for your lives," Afarin screamed at them in English, knowing the Kenyans would understand.

One of the fighters was opening the driver's door of the technical, another one climbing on the back to get to the machine gun. Afarin dropped the man on the back first with two rounds, then shot the driver through the window. She double-tapped him to make sure. While Timothy was keeping them busy, Afarin went round the front of the bus. The stupid ones were still gathering their belongings. The smarter ones were disappearing into the bush. The second technical was reversing onto the road, a gunner swinging the machine gun towards Timothy's position. She dropped him and shot out the vehicle's rear tyres. Again, she double-tapped the driver. The would-be gunner was screaming, holding his bloody crotch, *must have snatched that one,* and she dispatched him quickly.

A burst of fire showered her with glass from the bus's windscreen, so Afarin peered round the front of the bus and fired three rounds at a fighter who was torn between firing at Timothy and this new threat that was frankly so un-Islamic. By now, Afarin had learned to count her rounds and fumbled between her legs for a fresh magazine, the empty one dropping onto the dusty road. Her body was in cover; only the Glock and her right hand was visible.

The 7.62mm round hit the body of Afarin's Glock on the top slide, just above the trigger housing and by a bizarre quirk of ballistics, the flattened round ricocheted off at right angles. The tumbling round had demolished the pistol and her hand, entering her lower arm just above the scaphoid bone. It tracked upwards between her radius and ulna bones, shredding the radial and ulna arteries, and lodged near the neck of the radial bone. Afarin grunted in agony and went down on her knees. The Al-Shabaab terrorist came round the front of the bus, raised his AK-47 and fired a burst at Afarin, and at least two rounds hit her in the chest. She was blown backwards by the impact and stared up at the sunlight coming through the acacia tree above her and she thought: *This is the way the world ends. Not with a bang but a whimper.*

She heard the rounds thwack through the terrorist's body before he could make sure. But she was losing peripheral vision. Soon the view of the tree was like looking through the wrong end of the telescope and then she went blind. As she fell into herself, Afarin heard Timothy tell her gently that she was going to be all right. *Liar*, she thought.

Timothy worked quickly through the protocols. The primary survey was easy. The remaining hazards were dispatched quickly and dispassionately and he ruthlessly ignored the remaining panicked and wailing passengers from the bus. He performed the jaw thrust to open her airway and Afarin coughed bright red blood into his face and he tasted her ebbing life. She only groaned weakly when he twisted the hair above her ear and she did try to pull her good arm away when he pinched the web of skin between her fingers. That gave a GCS of six, which wasn't good. Her airway was clear but already her neck was twisted and displaced from the hemothorax. Her breathing was fast and shallow because of the air and blood being trapped within the pleural cavity. Her pulse was fast because not enough air was being oxygenated. Afarin's lips were blue, her lower right arm was shattered and shredded and he had no means of tying off the blood vessels, so he applied a tourniquet because she would lose the arm below the elbow anyway. Timothy ripped open her dirac and saw the two purple-ringed entrance wounds, bubbling blood. The first a few inches above her right nipple, the second slightly higher. He gently rolled her over and found the single exit wound, big enough to put his fist in. He could see the whiteness of shattered ribs and the lung bubbling with frothy blood.

Timothy ran for the car and dragged out the trauma kit, a roll of black bodge tape and some plastic sheeting. He went through the trauma kit and found the coagulation powder that would help to stop the bleeding. Then he applied the powder and a Celox haemostatic wound dressing to the exit wound, covering it with a cut square of plastic sheet and taping it in place so that it was airtight. A second square of plastic sheet was taped over the entrance wounds, not so easily this time because of the contour of her breast. It was only secured on three sides. The theory being, when she breathed in, the lungs would swell and expel the air trapped in the pleural cavity. When she breathed out, the patch would seal, preventing any more air getting in. In theory anyway. He didn't feel confident enough to insert a chest drain. The trauma kit didn't have a Seldinger chest drain kit and he doubted he could find her fifth intercostal space anyway, let alone cut into it. Because she was unconscious, he didn't want to administer morphine. If she woke up screaming, he would. But at least her breathing had slowed a little; the cyanosis around her lips seemed less and her neck displacement didn't seem as twisted.

"Come on, Afarin, fight for me, please."

She needed top trauma care in a specialist unit. He could radio for a military helicopter, but that could take hours and they wouldn't have the necessary in-transit care. Nairobi was 200 kilometres away, at least two hours. Timothy gently lifted Afarin and carried her to the car, laying her on her wounded side on the back seat. He jammed her unconscious body in as best he could with their kit and then he drove west like the devil was chasing him.

Chapter 38

# EPILOGUE TWO

––––––

Former Detective Inspector Charles Hope became a very successful novelist. He wrote scathingly satirical comedy novels about the police service, which won him few friends among serving officers and the Police Federation, but a huge following among former officers who had seen and had enough, and the general public who had been involved with dealings with the police and for whom it was all too realistic. He even wrote under the *nom de plume* 'Forlorn Hope' to rub the noses of the Thames Valley Police in it.

When the situation in the Home Counties became intolerable, Hope moved with his family to Shropshire and bought a country house for cash. He is still visited by a member of the Inkspots every six months and they catch up. Like all of them, Hope remained unmolested by the Security Services, who by then had far more pressing issues to deal with.

*

Major Gardner left the Army after a full career, having discovered there was a glass ceiling for those of his background. But mainly, he preferred soldiering and command and leadership to the politics of the headquarters and staff officers. He never made colonel but was respected and liked within his battalion, and his colonel stopped pestering him to go on and complete the Intermediate Staff Studies Course.

Ironically, although he detested politics within the Army, Gardner stood as a member for parliament as an independent. The sitting Tory MP was a noted expense fiddler and general trougher, and her Labour rival was a known Momentum and Union plant. Much to his amazement, Gardner was elected to the Mother of all Parliaments and became very quickly disillusioned and frustrated. The only realistic means an individual MP had of making a difference was to be elected onto one of the select committees, and as an independent, Gardner had no chance, due to the death grip of the party system and the whips, who maintained a system of status quo and mediocrity. Gardner served one term and didn't stand for re-election.

It was the actions of the ruling class that made civil insurrection inevitable. The betrayal of a legitimate and legal referendum vote to leave the EU and the clampdown on free speech inflamed a normally docile and compliant population. The zombie Labour Government proved to be incapable of governing and the previous summer's 'Race Riots' in northern town and cities, and the reaction to them, caused a powder keg of resentment to explode. When the police actively supported the rape gangs, the anger of the indigenous population was directed against them and it knew no bounds. In one shocking incident, a riot van was isolated and ambushed in Leeds and the nine police inside were slaughtered, bludgeoned to death, and the bodies hung for display at Elland Road football ground.

It was a sickening act that shocked the world, but the feeble government's attempts to crack down on the rioters backfired, and insurrection broke out in all major towns and cities throughout the country. Many Army units refused to obey orders. Given the mass prosecutions of military personnel for 'historic war crimes', who could blame them? And this insurrection wasn't rioting to loot in a spasm of anger and greed, the 'Insurrection' was well coordinated and led, and it became obvious that some key units had received special training in urban warfare. Britain had become ungovernable and quasi-independent areas were set up in the South, the West Country, East Anglia, Cumbria and the Northern Marches. Most of the major cities were ungovernable hellholes of crime and lawlessness.

When what the zombie government called the 'Insurgency' and the people called the 'Fight for Freedom' continued to spread, it was inevitable that Gardner would be involved. His former constituents more or less demanded it. He was instrumental in the formation of armed groups in the part of the country Hereward the Wake had once operated. The Security Services had forgotten how to police the countryside and they were easy meat for the well-organised armed units, who knew the land and how to operate in it, thanks to men and women like Gardner. Their vehicles were ambushed, the police stripped of their weapons, equipment and vehicles, and the humiliated policemen and women were driven to cities such as Northampton and dumped off. The vehicles were resprayed in camouflage and the arms distributed to those trained to use them. When the Security forces came *en masse,* the Freedom Fighters declined combat until another outbreak flared up in another part of the country and the police went away.

Gardner met Edge once again, at a frightfully civilised conference for Insurgents, held near Berkley. After the deadly business of the day, they got drunk together and reminisced about court marshals, the Balkans and a Croatian forensic anthropologist. Gardner still never told him about the note that had been rammed in her mouth.

*

In the foyer of a television production company in Norwich, a man came out of the stairwell doors at the same time as the lift doors opened across the other side of the lobby. The man wore a suit that was a little tight across his shoulders. His hair was closely cropped to be non-existent and his face was hewn by a life spent outdoors and battered by the slings and arrows of outrageous fortune. He stared across at the two women who had come out of the lift. One obviously worked for the production company because of the identity badge on a ribbon round her neck. The other was a striking Muslim woman wearing a hijab.

The man's eyes narrowed and he strode across the foyer. The company woman gave a start and placed herself between the Muslim woman and the advancing man, who ignored her and went up to the woman in the hijab.

"As I live and breathe," he said pleasantly, "if it isn't the Tinge with the Minge."

The woman from the television company looked at him with disgust and beckoned to the armed security guard by the main doors. She was amazed when the Muslim woman gave a gasp of pleasure and threw her arms round the man's neck, which was slightly awkward because of her artificial right arm.

"Oh, Jarvis! It is you, isn't it? When was the last time?"

"Basra 2005."

"And you remembered me after all these years. You haven't changed a bit. Well…"

"I never forget an arse," he told her solemnly. "And you're a bloody liar. But in your case, you haven't, apart from…"

"Can you wait for me? I just need to say goodbye to this lady."

He nodded and the security guard stood down. He didn't really relish having to try to forcibly eject the man in the suit. Outside on Edward Street, Afarin put her good arm through Jarvis's. She leaned into him; it was like their shared fears and hardships made the years irrelevant. They were a diminishing band of brothers.

"You fancy a spot of late lunch?" he asked her, and she nodded gratefully. "But isn't it your Ramadamadingdong?"

"I don't bother with that crap," she said light-heartedly.

They found a pub and as he waited for the drinks, Jarvis looked at all the fading photographs of American airmen. He wondered how many of the monochrome ghosts had died in spinning and burning bombers over Germany. They both had soft drinks and he carried across a couple of menus.

"Right", she said, "you first, why were you in that television company and what the bloody hell happened to your hair?"

"I've been hired as a 'military advisor'. Ross Kemp is doing a documentary of special forces operations in Afghanistan, particularly the Tora Bora cave complexes."

"Seriously?"

"Yep."

"Am I in it, and who plays me?"

Jarvis grinned. "Well, we first thought of Kim Kardashian, but her arse wasn't big enough, so we went for Nadiya Hussain. You set up your mobile bakery on the gun line, and when the plucky blades come back in, in their Pinkies, they can tuck into a nice Victoria sponge with a mug of char, while you, or rather Nadiya, smile demurely at the camera."

She laughed out loud, something she hadn't done for a long time.

"Right, your turn. What happened to your arm?"

"I got banjoed by Al-Shabaab on the Kenya, Somali border. Took two in the chest as well. A Kenyan SF guy I was with saved me. Luckily, he'd done a battlefield advanced trauma and life support course with the Israelis, under the reciprocal training agreement. They couldn't save my arm, though, too much damage. I wear this arm so I don't frighten the kids. I've got a much better bionic one that gives me almost full function. It looks a bit scary, though."

"And what's with the headscarf?" asked Jarvis bluntly.

"It makes me invisible in the town and cities and I can move around. It's essential for my charity stuff. That's why I was at the TV company."

He put his head in his hands. "Charadee, oh, no way."

The girl who had spoken up against a colonel in Afghanistan flared up at him. "Don't you fucking judge me, Mr Jarvis, until you know what it is I actually do!"

Some people looked at them and she lowered her voice. "I do stuff that you bloody cowards daren't. I have founded an organisation that goes up against Muslim paedophile rape gangs. We target the enablers and the organisers. We go against their assets and we publicly shame them. Our workers are mainly Sikhs and former Gurkhas and they've all had military training for the strong-arm stuff. Our female workers are all ex-forces from medical, police or educational backgrounds. We work with the young white girls who have been raped and trafficked, because you weak and feeble lot fucking daren't. We target the imams and the councillors who encourage and protect the perpetrators, and sometimes senior police officers. We destroy them.

"And it's difficult for the police, politicians and media to ignore what I do, or rather try to close me down. I've learned from them and play the Muslim card at every cut and turn. The fuckers are terrified of me."

Jarvis blinked at her. "Christ, I bet you're popular! And I see your language hasn't got any better."

"Oh, I've had death threats. They call me the 'One-armed Whore of Satan'. I had a contract put out on me and two men came for me one night."

Jarvis was staring at her, a cold feeling in the pit of his stomach. "And?"

"And now they're at the bottom of Wastwater, wrapped in carpets with breeze blocks. The man who put out the contract was hung outside the mosque with a pig's trotter in his mouth, *pour encourager les autres*. Generally, I'm left alone now, although I make a point of checking under my car and varying my routes."

"Are you carrying?"

"Always. You lot taught me that."

"Jesus, Treacle. You forgot to tell us you're a fucking psychopath," Jarvis said in a passable cockney accent.

Afarin smiled. "Henry said that to me, so, so long ago. Where is he? What's he doing?"

Jarvis's face became drawn with sadness. "I'm sorry, Afarin, love. Henry died in the Congo a couple of years back."

She bent her head forward so Jarvis couldn't see her tears. He reached across the table and grasped her hands, both real and prosthetic.

"I really loved him, you know. He was the first man I ever… The only one, if I'm honest."

They ate their meal when it came, exchanging lighter chit-chat, avoiding the subject of Henry Morrison and his marriage to Angela Keeble. Over coffees, the afternoon dragged on into early evening and they seemed reluctant to part company. Finally, Afarin said, "Jarvis, it's been lovely, but I had better head off."

He looked at her beautiful eyes, the empty years, and decided, what the hell!

"Do you have anyone in your life, Afarin?"

"Err no, what about you?"

He had something in his eyes, a faraway look that reminded her of leaning against a Hesco bastion in Afghanistan, nearly twenty years ago. It was a look of tender sadness.

"No. Never have. Nothing meaningful, I guess. It's one of the few things about my life that I regret. Look, you can laugh at me, or tell me to piss off, but the truth of the matter is, we're a pair of misfits. You have your admirable work, and I always said you were the bravest person I'd ever known. Why don't we try to make each other happy for a little while at least? It probably won't work out and we'll devise intricate ways of killing one another, but in all honesty we deserve a chance of, well, happiness or something, and what do we have to lose?"

"As I once said to Henry, I'm not very good at this sort of thing, because I'm just not."

"Well, you're in luck then, because neither am I."

She looked at him evenly, a worried smile playing around her mouth. "Why not?"

And they did share each other's lives and after a while, each other's bodies. And were they happy? Well, they made a decent fist of it…

*

Horace Cutler QC died on the A1 just south of Newark on the 21st of September 2023. It was just after 07:30 while he had been returning from a court martial at Bulford, the previous day. He was anxious to keep an appointment in his Lincoln chambers and had set off from Wiltshire at 04:00. His Bentley was travelling at 115 mph in the outside lane, when a lorry driven by a Latvian swerved out from the nearside lane. The lorry driver had been looking down, trying to change the track on his iPod. He had had six hours' sleep in the past forty-eight.

The Bentley was side-swiped onto the central reservation and in a case of the bloody-mindedness of Lady Luck, there was a gap in the central reservation where a side road crossed the main trunk road. The A1 in Lincolnshire is notorious for these anomalies. The Bentley rode up the crash barrier, flipped over, landed upside down on the southbound carriageway and was hit by a lorry travelling south to a Channel port. Horace Cutler was killed instantly but was pronounced dead at 08:52 at Nottingham's main hospital. His wife was advised not to view his remains, and Cutler was identified by a signet ring and a personal letter in his coat pocket, written and signed by 'Mark', inviting him to visit North Devon for some fishing, shooting and poaching, to get away from the madhouse.

Horace Cutler was laid to rest in Branston, near Lincoln, and apart from his close family, friends and two daughters, the funeral was attended by over fifty serving and former members of the Armed Forces, some in uniform, some in their veterans' uniform of blazers and medals, all of them Service personnel who Cutler had saved from the military justice system and had gone on to have distinguished careers in the military. There were also some twenty women elegantly dressed in black, some with black veils, discreetly filling the rear pews of the church, and they all disappeared as soon as the service ended. They were of all ages from quite young to middle-aged and they were all strikingly beautiful.

The man who sat alone in a long overcoat recognised one of the women as having been the station adjutant at RAF Akrotiri, when he had been waiting for his court martial. She had been a junior officer then and had treated him with sympathy and kindness, despite the severity of the charge he was facing. He smiled to himself, knowing that during his life, Horace Cutler had spread a great deal of kindness as well, and good luck to the randy old bastard.

He left at the same time as the striking women, placed the Mossberg in the passenger footwell against the transmission tunnel, butt uppermost and covered with a blanket. He drove south-west in his Land Rover, on the B and C roads to avoid the burning cities and lawless motorways. He felt as desolate as the empty countryside.

# Chapter 39

# EPILOGUE THREE, EDGE'S SWANSONG

———

*He was a man, take him for all in all,*
*I shall not look upon his like again.*

WILLIAM SHAKESPEARE

The virus came and the Deep State was given its opportunity to eradicate non-conformism and finish the work of Common Purpose. Inevitably, the country burst into flames. It started in the unpoliced cities that had largely become a no-go area for the indigenous population, and spread to the former industrial towns. This was no violence driven by drink, looting and greed. It was driven by a core element of society that had had enough. Civil disobedience begat violence against the invaders and their support arm, the police. This time, it was sustained and organised and the zombie government and its enablers couldn't understand what hit them. It ranged from refusal to pay fines, to failure to turn up for work, targeted vandalism of infrastructure to ultraviolence against a paramilitary police that had lost the ability to police by consent. Bristol, Exeter, Plymouth burned, and

Edge and Moira watched, made preparations and constructed defence in the depths of their property.

It soon became clear that spirited amateurs, no matter how committed, could not prevail in the longer term against the authorities. They lacked expertise and an infrastructure to sustain a long period of insurrection and leadership. Ground and towns were taken back. The authorities cut off power to the areas controlled by the insurgency and petrol became very difficult to source. The Edges rode out the storm in their citadel.

"They need you, you know," she told him one evening over a dinner of venison casserole. Poached venison, naturally.

"They can piss off. A bunch of Walts, saddies and psychopaths."

"Not all. Daddy helps them with money and fuel. God knows where he gets it."

Edge grunted.

"Part of me is so very glad you don't want to join them, but another part knows that you'll regret it."

"This elderberry is very good. You're getting to be quite a dab hand at this, Moira."

*

Edge finally got round to fixing the loose slates on the outhouses. The rain had got in during the winter and shorted out the electrics on the generator, which had been expensive to fix. It was a cold spring morning and as he rested, he looked at the bright green new growth on the willows down by the flood meadow. The replacement slates had been raided from a disused barn and while not perfect, they would do.

He clocked the black Range Rover coming down from the north, through the sparse growth of the narrow lane. It slowed by the junction and pulled into the part of the drive off the road on the other side of the gate. Two men got out. One wore a long ranchman's coat and by the way he scanned the area, Edge knew straight away what he was. The second man was very much dressed for the countryside but not for work. He wore a tweed jacket and cap, wine corduroys with gaiters and walking boots. He looked with interest at Edge's improvised stinger, buried in the drive just under the double gate. He failed to notice the two homemade claymores hidden in the shrubbery, commercial blasting sticks in ice cream containers, packed with nails, nuts and bolts covering the front of the cottage. There were two more round the back.

Not plod, Edge concluded. Not spook, either. Bodyguard was ex-military, not watching Edge but constantly scanning the surrounding area. This man visiting was important, but was he a threat?

"Moira, you had better fire up the AGA!"

She had been upstairs, writing her long, intricate journal in the spare room when she heard Edge yell. Moira had no idea what she would do with it. It was a journal of their lives, tidily illustrated in a slightly cartoon style she used. Edge had scoffed, but he was secretly jealous of her natural style. She was quite the homemaker now that the glass factory had shut down. Nobody needed expensive and elaborate glass anymore. Sometimes she helped her father since her mother had died, cycling to Bishop's Tawton, and she was as fit as a butcher's dog. Moira opened the window and leaned out.

"What?"

"Fire up the AGA! We've got company."

Her stomach lurched when she saw the car and two men, and she ran down the stairs to the cupboard underneath. "Oh no, oh God, no."

There were two shotguns in the house. A Remington 870 in the wardrobe in constant readiness for a last stand, although Edge unloaded it each week to ease the spring, and a heavier Mossberg 930 in this cupboard under the stairs. Moira grabbed the biscuit tin from the shelf and the leaning shotgun. She pointed it away, made sure the safety was on, opened the breech and then turned the weapon over. She fumbled with the tin lid and dropped two cartridges, but fed in the first one with her thumb until she felt the click of the magazine catch. Edge had showed her how to do this what seemed like hundreds of times. Her hands were shaking as she fed in the eight rounds, closed the breech then went through to the kitchen and cocked the weapon.

A man in a tweed suit was leaning over the gate and seemed to be conversing with Edge. The man behind was looking around, his hands crossed in front by his groin. Her bladder felt loose with fear. She sat down at the table, the Mossberg pointing at the door, waiting for the shooting to start, knowing she would be left to defend herself and the property. She flicked off the safety catch while she remembered. *Fumbling kills you*, Edge had told her.

The man in the jacket and cap smiled disarmingly at Edge. "I really am so sorry for dropping in unannounced, Mr Poulsom, or whatever you're calling yourself these days."

"Who are you and what do you want?"

He introduced himself as Air Commodore Stanhope, the Deputy Lord Lieutenant of Devon and explained, "Former Staff Sergeant Edge, because that is who we believe that you are. We need your expertise."

Edge recognised the man's ceremonial rank, rather than his former military one. "Look, sir, there must be plenty of other people who have served in the military and can help you form, what I expect, is a militia force."

"There's much more to it than that, but you're right, we have reinstated the 1921 act to call upon men to bear arms. You would be invaluable to us and we already have a network of like-minded and trained people. I would be grateful if I could outline our plans to you. Do you mind if Martyn stays outside? He takes his job very seriously."

"I'm glad for your sake that he does."

Edge led the way into the kitchen and the Deputy Lord Lieutenant didn't show any surprise at the Mossberg semi-automatic shotgun on the table, pointed at the door and him. He removed his hat politely and said: "How do you do, Mrs Edge. I'm delighted to have finally met your acquaintance. You are exactly as your father described you, but if I may say so, his description doesn't do you justice."

*Smooth as a sewer rat*, Edge thought, and made the introductions.

"Can I get you anything?" asked Moira, moving the shotgun off the table. She put it on the sideboard where she could reach it if necessary.

"A cup of tea would be most welcome, thank you."

"All right, Air Commodore, what do I call you?"

"As I'm not on ceremonial duties, Bernard will do."

"Okay, Bernard, let's keep it simple. I'm Edge. Now never mind what you want me to do, what is it that you're trying to achieve?"

The Deputy Lord Lieutenant leaned forward earnestly. "We want to make the majority of the West Country an autonomous, self-governing area, mostly self-sufficient and able to defend itself from 'interference' by that which laughably calls itself the British Government."

"There's more to running your own canton than training up some hired killers. That's the easy bit. The hard part is having all the necessary infrastructure, logistics, communications, and being able to sustain this in the longer term."

Moira put the teapot, milk and sugar on the table. "I'll make myself scarce while you're talking. I've made a mug for your chap outside."

"No, I wish you would stay and listen to this, especially after the invaluable contribution of your father. I'll take it out to Martyn."

Moira and Edge looked at each other. "Walts," he said softly.

"Let's hear him out, Mark."

When the Deputy Lord Lieutenant returned, he sat down and began to explain: "The Lord Lieutenant is the British monarch's personal representative in each county of the United Kingdom. Historically, the lieutenant was responsible for organising the county's militia. While the legitimate monarch may be in exile, the conditions must be met, should he ever return. We have recruited engineers and specialists in logistics and communications. We have financial backing and, we believe, the support of the rural population. We need to be able to prevent the government from thwarting our plans."

Edge put his elbows on the table and rested his head on his fingertips, deep in thought. He was quiet for a long time, and then it started pouring out.

"First of all, Bernard, this isn't *The Good Life*. You are going to have to make some pretty harsh decisions and people may well die because of them. I know you're an ex-military man, former winged master race?"

The Deputy Lord Lieutenant shook his head. "No, I was a loggie, A4."

Edge nodded approvingly. "That's good. So you're not playing at it. You will lose a lot of people, many of the younger ones, I'm afraid. The ones you need. Life will be too tough for them when the government close down the mobile network or the internet and they won't be able to cope. Some may come back and some may filter in from the cities, but it will be a self-selecting bunch. You need to induce the youngsters to stay. There are a lot of retired people staying in these parts. If they're useful, great. If they are retired bankers, lawyers or politicians, get rid of them and make the houses available to the indigenous population. I hope you've managed to identify some handy and tough administrators, because one of the first things you should do is conduct a census. Put all the information together like a Doomsday Book."

Moira started to take notes on a pad.

"Forget the cities. Their populations are largely unproductive and they will take more than they would provide. They are lawless and you will never have the manpower to police them. Isolate places like Bristol, Exeter and Plymouth, although you must vet everyone who wants to leave what could well turn into hellholes. It's already happened in the north with the Caliphate. Let the government look after them. You'll need a port capable of handling large ships. I would suggest Falmouth. It's small enough to be occupied, policed and defended.

Reactivate Pendennis and St Mawes Castles that guard the entrance to the harbour and garrison them. Keep the roads maintained, but don't worry about motorways or the major trunk routes that connect the cities. The government will want to hold on to those. You will need to move stuff by coastal convoys and these should be defended. The shipyards at Appledore have the necessary expertise to build fast boats that can be armed. These can also be used as fishery protection vessels, to get the fishing fleet back on its feet. Impound any foreign boats in the Bristol Channel and Western Approaches, and that includes Irish and Scottish vessels. Dump the crews off somewhere. Alive!

"You'll need weapons, including heavy weapons for the boats. That will require raids into Plymouth, Yeovilton or the RM and TA garrisons. The early hours of a Sunday morning would be best because viable manpower on military bases is the lowest at these times, but expect casualties. Oh, and you'll need explosive experts and heavy plant to get into the armouries. Have you recruited any pilots?"

"Yes, both fixed wing and rotary, mainly ex-military."

"Good, start commandeering aircraft when it kicks off. Any raids will provoke the government, so you must be ready for it and go in very hard. The police already hate and fear the countryside, as they abdicated responsibility for its citizens years ago. Don't stand and fight them when they come. Draw them in, isolate them and pick them off. Remember, always live to fight another day, and under no circumstances should they be harmed if they're captured. They're just doing their jobs for their political masters, so no repeat of that disgusting shit that happened in Leeds. Try and turn them if you can. After all, they are just plod, not the Gestapo.

"The authorities will always have the technological advantage, so fight them asymmetrically. No routine use of mobile phones and no internet. The signals can be jammed and are constantly monitored. We go back to a closed postal system, dead letter drops and dispatch riders, to which end you'll need shitloads of bikes and dispatch riders. You will also need a network of watchers who can maintain a permanent ear on the ground. Go with the Miss Marple option, because nothing escapes the attention of elderly women who know their community. For quick comms you will need to use mobile phones or CB radios. Go abroad and buy shitloads of pay as you go phones and sim cards. You can get cheap radios in the Eastern European countries.

"Medical services are bound to decline, so we'll have to go back to local cottage hospitals with a more rudimentary service. People will have to become more stoic and pay for healthcare, either at point of delivery or through insurance. There won't be any requirement for boob jobs or gender reassignment. Start a training programme and have one, possibly two, major units. That will not be easy, and to put it harshly, the long-term sick will almost certainly suffer. I hope you've thought about recruiting healthcare professionals, identifying buildings and sourcing medical supplies.

"There will be absolutely no room for criminals or freeloaders. Already we've noticed gangs of travellers capitalising on the lack of police. They have to be removed, either by forcing them to move out, or more permanently for the greater good. You'll need some form of justice system, I would suggest based on the military inquisitorial system, and under no circumstances should venal, smart-arsed lawyers be allowed to turn the law into their own personal cash cow. No prisons, just work gangs or banishment for the repeat offenders.

You must keep your cells of people as small as possible, and then if they are captured or turned, they can't bring down the entire organisation. You must have contacts of former police and as distasteful as it sounds, you will need some kind of secret police organisation. Choose your people carefully, because power corrupts.

"You might want to think about setting up your own news network, to counter the lies of the mainstream media, when people can get a signal. Report truthfully and keep it light-hearted where possible. People appreciate hearing about the latest conviction for sheep shagging and not propaganda.

"So now my bit. Out of every group of one hundred men or women who you want to fight for you, you will be lucky to end up with five who can handle a weapon and operate in a dangerous and chaotic situation. Of the ninety-five who don't make the cut, you may have to discount thirty who are just plain useless, dangerous fantasists or psychopaths. Twenty will never meet the level of fitness required. Twenty will be unable to commit in the long term and fifteen will drop out in training. Ten will drop out when they realise just how bloody awful fighting is. But don't disregard these people. They may have the admirable skills required for support functions such as analysis, intelligence and logistics support. I would suggest you instigate a form of psychometric evaluation for all volunteers. It will save a lot of time in the long run.

"You will never have enough weapons to issue everyone with a firearm. Make an inventory of all weapons such as shotguns or even illegally held stuff.

Forget raising a host of archers. It takes years of training to draw a longbow. There is enough expertise on the farms and in garages to start producing crossbows. They are bloody effective and can be made out of old vehicle leaf springs. There's enough blacksmiths still knocking around to make a few thousand bodkin bolt-heads, which will go through modern Kevlar like it isn't there. The same goes for improvised explosive devices. A pipe bomb will disable a Land Rover, and you can make a bloody good napalm from petrol and a few ingredients found in an average workshop and kitchen.

"Most importantly, don't provoke the government too much. If you are completely outrageous, they will have to react to you. Only fight as a last resort and remember to fight the war of the flea. They are vulnerable and stick to main roads, and no matter how scared your people will be, they will be terrified, because they will have heard a lot of bullshit about what you do to them if they're captured.

"There will have to be a spearhead force, mobile with vehicles or even aircraft, on a high readiness state, say, thirty minutes' notice to move. Much like the RNLI. They must be your best troops with the best equipment. And capable of fighting anywhere. These must be carefully selected and rigorously trained. There should be enough retired Bootnecks round these parts to know the qualities you will need."

Moira ripped the pages off the pad and handed them to the Deputy Lord Lieutenant. "Thank you, ma'am. You have certainly flagged up a couple of issues we have only just touched upon. It would be invaluable to us if you would agree to meet with our J5 plans expert at a mutually convenient time and place. We've organised along the military headquarters lines, Js one to nine. It would be wonderful for us if you would agree to join the J3 cell."

"I'll need to have a long, hard think about that, but I will meet with your J5 people. Let me know the time and place," Edge said cautiously.

As Edge opened the door for the Deputy Lord Lieutenant, he saw the bodyguard squatting down and rubbing the head of an old tabby cat.

"Come on, Monty. Stop being a tart," Edge told the cat, and the bodyguard stood up guiltily.

"Looks like your old puss has been in the wars," the Deputy Lord Lieutenant remarked, looking at the jagged scar down the side of Monty's nose. "Goodbye, Edge, and you, ma'am. I hope that we meet again."

The bodyguard handed Moira the mug and smiled shyly. They watched the two walk back to the Range Rover.

"Well, what do you think?" she asked.

"You forgot to apply the safety catch," he told her.

*

Edge did reluctantly join the insurgency and led three raids on military establishments in Plymouth and on Dartmoor and the old airfield at Chivenor. He wrote a training plan, or rather Moira rewrote his chaotic notes, and it became established doctrine for the West's Irregulars, now rebranded as the Dumnonian Militia. It was called *Rural and Urban Fighting for Irregulars, or the Art of Knowing When to Run Away*. She also illustrated the manuscript and when Edge saw her drawings, he didn't speak to her for two days. The counties of Cornwall, Devon and parts of Somerset and Dorset grew rich and prosperous, producing a surplus of crops for export. The fishing fleet was revitalised with captured Irish and Spanish trawlers, and Edge was instrumental in setting up the Stop Lines on the Exe, Dart, Taw and Tamar rivers. He designed the covert defensive forts, constructed along the lines of Special Auxiliary Units of the Home Guard, The Scallywags. The population decreased quickly to a sustainable and manageable level. Life was hard. People died who may have lived before, and life expectancy decreased as well. But people seemed more accepting and phlegmatic and Christian worship made an astonishing revival. Edge and Moira slipped gently into a dignified late middle age. Edge absolutely refused to listen to ABBA's *Fernando* under any circumstances.

*

Monty was asleep, lying on the grimy woollen blanket (which he wouldn't let Moira Mother wash) in his cardboard box in the kitchen, his legs twitching as he dreamed. It was the rare but recurring dream of the beautiful vixen and how she had sustained him with a dead chicken. Monty liked that dream.

He opened his eyes and the moon cast shadows across the flagged floor. It was a full moon and very beautiful. Snowflake was standing away from his bed in the moonlight and he gave a little yowl and purred loudly in greeting. She walked gracefully towards him and head-butted him gently. Monty was overjoyed because he could actually feel her.

*Snowflake?*

*Come on, Bernard Law Montgomery, First Viscount Montgomery of Alamein. Get up, you useless waste of fur.*

Monty stood up and stretched luxuriantly. The pain of his arthritis had vanished, as had the dull ache in his hind quarters. Monty stepped out of himself.

*Is it time?*

*Yes.*

*Will it hurt?*

*No.*

*Are you coming with me? I'll miss my human mother and father.*

*Yes. I'll be with you forever now.*

*Why?*

*Because we saved a human life and it's time for both of us to move on.*

*Into the light?*

She nuzzled against his neck, *Yes, Monty, into the light.*

\*

Moira was always the first to wake up, a habit from when their children still lived with them. It was cold in the bathroom while she relieved herself and as she washed her hands, she looked at herself in the mirror and pouted. *Bloody grey hairs. I'm beginning to look like a bag lady.*

It was cold downstairs as well; autumn had given way to winter. She would get both the wood burner and the AGA cranked up to heat the place before he got up. *You're not the only one who can light a wood burner, Mark Edge.* She hopped on the cold flagstones. *Was that a frost under the hedge?*

"Well, Monty Edge, I don't blame you for staying in bed, coz it's bloody cold this morning. Where the hell are my wellies?"

She went out with a trug to bring in some logs and kindling, being careful to make sure there were no lurking spiders. Back in the kitchen, she looked at Monty's bed, so she could pull it back to light the wood burner. Moira was puzzled because the cat would normally be weaving in and out of her legs, demanding his breakfast. He was still lying in the cardboard box. "You've got a handsome wicker basket and you prefer to sleep in a cardboard box with a manky old blanket."

Monty lay immobile, looking so unbearably cute. "Monty?"

She touched him and he was cold. Moira gasped and sat down heavily on a kitchen chair. "Mark... MARK!"

Edge thundered downstairs with the Remington shotgun and stared at his weeping, distraught wife.

"It's Monty. Mark, he's dead!"

Edge bent down and examined the cat. He gently opened Monty's eyes and both of the inner lids were closed. He was cold. Edge pulled up a chair and sat next to Moira, who was sobbing. He put his arm round her shoulders, which were heaving in grief.

"He was all right last night. I gave him his cuddly mouse and he seemed fine."

"Moira, Monty was eighteen. I don't know how old that is in cat years, but it was his time."

"Oh, please cover him up, Mark. I can't bear to look at him."

Edge draped a tea towel over the box and moved it into the scullery. "He's got a smile on his face, like he's laughing at us. He wasn't in pain, he just slipped away."

They sat and had a cup of tea and waited until their grief was manageable.

"What shall we do with his body?" asked Edge.

"I don't want him cremated with loads of other dead cats."

"What about a Viking funeral? Cast him down the river in a burning boat, with a dead rat at his feet. Like the book *Beau Geste*."

"For God's sake, be serious, Mark."

"Actually, I was," Edge said quietly.

"We'll bury him under that tree in the house over the lane, where his little friend was buried when she was killed by that car. They were inseparable and Monty really liked her."

"Do the same people live there and would they let us? How would you feel if your garden was being used as a pet cemetery?"

"Yes. The Adamsons. Their kids have left as well," Moira told him, as though this made them kindred spirits, "and we won't know until we ask, will we?"

"In which case, you'd better do the asking. I think I rather scare the locals."

Moira must have been persuasive, because two hours later, Edge was digging carefully around the roots of a by now mature beech tree. He had to go down three feet, excavating the hole carefully until he came across the little rib cage and the cat's skull. He marvelled at how big the holes in the skull were to allow for the species' sense of hearing. The tree had taken possession of little Snowflake, but it was as though it had left a space between the roots close to the skeleton, a Monty-sized space. Edge excavated carefully with a trowel. *Like Carenza's trench in Time Team*, he thought with a little smutty snigger.

*No, more like…* The smell of the earth made him think of another place and another time. Edge rocked back on his heels and groaned with anguish. Suddenly he couldn't see properly and he realised with shock and a burning throat that he was weeping. Edge was engulfed with grief. He wept for a Croatian woman that he had loved and lost. He wept for his mother, and not being there when she died. He was weeping for his father and uncle, for all the dead, for the years of happiness with his wife that he had missed. He thought about the way he had treated Kimberly as well as Bia Vargas, the son he had never seen, and groaned aloud in guilt. He was weeping for a Puerto Rican woman whom he had held while she died in Bolivia, but most of all for a tabby cat called Bernard Law Montgomery, First Viscount Montgomery of Alamein. Edge put his head in his hands as all the years of bottled-up grief, anger and emotion buried him.

It took a long time for him to pull himself together and he excavated a space behind Snowflake's skeleton. He picked up the stiffening Monty and gently placed the cat's body down into the grave. It was as though Monty had died in a perfect position, and Edge draped Monty's front paw over Snowflake's remains. He sat in silence for a few moments then carefully backfilled the grave. Moira had given him a few snowdrop bulbs which he put on top of the grave, then picked up the cardboard box and grubby blanket and trudged home. Despite his monumental sadness, Edge realised with some surprise that he no longer felt afraid. The worry had gone, along with all the mental baggage.

That night over dinner, they toasted absent friends with Moira's elderberry wine. They linked hands over the table, like they had done years ago.

"What will become of us, Mark?"

"Well, either the government will come for us and we'll go down in a blaze of glory, or we'll go like Monty and hope there's still someone around to put us under that tree."

"And in the meantime?"

"We'll just have to take what life throws at us. Together, and with Guy Jarvis and Afarin. And I know I don't say it as often as you would like, i.e., constantly, but I do love you, you know. Cheers."